TOMMY

HOMO
NOVA

and the House of Abraham

BOOK ONE

Fireside Publishing, Wakefield, West Yorkshire, United Kingdom

First published in Great Britain in 2021 by Fireside Publishing Ltd
16 Mill Lane, WF17 6LE

www.firesidepublishing.co.uk

This edition published in October 2021

Copyright © Tommy Crabtree, 2021
Cover illustrations by JD&J

Fireside

PUBLISHING

A CIP catalogue record for this book is available from the British Library

Paperback ISBN: 978-1-9163-0060-6

Typeset by Falcon Oast Graphic Art Ltd, Tenterden, Kent
Printed and bound by CPI Group (UK) Ltd, Croydon, CR0 4YY

For Elleri and Rune,
my reasons why.

CONTENTS

WHOEVER IS LED TO BELIEVE THAT SPECIES ARE MUTABLE, WILL DO GOOD SERVICE BY CONSCIENTIOUSLY EXPRESSING HIS CONVICTION, FOR ONLY THUS CAN THE LOAD OF PREJUDICE BY WHICH THIS SUBJECT IS OVERWHELMED, BE REMOVED.

— CHARLES DARWIN —

CHAPTER ONE

AN UNEXPECTED ARRIVAL

When going about her business alone at home, a sudden burst of warm fluid trickled down the inside of Astrid's legs. She gasped, then hovered in a state of suspension, wondering if her bladder had relieved itself of its own accord. Without the aid of a mirror, she had great trouble seeing beyond the hemisphere of her bump, but in rummaging about in her underwear her hand met with the severest damp, though no smell of urine accompanied it. Drawing out her hand, she saw a sort of syrup clinging to her fingers; a mucus that, under the candlelight, seemed brown, red, and silvery all at once. And she knew that this, the harbinger of motherhood, the breaking of her water, announced the beginning of a journey of extreme and inescapable torment: the baby was coming!

"Something's not right," she said, in a faraway voice. "I can't be going into labour … Only seven months have passed. It's too soon." But a contraction of her womb made it known to her that her time had come.

Her cries for help went unanswered, for strangers seldom wander the Arctic for leisure, least of all in the dead of night. It was more likely for her cries to disturb the ears of nearby polar bears than to alert the faraway societies of man.

"Thorsten, where are you?" she called, stumbling in no purpose-ful direction and not allowing her hand to part with the underside of her tummy. A temporary dizziness robbed her of her senses, the like of which is incurred when standing sharply to attention; the room seemed to roll into a brown and yellow blur. She pressed her other hand to her temple and gradually the interior of the cabin came back into focus. The timber web of struts and beams that stanchioned the roof was scarred with Viking knotwork; painted shields decked out every wall—blue, black, and blood-red; every chair and stool was festooned with pelts; the candles billowed and their serpentine vapours filled the air; the narwhal tusk affixed to the chimney breast appeared like a great ivory javelin; and the scant light from the fire below was in danger of imminent expiry.

Beside the fireplace stood a basket of pokers and shovels, out of which Astrid snatched a pair of tongs. With them, she stole a chunk of kindling from the heart of the fire. Then, she took an oil lantern from the mantelpiece and, having unfastened its window, passed the flaming tinder over the whale blubber inside, transferring to it a blaze of its own. She clasped the lantern window shut and returned the tongs, and then another contraction gripped her womb. Reaching out blindly, she leant against a timber stanchion while her face wrung into a feverish scrunch. When the wave of torment passed, she flung on her furs and scrambled to the cabin door with the burning oil lantern in hand.

Upon opening the door, a blast of wind almost ripped it from its heavy hinges, causing the cabin's timber frame to judder to its core. Baubles of snow sought refuge inside, and there they melted away into the silver strands of reindeer hide that furnished the floors. Astrid held her balance at the porch and squinted as the dew in her eyelashes crystallised. Still no sign of Thorsten. Assuming now the gravest of circumstances, her thoughts turned to polar bears: was that the howling of the wind or of hungry hunters?

"Don't be late, Thor. Please, please, please; not tonight."

She set the oil lantern upon a wrought-iron hook, and there, in a riotous swing, did it serve as a beacon to steer Thorsten home against the blackness of the polar night. Then, grasping the door handle with both hands, she hauled the door back into its frame against the rebellious gale.

The outside world sealed off, Astrid waddled in helpless apprehension throughout the cabin. It was a womb itself, the cabin. And looking down at her bump, she supposed it might be a good thing if her baby stayed inside her forever. Sheltered and isolated, yes, but so too from the dangers of a forbidding modern world.

To occupy her mind, she set about adding more coal to the hearths and fire baskets. Every spare candle and oil lantern was lit, not for light, but for the meagre agglomeration of their heat. And as she went about her domestic errands, the intermittent twinges pulverised her abdomen.

She sank into a tanned-leather armchair and found herself consumed with regret. Her lust to escape the city and be far removed from people had seemed romantic. A clean break from the everyday swooning over of modern arrangements; liberation from the bonds of the man-made; disconnection from the talons of technology; separation from the obsessive collecting of material trappings. The modern home had turned museum, brimming with ornaments and artefacts that had no practical use other than to massage the pride of their curators. They thought of themselves as homeowners, but they realised not that it was their homes and possessions which possessed them. Yet, in her current state, Astrid conceded her old life wasn't all that bad when compared to living here. Svalbard: that which had given her a peaceful retreat had also become a hostile place to give birth. Not for over three months had they felt the warmth of daylight grace their pallid cheeks.

"I'm not ready. Just contractions. They'll pass—"

The spasms of her womb returned, each time more powerful, and the rise and fall of her breast underwent a drastic rhythm.

"Why did we choose this life for you?" she said, looking down at her dome and letting slip a depressing half laugh, half cry. "To be foragers—hah; this was such a stupid fad."

The foragers had no device with which to call for help. No connections of any sort. No vehicle for transport. Not even a device to tell the time. If it didn't exist a thousand years ago, it was forbidden. Even visiting the hospital, they agreed, was a breach of their ways; no health scans of the baby were ever conducted; no clinicians were ever consulted; no medication was ever consumed; intervention was never condoned. Not even after her first miscarriage. There'd been excessive bleeding. A shedding of her insides. A passing of foetal tissue. She remembered it now: its searching black bug-eyes gave it the semblance of—she hated herself for thinking it—a pale alien. And she couldn't shake this haunting image of a baby stillborn—or, at best, crippled.

Tears of candle wax spilt in great quantities. Her hands shook with terror. To steady them, she took up a thick plait of blonde hair in her mouth and trimmed the ends incessantly.

Unable to turn her thoughts away from miscarriage, her eyes became suffused with tears. Two months premature—something had to be wrong. She blamed herself. This could only be the consequence of their migrating to this unrelenting clime. And now it was a stretch beyond her imagination to envisage a life in which she held a baby, believing herself to be destined to spend the rest of her life with faulty female faculties, without a child.

A pang of cramp punished her as though in retaliation for her rueful thoughts. But each one, uncomfortable as it was, offered hope. A signal from her bump: *here I come, Mamma.* In response, she massaged the underside of her belly, straightened her back, and dabbed at her runny pink nose.

"We're going to fight our way through this, bump." The torturous contractions doubled in frequency and intensity.

To stymy the pain, she dug her fingers into her palms, her nails carving divots into her skin. She sucked air through her teeth, regulating her intake. Upon relaxing, she felt the baby's position change and a new throbbing at her cervix.

"Thorsten—agh! I can't be doing this. Not on my own." But to wait any longer was a danger to the baby.

In haste, she completed a lap of the room, collecting the necessary articles for the delivery. She undressed the throne-like chairs of their thick pelts and gathered pillows stuffed with eiderdown; with these, she arranged a couch by the fire. Stopping at a cask of mead, she deliberated, though not for long. If she had to do this alone, without painkillers (forbidden), then being sober was an agonising thought. So she supped from the mead cask, and the draught became a burning ravine throughout her insides. Then she stripped off her trousers, stockings, and underwear. All save her frilly socks were removed from her lower half, but the hairs of her legs offered some relief from the wintry air. (The common obsession with removing hair in more southerly countries was a practice mocked by foragers of the Arctic, where every additional strand was regarded as a tally of one's beauty.)

At last, she lay in the mound of furs by the fire. Upon settling, she was overcome with the maternal urge to push. But pushing at this stage was a terrible idea, for both her bowels and bladder threatened the foulest mutiny. There was to be no getting comfortable, and at each successive contraction she shook with more feverous fervour, while the network of stretch marks on her belly flared up like purple bolts of lightning.

The clouds were pregnant with snow, and as the upside-down blizzard beat on, Thorsten trudged up the twisting vale, leaning his seven-foot frame into it to keep himself from being blown over, the frost crunching underneath his ragged wet boots as he went. He towed his sled behind, but it hauled no cargo: no winter's catch, only the dead weight of tackle. He'd gone to great pains that day, having tracked reindeer, hunted ptarmigan, stalked fox, and fished at the shore. Spear, trap, harpoon, net; none had brought any yield.

Two days had passed since any proper meal, but the thoughts of disappointing Astrid eroded his insides more thoroughly. She was losing weight, not gaining like she was supposed to during pregnancy. To compensate, she preserved her energy by reducing her activities to little more than a cycle of sitting and thinking—and overthinking. Her worst fears he shared; but if, as a result of malnutrition, their baby should be born with an unfortunate condition and into a life of uncommon struggle, the blame would be on him for his failure to provide.

He dropped to his knees and punched great holes in the snow with his cubic fists, leaving beaten-up patches of ebony slush. He roared, but the wind deemed his voice irrelevant. Angry at the blizzard, he took up his spear in both hands. Then, holding it high, he drove it into the ground, the shaft puncturing the frost—and something soft beneath. A piercing squeak cut through the wind at the point of the spear's entry.

With difficulty, he unstuck the spear from the ground, and when he brought it up for observation, he saw a vole writhing on its point. He slapped his chest and laughed. This was a fat one, worthy of roasting. In fact, it was the fattest he'd ever seen. In the frozen air, she gave her last breath, curled up, and turned rock solid. But then a savage thought occurred to him, and seconds later he himself froze over … This swollen-bellied vole looked to be carrying younglings of her own.

He flung his spear as though there was a real possibility of contracting some unfathomable bad luck through his kill which he might pass on to Astrid and their baby. Then he turned away and vomited the watery contents of his stomach. Not even in their hungriest hour would they—could they—dine on a skewered mother and baby, no matter what the creature.

"Still," he said, dragging his sled away and looking over his shoulder as though looking through a window into his past, "the dangers of this place pale when compared to those we fled."

As he waded on through the snow, he came to the latter part of his journey. He longed now for warm dry clothes, a pair of toasted socks, and a mug of strong mead. But as his excitement grew, so did his guilt. In a state of indecision, he sped up, only to slow down again thereafter. Then, at the sudden suspension of the weather, he halted in his tracks.

The blizzard parting and the wind dying, Thorsten lowered his scarf and rolled back his wet hood. He swept his long ginger forelocks away from his brow and brushed away the ice which clung to his dense beard. Belts of infinite stars glimmered as though a sequinned mantle had been drawn across the polar sky. Ribbons of emerald and ruby rippled to and fro—the magic of the Northern Lights. He could've passed an hour or two watching their undulations. He contemplated it, but in noting the position of the constellations he saw it was already getting late, so on he pressed.

A short while later, he saw it: an orange beacon in a pendulous swing. At such a distance, their well-camouflaged longhouse, Thrudheim, under its dusting of white icing, seemed a gingerbread house. To look at only made him hungrier.

After he'd tied his sled to the coal shed, he clambered up the porch one step at a time, ducking to avoid the hungry fangs of icicles. Here at the door, slouching with his hands in his pockets, his grass-green eyes dropped to the doormat and he let slip a pitiable sigh. When looking up again, he feigned his happiest whistle and went inside.

Chapter Two

SOLDAGEN

The net of hair strewn across Thorsten's face veiled his eyes, and he maintained his merry whistle, never looking up, for fear of meeting Astrid's eyes. In his periphery he'd seen her honey-blonde head rise out of a mound of furs beside the fire, but he turned away, hoping to defer her disappointment for a little while longer.

He kicked aside his boots, then hung his furs on the reindeer antlers and only paused in his whistling to please his nostrils with the smell of cinnamon that always lingered in the air. But it was a betrayal of the senses, since there was no tasting to satisfy it. Still, his bloodshot eyes rolled back, and as the dull aching of his heavy body waned, and as his bones thawed out from the frost, he almost drifted into a standing sleep.

"Thorsten."

His neck jarred as he whipped himself to attention. "Huh—wha'?"

Her explosive tirade had no effect on him, for dominating his senses was an irksome tickle spreading throughout his nose: "I need to sneeze. One sec—" *Tchoo—tchow—tchee—tchar—tchah.* He rubbed his bulbous nose with his palm as though he were erasing it from existence.

"Thorsten!"

Something came spinning towards him. He parried it with his arms, but not so quickly that he could deflect whatever it was from striking his forehead—a chunk of kindling. His cubic head turned red as a brick. Hot blood snaked around his temples, and his monstrous brow swelled to full capacity. But he drew in a deep sigh and accepted the punishment for his shortcomings.

"Are you deaf?" came a muffled voice from beneath the furs.

"Am I dead? There were several occasions during the day when I wished I was."

"*Deaf*, fool. Are you deaf?" She let slip a grievous moan. "The baby is coming."

He hurtled to her side and saw how her face was wrung and how the protruding tendons in her neck seemed to age her thrice. "But … you have many weeks remaining."

She was in too much pain to voice a reply, and when he realised it wasn't a trick, a gasp rushed past his lips with the vehemence of one resurfacing after having spent too long underwater.

"Astrid, tell me, how are we going to—when did you—what do I do?"

No verbal answer; the agony was too much. Her face twisted into the sourest scrunch as she shook her head.

They had no snowmobile for transport, nor did they have any Tech to call for help. If it didn't exist a thousand years ago it was forbidden. But gladly would Thorsten relinquish those self-imposed rules just this one night. Throughout her pregnancy he'd downplayed childbirth, supposing that if wild animals and lesser species could endure it without medical intervention then so too could Astrid in the comfort of their home beside the warm fire. But now that the moment was here two months too soon, the notion of a smooth delivery was little more than a fantasy. Gathering himself upon his feet and dabbing away the sweat congealing on his brow, he said, "I'll run to get help—as fast as I can."

"Thorsten, the baby's coming. If you walk out of that door—if you dare leave me …"

"I want you to be safe."

"Then don't leave me alone."

"Astrid," he said, taking a knee beside her and clasping her fretting hand in his, "you've got to be telling me what to do."

"Shh—" A hellish cycle of wheezing interrupted her speech, "you're supposed—to be—reassuring me."

But it was he himself who was most in need of reassurance. She'd always accused him of being unable to multitask, yet here he was, blinking, scratching the roots of his locks, and gnawing his fingernails into oblivion all at once.

"Stop wasting time," said Astrid, yanking his beard so their eyes were level. Her fair face turned foul. The smell of mead hung on her breath.

"You've been drinking, haven't you?" But having said this, he realised she was blameless. What else had she to sustain her energy other than the sugars from their mead reserves?

The sour expression was still spread across her face; he felt a set of fingernails digging into his wrist, seizing him like some wicked bear trap. Then she unleashed a drawn-out cry. Throughout this, he remained quiet, not unlike the naïve livestock that wears a civilised and patient look when queueing up for the abattoir.

"Tell me, Astrid, what do I do?"

She fended him away. "You're not coming near me until those filthy hands are clean."

He clasped her cheeks and kissed her on top of her head. She swatted him away with her slender hand, missing him by a hair's breadth. After drawing himself to his full height, he tied back his bedraggled red hair into a bun, rolled up his sleeves, and tightened his belt buckle a notch.

"Thor," she said, between heavy pants, "have we—got any—coal? I can't—feel my t-t-toes."

He stroked his beard in contemplation for a moment, then charged through the front door.

The moon shone like a cracked pearl suspended in the sky. The wind had died, preserving his deep footprints from earlier, and he followed one set of these prints to the coal shed. Across the double doors a horizontal wooden barricade held them fast. He delivered an uppercut to it, dislodging it from its bracket, and the doors swung loose. At the back, camouflaged in the darkness, was an anvil-sized black rock. He clapped his hands in self-congratulation, for he'd rationed their coal for this very moment. Carrying it in both arms, he lumbered back inside, leaving the doors of the shed flapping throughout the rest of the night. When he'd split the coal with a rock hammer and tossed it into the fire, tendrils of flame mellowed the air.

Astrid groaned and moaned; she drew her breath in and out through clenched teeth with such frequency that it would've been easy to mistake her for an oncoming steam train or some other industrious machine with no shortage of pistons.

Thorsten dusted the residue of coal from his tunic and, using a pan of melted snow (now tepid having had thirty seconds over the hearth), washed his muck-engrained hands, scouring them until his forearms were shiny with a new layer of skin.

"Is your knife clean?" she said.

"Knife? Tell me, please … not a caesarean?"

"Nuh, you fool. For the afterbirth."

"Oh, yah." He wondered what she meant by "afterbirth", but the precious little time remaining was better spent running errands and doing what he was told than wasting it on last-minute revision for his practical midwifery exam. "Yah, I'll clean my knife."

"Wait, tell me first what you see down there."

"Down where?"

"Down below. Between my legs, fool. Look."

After glancing below, his eyes were swift in averting back to hers. He feigned a smile, but an involuntary twitch—a circular scrunch of the nose—gave away his inner apprehension. The blood ran chill through his face; things grew faint; his vision became blotched. Hunting, skinning, and filleting deer, that was no trouble; nor was the practice of gutting, stripping tendons, or slicing fat. But the bloodiest of chores weren't preparation enough for this: a child bulging out of its mother, entering the world compressed against the walls of an airless chamber.

He tugged at his tunic's collar to allow some air to his neck.

"Thor," she said, yanking his arm like a bell ringer, "what do you see?"

"The crown of the head."

"I daren't push. I'm so scared. My hunger—being premature—the winter. What if—"

"Don't say it. Come; start pushing on three. One ... two ..."

"—what if our baby isn't born like other babies?"

"Stop thinking like that," he said, now shuffling between her legs and holding out his hands like giant mitts ready to field the catch. "Come now."

"After all this trying, I can't bear to cremate another. What if—"

"Astrid, please."

"I'm not supposed to be giving birth at seven months."

"Come. Together now. Strong, smooth, controlled breaths. Come on. Breathe with me now. In ... and then out ... in ... and then out. Good. Strong—smooth—controlled. Say it with me: *strong—smooth—controlled*. That's good; keep it up."

"Stick—stick—stick," she demanded.

Thorsten passed a chunk of kindling sideways into her snapping jaws, and her teeth almost split the wood. When he saw that tinder the following morning, it had the appearance of having been ravaged by teething woodworm and was pockmarked with the severest cavities.

"Keep breathing; just keep breathing," he urged, mopping away the pearls of sweat forming on her forehead. After a while, he discovered an arcane technique: massaging her jugular in a clockwise motion had an inexplicably calming influence over her.

Few spaces in Thrudheim went unoccupied in the moments that followed. After much position-changing—lying prone, lying supine, lying sideways, squatting, crawling on her hands and knees—the best relief for Astrid was in standing up and leaning against the wall while Thorsten dug his thumbs into her coccyx to quell her contractions.

"Come; standing is no use. Lie down beside the fire where it's warm." He took her by the elbow and eased her down onto the mound of pillows. "You need to be pushing harder to allow the head to come through."

"I can't, Thor," she said, spitting out the kindling. "If I push, it's going to split me in half."

"You can do this."

"I'm dying. This is it; I know I'm dying."

"You're not dying, fool." He grasped her hand and squeezed, though not as hard as she did. "Remember, every contraction is one step closer to meeting our baby. Hold on to me. I've got you, and you've got this. Focus on your breathing. That's it. Deep breaths now. Pay attention to the rise and fall of your chest."

Through gritted teeth: "So grateful to have you, Thor. Anybody would think you'd"—her face contorting—"done this before …"

The vain lament that followed was so shrill that it promised to send a tuning fork, if there were one present at the scene, into an endless tremor.

Outside, the screams startled a snooping snow fox. It abandoned its supper and scarpered across the snowy plains. When at a safe distance, it chanced a glance back, its head atilt in wonder. Another shriek pierced the wilderness, and the fox abandoned its ambition of ever finishing its supper; and not a single paw, or hoof-print, was seen about Thrudheim for several winters.

After growing somewhat in confidence, Thorsten lowered his head between Astrid's legs. But during his motivational urging of her to squeeze, a yellow fountain sprang forth from between her legs and sprinkled a steamy pattern across his chest. He shook the fluorescent droplets from his beard and concealed his snarl as best as he could. (He afterwards learnt that he should consider himself lucky that the grotesquery was limited only to this light soaking and that good fortune had spared him from the common soiling.)

"It's coming, Thor—agh." Her perineum tore asunder; and as through a burst dam, an excited red river ran its course, making contemporary artwork of the deer hide beneath her. The baby's head appeared beyond the outer walls of its crimson cage.

Thorsten reoriented himself and shielded the baby's face from the frigid air with his hands. "After the next push we get to meet our baby," he said, blinking away the tears. At the close of his sentence, Astrid held her breath; her face reddened so much that she looked in danger at any moment of detonating. She gave one last shriek—a shriek that promised to hoarsen her voice forever—and the baby's shoulders slipped free, thereafter falling into Thorsten's blanketed hands. But when holding the baby, his joy was overturned, for the little creature was still, its inky-blue skin awash with blotches.

"We did it," said Astrid, beaming with delight. "My baby—let me see."

Everything slowed. Thorsten hovered like a pendulum, caught in a languid rocking back and forth on his knees. His mind became hollow. All thought ceased its chatter. A prolonged ringing and singing of steel seemed to slice through his eardrums. And when order was restored to his mind, his tongue swelled to fill the vacuum of his mouth, denying him speech.

"Thor, you're scaring me," she said, sitting up and aggravating her wounds in doing so. "It should be crying. Why's my baby not crying? Is it the cord? Is it tangled? Do something!"

Looking down, he saw that the baby was free from any umbilical noose. Yet, behind his own foggy vision, his eyes were drawn to a faint movement: a twitch or a faint cough. A sniff, perhaps. There, again. Its tiny face puckered, and a bubble spluttered from its nose.

"Oh, my baby, my baby, my baby," said Astrid, driving her fists into her eye sockets like a pestle in a mortar.

She hadn't seen what he had, and some instinct now compelled him to dab the baby's nose with a knuckle. Dab—dab—dab. A sticky fluid oozed from its nostrils. Dab—dab—dab. More trickled out. And when the baby's airways became unplugged, a chain of sneezes ensued: tchoo—tchow—tchee—tchar—tchah. Then it trialled a cry for the first time, which sent all three of them into a chorus of crying.

"With a sneeze like that, there's no doubt about him being mine," said Thorsten, handing the baby into Astrid's outstretched arms while still tethered to the cord. His hands were shaking; he was a bag of nerves with handling this fragile little fledgling. Yet, at the same time, a joyous tickle spread throughout the fibres of his sternum.

"*Him*, you say? Oh, a boy. We have a baby boy." Astrid beamed down at him, but a moment later a shadow seemed to pass over her that eclipsed her elation; and she was quick to cocoon their baby in a shawl and thereafter draw him to her bosom.

"Is something wrong?" said Thorsten, trying to gain a better vantage. At that exact moment, the slumbering sun awoke from its three-month hibernation; a razor of light snuck in beneath the front door. "Look, Astrid—Soldagen; the sun has risen above the mountains."

She was in no mood for celebration and told him instead to prepare for the afterbirth.

There she goes again with this *afterbirth*, he thought.

Off he sped and came back with a sterile knife. On Astrid's instruction, he took up the rubbery cord, which had the aspect of a white snake. When turning it over in his fingers, he could trace no pulse. So, with some string, he tied two knots about an inch apart and severed the fleshy chain, disconnecting mother and baby.

How had she come to know that which he knew nothing of? When asked, she likened childbirth to understanding a language with no prior knowledge and said it was as though she'd spontaneously inherited the keys to the library of motherhood and with it the ability to read instincts she had never before experienced. "You just know what to do," she said, shrugging.

A short while later, with great pain on Astrid's part, the tail-end of the cord slithered out from within her, towing behind it a clump of flesh.

"What the hell is that?" said Thorsten, his eyes widening with horror. He mistook it for a brain until Astrid corrected him.

"It's the placenta. Why are you looking at me like I'm some kind of freak? It's natural."

"I didn't even know such a thing existed. What else are you hiding up there?"

Having no other alternative for breakfast, she suggested they cook it: "I've heard placenta is tasting like beef." He retched incessantly until the subject was changed and the thought forgotten.

Reclining together with the baby in their arms, they lay with their heads conjoined. Thorsten scooped his hand around the baby bundle as Astrid gave suckle. Looking at his hand, he realised the bloodiness of what had occurred; there were red handprints on many surfaces, and the longhouse resembled a crime scene. But they'd done it. Alone. Without aid. It was all worth it, for here was his son.

When Thorsten drew the blanket away from the baby's face, and having now had chance to look upon him with clear eyes, without that excessive magnification and prickly irritation caused by tears, he noticed something was different, although he hesitated to say so. He felt Astrid's eyes weighing down on him. Did she expect him to say it aloud? The worst of words any new parent could contemplate? Eventually, it was she who, looking up at him with the gravest dread, broke the silence.

"I think there's something wrong with him."

The baby did look different, yet he seemed happily unconscious of his condition. His jaw protruded with a hideous yet pitiable underbite. His nose was broad and his brow was dense with bone. So fine was the white-blond lanugo that grew in abundance over his body that it could only be seen under a certain light, but there it flourished in all regions save the soles of his feet and palms of his hands.

"He *does* look different," said Thorsten. "But then, he's in no pain. See how he sleeps."

"I know, but maybe we should take him to—"

"Hospital? Astrid, we've come this far on our own. We did it. He may be premature, but he's not scrawny. And the journey is long, and we should let him rest. You should rest, too. Trust me, I don't think this is a disability. For all our guesswork, it could be the opposite. Don't always look for the negative."

"But I worry about what people might say. I don't want people to say hurtful things about him."

"Then let's stay here. Keep him hidden. Protect him. Forget about anything else—about anyone else. Today is a great day. Let's not spend it worrying about what might or might not be."

Thorsten leapt up and threw open the front door. Splendid sunbeams drenched their pallid faces. He looked down across the coast of Isfjorden, where the ice floes meandered in and out of the bay and where clusters of homes—sea-blue, pale-green, and ash-yellow—were buried under blankets of snow. As the sun crept low across the glassy blue skies, the frost-ridden tundra twinkled, and beneath the white crown of the mountains the entire town of Longyearbyen seemed to kneel to its majesty. An eruption of cheers could be heard; the townsfolk were celebrating the sun's return and, in keeping with tradition, would no doubt be gorging on brunost (a brown cheese with caramel flavourings).

"Soldagen," he added, planting his hands on his hips and looking out with profound appreciation oozing from his every pore.

"Ulrik Magnusson," said Astrid, still occupying her spot beside the dwindling fire.

"Ulrik?" said Thorsten, stroking the tip of his beard.

Astrid looked down at their son and repeated, "Ulrik Magnusson."

"Ulrik Magnusson. A strong name. A powerful name. A leader's name." Delighted with the choice, Thorsten took his knife from its sheath and marred the floorboards at the place where Astrid had birthed him (much to her annoyance, as she still lay there suffering with her lacerations):

Ulrik Magnusson
Soldagen — 2058

"You are deft with a knife," said Astrid, "but can you show the same skill with a needle?"

"Needle? What do you mean?"

"My wounds—I need you to be stitching them."

His stubby, clubby hands were ill suited to fine sewing, and in his most recent attempt he'd accidentally sewn up the ends of a pair of sleeves so no arm could reach out. With that in mind, she had every right to fear his patchwork, so she demanded he bring her whatever mead they had in their reserves before risking the botched operation.

Upon its completion, Astrid took Thorsten's callused hand and caressed it in hers. She flicked her lashes at him and then, in a swift turn of mood, seized him by the beard: "Never again, Thor. Never again will I go through the agony of childbirth."

"Understood." Though he had strong doubts about Ulrik being an only child forever.

Huge smiles stretched across their haggard faces; their cheeks swelled with parental pride. But behind their eyes was an unspoken anxiety. Their prolonged silence was an admission: at less than a few hours old, even then they knew baby Ulrik was destined for a life fraught with hardship and uncommon strife.

"You're right, Thor," said Astrid, nuzzling baby Ulrik's prominent nose. "For his sake we must keep him hidden. Keep him out here in the wild. Only venture into society when we have no other choice. We must never let him stray from our side."

"And not only for his sake, but for our sakes, too."

Chapter Three

THE VAST SUPPER

Meanwhile ...

Her architecture was akin to some contemporary Camelot.

Out of the sandbanks of Normandy she rose like a magic kingdom, the enchanting spire at her zenith bursting the winter sea-fog. The low tide lapped against the ramparts of Mont-Saint-Michel, and by the grace of her foundations she sustained no erosion. There she stood—as she had done for centuries—like the proudest entrant to a sandcastle competition, her purple and golden banners fluttering like ribbons of self-congratulation in response to the silver trumpets and the peals of her abbey bells.

These purple banners had a familiar aspect to them, perhaps in the same way that you might happen upon an old friend after long years of absence. At first, you look with neck outstretched, then you cock your head, and lastly you squint; and you conclude that it *is* them after all, though their alteration has been radical. Even so, the crest emblazoned at the centre of those banners was a most familiar-looking sword; yet if you were to stretch out your neck, cock your head, then squint, you'd notice a stark union therein: a crucifix, the star of David, and crescent moons engulfing stars: an amalgamation of the symbols of Christianity, Judaism, and Islam.

At the heart of the sandcastle, twisting cobbled streets forked here and there, giving rise to various pathways up the mount. Lining the narrow streets, standing shoulder to shoulder, were parallelogram homes; and it wasn't uncommon behaviour for the townsfolk, upon finding themselves passing in their shadows, to quicken their pace, the anxiety of these edifices toppling over being a thought too extreme to ignore. Yet none ever fell. These diagonal structures had been molested by the hand of time and yet had since been restored by the hand of affluence. To reimagine these houses into any shape other than their immediate form was a skill possessed only by the town drunkard, who attested to their being entirely perpendicular. With his own wife, he'd argue long into the night; if she wished to see buildings at right angles, then she ought not to go about with that dreadful single earring anchoring down one side of her face and instead straighten up her posture.

But long gone was the town drunkard, his wife, her dreadful earring, and all trace of their ever having lived there. No, not dead ... but evicted, and not through any disgrace. There were no residents in Mont-Saint-Michel anymore, save the Chancellor—whose only neighbours were his guardsmen and servants.

In a state of impatience, the Chancellor stood at the abbey window and peered out across the shore. He was a suit-clad, bent-over fellow, and his silver hair was long and brittle, as though it was a willow affected by a bout of hoarfrost. Gaunt was his posture, and squint were his olive eyes, like one who spends years underground tinkering and mending model trains and planes under dingy lamplight—as so often men do in the winter of their lives, having rediscovered the delight of child's play. Except Emmanuel Saint-Pierre never confined himself to any sort of underground workshop, nor did he tinker with toys; he'd elevated himself beyond all reputation as Chancellor of the Democratic Republic of United Europe (DRUE). Law and order were his toys for the tinkering.

After pressing his face to the window, he drew in a sigh of disgust and withdrew. No sign of his esteemed guests. The abbey bells pealed above to mark the passing of another hour.

20

The Chancellor slumped back into his armchair by the window, uncrossing and re-crossing his legs at rapid intervals. His thumb and forefinger underwent a massage at their tips, as though between them was a wad of plasticine in need of thorough moulding, or a miniature world in need of creation. Something grave dominated his thoughts.

"Lord Almighty," he said, fixing his olive eyes to the ceiling, "I'm a patient man, but my age exceeds my patience. I have no time to waste. Why do they keep me waiting?"

At last, his prayers were answered: a final clang of abbey bells sounded from the top of Mont-Saint-Michel. The Chancellor stirred and darted to the window again.

"Blessed be God! They're here."

Burly servants were heaving two sedan chairs (one emerald, the other sapphire) and making their ascent to the abbey at the summit of Mont-Saint-Michel. Behind, there followed a party of men clad in illustrious cloth.

Within seconds, the Chancellor adjusted his cufflinks, fixed his tie, swept his silver locks behind his shoulders, and hobbled away.

Earlier, these stone hallways had been grey and dark, but the fires had since been lit, the chandeliers lowered, and the candelabras ignited so that now all that had been cold was gold.

Passing through the knights' hall, the Chancellor found himself in the company of statues—no, not statues, but flawless waxworks; waxworks that were dressed and groomed so that they seemed alive and pausing in philosophical thought. They were the prophets of old. Noah to his left; Moses to his right; then Aaron, Jacob, Isaac, Job, David, Solomon, Abraham, and Jesus. It was a habit of the Chancellor's to zigzag his way through this section of the abbey, going from one alcove to the next and kissing the feet of each prophet, perhaps hoping for their favour and blessings.

The click of his polished heels announced his coming, and he passed from one room to the next. By the time he appeared in any room, his servants had already drawn themselves to a halt and taken a knee. There they waited. And when the Chancellor flicked his wrist, they resumed their positioning of ornaments and their preparing of furniture, and they took the greatest care in unfurling those purple and golden banners.

Following his nose into the refectory, Chancellor Saint-Pierre stumbled upon a vast table of inestimable length. It was laid with fresh loaves of challah bread, olives, figs, cheeses, and exotic roots. The crystal goblets sparkled and the ornate silverware twinkled; it was as though the firmament itself had collapsed and was suspended in the hall, such was its starriness. Happy that the preparations were under way, the Chancellor gave thanks in abundance: "My lambs, to you—and indeed your families—will I dedicate a prayer to before this day expires."

There was a collective inhale of excitement.

After quitting the refectory, the Chancellor brought himself to the main doors of the abbey, where his most venerable bishops waited. Not wishing to be a rude host to the guests about to arrive, he stepped outside into the unfavourable weather and ordered his retinue to do the same.

Out here, the wind ruffled his long silver hair and then in the next instant threw it upside down, exposing the elongated crown of his head. Like the willow that disguises its trunk with its drooping fronds, he covered his conical skull. It was as though upon his delivery into this world the supple marrow of his crown had suffered an atrocious phase of clenching and wrenching upon its encounter with the midwife's forceps; and it seemed, in its extended capacity, to be the most ideal warehouse for the storage of facts and figures—and, more importantly, Bible quotes.

With arms out wide, the Chancellor beamed a smile towards his guests, who were alighting from their sedan chairs. The parade of imams and rabbis accompanying them fell into silence.

"Shalom, brother," said the Chancellor.

The Chief Rabbi of Israel, Levi Ben-David, came forward with open arms. He was robed in blue and white, and he wore a dome-shaped turban upon his head. Regal ringlets spiralled past his happy cheeks like cords of vintage telephones and mingled with his beard.

"Shalom, Chancellor Saint-Pierre," said the Chief Rabbi, in the gentlest voice detectable by human ears. "I'm honoured to be of the select few to receive the invitation into your home."

"Nonsense, Levi. I'm honoured to have you in it."

Then came forward the Caliph of Babylon, Sultan bin Ibrahim, an immense figure wearing garments of green silk and bracelets of gold and pearl. At the mercy of the elements, his dangling bangles appeared to be the most exquisite set of wearable wind chimes. Like the Chief Rabbi, the Caliph, too, wore a turban, though the Caliph's was of striking emerald. Dark were his brows; his beard was black; his teeth were yellow from a fondness of turmeric; and his crescentic smile was wide from a fondness of laughter.

"As-salaam-alaikum, Sultan," said the Chancellor. "It's been far too long."

"Wa-alaikum-salaam," replied the Caliph in his bass voice, thumping his barrel chest with his palm, bangles rattling like a tambourine. "It *has* been too long, Chancellor."

They stood like distinguished kings of the Orient, or like an ancient triumvirate of power; the Chancellor of DRUE, the Chief Rabbi of Israel, and the Caliph of Babylon. Together they stood, men of spiritual similitude, in political harmony.

The party behind caught up and formed a semicircle around their leaders. In their colourful gowns, the imams, rabbis, and bishops all seemed a rainbow of tolerance.

Despite the weather, Chancellor Saint-Pierre wouldn't admit a soul inside until he'd bidden shalom and salaam to each guest. Having rehearsed the names of the imams and rabbis, and having tapped their shoulders and nudged their elbows, he ushered them in and sealed the great wooden doors behind them.

"Chancellor," said the Caliph, commencing a stroll through the halls, "it's been almost—"

"Tut-tut-tut, please, no more titles," said the Chancellor. "We are friends here, Sultan."

"Indeed, Emmanuel. It's been almost four years," continued the Caliph, "almost four years since you were an ambassador brokering a lasting peace between our flocks; almost four years since the Peace Treaty; almost four years of harmony between Muslims, Christians, and Jews. Never did I expect to see this miracle in my lifetime."

"Behold," said the Chief Rabbi, "behold how pleasant it is when brothers dwell in unity."

"Mashallah," said the Caliph, his voice booming throughout the abbey with such power that it threatened to snuff out the nearest candles; "Muslims, Christians, Jews—we are the People of the Book. And in the Quran (Surah Al-Ankabut 46) it says: 'We Muslims believe in the Revelation which has come down to us and in that which came down to you; our God and your God is One.'"

"Indeed, Sultan, that's our entire foundation," said the Chancellor, stopping to collect the Caliph's hands in his and bowing. "The tenets of our beliefs are much the same, though our traditions differ. As I always say: the paths of religion are fingers of the same loving hand. We are the sons of Adam, Noah's heirs, sheep of Moses; ours is the House of Abraham."

A chorus of praise echoed through the halls, and fists were thrown in the air.

"Tell me, Levi," said the Chancellor, "how are the chosen people of Israel?"

"Wonderful," said the Chief Rabbi.

"And, Sultan, in Babylon, I take it things are well?"

"Emmanuel," said the Caliph, holding out his clanking arms in surrender, "our nations were riven by war. But you—*you*—it was you who gave to us a new home: New Babylon! How prosperous we've become. Dubai? Abu Dhabi? Doha? What are they but shanty towns when compared with the grandeur of New Babylon?"

"I'm happy to hear it, my brothers. I really am." The Chancellor smiled; then he looked at the ground with solemn longing.

"Are things not well in DRUE?" asked the Chief Rabbi. Despite his shock, he'd never been heard to raise his voice a single decibel at this or any other news.

Like the consummate conductor, the Chancellor drew up his fist and snatched at the thin air. The orchestra fell silent. A nerve had been struck like the wrong chord. "My sincerest apologies," he said. "I've had much on my mind ... and that's why I asked you to come. I'm in need—dire need of advice. And, in matters of the strictest confidence, I trust only you."

"Whatever you need, Emmanuel. That's why we're here."

"I know—I know. You're good to me. But first, you must be hungry; let us eat."

Before the feast, much of the party disappeared to conduct their ablutions, while others prayed. When they reconvened, they were led into the refectory and seated at the never-ending table. The imams, rabbis, and bishops were seated first. There they glowed, as people so often do when presented with food on an empty stomach. All chatter ceased when in came the Caliph and the Chief Rabbi; but everyone scrambled to their feet and every mote of dust seemed to hang in mid-air when the Chancellor entered. Having taken his seat at the head of the table, he gave a subtle flick of his wrist and the guests resumed their seats and gravity was applied to the dust once more.

Salmon, much to the appeasement of all, was the main dish (fish being a dish with little religious regulation). Course after course came, and the people of the table grew bloated and tired. One bishop, who'd consumed one goblet of wine too many, called out, "Sultan, I notice on your head you wear a turban. Which sect of Islam are you, then? Shia? Sunni? Salafi? Ahmadiyya?" The Chancellor was ready to dismiss the bishop for his obscene etiquette, but the Caliph, smiling, asked him not to. "Emmanuel, I have great pleasure in answering this question." Turning to the bishop, the Caliph said, "I'm of no sect because a sect only exists in the heart of the corrupted man. There is only Islam in the eyes of Allah. I am Muslim. This is the only title I choose."

The Chancellor clapped and everyone followed, and the banquet resumed, though he himself rejected his plate, having no appetite for anything other than conversation. He pushed aside his dinner plates, the salt and pepper jars, cutlery, even his wine goblet, as though clearing a path of dialogue between him and his most trusted friends.

"Emmanuel?" said the Chief Rabbi.

"I've not the appetite tonight, Levi," said the Chancellor in a low voice. At once, the Caliph and the Chief Rabbi folded their napkins and pushed away their plates. Then they drew in their chairs and turned in their ears. "Brothers, my leadership is failing."

The Caliph's eyes widened; the Chief Rabbi's eyes narrowed; their heads flitted between one another.

"I don't believe it, Emmanuel," said the Chief Rabbi. "Your people love you."

"They love themselves, Levi. You see, their love of this life is greater than that of the hereafter."

"Ah!" said the Caliph. "What is the life of this world but goods and chattels of deception?"

"Precisely, Sultan. My people are distracted by material things. They've turned away from the Lord. The churches, the mosques, and the synagogues of Europe—they're empty. Tell me, Sultan, are the mosques empty in Babylon? Levi, are the synagogues empty in Israel?"

Both shook their heads. Their houses of worship were oversubscribed.

"There may be peace in my republic," added the Chancellor, "but there's also grave doubt; and where there's doubt, there's sin; and where there's sin, sooner or later, there comes retribution."

"Doubt," said the Chief Rabbi, "is a struggle we've all faced, Emmanuel."

"Yes, individually. But doubt has infected the entire continent like a disease."

"What reason is there for such widespread doubt?" said the Caliph, inclining his head towards the ceiling in the search for an answer. After much rummaging, he found no answer in his beard either.

A moment after the Chancellor's goblet touched his lips, not a drop remained. When he returned it to the table, one servant ready in waiting uttered, "Your Excellency," and renewed its contents again.

"Science," said the Chancellor. "Science teaches the masses to doubt our faiths."

"Some science in particular?"

"Oh yes ... Darwin's theory of evolution."

"Emmanuel," said the Chief Rabbi, "evolution and faith—are they at odds? My understanding is the Pope accepts evolution. Does the Pope, and the many popes before him, not admit evolution is God's method of creation?"

"The Pope is advancing a lie," said the Chancellor. With his shaking hand, he swept back the silver strands obscuring his view. "Times may change, but the Bible does not. The word of God is absolute. Women priests? Same-sex marriage? Tut-tut-tut. The relaxing of God's laws has weakened His message and has seen to the diminution of His congregation. And all this talk of evolution—and its acceptance by the Pope—is the latest in a series of Trojan horses to have infiltrated the Church with pagan views. But we're not to be yoked with the unbelievers, 'for what partnership has righteousness with lawlessness? What fellowship has light with darkness?'. Evolution—or *evilution*, as I refer to it—is the greatest enemy of faith."

"What is it about evolution you find threatening, Emmanuel?"

"Genesis. Genesis is the history book of our universe. And we three— Muslim, Christian, and Jew—we believe Adam and Eve were the first humans on earth, do we not?"

"We do," assured the Caliph and the Chief Rabbi. The imams, bishops, and rabbis were all eavesdropping, but the Chancellor showed no hesitation in speaking so openly, for they ought to be privy to his message in order that they might propagate it.

The Chancellor added: "If evolution were true, as the scientists insist, Adam and Eve couldn't be the first man and woman. Understand? Evolutionists teach that life began out of nothing and that somehow a single-celled organism came into spontaneous existence. Then after a series of biological accidents over millennia, those single-celled creatures transitioned, somehow, into the billions of different forms that inhabit the planet today ..."

"Ridiculous. In His image was man and woman created," said the Chief Rabbi, bowing his pious head.

"Not according to the evolutionists. Do you know what else they teach in our schools? They teach that your great-great-grandfather was a fish; you are a distant cousin of a banana; you are related to made-up species of dinosaurs; and they even have the audacity to teach that you are kindred with killer diseases such as HIV and coronaviruses. The Old Testament prophesied such lunacy long ago: in Jeremiah 2:27 it tells of nonbelievers and pagans who'd say to a tree, 'You are my father', and to a stone, 'You gave me birth'. Indeed, the evolutionists teach that all living organisms are related; they say *all* life shares a common ancestor. Lord have mercy on their souls."

"Emmanuel," said the Caliph, "remember: it is but a theory. What is a mere theory when compared to the Revelation? 'The Unbelievers, they are the worst of beasts' (Surah Al-Anfal 5). Pay them no heed."

"Nevertheless," sharpening his eyes, "they're steering children away from the Lord with their science fiction."

"They are a misguided people."

"'People', did you say, Sultan? *People*? I wish they'd see themselves as people. Their view is that man is merely an animal. An animal! Nothing but a naked ape. If we teach our children that they've evolved from monkeys, we can expect them to act like monkeys."

"Monkeys? A contemptible view of humanity," said the Chief Rabbi. "They are educated beyond intelligence."

"What does that leave us with but a society of animals? A herd following bestial instinct. And when there is no absolute morality, men stray into lawlessness. I've become weary of the uglification of my continent: I've inherited the keys to a continent of blasphemy and buggery, a continent of sodomy and suffering. These thugs and their penchant for the abortion of innocent children are worse than my blackest dreams of hell … No, I can't abide it any longer. So far I've been a good politician—a people-pleaser—but a terrible Christian to allow such devilry to continue. If ever I get to heaven, it won't be for my liberal governance."

"That's deeply concerning," said the Chief Rabbi. "But the fault isn't—"

"Concerning, you think, Levi? My deepest concern I'm reluctant yet to announce."

"If something is worrying you, Emmanuel, tell us so we may offer you advice," said the Caliph.

The Chancellor drew in a breath and released a pitiable sigh.

"Very soon they'll replace our Lord. That's the intention of the faithless. I know it. I've spoken with Him. The Lord has shown me."

"You have?"

"Replace with who, Emmanuel?"

"Themselves, Sultan. Themselves."

"They could never—"

"Don't underestimate the lure of their lies," said the Chancellor, drawing in his chair. "Scientists have all the tools they need. They've already hacked into the genes of a woolly mammoth and resurrected an extinct species. They have all the knowledge they need to modify man. They're already creating babies in laboratories using artificial wombs— all from a single strand of hair. Skip forward a few years, and they'll be creating designer babies—choosing their hair colour, eye colour, height, intelligence."

The Caliph plucked a black beard-hair and observed it under the light as if it was the first time he'd ever beheld one.

"There will be," added the Chancellor, "attempts to design a new species and evolve mankind. They'll try to make savants of themselves, and when the biohackers succeed, they'll say, 'Rejoice, for I am God.'"

"And the Lord revealed this to you?"

"Yes, in a dream. There will be claims of a new species of man; I know it. And it's my mortal duty to silence the first claimant. Otherwise, the floodgates of heresy will burst open."

"New species of man? A blasphemy!" declared the Caliph.

"Indeed; and the Pentateuch is clear about what to do with blasphemers," said the Chief Rabbi.

"Remind me, Levi."

"'One who blasphemes the name of the Lord shall be put to death; the whole congregation shall stone him,' (Leviticus 24:16)."

The Chancellor hummed while in deep consideration.

"Grievous," said the Caliph, "will be the day of judgement; 'they will be bound together, their garments will be liquid pitch, and their faces will be wreathed in fire' (Surah Ibrahim 49–50)."

"Sultan is right," said the Chancellor. "Authority is not mine to deal out their chastisement. It's for Him to judge the faithless on the day of judgement."

"What, then, will *you* do?" said the Caliph.

"Brothers, what can I do?" He orientated his body to each of them.

"It's clear to me," said the Chief Rabbi.

"And I, also," said the Caliph, swallowing an impending belch.

"You must," said the Chief Rabbi, prodding the table with his index finger, "enshrine your biblical laws into the laws of your land. Do as I've done with halakah law in Israel and as Sultan has done with sharia law in Babylon."

"Levi, they'd try to unseat me as Chancellor."

"Some may *try*."

"Emmanuel, you're the most powerful man in the world. If anybody can …"

The Chancellor turned the thought over in his mind. His thumb and forefinger underwent their routine massage: the moulding of a miniature world in his hand. "Canon law, hmm." His thumb and forefinger intensified their work. "My brothers, faith and evolution are incompatible—that much to me is clear, and my mind will never, ever, be changed." His olive eyes looked yonder.

"Then you already know what you must do," said the Caliph.

"I'm just afraid to do it."

"We are with you," said the Chief Rabbi, placing a hand on his shoulder. The Caliph placed his hand on the other.

"You're right. I can't deny that all you've said hasn't crossed my mind already. But your love and support comes when I'm in greatest need of it.

I ought to do what I should have done from the start of my administration as Chancellor: rehabilitate the Continent. Reset our government, with God at its very heart. Draw up canon law. Yes, it shall be the Journal of European Law (JOEL), wherein blasphemy will be decreed illegal, in both speech and literature. The theory of evolution must be taken out of every school curriculum and replaced with prayer. And those university professors who are the prophets of this scientific dogma will be dismissed, and I'll see their research shut down. For the sake of love; for the sake of peace; but more importantly, for the sake of truth, I must expunge this brainwashing. Our children do I pledge to bring up in the discipline and instruction of the Lord. I must restore His religious republic."

"Chancellor, you know I agree with you, but your critics will say you're denying your citizens the right of free will."

"Then I'll say unto them, 'Do you allow your sons and daughters to cross the road without first teaching them how to cross safely? Or do you allow them to learn by trial and error? No, not when the cost of error is fatal. And when it is, it's right to teach our children the safest ways to cross the roads of this world.' My brothers, my love for my lambs is unconditional, and I'm not so cruel as to condemn the children of God to the eternal fires of hell."

Goblets were raised and chinked.

"Yes … thy kingdom come, thy will be done," said the Chancellor, grooming his beard in contemplation. "On *earth* as it is in heaven … yes. On earth. Hmm."

"Are you feeling quite well, Emmanuel?" said the Chief Rabbi, lending extra support to his shoulder.

The Chancellor turned colourless and fell into repetition of the same prayer: "Thy kingdom come, thy will be done … on *earth* as it is in heaven …"

"Emmanuel?"

"Uh, hem—oh yes. Sorry. There's something I need to do."

Some colour returned to his face, and he became present again. Without a word, he rose from his seat, slackened his tie, threw down his jacket, and excused himself. The Caliph called and asked him where he was going.

"Sultan, you are the Caliph; Levi, you are the Chief Rabbi; your positions are holy, whereas mine is purely administrative. If I'm to be the head of a theocracy, the leader of God's kingdom here on earth, my status should represent something beyond my current office. Wait here till I return."

Deep confusion ran through the hall, especially among the members of the Chancellor's own clergy.

The Chancellor came upon the waxworks of the prophets. When standing before Abraham, he borrowed his white mantle and draped it about himself, fastening the belt about his waist. At the feet of Jesus were a pair of sandals which were about his size; these he unbuckled and then buckled onto his own feet. Lastly, he took the shepherd's crook from Moses—a beautifully warped white branch almost as tall as him. And having surveyed its knobbly edge, he pounded the stone floor with it. Then he reappeared at the head of the table in the guise of a shepherd. He was no longer burdened with the aspect of a sclerotic old man, but now had the visage of a humble demi-deity.

At first, the Caliph let slip his golden laughter and issued a thunderous thump to his chest, but his humour was swiftly corked when he saw the sincerity in the Chancellor's burning eyes.

The Chancellor spread his arms wide as though he were some vicegerent of Jesus Christ, the long mantle about his arms falling like angelic wings. At the stamping of the white crook, the entire hall fell into silence as though a spell had been cast upon them. Never had wood put so grave a dent in stone.

"There are sheep that are not of this fold"—with his crook, the Chancellor hooked in a fearful servant by the neck—"I must bring them so they can hear my voice. And there will be one flock, and I will be their Shepherd (John 10:16)."

A slow clap commenced. The Chancellor, or the Holy Shepherd as he now took to calling himself, released the fearful servant from his crook. Soon the whole place was in a general state of foot-stamping and cutlery-clanking and table-drumming which ran long into the evening. But the Holy Shepherd skipped the frivolities, bade his guests farewell, and retired early to bed.

In his bedchamber he dedicated a prayer to each of his servants for their good work and paid thanks also to the Caliph and the Chief Rabbi for their loyalty and wisdom. Then, having brought himself up from his knees, he, with crook in hand, got straight to work on rehabilitating the Continent.

CHAPTER FOUR

RAGNAROK

Year 2072 – Fourteen years later ...

With each year that passed, life, harsh weather, and indeed parenthood engraved more deeply the emergent wrinkles on the faces of Astrid and Thorsten. Their furniture remained the same, as did their clothes, the food they ate, the places where they walked, and the matters on which they talked.

Having bypassed puberty in the swiftest duration the human anatomy allows, Ulrik found himself at fourteen to be almost his father's height—on the verge of seven foot. In fact, virtually all his features engendered the Magnusson aspect, many being square: head, teeth, kneecaps, elbows, shoulders, and great snow-shovel hands; and his pappa's grass-green eyes shone like marble planets underneath his brooding brow. He had no substantial trace of Lillegard (from his mother's side) in his outward appearance, save the lightness of his hair. But that hideous yet pitiable underbite was entirely his own, and so too was the spread of body hair that forested his every inch of skin. These traits gave him the most arresting appearance: he was agreeable to the eye but also rather frightening at the same time, perhaps not dissimilar to the way you might appreciate a polar bear from a safe distance, but less so if you were to find yourself in one's immediate company.

On Pappa's strict advice, he avoided urban areas, never setting foot in any school, club, or society. The wilderness was his classroom, the fauna his classmates. Trekking and tracking were the features of his timetable. No exams, only tests of survival. And fishing was his chief hobby, or rather swimming was. Being of a permanent hot and bothered disposition, many summers ago—if it could indeed be deemed a summer, since Svalbard is seldom warmer than an Oslo winter—having the urge to cool himself off, he submerged himself naked in an icy fjord.

There, under the waves, Ulrik saw with crystal clarity the aquatic affairs of crawling creatures; krill tickled along the fronds of kelp, starfish scoffed mussels, urchins impaled sea cucumbers with their crimson spikes, and spindly snow crabs tried to mate with the destitute drones that had the semblance of their plastic doppelgangers. As he swam, he saw a single beluga whale heading along the same channel (having most likely been separated from its pod). For a moment, he came within petting distance, before it turned back and made for the seas of Greenland.

Ulrik returned daily to that spot, hoping to see that whale again while swimming. Though he never did. But at the changing of the seasons, he grew, by rapid degrees, accustomed to the icy waters and casually emerged from them free from injury every time.

One day, upon deciding to confess all this to his parents, it occurred to him that he'd stand a greater chance of convincing them of his Arctic scuba diving obsession by fetching home for them a supper of krill and mussels. At first, they were shocked; then hungry; then impressed; so much so that Pappa equipped him with the sturdiest net for the fishing of char; stock which he'd later go on to trade with other foragers for their wares: kohl, wood, pelts, and the like.

It was through Ulrik's newfound occupation that he discovered a love of swimming, and a talent, too, for those snow-shovel hands were also the best of oars. He spent hours paddling, undulating, and darting among the ice floes even at the height of winter. On those solitary shores, his brilliance went unnoticed for years. Until, that is, some local intrigue passed about the tongues of children (who are always first to discover such things). They watched from afar and often returned with siblings and friends, thereby settling the rumour of Quicksilver's existence (for that's what they called him at first, owing to the water droplets that crystallised on his body hair when emerging from the water). He was named a great many other things, and the nickname which eventually stuck was Troglodyte, before its abbreviated form, Troggler, was settled upon.

One such child, Brynolf Grimstad, having taken an especial dislike to Ulrik, led a regular cavalry of growling snowmobiles, ambushing him on his way home across the snowy plains; teasing, taunting, and tormenting him. At first, they pelted abuse, then snowballs, then rocks—sharp rocks disguised as snowballs.

These juveniles had at their disposal an entire language dedicated to causing offence. Ulrik kept silent under this volley of abuse, but the bulging of his temple, and the fidgeting of his hands, and the chewing of his lips rendered his anxiety impossible to hide. And like a fish, he bit their teases, taking their bait, only then to be snatched by the rusty hook and reeled in, flapping as its damned fate closed in around it.

One day, having finished his mid-afternoon swim, Ulrik found that his kicksled had gone, or rather had been reduced to a pile of cinders and ash on the beach, with today's krill barbecued into oblivion. His furs, too, had vanished. Some way off in the distance, the rotund silhouette of Brynolf was mounting his snowmobile with a bundle of stolen furs tucked under his arm. With the biting wind at his naked back, Ulrik sprinted across the pebbly beach and onto the snow (which was itself as coarse as concrete), shrieking like an escapee from an asylum. But rather than flee in terror, Brynolf wheeled around on the snowmobile to face him head on, the headlamps blinking, the engine revving, and the horn bleating. Without warning, the snowmobile charged forward like a rampant ram, unerring in its path and throwing up showers of snow in its wake. Ulrik's unintelligible yelling was drowned out by the riotous honk. All his muscles braced for impact as he leapt up shoulder-first into the air, man versus machine. All his consciousness and all his bravery were knocked out of him as he collided with Brynolf's snowmobile. He toppled in mid-air, and when he landed on his opposite shoulder, there sounded an audible pop at his collarbone.

When he woke it was to distant laughter, chants of "Troggler", and fading pastel skies. A scattered scarf was his only defence against the wind; this he used as a sling to take the weight of his floppy arm. In a tearful state, he dragged his bludgeoned body homeward, naked, much like the lands he roamed (for there were no forests or woodlands on Svalbard in which he could take cover. It had always been a chief regret of his, never to have borne witness to a living tree; he could only recall their wooden bones being used for the construction of longhouses and the building of fires).

The clank of a distant engine, the roar of an ocean wave, the whisper of the wintry wind; enough were these to strike up visions of Brynolf's return. His pacing eyes flitted from east to west, searching out his aggressors, and he was prepared at all events to drop to his knees and surrender. But for today, at least, they were gone.

He was slow in ascending the veranda, not through any growing fatigue or ache but being keen to defer the interrogation of his coming home injured.

Inside, a blast of heat spread over him and melted the diamond droplets clinging to his body hair and ponytail. That was the first time he'd shivered. He must've taken a blow to the face when hitting the ground, for his eye began to puff, the heat inside Thrudheim amplifying the conditions for the sudden swelling of his eye, so much so that it eventually closed.

He made a beeline for his bedroom, leaving behind a trail of wet patches like some Arctic slug (if ever such a creature existed)—until Pappa greeted him. "Any catch today, Ulrik?" he said, not fully looking up from tending the fire.

"Ulrik, your clothes!" said Mamma, casting him a tweed blanket to cover his nudity. "You'll be freezing to death."

Pappa scrunched his thick brow, pushed himself up from his knees, and left the fire to tend itself. With the poker in his hand, he pointed to

Ulrik's arm, elevated in its sling, and said, "You did that ... swimming? Where are your clothes?"

In the meantime, Mamma scurried out and in again with warm furs, thereby swaddling Ulrik as though he were fourteen years younger. She'd have sat him on her knee, too, had he not made a wild protest. Then he sat down, or rather was placed down by Mamma in a chair, and he winced at the disturbance to his collarbone.

"Who's done this to you?" said Mamma. "Brynolf Grimstad again?"

Ulrik pressed his face into a cushion. Its ghoulish imprint was absorbed into the fabric, leaving three damp patches: two small irregular blobs where tears erupted and one patch below, where drool pooled.

"Tell us what's been happening," said Pappa, heaving in and out tremendous gusts of breath.

"This is all your fault," said Ulrik, throwing down his cushion. "I hate my stupid life; I hate this stupid house; I hate these stupid clothes; and I hate the stupid food we eat. My only joy is swimming, but I can't even swim in a real pool because you won't let me. I hate everything about living here. I hate not having friends. I have nobody but you and *you*," eyeing Pappa with contempt. "You won't even let me be going to hospital when I'm in pain like this. You won't let me do anything 'if it didn't exist a thousand years ago'. I don't want to be living a thousand years ago. I want to live now, in the real world. And to get away from here. To make new friends. To swim. To compete. To dream."

Tutting at the sight of his tremendous black eye, Mamma nursed it in that rough maternal way, compressing against it a chunk of ice (having retrieved it, rather resourcefully, from the endless supply outside). "Ivar is to you a good friend?"

"Yah, when he's present. But he wasn't with me today."

"Ulrik," said Pappa, kneeling down to his level, his bass voice causing the entire house to vibrate, "you need to tell us what happened. You didn't cry, did you? You must never let anybody see you cry like this."

He made no reply.

"You can tell us what happened, Ulrik," said Astrid. "I promise, if it gives you peace, neither your pappa nor I will go threatening anybody."

Between intervals of throat-kinking and flowing tears, Ulrik told them all that had taken place.

"It's not my fault I'm different," he said in a strained voice, his collarbone a source of grief.

"We're all different," said Mamma, taking his chin in her hand. "Like snowflakes, no two of us are the same. You were born to be different."

"Yah, Ulrik," said Pappa, "be proud to be different."

"That's not what you're always telling Mamma. You say it's dangerous for me to be different, and I know that now. My life would be safe if I looked normal like them."

"Son, there are clinics on the Continent where surgeons can alter how you're looking. They put you to sleep, knife open your face, and mould plastic beneath your skin. Like a doll, they remodel you. Would you want that? To change who you are?"

"Nuh, I don't want to change." He lowered his gaze, and his leaf-green eyes darkened, turning red as though struck by a sudden autumn. "I want everybody else to change."

"That's my son." Pappa nodded and rumpled his hair.

Ulrik continued: "I want to stand up to him. I want to make *him* hurt. I want to punish him. I just don't know if I can take him."

"You're much taller and stronger than Brynolf," said Pappa.

"Nuh, there won't be any fighting," said Mamma. "Ulrik, bear, you might have to stop swimming. Just for a while. Until things settle back to the way—"

"You can't stop me." Ulrik stood up, though too quickly, for the movement tremored throughout his body and aggravated his collarbone. "I'd rather die. Swimming is all I have. My only passion."

Mamma glanced towards Pappa as though seeking support, but he dismissed her, pretending to be occupied by other pressing ideas. Her lips tightened and her eyes twitched, but turning back to Ulrik, her face changed to one of pity for him.

"It's not *all* you have, Ulrik; you have us, you have Ivar—who is as good as any friend I've ever had. Together we hunt, we fish, we forage, we make clothes, we trade—"

"Nuh," said Ulrik, attempting to retreat to his room, though he was shepherded back into his chair by the hand of maternal empathy. "We scavenge. We don't live; we survive. I don't want to be living this kind of life anymore."

"Ulrik," said Pappa, trying to collect his hand in his, "I understand you're hurt—you're upset."

"I won't be changing my mind, Pappa." Ulrik retracted his hand.

———

Evening came, and the subjects of discourse changed, and the mood lightened while Ulrik's black eye darkened. This turgid sack of fluid caused his eye to clamp shut so that his vision in it was entirely blinded.

Suppertime was upon them, and Pappa volunteered himself as the cook. He was to treat Ulrik to his favourite dish: spiced char broth, which had thick white flakes of fish swimming in a light orange soup. When it had been served, they sat huddled together on the hide rugs, inhaling their broth from their bowls, and, without the hindrance of a spoon, vacuuming it up with the nozzles of their mouths. Ulrik stained his blond beard in his attempts to lick his bowl dry. So clean was the bowl that there was no evidence of it ever having been used, and it could instantly be reused for the next meal without threat of contamination.

Suitably full, Ulrik thanked them both, bade them each a good night, and withdrew to his room, but not without first stubbing his toe—owing to his temporary blindness in one eye. Pappa guided him the rest of the way, plumped his pillows, and lit a few candles. When Ulrik heard the door click shut behind him, he sat on the end of his straw mattress, only to see, out of the corner of his good eye, that Pappa had remained behind. Pappa shuffled up next to him, slapped both his knees, and drew a great quantity of air into his lungs.

"How's your eye?"

"It doesn't hurt so much, but I can't see anything. Though my collar-bone—agh—I think I'll be sleeping upright tonight." He shuffled back to the wall, with his floppy arm elevated.

"You know the All-father had one eye?" said Pappa, with a mysterious glee about him.

"The All-father?"

"Odin, the Norse god."

"I didn't know Odin also had this name, and I never knew he had one eye."

Ulrik heard the skitter of feet outside: Mamma listening in, no doubt.

"Yah," said Pappa. "Odin plucked out his own eye and sacrificed it into a well so he could drink from its waters. You want to know why? Because after drinking from this well, he gained insight into a deep and ancient knowledge."

"He plucked out his own eye?"

"Yes. Because Odin understood the value of wisdom and was prepared to make sacrifices for it. Hey, it's been a while since I told you a story. Want me to tell you one now?"

"Pappa, I'm not a youngling anymore."

"I know, but you don't have to be a youngling to enjoy a good story. They're good for taking our minds off things. To help us unburden. Forget our troubles. They give us hope."

"Mamma says you shouldn't be filling my head with your stories. And the other younglings—they get to watch things called movies on their Tech. Do you know what a movie is? It's a story. I've never seen one. Ivar says it's like real life, but the people in it aren't real. Tractors, I think they're called. I'd like to see one."

"Actors, Ulrik." Pappa chuckled. "Movies, yah, I remember them. You aren't missing out on much. Folk waste their whole lives watching them. Okay, why don't you let me tell you the greatest Viking story; the story with the *biggest* battle and the *bravest* warriors?"

They butted foreheads in agreement, as was their custom; a custom practised upon greeting and farewelling, in both the morning and evening, both before food and after; it could be employed to express to someone that they were liked, although at times it was even more apt to express dislike. It was a savage equivalent to that of the handshake practised by southerners. But in Ulrik's tender condition, they met with only a gentle connection.

"Ragnarok: the doom of the gods," said Pappa, clenching his fist like a hammer. "Chaos, Ulrik. A great battle will be fought, and the mightiest will fall. It'll be the end of the world as we know it—so said our ancient fathers."

"The end of our world? You say it like you believe it, Pappa."

"So you think me a fool to believe in such things?"

"They're just myths—old legends."

"Billions of people believe Jesus Christ walked on water and rose from the dead. Billions believe the Prophet Muhammad flew to the moon on a winged horse. Billions believe we are the descendants of Adam and Eve. Do you consider these myths and legends?"

"Nuh, Pappa, they're actual religions."

"And yet no more believable …"

"Well, I'll decide myself what to believe in one day. Too many people believe a thing just because their parents have told them to. I'd like to make up my own mind about what's true. Anyway, on with the story."

"Indeed. Unlike many endings, we will foresee the end of the world coming: a world under snow; a cock will crow; a horn will blow; at these three signs will the entire world know."

"A world under snow? But it's always snowing here on Svalbard, Pappa; it's always cold."

"Well, there are countries south of here where it's always summer. The high sun cooks and cracks the skin of those who stray from the shade. But even those golden sands will be swept up in favour of dunes of snow."

"And that will end the world? Pappa, we've survived the harshest winters. If we—"

"Some will perish in that winter, but this is only an omen of the chaos to come. The factions of the world will wage war upon one another.

Cities, countries, empires will fall, and thereafter the greatest treachery of all will happen: brothers will kill brothers."

"Good job I don't have any brothers, then."

"Ah, Ulrik," said Pappa, and a solemn look befell him. "You wouldn't be wanting my brothers."

"Why, Pappa? Tell me."

"I'll tell you when you're older."

"You always say that because you're hoping I'll forget and never ask again. Tell me about my uncle Karsten and Sigsten. Karsten is your twin, right? Mamma says he looks exactly like you. A clone. Tell me the stories of your youth."

"My brothers—nuh … I can't. We were the best of friends some days; other days, not so much. That's all. Some other time, perhaps. Now, about Ragnarok."

Before Pappa told any more, he removed a layer of fur, then another, and kept going until he looked in danger of stripping off his outer layer of skin, so unbearably itchy were those questions for him.

"Ragnarok, Ulrik; Ragnarok. Those who remain will mourn the slain. The dead will be strewn across the land like a table set out for ravens. The scavengers of the sky will descend upon the cemeteries of the world, but there will be little worth a peck after the world is clad in a robe of hellish flame. Think you that you would hide underground from the fires? What then when the ground quakes and the rubble of your house becomes your burial mound—when all houses are reduced to rubble and become the graves of their tenants? Think you that you would scale the highest mountain? What then when the rains of falling soot and ash choke your lungs and poison your bloodstream? Think you that you would favour the air at sea, set out with a crew, and live a waterman's life? What then when the serpent of the sea whips up its hind, causing violent tides and watery wreckage? Think you that if you survived this you would be a creature of fortune? What then when the black wolves rise and swallow the moon and all the lights of the sky, leaving the world in absolute darkness? What then, Ulrik? What then?"

"Pappa, you're a little too much absorbed in your own delusions some-times. We're living in the twenty-first century, not the *first*."

"Delusions, you say? Maybe ... But aren't we all deluded to some extent? Isn't that why we tell stories? Isn't that their purpose? To delude our reality?" Pappa fingered his pewter pendant—fashioned into the shape of a short-handled hammer—which hung from a plain band of twine about his neck. "You think I'm crazy, Ulrik; but the Vikings were closer than any before them to understanding the secrets of our origins: from our fiery father and watery mother, among the hissing and sputters there came into being the first of creatures, so the *legends* tell. Now, even scientists today say life began at such events, supposing life began in hydrothermal vents. Bah! Our legends have as much authority about our beginnings as any other belief or science. So, if our Viking ancestors were right about our beginning, should we be dismissive about their prophecy of our ending?"

"So what happens when our world dies?" said Ulrik, in a tone of extreme scepticism.

Pappa held out his index finger: *wait one moment*. He quitted the bedroom in a hurry and came back with a leaf of browned paper. There was some runic inscription upon it that had been penned in charcoal. It was an alphabet (Old Futhark) that Ulrik was a great deal more fluent in than that of the swirling letters of the English language. Suitably reclined (as well as could be, given the sting at his collarbone), Ulrik sat in anticipation, the candlelight dancing under Pappa's brooding brow as he commenced a rhythmic tapping on the wooden wall.

"Hum in a low, steady tone, Ulrik."

"Why?"

"Because we all have our part to play in this story."

To please his pappa, Ulrik hummed.

"Now, here is what I've written of Ragnarok:

I counsel you, do not forget
Beware the fell winter and the crowing of the cock

Ragnarok

Hearken to the horn's call or sense you regret
For these are the shadows of Ragnarok

Come will the chaos where brothers slay brothers
Where sundered be shields and reddened be spears
This flashing of swords; this bane of all mothers
Summons a lament of unnumbered tears
Though, I counsel you, do not forget
Beware the fell winter and the crowing of the cock
Hearken to the horn's call or sense you regret
For these are the shadows of Ragnarok

From the temper of fellow man will the Last Dregs hide
Upon ships which have all storms withstood
But yet have they to endure a heaven-high tide
No faraway shores shall escape the Flood
Though, I counsel you, do not forget
Beware the fell winter and the crowing of the cock
Hearken to the horn's call or sense you regret
For these are the shadows of Ragnarok

Cities be razed, and the mountains will quake
Blackened be greensward by the Roaring Red Riot
The lamps of the sky will the hellhounds break
Their snapping jaws sentence the world into quiet
Though, I counsel you, do not forget
Beware the fell winter and the crowing of the cock
Hearken to the horn's call or sense you regret
For these are the shadows of Ragnarok

Two survivors the cemetery underfoot hides
Their green eyes bud amidst the lingering smoke
Rising from black snows of ash side by side

The seeds of Ash and Elm be woke
Though, I counsel you, do not forget
Beware the fell winter and the crowing of the cock
Hearken to the horn's call or sense you regret
For these are the shadows of Ragnarok

A hatching sun spills forth its golden yolk
Paying dale and vale a dowry of grain
Naked lands be clad in a new green cloak
White rivers froth with shoals of fish again
Though, I counsel you, do not forget
Beware the fell winter and the crowing of the cock
Hearken to the horn's call or sense you regret
For these are the shadows of Ragnarok

Cries return at the new world's dawn
Milk from the bosom be once more drawn, they gleam
And open their eyes, this litter of fawn
The world their birthright, or so they dream
Though, I counsel you, do not forget
Beware the fell winter and the crowing of the cock
Hearken to the horn's call or sense you regret
For these are the shadows of Ragnarok

This be the origin of all things living
Winter; the requisite for the coming of spring
Amidst the heart of darkness be a stout light renewing
Fire—ice; Father of creation and Mother of undoing
Marry they in Hvergelmir ere the New Era brewing
But profit you will to remember the harbingers of ruin
And I counsel you, do not forget
Beware the fell winter and the crowing of the cock
Hearken to the horn's call or sense you regret
For these are the shadows of Ragnarok."

All tapping and humming ceased.

"What does it mean?" said Ulrik, rolling his eyes in ignorance.

"The cycle of all that will come to pass. After the end, there shall be a new beginning," said Pappa, pinning the paper to the wall with his thumb and a loose nail, pressing the nail till its head sank completely in the wood. "I'll pin it here should you wish to remember it."

"And you really believe all that?" asked Ulrik. Pappa always tried to weave lessons into his stories, but Ulrik struggled to draw any inspiration from this account. "Pappa, you're crazy for the things you believe in."

"Perhaps ... but then perhaps I'm no crazier than those folk on the mainland who believe in their one true god. They spend their lives on their knees in worship. Anyway, there's something I want you to be having ..." Ulrik's eyes followed Pappa's hands as they took the hammer pendant from around his neck. Pappa secured it longingly in his fist one last time. "Mjolnir; the hammer of Thor."

"Pappa, I'm not sure—"

"I haven't taken this off since we came to Svalbard. It was the start of something new for me, and it's been a part of everything important in my life. I think there's a new start awaiting you, Ulrik, and that's why I want you to have it."

Pappa let his fist flex open and he looped the necklace over Ulrik's head; which wasn't the cleverest thing to do since, despite its relative lightness, it seemed to weigh heavy on his collarbone. Though he was gracious in acceptance, if only to please his pappa.

"Thank you, Pappa."

"You know what 'Mjolnir' means, Ulrik?"

"I think—"

"It means 'crusher' in old Norse. Wear this and, at the very next occasion, crush Brynolf Grimstad. Will you do that for me, Ulrik? Will you crush him?"

"I'll try."

Pappa drew himself up to his full height and took a last look at him before he pinched out the heads of the candles with his fingertips. The door creaked open and clicked shut behind him.

"Dream well, Pappa," he said, but he'd already gone.

Ulrik sat upright in the absolute darkness of his room and at once fell into a broken sleep, waking often throughout the night, disturbed by the agony of his collarbone.

———

Astrid snuck away onto the veranda moments before Thor quit the bedroom. On her way, she'd snatched a giant flagon and topped it up with mulled wine. She tidied her hair, leant over the balustrade, and gave off the impression that she'd spent the entire evening out here counting the stars and gazing into the cosmos.

Heavy, hollow footsteps came upon her from behind. A tender hand massaged her barley-blonde hair, gliding through it and working out the knots. She felt the twirling of one of her plaits (presumably around a finger) and then a gentle tug, causing her to turn in the direction of its pulling.

"Glogg?" she said, offering the flagon to Thor's face.

He lifted it to his nostrils and drew in a prolonged sniff; the steam drawn into his nostrils caused them to loosen and flare wide.

"Smells great, as always."

"Liar."

"Nuh, this time it smells great. I can see you've put effort into it." He took a modest sip. "Though it tastes like piss."

She elbowed him in the chest, but he stood unflinching as a stone pillar; not a single millimetre of ground did he concede, yet she herself almost tumbled backwards. "And how would you know what piss tastes like?"

"Well, I remember a time when my wife couldn't control her bladder, and—"

"I was giving birth, you stinking troll." This time she twisted his nipple and only released him after he pleaded for mercy. Then she leant against him, crossing her arms, trusting him with her entire weight. He reined in her waist and engulfed her in his warm furs. "You're good for body heat," she said. "That's all I want you for." She blew a mist of whirling fog into his blinking face, then turned around and looked across the snowy wilderness; his arms were like a great harness across her midriff, and his beard acted like the woolliest scarf at the back of her neck. Then a silence befell them; her thoughts dwelt on Ulrik.

"It has me worrying all the time, Thor. I don't want him to go swimming out there, but I don't have the heart to stop him."

"I don't think we could stop him if we tried. He never listens."

"What can we do?"

"There's nothing we can do. It's for him to resolve. He needs to fight back."

"But he isn't like you, Thor."

"He isn't like you, either, Astrid. Hasn't it occurred to you that he's unlike anybody else who's ever existed? Swimming naked in frozen water?"

She slipped away and sat on the lowest veranda step, caring not if it froze her haunches. She bit away at strands of her hair, trimming the split ends and letting the wind carry them away.

"Stop chewing your hair," said Thor, taking up a seat behind her and holding her hand to prevent any more of the like. Their fingers interlocked and clanked where their wedding rings collided; each was the same token, the shape of a lindworm, a wingless dragon coiled about their finger.

"Our wedding was the best day," she said. "I think about it all the time."

"I was thinking about it only yesterday."

"I like to imagine walking barefoot on the grass, in our grove alongside the riverbank. Trees half fallen into the stream. Blackbirds tweeting. Hares frolicking. Frogs croaking. That was the hottest summer I can remember. I'd do anything to go back for a day—or even one hour."

"You made me cry, seeing you in your dress walking through the glade. If you ever tell the boy I cried—don't you ever."

"It was a beautiful dress until you tackled me into the grass."

"I fell into you."

"You wrecked my dress."

"I was drunk."

"And I don't blame you." She laughed, then rested her face on her fist. "Oh, Thor, I know you don't miss your family, but I'm hoping to see mine again soon."

"It's not that I don't want to, it's just—"

"Let's take Ulrik. Show him something new. Give him a new sense of who he is. Let him discover his own identity instead of always trying to make him be like us. He needs his own adventure. If we cage him up here, he'll resent us forever."

"Why do you forget, Astrid? The whole reason we came here … I'm trying to protect us."

"Well, why not invite my parents here? They would come in the summer, if their health allows it. They're getting old, Thor. I might never see them again."

"Nobody can know where we're living. If you've told anybody—if you've risked our safety—"

"Relax. I haven't told anyone." She let slip a great sigh. He stroked her cheek with a finger, but when she bared her teeth he must have sensed the danger of losing it. He drew his hand away from her face and linked arms with her instead.

"I know you're thinking it would be good for Ulrik, but I don't. You've seen how people look at him. Not just fledglings, but adults, too. Nuh, I can't. We need more time to consider."

"Nuh, we won't consider anything. You'll let me forget or try to convince me until I give in. But you won't be changing my mind. Not this time. With or without you, I'll be taking my son home."

"Home?"

"Yah, home. And I don't want him hearing any more of your stories, either. Don't you think he has enough on his mind without you telling him 'brothers kill brothers'? You think you're being clever?"

"Maybe it's preparing him; preparing him by telling him the

consequences of what will happen if we should return. Maybe you should remember that, Astrid."

"You choose to be exposing him to the same thing you want to protect him from. Sharing your pain won't halve it; it will double it."

"Why do you always talk to me like I'm stupid?"

"Because you say stupid things, Thor. You promised me you'd never tell him of Karsten or Sigsten—or our past. Why are you now saying you'll tell him when he's older? I overheard you in the bedroom just then. I don't want to be having this conversation again."

"And I don't want to hear about going back to the mainland again. Do you think if we return, Karsten won't find out? You talk about keeping our past from Ulrik, but here you are begging to return to the place from which we escaped."

Astrid waited for him to retract his comment, though his lips remained steadfast; so tight were they that they curled inwards, exposing his square teeth. She unhooked her arm from his, stood up, patted him on the head, and excused herself.

"Where are you going?"

"Nowhere. I'm trapped here, aren't I? Like a bird in a cage. Right where you want me …"

He gave no reply.

She left him alone on the veranda and took shelter inside, hoping he'd follow her and agree to some compromise. But he didn't. From behind a razor-thin gap in the doorway, she peered out. Thor seemed relaxed, uncaring, happier now he was alone and engaged in sprightly conversation with himself. She pressed her ear close to the gap, trying to make sense of the murmurs he made, but the wind was wuthering wildly. When it abated, she heard his delusional reciting of the same portentous poem he'd read to Ulrik as a bedtime story. Never was a man more absorbed in his own delusions.

Her crumpled chin assumed the shape of a craterous moon as she fought back tears. She looked down at her wedding ring and for the first time resented it. With great friction, she twisted and prised it off, leaving a pinkish scar where it had been clamped all these years. She placed it in an obvious place where she hoped it would be instantly noticed: dead centre of the supper table: a statement of intent. As she went further into the passageways of the longhouse, the rumble of Thor's prophecies seemed to pursue her like a foreboding shadow.

"... For these are the shadows of Ragnarok," echoed Thor philosophically. "Hmm, Ragnarok."

CHAPTER FIVE

A FEUD IN THE MOUNTAINS

The night treated him with contempt.

Ulrik dreamt, as he often did, of floating weightless in a real swimming pool. Not tossed this way and that by the volatile ebb and flow of the ocean surf, but levitating atop the crystal-clear water. Lying idle. A weightless ghost in an aqueous heaven. But all at once his every feature turned to solid gold, and his weight intensified under some unrelenting gravity that sent him crashing beneath the surface. As he sank, he lunged for the air—and in doing so lunged in real life and awoke to a hideous sting at his collarbone that sent a sharp pang throughout the conduits of his bones.

Groggy, he groped at his bedside table and picked up a hand-mirror, thereafter checking himself over. He appeared to be growing a prize plum out of his eye socket, so puffy and purple had this tumour-like injury become. It seemed like a water balloon liable to burst should a coarse finger-nail make accidental acquaintance with it. The temptation to scratch it was almost impossible to resist, yet somehow he suffered it without doing so.

There was a disturbance outside his bedroom: a slinging of baggage and rummaging of goods; a great huffing and puffing that was usually heard about this time on market day. Mamma and Pappa, late, no doubt, for their day of trade; a day on which ships from faraway places dock and offload throngs of affluent passengers who come not with money but wares to trade with the forager merchants of Svalbard in return for their handmade goods.

His bedroom door flew open and Mamma slouched in the doorway. Her arms were loaded with wooden carvings of narwhal, bear, and fox—each encrusted with signature white stone eyes—and over her shoulder was slung a fat sack of knitted hats, scarves, and mittens.

"How are you feeling, bear?" asked Mamma, dropping the contents of her arms onto his bed and making a fuss over him.

"Tired," he said. "Hungry."

She took his chin in her hand, tilted his head, and surveyed his eye. "See that you get some ice on that; but before you do, go and toast the last of the bread before your thieving pappa eats it all. Oh, and there's some lingonberry yoghurt, too. And if you're still hungry, there are some left-over sweetmeats in the store. Have that for lunch."

Just then, he noticed that her wedding ring was missing. "Mamma, your ring ... have you misplaced it?"

She kissed him on the head, scooped up her merchandise, and told him not to worry. Passing through the doorway, she craned her neck and said, "Are you sure you'll be okay alone today?"

He returned an impassioned nod. She said she was proud of him and dashed outside to load up her kicksled.

After shuffling out of bed, he rotated his good shoulder, and there was a temptation to loosen his other shoulder, too, but the threat of aggravating his collarbone stymied the urge. Instead, he rotated his wrist and, with great care, flexed his stiff elbow. But once he sensed the smell of food, he forgot all about his injury and became invigorated, like a bloodhound at the scent of prey. He lumbered out in search of it.

"Savage boy," said Pappa, slapping his pockets and striding about the longhouse with his boots on, searching, it seemed, for his house key. "You look like you've returned from battle. Makes you look tough, that eye."

"Pappa," said Ulrik, his mouth full and churning like a cement mixer, "your key is on the antlers."

"Gah, course it is. Thanks. Now, make sure to get lots of rest today, you."

"I've agreed to meet Ivar at our halfway point, so I was thinking—"

"Leave the house? I don't think that's a good idea, what with your collarbone. You can't."

"Pappa, Ivar is the only friend I have." He dusted the toast crumbs out of his stubble. "He'd wait for me all day. I can't keep him standing there forever. I will go, if only to tell him I must return to Thrudheim and rest. Please, Pappa; once I've seen Ivar, I'll come back here and eat and sleep and rest as much as I can."

"Nuh. The reindeer herdsmen and the trappers have reported bear sightings. They're on the increase. This isn't a negotiation. You are to stay here and rest. Now, we're late;"—throwing a fur cloak over his shoulders—"we need to be moving. Astrid … ?"

She was already waiting outside.

Ulrik bit down on his bottom lip and wrung his face into a hideous scrunch. He followed Pappa out onto the veranda; and then he watched on through the narrow slits between his scowling eyes as they slalomed down the hill on their kicksleds; kicksleds that were brimming with stock to barter and haggle with.

Breakfast having been devoured, Ulrik now got dressed, though he abstained from layering up too many furs that would weigh heavy on his shoulders.

"I'm not staying here on my own, only to be bored out of my mind. Curse them. I'm old enough to do what I want, when I want."

With one dextrous hand, he laced his boots and was ready to defy his parents and set out in the opposite direction—into the mountains. While in the doorway, he gave one last look at his bow and quiver of arrows hanging from the reindeer antlers, judging it for a good deal of time; speaking with it, insulting it, even. Such a lame weapon was this when compared to those of the other younglings, whom he often saw carrying rifles on their way to school. A bow was a worthless, primitive weapon—a stupid weapon—and not worth the girding around his collar and risking further aggravation to it. He abandoned the bow, the arrows, and thereafter, Thrudheim.

Up a steep, rocky ascent he trudged, kicking snow as he went and cursing his pappa for his cruel rules. A short while later, his mood was lifted when a stout figure emerged in the distance and advanced with a confident gait, both fluid and purposeful. Scorched tangles of raven hair fell from the hood of the pale-faced wanderer. Ivar had ventured beyond their halfway point and come in search of him (owing to his lateness). Ulrik thrust his good arm into the air, and Ivar signalled back with a spirited wave. When they neared one another, they grinned; but when Ivar saw his eye, all the features of his face drooped south as though surrendering to an intensified gravity. Ulrik stooped down to Ivar's height, insisting they still butt heads regardless of his injuries.

"Ulrik, your eye," said Ivar, lowering his hood and thereafter butting heads with him. "It looks terrible."

"It's not too painful. I'm suffering more because I want to scratch it. My collarbone, now that hurts. I think it's cracked."

"Let me see. Who's done this to you?"

"Who else?"

"Didn't you fight back?"

"I wanted to, but he's much older, and there were many of them, and he struck me with a snowmobile."

"But you could break Brynolf in two."

"If it happens again, I won't be giving him the same chances, that's for sure."

"You mean you'll fight him next time?"

"I think it's the only way to stop him."

"That's brave. Now come; we've got better things to be doing than wasting our time talking about trolls like Brynolf Grimstad. Let's go for a hike."

Ulrik insisted on returning home, but since Ivar had covered a greater distance to meet him, he felt obliged to spend a little longer in his company. So the two of them went about the snowy country, chatting without pause about whatever subject sprang to mind.

"If you could choose to be anything in the world when you grow up, what would it be, Ulrik?"

"Sometimes I think anything but a stinking forager, and anything that would get me out of this cursed place—this frozen hell I call Niflheim. But if I could choose to be anything, I'd be a swimmer, swimming in a real pool against other swimmers. And I want to be famous for winning medals."

"You'd be the best swimmer, Ulrik. You swim every day without fail. I bet you could actually do that one day."

"Doubt it. I'm a forager. I'll probably never leave this place. Anyway, what would you like to be when you're older, Ivar?"

"I saw the white mammoth the day before yesterday. You know, the one at the Arctic Sanctuary? Onyx they call him. I think I'd like to work there as some kind of ranger."

"I haven't been lucky enough ever to see that mammoth," said Ulrik. "Must be terrible being the only one of your kind. Nobody else to relate to. Yah—a lonely existence."

"It's sad there won't be any more mammoths for him to make friends with."

"Why is that? They made him in an observatory, so can't they just make some more mammoths?"

"*Laboratory*, you mean, Ulrik. He was made in a laboratory—and my uncle says it's because of the laws of United Europe."

"What laws? I don't understand."

"Uncle says the government doesn't trust scientists because scientists have taken their research too far."

"But Onyx—they shouldn't be keeping him in bonds, and all alone. That should be legal."

"You mean *illegal*, Ulrik."

"Yah, it should be illegal. He needs to be set free."

With the best intentions, they concocted half a plan of how they might emancipate the white woolly mammoth. They might've been bold enough to enact it, too, but their attention evaporated like a puddle under a summer sun, and they soon forgot about the storming of zoos and the rescuing of lonely creatures. Instead, they sat themselves on two humps of rock, deciding that now was the best time to satisfy the growls in their bellies.

Ivar took out a ruby-red apple from his satchel and tossed it to Ulrik. In less than ten seconds it had vanished; pips, core, and all.

"How are you not getting fat when all you do is eat?" said Ivar. "You grow only upwards like a pine and never outwards like a yew."

"I don't know what you mean, Ivar."

"Trees, Ulrik; they're types of trees."

"Oh, I knew that. Hey, pass me your knife for one moment."

"What for?"

"This tree"—pointing to his face—"needs pruning."

Ivar tossed Ulrik his sheathed pocket knife. Perhaps Ivar thought he was going to trim a few stray ends from his forelocks. Instead, with no explanation, Ulrik took the tip of the knife and perforated the edge of the fluid-filled sack molesting his eye. Red dribbles trickled out, commingling in his stubble, where it froze over; and when he squashed it with his fingertips, a bloody fountain squirted forth. His eyelid opened, and he became dazzled by the sunlight streaming in. When he looked upon Ivar with clear eyes again, he saw him shaking his head, his jaw unhinged and hanging low.

"Why the hell did you do that, Ulrik?"

"Because it was itching, and I couldn't take it any longer. See; it's better now."

"Don't you know anything?" Ivar snatched his knife, wiped the bloody blade in the snow, then took off hiking. "A bear's sense of smell is seven times as strong as a bloodhound's."

"Ivar, where are you going?" Ulrik strode after him, then broke into a jog. "What's all this talk of bears?"

"Bears, Ulrik; the polar bears," he said, over his shoulder. "They'll catch the scent and be drawn to us. They can smell prey from miles away."

At once, there came a growl in the distance. Both boys froze; their eyes panned across the country in search of prowling predators. As the growling grew louder and drew closer, they saw it was produced by a pack of beasts; beasts of a metallic kind: snowmobiles, throwing up powder as they rallied across the snow. Three figures rode atop, clad in luminous mountain wear and helmets. Their voices broke out in a raucous whooping, like cavalry routing a helpless band of peasants from their homes; encircling them now, and pelting them with rocks. Ulrik and Ivar shrank back to back, and when the barrage of rocks came to a halt, the invaders closed in for negotiations.

A figure dismounted from the shiniest, glossiest snowmobile. He approached with exaggerated swings of his arms as if he were up to his chest in clods of mud and was having great difficulty in wading through it, so taxing did the most rudimentary act of walking seem to him. Then he lifted off his helmet and slid his eyeTech to the top of his head. Brynolf Grimstad. If it could be said of Ulrik that his own features were square and cubic—head, jaw, teeth, joints—owing to his broad frame, then it could also be said of Brynolf that the geometrics of his anatomy were constructed entirely of spherical matter: a round head, paunchy body, discoid ears, hands swollen like soccer balls; no knuckle, knee, or elbow in sight; only via the agency of x-ray could a bone be identified. The only exception to this rotund arrangement was the two sharp horizontal slits where his eyelids parted; two piercing black pupils staring out from within and threatening the severest retaliation for meeting their gaze.

Ulrik's eyes fell to the snow.

"Aren't we lucky?" said Brynolf. "We go on a safari and see not one but *two* trogglers."

His fellowship laughed on cue.

"I might be a trogg—I mean forager," croaked Ulrik, clearing his throat, "but one day I won't be. I'll find a new home. Not a grotto, tent, cave, or igloo. A home of bricks, not sticks. And I'll work my way into a respected ..." In raising his eyes again Ulrik saw that Brynolf brandished a rifle over his shoulder, hogging it like a child does a favourite toy: happy to let others lay their eyes upon it, but never a sticky hand.

Ulrik had earlier contrived, upon such an occasion, to land a flurry of furious fists about the equator of Brynolf's skull and send him rolling off for good. He'd choreographed the event in his mind with perfect clarity, the outcome most favourable to himself, standing triumphant over his defeated foe. And after hearing out Brynolf's pathetic pleas, he'd find himself prone to a show of mercy and thereafter be showered with applause from some fictitious audience of weeping mothers and doting daughters. But now that the moment presented itself, the agony of his collarbone returned, and all the courage within his heart seemed to shrivel like a sun-dried tomato.

"You owe me, Troggler; you owe me for the damage done to my snowmobile." Brynolf rotated his globe-head on its axis towards his vehicle, then demonstrated, with a sequence of karate chops, the entire area of the dent.

"But you drove into me."

"You shouldn't have been standing there."

"If I had money, Brynolf, I'd pay for the damage."

"Course he has no money," announced one of Brynolf's companions. "These dirty trogglers don't work. They contribute nothing yet expect everything."

"And I've seen them," said the other, "wiping their asses with snowballs and moss."

"Ugh. You don't belong here, Troggler," said Brynolf, his narrow eyes engulfed by his rodent cheeks.

"Is it true you're only fourteen years old?"

"Why do you have blood in your beard?"

"And why do you have so much fur on your face? I can't tell where your eyebrows stop and where your hairline starts."

"Why do you swim in freezing waters?"

"Why do you look so stupid? Guh-gah-gurgh."

"Neanderthal—Neanderthal—Neanderthal."

"Enough," said Ivar, advancing to Ulrik's side. There was an electricity in the air, like the close humidity before a storm.

"*I* say when we've had enough," said Brynolf, aiming down his rifle at Ulrik, his wobbly cheek overhanging the butt of the weapon. "Say sorry for being so ugly, Troggler."

"We've done you no wrong," said Ivar, pressing his forehead to the muzzle of Brynolf's weapon. "Why do you keep doing this?"

"Because I can," said Brynolf. Turning sharply, he beat the muzzle on Ulrik's shoulder, and in that instant agony Ulrik fell to his knees, heaving in and out huge gusts of Arctic air. "Now say sorry."

"Agh. Please, okay, okay," said Ulrik, resting his hand upon his collarbone as though holding the shards of it together. "I'm sorry for being ugly. I'm sorry for being ugly. I'm sorry for being ugly. There, I said it."

"Enough," said Ivar, snatching the barrel of the rifle and attempting to wrest it from Brynolf's grip. But Brynolf lunged forward at the same time and rammed it into Ivar's sternum, winding him.

"Look, he's protecting his boyfriend," said Brynolf. "Come; kiss your boyfriend, Troggler." He poked the back of Ulrik's head with the rifle. After ordering him to stand, he was guided to Ivar's face—whose head was being twisted like a corkscrew in the hands of one of the bullies. A hand from behind seized Ulrik's scalp, and his head was pressed to Ivar's. They curled their lips inward to prevent contact.

"Ugh, look at them kissing. These trogglers aren't real men."

"Fight me," said Ivar, wresting his head free. A clump of hair was torn from his scalp as he did so. Standing head to head, his breath billowed between their faces. "Only you and me, Brynolf. Fight me without rocks and rifles."

"I would fight but, ugh,"—with one hand Brynolf wafted the air as though a rancid agent was borne along with it; with the other hand he pinched his nose—"your breath stinks."

"Put down the rifle and fight me, walrus," said Ivar, eyes bloodshot with red lightning bolts, speech imbued with thunderous tones.

"Don't be letting him talk to you like that, Brynolf," said one of Brynolf's companions. "Take the troggler down."

"My rifle," said Brynolf, "is worth more than everything you'll ever own in your lifetime. I'm afraid if I touch you it'll make me diseased like you." He hugged his weapon tight: there was no fight in him without it. And he was spared the embarrassment, for an opportunity arose which allowed him to flee with his ego intact.

"What's that noise?" cried the youngest of Brynolf's companions.

Berserk was the threat which sprang out from hiding and stood up on hind legs. Black nostrils snooped from a coat of white camouflage; hungry jaws agape revealed rows of monstrous fangs like an armoury of ivory daggers. She grounded on all four paws and cantered towards them.

"Bear!" screamed the companions, who mounted their snowmobiles and started their engines. "Shoot it—shoot it, Brynolf."

Brynolf took out a clip of brass bullets, then clicked, knocked, and cocked the various catches and levers on his weapon. But in his frantic fumbling, the magazine slid out of the base of his weapon without him realising; and when the trigger was depressed, only a puff of mist discharged from the chamber.

"It's not working," said Brynolf. "Run!"

"You can't leave us!" shouted Ivar.

It was the fastest Brynolf had ever waded through the clods of air to get to his snowmobile. One of his companions hesitated; perhaps out of remorse for leaving Ulrik and Ivar for bait. And for that display of humanity, Brynolf bashed him on his helmet; a fierce reiteration of his place in the hierarchy of bullies.

Engines revved and thereafter they fled. The bear, in her loathing for engines, changed her course to intercept them on the snowy plains, hunting them until they passed over the threshold and down into Longyearbyen. But having lost her prey, she wheeled around, searching. Then, finding Ulrik and Ivar fleeing into the heart of the mountains, she cantered after them.

All the pain in Ulrik's collarbone abated, and his makeshift sling was thrown like a kite to the wind as he flew across the wilderness. His pace was swift, his strides long, but Ivar lagged, and the bear made rapid gains on them. Fatigued and foolhardy, Ivar abandoned his retreat altogether and readied himself for a fight.

Ulrik watched on in horror. Ivar was poised with knife in hand, not holding it by the hilt but by the blade, his other arm outstretched for balance. The bear nearing, she drew herself up on her hind legs, accepting the showdown. At once, Ivar drew back his knife hand, then thrust it forward. Nine inches of shimmering steel cut through the air, and with a violent thud the spinning dagger buried itself deep within her midriff. In the shadow of the mountains, the guttural howl echoed, sounding less like a maimed bear than a falling tree groaning before its eventual crash to the ground. But there was fight in her still. Off the boys pelted again, this time hoping to have the better legs for escape. But she slunk after them, her ivory daggers and obsidian claws intent on perforating her puny prey.

At once, from some higher terrace of the surrounding blunt mountains, there came a clatter of rifle fire ricocheting throughout the sky. The bear halted and swung her skull around this way and that, then cowered. She knew that sound too well, the cause of so many of her kin's suffering. Knife still lodged in her breast, she abandoned the chase and cantered through a gaping pass in the mountain.

Ulrik hunched over his knees, panting and shaking, almost spent. After a while, he stood upright again, enabling his lungs to fill to capacity; he planted his hands on his hips and purged the phlegm from his throat. When his senses were restored, he saw Ivar collapsed on the ground to his right. Ulrik staggered over to him and nudged him with his boot. Ivar groaned, rolled over, and held up his arm, making a visor with his hand to screen his eyes from the westering sun. Ulrik yanked his arm and hauled him to his feet, though he hobbled like a hamstrung horse and could hardly stand.

"It's okay, Ivar. It's okay." Ulrik tried to contact his wandering eyes.

"I'm okay, Ulrik. I'm okay. We're okay, aren't we?"

"Because of you, Ivar." Ulrik grasped his shoulder, butted his head, then slapped the nape of his neck. "We're okay because of you."

"That gunfire—where did that come from?"

They looked around. No sign of any presence.

"Who knows. But I don't want to be sticking around to find out. The bear headed that way, so we can't go back. We'll have to take the long way round. Come; let's head towards the mountains."

"But it'll be getting dark soon."

"Even if it takes longer, we'll be safer, Ivar."

Ivar buried his satchel under a heap of snow lest the scent of cinnamon cakes lure a snooping black snout. Then they made haste on their general course of up, down, and around over rocky terrain, remaining silent for much of the way in case their voices aroused keen ears. After trekking at length, they arrived at a clearing: the flat expanse looked as though a white canvas had been stretched across all four corners of the terrain; perfectly level, unspoiled by footprint or paw print. They ventured from the shade of the mountain and across the clearing, but when crossing the halfway point of this supremely flat terrain, Ulrik found himself at the mercy of a prolonged skid.

"Huh, I don't remember," said Ulrik, skating to a halt, "I don't remember there being a lake here when I last trekked with my pappa."

"Lake?" said Ivar. "What lake?"

"See here." Ulrik kicked away a layer of snow from the glassy crust beneath his boot. "Maybe it formed because of the new mountain rains. There wasn't always this much snow here, I'm told. Now there's enough to build every forager a snow castle of their own."

"You're right." Ivar gasped and took a step backwards. "Strange seasons we've seen on Svalbard with the warming of our world. We should go back."

"Go back? But we've already crossed halfway, and that's the weakest point of any lake. And the ice we've crossed was strong enough to support our weight, so we should be fine to continue …"

"I'm not sure that's a good id—"

A sweet cracking sound ensued as the tension underfoot grew; the glassy floor was failing. Both were suspended in motion with arms and legs outstretched for greater balance. Not even when faced with the bear were Ivar's features so badly wrung with fear.

"Get low like me," said Ulrik, spreading his limbs like a water spider, with great anguish to his collarbone.

Ivar lunged his lead leg forward. As he lowered his rear knee—attempting to manoeuvre into the prone position—he lost control of his front foot, his legs gradually sliding apart. He seemed to place a great deal more weight on his front foot to counterbalance it, but when he did, a web of cracks spun around the circumference of his boot and grew outward.

"Steady—steady."

The cracks grew into wicked striations. A violent scar tore across the skin of the lake between the two points of tension: Ivar and Ulrik. Ivar's lunge continued to elongate, though he hadn't the groin for such a splits. Groin on the verge of rupture; lake on the verge of rupture; one had to concede. "Ulrik, if we go under … I can't s-swim." Ivar slid one inch too far before he tumbled backwards and crashed like a wrecking ball onto his buttocks and through the ice. A gaping mouth opened in the ice sheet and exposed its jagged teeth; it frothed and bubbled—belched, even. And yawning wide, it swallowed Ulrik, too.

When fully submerged, Ulrik's furs felt like a costume of anchors upon his body. With his good arm, he'd stripped all save his trousers in a matter of moments and floated towards a bright shaft of light cascading on the broken ceiling. He was in no torment—this being his preferred environment—but for Ivar this would be the iciest hell.

Out of the open mouth Ulrik emerged, sucking at the air. A dogged cough saw off the briny contents that filled his chest, and he spent a few moments spluttering through his nostrils. No sign of Ivar. Not much time, then. Deep breath in—hold—down again.

Down he plunged in search of signs of violent thrashing. His collarbone was a nasty hindrance to his stroke; his flipper-feet paddled harder to compensate. Out of billions of humans, only he was acclimatised to such frigid realms, yet, with his cracked collarbone, he was encumbered with the severest inability to navigate them.

How far had Ivar drifted? Ulrik cut through the waters—undulating like an eel, relying mostly on the strength of his kick—looking for a silhouette; a body moving or still. There! Not tangles of seaweed but black locks of hair. And a face, pale like the weak glow of winter sunlight. He darted towards his friend. A white hand stretched out. He reached out to clasp it. It returned a meagre grip. A gasp escaped Ivar's mouth, sending bubbles to the surface as he himself sank lower and lower. His chest convulsed as his lungs flooded, and they lost all their buoyancy, being utterly spent of air. With his good arm, Ulrik scooped Ivar's body over his shoulder. No matter how extremely his feet propelled and eddied, though, Ulrik himself sank. His weak arm being free, he chanced a stroke with it. A sharp sting. Bubbles from his own lungs escaped; air running out. He tried to unburden Ivar, tried to strip away his furs. He fiddled, snatched, yanked, but the buttons and clasps were too many. Consciousness diminishing, Ulrik returned to the cleft of the lake—without Ivar. There he floated, face puckered, regaining his whereabouts.

His vision welled up with tears, and he wore the deepest corrugated frown. But he stifled his sobbing and readied himself for a better effort; and thereafter he returned to the deep of the basin.

He dived down and scrambled up several times over, each time gradually weakening, each time his hopes of a heroic rescue dwindling like a candle near the end of its wick. And when, on his last journey, he arrived at Ivar, he saw him floating—limbs flailing, orifices all agape and bubbling, stark white snowball eyes lolling back and forth in their sockets. He himself was in danger of sinking and becoming the second hostage to that aquatic underworld, so heavy did his leaden heart weigh, and so gruelling was the pain in his collarbone. Alone and defeated, Ulrik retreated to the cleft of the lake for the last time.

He tossed his good arm over the threshold, using it as a grappling hook to claw himself out. But each time he dragged himself up, the ice-shelf broke away. So he clung to the edge and bobbed atop the water, waiting for night to draw in—waiting for the ice to reinforce.

Twilight came on swiftly; the moon was little more than a fingernail.

The wind hastened. Tresses of Ulrik's hair solidified like iced dreadlocks. His tears crystallised, and his eyelashes became rigid. Upon each individual eyelash there congregated tiny snowflakes, the likes of which collect and balance in weightless heaps on branches of naked trees.

Now that the crust of the lake had formed around his neck, it was time to stress-test it. But his grappling hook arm was glued to the ice by the skin of his forearm. He'd have to make the best of his bad arm. Whether by fortune—ill or good—that side of his body was entirely numb. The only detectable sensation was his pulse limping around his sullen face and the sluggish thump of his heartbeat thudding against the walls of its cage. He summoned his last store of strength and dragged himself out by his secondary hook. The anaesthetic of frost made the ripping away of his arm seem a trivial thing; not a murmur did he offer up at the severance of flesh. Free from polar ensnarement, he crawled away, leaving red-velvet stains in the snow each time he rested on his wound; but he only managed a few yards before collapsing. At the mercy of the Arctic elements, he stiffened like petrified wood and fell into a subconscious torpor not unlike a hibernating creature.

Later, amid the howling of the wind, he stirred when he heard what he thought was a skitter of paws followed by a savage growl. He was too weary to do anything but lie between this world and the hereafter as the speedy paws and greedy jaws advanced towards him. Its two effulgent lamps for eyes penetrated the fog and beamed down on his lifeless body; its guttural breathing sounded like that of a tired engine. Then voices. Frantic voices in the air … or in his head?

Chapter Six

THE HOUSE OF ABRAHAM

Earlier that same day ...

Thorsten whistled a merry melody while making his preparations for trade. He strung up char (red-bellied fish) by their tails to a wooden track overhead; others were laid on beds of ice among sprigs of herbs, where they stared with their cold, moralising eyes at those who intended to make their purchase. Between these fat fillets he positioned jars of his homemade wild sauce—a vomity-looking concoction; but they were an upsell impossible to decline, for the necks of these jars were decorated with fantastic scarves of beige twine, thanks to Astrid.

His set-up complete, he moved on to the neighbouring Sami tents in search of Astrid. By now, the other foragers had erected a whole lane of these conical silver tipis, each one with its own unique patchwork of hides and each offering the warmest sanctuary for those inside. Merchandised within were all things homemade: pelts and skins, trousers and tunics, pendants and charms, earthenware, chess pieces, ornaments, baubles, candles, carvings, mulled glogg, soups, sweetmeats, cheeses, and milks. None was to be bought with money; the only currency accepted being commodities for the trading (fruit, firewood, tobacco, wine, medicine, spears, knives, bows and arrows, nets for fishing or catching puffin), the price determined according to the strength of the tourists' desires. If the tourists wanted forager souvenirs, they had to come prepared to haggle for the rarity of their charms. It was a quirky inconvenience to visit a world in which money and Tech were obsolete.

The merchants were poised for trade; standing outside their tents, these long-haired men and women wore dark kohl about their pagan eyes, looking somewhat like their yammering huskies, whose eyes were like icy rockpools amidst volcanic sand. Thorsten shooed one stray hound out of the way, stooped low, and entered Astrid's tent.

She was absorbed in her own creations, arranging them in particular spaces, turning them this way and that to catch a certain light, and widening the spaces between them, only to narrow them again thereafter. Thorsten intervened; and when he'd finished, the collection of wooden carvings had the semblance of an orgy of frustrated beasts in which there featured a mammoth straddling a vulnerable-looking walrus as well as other obscene arrangements of illogical zoological sodomy.

"Why do you always insist on acting like a teenager?" said Astrid, tutting. "You're ruining my work. Now leave me."

He slumped his shoulders and retreated to his fish market. It was always best to steer clear of her when she was in this mood.

The day under way, Thorsten saw (as he always did) much traffic pass by his stall. Lured by the tresses of Astrid's flowing hair, the tourists were willing to pinch their noses and endure the pungent torment of his seafood to crowd outside her tent. Here they clustered like ferrous filings around a magnet in wonder. Not a lady, prim, well-spoken, and in exquisite dress, but a woman of spirit, fierce speech, and wearing roguish dress; not a woman of suppression but of expression—and she was all the more delightful for knowing it. Her attitude was conducive to clinching the best bargains, and she clinched her first trade of the day having festooned one particular man with an array of scarves, complimenting him even as his wife peered on from the corners of her narrowed eyes, harrumphing, with her arms tied up in knots. After exchanging with him a sack of mixed root vegetables for a single scarf,

Astrid gave her thanks, landed a gentle headbutt, and moved on to the next customer.

Thorsten rested his face on his cubic fist; he was yet to make a trade. But then a distinct laugh interrupted his boredom; one which sounded like a swift repetition of the word "egg": "Egg-egg-egg-egg-egg."

Above the scrummage of bobbing heads, Thorsten saw that the owner of this laugh had, rising out of a nest of side-hair, a most unfortunate egg-shaped head. He was a man of advanced age and went about with a contemptuous snarl upon his upper lip. He had bulldog jowls suggestive of an overindulgent diet and wore an open velveteen jacket that would be impossible to button owing to his porky belly: a terrible defence against Arctic winds. Tethered to his side was a young boy, bereft of suitable clothing. A grandchild, perhaps? No. He referred to Mr Egg as "Father". And now their lack of clothing had the nearby foragers riled and speaking in vexed whispers, the welfare of fledglings being of the utmost concern in forager society.

"Father, it stinks of fish," said the boy.

"Egg-egg-egg-egg-egg; it's a strange place the Holy Shepherd has posted us to, isn't it? Egg-egg."

"Are these people beggars, Father?"

"Egg! I'd say so judging by their appearance. Stay close; they'll smell that we have money, and they'll try to swap their hideous souvenirs for the contents of your purse. May the Lord have mercy on their souls."

All fell silent. The black eyes of the foragers and their hounds fixed on Mr Egg like assassins in the shadows. Thorsten drew up his hood and slouched inconspicuously behind his fish stall. Even in his shrunken state he towered over the heads of others, so much so that he knew of every person suffering from bald patches upon the summits of their heads.

"We wouldn't," said Astrid, abandoning a customer mid-haggle and producing herself in front of Mr Egg, "we wouldn't be wanting your money; *you* who know the price of everything but the value of nothing. Have you no manners?"

"Egg-egg!" Mr Egg turned to the young boy. "Cavewoman speak English."

"At least cavewoman has the intelligence to dress appropriately." Astrid unravelled her scarf and squatted to the height of the youngling, who'd tucked his tiny pink hands underneath his armpits. Men of no shame wagged and panted like puppies, taking this as an opportunity to ogle her haunches. After draping the scarf around the boy's bare neck, she cupped his cheeks with her gloved hands, then turned to Mr Egg and said, "Your son is almost frozen."

"Egg! He's not my son."

"Didn't I just hear him call you Father?"

"I'm Father Eggert, his priest, and I'm Svalbard's new governor. Now, take the scarf; take it back." The boy was smelling Astrid's scent on the scarf when it was robbed from him and flung to the wind. Father Eggert turned in a full circle and extended his finger at the theatre of bystanders, announcing, "We won't be trading with you, you, or any of you."

Thorsten's fists throbbed like aspiring meteors.

"You think I'm wanting something in return?" Astrid rumpled the hair of the boy, pinched his nose, and arose. "It was a gift for this little fledgling."

"A bribe, I suspect. Hoping that I, the Governor, might turn a blind eye to all the wrongdoing here?"

"I don't—what wrongdoing?"

Bass rumblings of discontent were amplified among the foragers.

"All this trade is," said Father Eggert, rubbing the shiny shell of his head, "I suggest, a clever medium of tax avoidance. When I take up my office, it'll be my first duty to launch a full investigation into the practices conducted here."

This threat to his wife and fellow foragers inflamed Thorsten. He'd never had the urge to crack an egg and scramble its contents as much as he did now. When he drew down his hood, tendrils of his hair were thrown skyward by the wind, and he appeared coronated with a crown of fire. "Thorsten," said the townsfolk, who thereafter bade him good health as he shouldered through the crowd. ("Good health" is the forager greeting considered the sincerest form of "Good day"; for bidding a person only a single day of goodness was to deny a person any goodness beyond the stroke of midnight, but to bid someone good health was to bestow an indiscriminate blessing of vitality that would never expire.) Arriving behind Father Eggert, Thorsten leant his elbow on a stranger's shoulder who seemed proud that his shoulder was a worthy pedestal for the fire-giant.

"Father," said the boy, teeth chattering like castanets owing to the cold, "these people are poor. Why don't they want our money?"

Astrid took a knee again and whispered, "Sometimes, little fledgling, those with the least have the most to give." She slid a woollen hat over his pink ears, and he blinked with delight. His attention was then stolen by the presence of Thorsten, and looking up, he rubbed his eyes in wonder at no doubt the biggest man he'd ever seen.

"Thor ..." said Astrid, as she flicked her eyes from the boy to him.

Father Eggert pivoted on his polished heels, craned his neck, and looked at Thorsten in the manner of one suffering from a pre-frontal headache. Thorsten extended his hand and waited for him to shake it. When receiving Father Eggert's slender palm, he noticed it felt like an infant's. But no onlooker was so oblivious as to assume they were exchanging a gesture of friendship. Thorsten drew in a deep, pondering sniff and knitted his brooding brow, trying to lock on to those close-together eyes at the centre of the egg. Their hands still joined, Thorsten's grip tightened and threatened to crush and calcify those frail fingers into bonemeal.

"Peace be with you," said Thorsten.

"And also—" grip tightening; teeth grinding, "and also with you."

"Now, it's customary to headbutt when we foragers greet, but I wouldn't want to spill any yolk from that delicate egg."

Laughter broke out among the foragers. Even the huskies seemed unable to contain their howls.

Father Eggert scoffed and retracted his arm into his sleeve, where he flexed and straightened his fingers. Then he smoothed down the nest of his egg and adjusted the lapel of his jacket, upon which was emblazoned a union of symbols: a crucifix, crescent moons, and a six-pointed star—all joined in the shape of a sword. Thorsten recalled seeing it on stickers in windows, on the bumpers of snowmobiles, and embroidered on a purple banner outside the Governor's chambers.

"Father," said the young boy, "we're going to be late for mass."

Father Eggert flicked his wrist, exposing his watchTech, and in noting the time became stricken by a mild panic. He gave a swift bow before groping his way through the crowd. The boy mouthed a thank you to Astrid before fleeing after his guardian. The crowd resumed their haggling.

"I recognise that symbol from somewhere, Astrid," said Thorsten, stroking his beard. "That symbol on his jacket."

"You do?"

"I do. I've seen it appearing in many places now."

"I wouldn't be giving it any more thought," said Astrid. "Anyway, thanks for coming to support me." Beaming up at him, she closed her eyes, her lips drawn into a crimson crescent.

He girded his arm around her waist and kissed the crown of her head.

"Are we done for the day?" he said, smacking his belly. "What I really mean is: is it time for food, yah?"

"We have to be getting back to Ulrik, Thor. I'm worried about him."

"Don't be. I remember what it's like being a teenage boy. If he's anything like me, he'll be glad of the privacy … if you know what I mean."

"I'm not sure," she said, whipping herself around at such speed that one of her plaits lashed his cheek, before strutting away.

"Trust me,"—he caught the fluttering end of her grey cloak and reared her back into his arms—"he'll be fine."

"Fine, but we go only for food. No drinking, no smoking, and no loitering."

"Understood."

No sooner had they set about closing their markets than a man with graphite hair approached—coloured like that of a virgin paintbrush, like black bristles dabbed for the first time in white paint. He had an infant's complexion; his smooth face looked in little danger of ever sprouting a single whisker or conceding so much as a wrinkle. And when he smiled, his smooth cheeks reflected the glare of the sun and shone like a golden bust. He might've been aged anywhere between forty and eighty—aged well or aged terribly—for silvering hair can add a decade or two to a person, while soft skin can reverse the effect. With such golden tones of skin and yet such silver strands of hair, there was no guessing his age.

"Hello, please, I'm sorry," he said, fumbling with a credit card in hand. "I know you're about to close, but—"

"Oh," said Astrid, "nuh, nuh, nuh; don't say sorry. You're no trouble. It's just that we don't accept money. We're foragers; we trade in goods."

"Ah, sorry, sorry. I should know that by now. I've lived here a long time. It's just, I was passing and saw your woolly mammoth carving. The big one. How much? Sorry, I'm not very good at haggling. I'll just pay you the asking price."

"We'll be open again next week," said Thorsten, slamming down sacks onto his kicksled with great exaggeration. "Bring us two sacks of wheat and it's yours."

"Thor," said Astrid, striking him in his belly, "don't be rude." She turned to the badger-haired man and asked, "What else do you have to trade?"

"Only the money in my pockets, but I *do* have an idea. Did I overhear you say you're hungry? I could take you for food. Would that be fair?"

"Food, you say?" Thorsten stuck out his lips like a duckbill, looked up to the sky, and for a few moments became suspended in deep consideration. "How about Isbjørn Huset?"

"You want to go there?"

"Yah, Isbjørn Huset; they serve the best whale meat."

"Hmm, whale meat is expensive."

"Yah," said Thorsten, in his usual blunt manner. "Very expensive ..."

Astrid produced a woolly mammoth carving from a sack and handed it to the customer. He stretched out both hands to grasp it and thereafter cradled it like a baby.

"Do we have a deal?" pursued Thorsten.

"Of course. Such a carving is priceless to me. Thank you."

Astrid's expression turned to one of adoration. She clasped her hands together and drew them to her breast. "What's your name, friend?"

"Chenglei," he said; "but my friends call me Cheng." His face became animated. "You can call me Cheng. And you are?"

"I'm Thorsten Magnusson;"—a polite butt of heads—"and this is my wife, Astrid."

Their bellies were rumbling, so they were quick to press on with their packing. Chenglei took great offence to the idea that he should spectate while there was work to be done. For an older man, he had a youthful spirit about him.

Thorsten gave all the leftover fish to another forager named Sigurd Stormhammer, who'd prepared a fire and was now stirring a cooking pot over it, adding the ingredients to a broth, soon to be shared among the other merchants. They were always grateful to the Magnussons for their surplus stock. And because of their generosity, an entire community of black eyes always looked out for their interests.

Kicksleds loaded (with more sacks than they came with, owing to their profitable trades), they made off in the direction of Isbjørn Huset. Chenglei sat in the passenger seat at the front of Thorsten's kicksled like a lapdog in a bike basket, while Thorsten drove his boot into the frozen ground to initiate transit. As they glided up to a steady speed, they entered into wholesome prattle.

"Astrid," said Chenglei, using his hand as a shield against the headwind, "what you did back there—that was too kind."

"Oh, you mean with the new governor and that poor boy?" In squatting on her kicksled, she became more aerodynamic, and her plaits were thrown up horizontally as they sped on. "That poor fledgling was almost frozen."

"Father Eggert," interrupted Thorsten, driving his boot harder to keep up with Astrid; "the Governor—whatever he calls himself—he was wearing a symbol on his jacket. What was that symbol, Cheng?"

"I didn't see, Thorsten," said Chenglei, craning his head to see Thorsten behind him, "but I can imagine … Did it look like a sword?"

"Yah, it did."

"Then I expect it was the Sword of Abraham. That's the symbol of the House of Abraham."

"The House of Abraham? Where is this house? Is that where Father Eggert lives?"

"Ha, silly. You're joking, of course … Oh, but I see you're not. You don't know, do you? Godlings, Thorsten. They're a bunch of *godlings*."

"What's a godling?" Thorsten's concentration being diverted, a hump of rock in the snowy road escaped his attention until the last moment. With no time to steer around it, he held his breath and clenched his eyes. The kicksled took flight, wobbled mid-air, and grounded a few milliseconds later.

"Agh." Cheng rubbed his coccyx.

"Gah, sorry for the bumpy ride. You were saying?"

"A godling: someone who believes in God."

"I believe in the gods." Thorsten drove his heel into the ground, propelling them forward with greater strength. "The Viking gods: Odin, Thor, Freyja, Tyr. Am I a godling, then?"

"Well, not quite. You see, none of those is the God of Abraham."

"Then I care little for that god," said Thorsten through clenched teeth. "He never cared much for me."

"You keep saying 'Abraham' like we're supposed to know what you mean," called Astrid, veering her kicksled closer. She cut in front of them, and Thorsten dropped his heel in the snow just in time, grinding to a halt.

"Why are we stopping?" he said, extending both arms wide as though waiting to receive a proper explanation. A white fleece of cloud was drawn across the sky. The horizon vanished and merged with the polar landscape. The world was in tumult, it seemed; shaken up like a snow-globe.

"We're stopping," said Astrid, "because I can't hear with all this wind rushing by. Sorry, Cheng, what do you mean?"

"The House of Abraham ... you really don't know, do you?" Chenglei stood up from the passenger seat and removed a glove. With a nimble finger, he drew sharp lines in the snow: a cross, a six-pointed star, and then a duo of crescents.

"That's it," said Thorsten, thrusting forward a cuboid finger. "That's the symbol the Governor was wearing."

"The House of Abraham is a political union," said Chenglei. "A house of three religious states: Israel (the Jewish state), New Babylon (the Islamic caliphate), and DRUE (the Christian republic)."

"That's nice," said Astrid, with her hands fixed to her hips, "but odd. What do these religions have in common that warrants such unity? I always understood them to be hostile to one another—at war, even."

"There used to be great unrest between them, but as factions of the House they now see themselves as brothers and sisters. You see, their stories are similar; so, so similar. Why do you think it's called the House of Abraham? Because Muslims, Christians, and Jews worship many of the same prophets—Abraham being one of them."

When Chenglei spoke, he did so with a turgid cloud of gloom above his head so that he now appeared closer to his true age. Under the shade of his hood, his golden cheeks became jaundiced, his clean attitude contaminated by a toxic subject. It had escaped Thorsten's notice before, but he saw that Chenglei had a pronounced Adam's apple which seemed, in all its excessive animation, to rise and fall with his moods.

"Cheng," said Astrid, "is unity not a good thing? Has that not brought about peace?"

"It *was* a good thing, Astrid." Chenglei now seemed at odds with his Adam's apple, as though he were choking on the barb of an arrow and was unsure whether he should cough it up or swallow it down. "It was a good thing to begin with. The Holy Shepherd built the House of Abraham as a way of bridging divisions and bringing peace."

"Wait, who is the Holy Shepherd?"

"The Holy Shepherd?" said Chenglei. "Chancellor Emmanuel Saint-Pierre ..."

"Emmanuel Did-a-pee-where?" said Thorsten.

Chenglei took the passenger seat of the kicksled again, perhaps out of self-consciousness, perhaps owing to Thorsten tracking the movements of his Adam's apple. At once they glided off again, this time at a walking pace.

"You must have heard about the Holy Shepherd? How can you not know who the most powerful man in the world is? Well, he founded the House of Abraham, and he won a peace prize for brokering the deal (the Treaty of Zion) which ended the 150-year civil war in Israel. That's how he got to where he is today. Then alongside him there is the Chief Rabbi of Israel, Levi Ben-David; and there's the Caliph, Sultan bin Ibrahim. All three of them are collectively known as the Triumvirate."

"You have my head spinning, Cheng. The Holy Shepherd, godlings, the Tri—Tricum—"

"Triumvirate."

"—Triumvirate, Chief Rabbi, the Caliph, the House of Abraham, the Treaty of Wherever. You've lost me, Cheng."

"Why is it such a bad thing if the Holy Shepherd brought peace?" said Astrid.

"Because, as time has gone on, the Continent has become a hostile place for people of no religion, the faithless, the unbelievers, the atheists, the heathens, the pagans, or whatever they call us. We live in a theocracy."

"Huh, a theo-what?"

"Basically religion is law." A look of outrage soured Cheng's face.

"Tell me, Cheng," said Astrid, "what's your grievance with religion?"

From behind, Thorsten saw Chenglei's jaw move in a pendulous swing from left to right. It was as though he was passing the question about between his molars and chewing hard to enable its digestion.

"I don't," began Chenglei after much deliberation, "have any grievance with religion when it's practised in private, but it's become a public affair. Shouldn't we all have a problem when so-called blasphemy and the denial of God carries jail time—or worse?"

Thorsten was beginning to wish he'd kept quiet and not asked any questions.

"Calm, Cheng, calm," said Astrid.

"Would you be calm if they'd taken away your career? Your ambitions? Your livelihood? I studied for years, and now my degrees are worthless."

"We're sorry to hear that, aren't we, Thor," said Astrid, baring her teeth at him and shouldering him. "Tell us your story, Cheng. We're listening."

"I'm a scientist, you see. A biologist, to be exact. A geneticist, to be even more exact. Well, I was, before genome editing was outlawed. I spent the last few years of my employment in a project that gave Svalbard the world's first woolly mammoth, Onyx."

"Scrapped? Why?"

"The Holy Shepherd's government outlawed genome editing. Said we were 'playing God'. Tinkering with the work of the Creator. It's a blasphemy, according to the Holy Shepherd. And that was it; all our research was censored. So, here I am fourteen years later working as a ranger at the Arctic Sanctuary. You see, I felt bad for bringing Onyx into this world only for him to be abandoned. Poor thing."

The trio passed through a precinct of coloured houses and came to a black longhouse with a turf roof below which creaked a weathered sign that read "Isbjørn Huset".

"Here we are," said Thorsten, glad for the conversation to branch in a new direction. "Ice-bear house."

They alighted from their kicksleds, parking them close to the longhouse where the wind was less formidable.

"So," said Astrid, taking off her gloves and fixing her hair, "vote the Holy Shepherd out of office."

"Can't," said Chenglei. "The Chancellor of DRUE is elected by the leaders of his European parliament: prime ministers, governors, and presidents."

"Can't the leaders vote him out?" said Astrid, pushing Thorsten forward and using him as a windbreak.

"Why would they? You see, he's been great for trade and has enabled the free movement of citizens, and their economies are booming. He's a politician who's promised change and delivered it. Not only that, but they're afraid that without him the Middle East will descend into war again."

"Ah, wait it out. Politicians come and go. How many years remain of his term before he must step down?"

Chenglei shook his head for a few seconds before he said, "Well, a chancellor of DRUE can only serve for two consecutive terms. He's already served two terms, but then he took a break, and now he's reprising his role and is promising more radical change. So we could have another two terms under his regime. Another decade."

Daylight was diminishing; the wind was picking up; the snow was beating down.

"Always, Astrid," said Thorsten, "always I'm glad of our decision to uproot and replant ourselves far away from society. You can't still be wanting to go back to the mainland after hearing all this. Sounds like we escaped DRUE at the right time."

"Escaped?" said Chenglei, standing in the doorway of Isbjørn Huset.

"Yah, here on Svalbard we're independent. We're self-governed. We foragers have protected status."

"Oh, is Svalbard not under Norwegian jurisdiction?"

"I think it must be."

"And is Norway not a member state of DRUE?"

"I believe it still is, yah."

"And did we not here today witness the arrival of our newly appointed Governor of Svalbard, who came wearing the badge of the House of Abraham?" Chenglei's Adam's apple dropped below the plinth of his collarbones. "Well, then, you may have escaped mainland DRUE, but not even here, not even at the edge of the North Pole, can you escape the Holy Shepherd's regime. We are his flock; we are his lambs."

CHAPTER SEVEN

OPERATION SNOWSTORM

High in the blunt mountains, the ranger unslung his rifle and aimed down the scope at the starved bear, tracking her as she pursued her prey at a determined speed. She was berserk in her hunt, owing to her hunger—and all the more for the dagger in her breast.

He rummaged in his belt-pouch, swiped a magazine, and slotted it into the base of the weapon. Lever cocked. Safety catch disengaged. Round in the chamber. Weapon loaded. Ready. As he panned the crosshairs over the bear, he took note of the wind speed and direction. His arms were steady; his mind clear; his timing sharp. Deep breath in. He clutched the trigger, letting loose a burst of glinting gold bullets. Miss—miss—miss.

"Schoolboy error, Tristan," he said to himself, looking down at his weapon with gritted teeth. "This bastard needs calibrating."

The bear halted, as though familiar with the sonorous pang of gunfire that came hissing through the air, spitting as the rounds penetrated the ground inches from her paws. She sniffed the air, reared back, and bolted over the horizon.

Despite missing his mark, the two lads (or was one a strange-looking older bloke?) now appeared safe. Tristan watched as their frantic faces looked around for the source of the gunfire. He saluted to them, but tentacles of cloud shrouded the terraces of the mountains—a sign of an impending snowstorm. At least the lads were clever enough not to linger, though they took a questionable route through a narrow pass which had lots of hiding spaces for ravenous beasts. From his high vantage point, he resolved to follow them to ensure they got home safely. He didn't need any more deaths burdening his conscience.

First things first: some tea. He twisted the cap off his flask and poured himself a brew. So badly scratched and scathed was this flask that hardly any of its original coat remained. It was the one they'd issued him when he'd joined the forces as a lad; and they'd suffered hard times and harsh climes together. This flask and the tea in it, when supped, tamed the severest passions; even the anxieties of being shelled and shot at. Tristan often said, when slurping his cuppa in the company of friends, that if Queen Boudicca and Emperor Nero, if King Arthur and Mordred, if Alfred the Great and Guthrum the Dane, if Harold Godwinson and Harald Hardrada, if Robin of Loxley and the Sherriff of Nottingham, if Richard the Lionheart and Salahuddin, if the Lancastrians and the Yorkists, if Guy Fawkes and King James, if Wat Tyler and Sir William Walworth, if Lord Nelson and Napoleon Bonaparte, and if Winston Churchill and Adolf Hitler had gathered themselves in the same room with a kettle and no small quantity of tea bags and biscuits, then countless lives would've been spared.

Down he sipped his tea, feeling a degree warmer for it. Then he splashed away the dregs, twisted the cap back on, and nestled it safely in the side-pouch of his Bergen. Time to move off again.

Tristan followed the lads from atop the shoulders of the mountains. It wasn't unusual for them to disappear from sight for a moment while he navigated the awkward crags and ledges. But Tristan was as sure-footed as a mountain goat, owing to the crampons strapped to his boots. When the lads stumbled out into view again, he saw them trekking across a flat white expanse; and suddenly, like two butter biscuits balancing atop a creamy latte, having become soaked and too great of a weight for the frothy lid, they vanished into the watery abyss.

"No!" Tristan yanked down his snow goggles and locked his hands at the back of his head. His patriotic, bloodshot eyes glistened red, white, and blue all at once as they filled with tears. Since he was alone, he tolerated a few to fall; and like glittering veins of silver ore they split a course down his rocky face, mellowing its usual ruggedness with streams of strife.

After drying his eyes, he took out his trinoculars, zoomed in on the frozen lake, and made a mental note of his bearings in relation to the cleft at its centre. Then, on his watchTech, he registered a distress signal. With any luck, a mountain rescue team would come. Though there was no immediate response.

To Tristan's relief, the strange-looking lad surfaced half-naked and seemed unaffected by the chill. But where was the other lad? At once, the strange-looking lad disappeared below again, presumably in search of his friend.

As the sun's fire arced low, and as the sky drew over its blanket of purple twilight, a pallid fog closed in. Tristan took one last look at the mouth of the lake, triangulating his position by eye.

Goggles down, ski mask up, Tristan ditched his Bergen with all its contents and unstrapped the webbing from his body. But he kept his rifle slung, and in one trouser pocket he stored a magazine of rounds and a handful of spare red tracer rounds. He kept his trinoculars hanging from his neck and pocketed his flask inside his coat (close to his heart). Hastening down the snowy fells, he took a snaking course: despite being the longest route, it was the swiftest. When arriving at a safe, gradual gradient, he took off his coat, sat on it, and tobogganed down the mountain's waistline, covering a greater distance than could ever have been made in the time on foot.

After reaching the foothills of the mountain, he stopped for a brief rest. While recovering his breath, he checked his watchTech for a response from mountain rescue: nothing yet. He tied his bootlaces, tightened his belt, and fastened his coat. Last, he tapped his breast pocket. Much to his relief, his flask hadn't gone AWOL in transit as he had, in his darkest thoughts, supposed.

With a regimented cadence he sped along the snowy plains, as though driven on by an invisible lash. He himself was both the slaver and in thrall: victim to his own torture, punishing himself with the cruellest speed. "Not far now, Tristan," he said, driving his crampons into the perfect blanket of snow; thereafter the clean field appeared acned by an outbreak of raging snow-pox. Strange it was to see thickening fog and raging snow in a place once known as the Arctic Desert. More precipitous was it now than ever in the history of modern man—because of modern man.

On he soldiered, groping his way through the impregnable fog. So dense was it that without the use of his trinoculars he might as well have gone about with his head bandaged up in linen like a mummified pharaoh, for all was opaque and white. Yet, under the trinoculars' infrared influence, he saw abstract, glass-blown-looking shapes in all their glowing glory—from burning-blue to blood-orange—the colour determined by the degree of their warmth. Thus engaged, Tristan searched for the presence of warm-blooded life. When he spun around, he realised how far he'd veered, for when orientating his trinoculars he saw a silhouette of diminishing orange at his feet: the strange-looking lad lying supine and half-naked.

"Fuck," said Tristan, grappling his own face and shutting fast his eyelids for a moment to blot out the ghostly corpse.

He'd seen countless casualties during his service, but being a spectator of death never got any easier. Being numb to death was a talent inherited, not a skill acquired like weapons-handling or map-reading.

Turning his back to the body, Tristan checked his watchTech. At last, a message, a response from mountain rescue: help was on the way. Upon receipt of this news, he unslung his rifle from his shoulders and rummaged around in his pocket for the tracer rounds. When armed and ready, he fired into the sky and the bullet left a trail of crimson vapour in its wake. With any luck, someone would see and be drawn to his petty fireworks.

Meanwhile, it was just him and the body, waiting to be rescued.

The temperature plummeted, and the hole in the lake sewed itself shut with seamless patchwork, leaving no trace of it ever being ripped open. Not wishing to chance any further disturbance to the ice, Tristan took to one knee on the fragile floor, then spread himself into the prone position and there lay facing the casualty. His eyes caught contact with two ghost-green eyes rolling about at their own will. Out of respect (and a selfishness to comfort himself), Tristan drew down the lids over the lad's languid eyes, but when he did, they sprang open again with living intent.

"Heurgh," said Tristan, recoiling and sitting upright.

A wisp of air escaped the casualty's nostrils, and there followed a faint rise and fall of his chest. The lad groaned. Only half-alive, but still alive! It was as though he were in the deepest torpor, like those hibernating creatures of winter.

Without delay, Tristan rolled back his fur hood and plucked off his woollen hat; steam emanated from his bald head like a power plant. He was quick to return his hood atop and pull the drawstrings tight, though, for the sting of frigid air attempted to freeze his brain. Hat in hand, he dressed it over the lad's head, though with great difficulty, as he first had to snap the long strands of hair that had stiffened like icicles. Hat now on, Tristan unzipped his mountain coat and attempted to cocoon the half-naked lad, but he'd bonded with the ice like a wet tongue to a freezing lamppost.

Tristan's answer to this lay concealed within his coat pocket, and, like a magician who pulls a snow-white rabbit from his hat, he pulled out his flask of magic tea and poured the contents over the seams of where the lad's skin had fused to the lake's surface. When the ice seams vaporised and vanished, Tristan peeled him away and resumed his insulating of him in as many thermal layers as he could spare; after which he lay tucked up beside him in a generous donation of his body heat.

Shortly after, a growling engine came as a welcome relief to him. His watchTech flashed an erratic blue and white, announcing an incoming rescue. Headlamps penetrated the fog. An engine of sorts rattled to a halt.

"Woah, woah, woah!" called Tristan, fending away the bright headlamps. "Stay back. We're on ice here," and muttered under his breath, "you thick twat."

The rumble of a reversing snowmobile. A plump figure advancing on foot. His large mouth, fashioned in the shape of a trumpet, was the first feature to emerge from the fog. He was a marshmallow-looking thing, dressed from head to toe in quilted layers, appearing akin to an oversized tardigrade. No other features were visible; no eyes, nose, ears, chin, or cheeks, only a hollow mouth trumpeting an irksome tune whenever he spoke.

"Ah, sorry, looks like I'm too late," trumpeted the lips.

"He's not dead, you plonker," said Tristan, dusting the snow from his salopettes as he stood to attention. "He has a pulse—though a weak one."

"Unfortunate creature to be born looking like he does," came the booming from those trumpet lips. "And such a tall creature ... Wait, that's Thorsten Magnusson's son—a forager. You called me out here for a forager?"

"What do you mean, a forager? I'm not from around here."

"Foragers—they're weird folk who live off the grid. They don't wash; they wipe their asses in the snow; they have no health insurance; they pay no taxes. I might not get my bounty for this." He seemed to be polishing his trumpet in the manner of one stroking their chin when pondering some great philosophical conundrum.

"Money," said Tristan, "is that all you're here for, eh?"

"We've all got bills to pay."

"Don't get lippy with me, sunshine, or I'll knock your bloody block off. Now, are you a paramedic or not?"

"I'm just the transport."

"Just the transport ... right. So, no medical experience, eh? Fucking great."

"Well, I don't see that you're any more qualified."

Tristan brought his face up to the trumpet; it was tempting to send his fist down into the primary orifice, thereby muting it for good. But he took a diplomatic approach and said, "Qualified? I'll tell you something: I've packed wounds, fixed a few tourniquets, plucked out shrapnel. Understand? I was in Baghdad while you were still in your dad's bags."

Trumpet-lips forgot how to play and retreated under the shroud of his hood. After marching to the snowmobile, Tristan found there a stretcher and a bundle of blankets, and he loaded up his arms and carried them back to the casualty. Having blanketed the lad's body, he rolled him onto the stretcher and tucked him in so that not a patch of skin was exposed to the elements.

"Oi," he said, "I see one guy busting his bollocks and one guy scratching his bollocks. Don't just stand there; cop hold of that side of the stretcher, and we'll lift him together."

"If I could, I would, but I can hardly lift a pencil these days. I pulled my back getting out of bed too quickly. Don't look at me like that; I'm serious."

Such an impotent, dithering bloke reminded Tristan of a lad years ago whom he'd met in basic training; a lad poised with an excuse for getting out of everything. A bulbous-bodied lad, who, upon discovering on one ill-fated morning that their day comprised a twenty-mile yomp, forged the swirled script of the medic's signature on a sick note that described how he'd pulled his back when slipping in dog excrement. Even so, the tardigrade stood in front of him—warm, dry, and replete with energy— tooting his exaggerated excuses from his bugle-lips.

After unbuckling his belt and strapping it to the stretcher, Tristan towed the casualty all the way to the snowmobile, where connected to the rear axle was a kind of passenger sledge, long enough for one to lie upon full length. Atop it was mounted an incubator that looked like a transparent casket. It was into this casket that Tristan hoisted and strapped the casualty, but being too tall, he had to fold his limbs in like a rag doll. Meanwhile, the tardigrade mounted the saddle of the snowmobile and made himself comfortable.

"Where do I sit, then?" said Tristan, marking time (walking on the spot) to warm the blood in his extremities. "Am I to piggyback?"

"Sorry," said the tardigrade, gesturing apologetically to his plump, marshmallow frame; "I only have space for one."

"Eh, you're joking, aren't you? So you're just going to leave me stranded? Is there anybody else coming?" The tardigrade shrugged and recommended that Tristan log another incident with the emergency help desk. "The f-fucking fuck are you w-waiting for, th-then? Christmas? Get your arse out of here before I rip your arm off and slap you with the s-s-soggy end. Move—move—move."

Moist air spluttered from the trumpet in a way not dissimilar to the child who, on their first introduction to a brass instrument, smacks their lips together and blows a sloppy raspberry. Tristan made little sense of all the spluttering excuses that followed, and it took extraordinary restraint on his part to bite his tongue and not get in the final word (as he always did) before the tardigrade departed—since any further conversation would've jeopardised the rescue.

Six twists of the ignition and one wild boot were necessary to kick-start the engine, which rattled, growled, and popped before rider and casualty disappeared behind a veil of fog.

These events had left Tristan sopping with sweat; his undergarments clung to his body like a loosely hanging skin. To be wet and rapidly losing body heat in the Arctic was to be in danger of hypothermia—or worse. He knotted his arms across his chest and hugged himself to offer some warmth to his core.

"N-need t-t-to keep m-moving." It hurt now to speak.

In the mediocrity of middle age, some men acquire a motorcycle, others prefer shiny golf clubs; some men turn to drink, others try drugs; some men wear a new hairstyle, while others adopt a new smile; some men get a tattoo, others holiday in Timbuktu; but in the crisis of middle age, Tristan wandered the extremes of the poles, hoping to find something out there to fill the void within. Yet, on the verge of freezing to death, those mundane snares presently being advertised to his imagination seemed alluring fancies.

Breaking into a jog, he followed the tracks of the snowmobile. But soon after, the range of his stride became restricted. His weary legs gave in and he was reduced to a rigid stumble. All feeling left his hands (despite them being gloved); his fingers were as solid as stone, and to clench them required a strength greater than could be summoned. He revived them somewhat by trapping them beneath his armpits, and it was a good job, too, for he heard a guttural growl that came not from his own hungry stomach but from that of hungrier company behind the white curtain of fog.

He whipped up his trinoculars, searching out the origin of the growl. A bright orange silhouette appeared ahead, rapidly growing in size. Too broad and squat to be man … It was a rampant bear! Within seconds, Tristan unslung his rifle and made ready, his frozen fingers hovering over the trigger, waiting.

The armchair adventurer, the aspiring argonaut, those with super-fluous confidence are quick to assert from afar that the best thing to do when threatened with being dragged away and dined upon by feral jaws is to remain calm; and with romantic pretence, they envisage themselves survivors of the direst circumstances. But in the darkest of hours, when the fright of nonexistence grips the hairs on the nape of the neck, we are all of us liable to the foulest mutiny of our bladders and bowels.

Tristan's frozen fingers hovered over the trigger, yet they remained in defiant protest against clenching. As when fighting or running away in a dream, all movement became lethargic the greater the effort he exerted.

Deeper into the shrouded path he wandered, balancing his rifle in his shaky arms. At frequent intervals he freed up one hand and brought his trinoculars to his furrowed face. And then, with the aid of their thermal imaging, he saw it again! Shapes of flaming orange—those of warm-blooded life—storming in a state of flux towards him.

CHAPTER EIGHT

ILL TIDINGS

Astrid, Thor, and Chenglei entered Isbjørn Huset, and having patted the snow from their cloaks and out of their hair, they handed their goods over to the storekeeper: a hunting bow, a sheaf of arrows, a sack of merchandise, and, since it was the custom to lounge in socks, they parted with their muddy boots. The storekeeper received them with one stressed eyebrow elevated right the way up to the apex of his receding hairline, and there was a reluctance to let out a space to them in his overcrowded cloakroom. But that was his problem; they had a problem of their own: finding a free table in this bustling tavern.

Thor shepherded them through the crowd, carving a path towards the fireside. There were no vacant seats, but Astrid knew he was up to his old tricks; he was going to launch an assault on the senses. Thus he stomped about, booming profane words and smelling as he did (of fish). Shortly after, a small party of mainlanders rose and, without finishing their drinks, abandoned their table.

When passing, Astrid overheard the words "foragers" and "filth" being used in the same sentence; so, in a show of defiance, she decanted the mainlanders' leftover drinks into a single flagon—mead, beer, and vodka—and drank it all without pausing for breath. Then, when she turned the flagon upside down and wore it for a wooden hat (proving its emptiness), the nearby foragers clamoured in unison and bade her good health.

"I thought you said no drinking, Astrid?" said Thor, scraping out a chair as he beckoned her to sit.

"I know," she said, wiping the froth from her lips, then sitting, "but they got me mad. They were looking at us as though we were dirt."

Amiable old Chenglei offered his amiable words, calming her while Thor disappeared to order food and drinks. Even after knowing him for less than an hour, Astrid knew Chenglei was a person to be relied upon by friends. When Thor came back, he did so bearing overflowing flagons, which he planted on the table before them. Thor finished his before Chenglei had even taken a sip of his cranberry and lime juice.

"So," said Thor, "city man, are you, Cheng? Out here in the wilderness isn't somewhere to be holidaying, if you'll allow me to say, for a man of your age."

"Not quite a city man. I'm here for work and have been working at the Arctic Sanctuary for a number of years now. You see, there's not much work on the mainland for someone with my qualifications these days."

"It must be interesting at the Sanctuary," said Astrid, trying to be polite but having little intellect to offer on the subject.

"Well, I'm a ranger there. It's work, I suppose. But it's not my passion. My true passion,"—his Adam's apple sprang to life—"my true passion is genetics ... Well, it used to be."

"Genetics, huh? Did you say earlier you had some involvement with that white mammoth project? My boy Ulrik is always talking about it."

"Is he now, Thorsten?" said Chenglei. "And yes, I did. But our research was shut down before we could introduce a friend for Onyx—a woolly rhinoceros. And that's why I'm here. Since I was involved in his conception, I've always felt an obsligation to look after him; to befriend him."

"Still, it must be a lonely existence," said Astrid, twiddling her plaits solemnly, "being the only one of his kind in the world."

"It's a fate I wouldn't wish on my worst enemy," said Thor.

Soon after, the smell of good food raised their spirits. When snow crab, puffin breast, reindeer heart, and seared mink whale were served up on rainbow-coloured beds of vegetables, they ate in silence, save for their chomping, chewing, munching, and crunching. Chenglei looked on in horror at Thor, who ate without a fork or spoon; instead, he spread his fingers to rake the salad to one side, then closed his fingers into the profile of a spade and served himself up great portions of meat before gulping them down his neck like an albatross—keeping his beak clean all the while. Bloated, they leant back in their armchairs and wetted their throats with golden mead. When the drinks flowed, so did their conversation, and deep conversation turned into drunk conversation.

For a moment, a sobering guilt stole over Astrid like a cold draught. It was getting late, and Ulrik was likely to need tending to. But Chenglei interrupted her thoughts with a direct question: "So, Astrid, Thorsten, what brought you to Svalbard?"

"We are foragers," said Thor, thudding his chest. "Not just us, but all humans. We're all foragers, including you, Cheng. Our bodies aren't suited to the office or warehouse—or laboratory. Man should roam the steppes and savannah with sunshine on his face and a breeze in his hair, not coveting and collecting wealth. No person can be content with life if they're always comparing their possessions to those of others. The certainty of knowing where your next meal comes from—it robs you of your true nature; and it robbed us dearly. See, it's the hunt, Cheng, which is our most ancient struggle—our primal occupation. And so, to answer your question, it was our ancestral longing for the wilderness that brought us to Svalbard. Here, at our own leisure, do we feast, do we fight, and do we fuc—"

Astrid karate-chopped him in the throat, causing him to choke on his last word. After all, there were younglings present at the adjacent table.

"But of all places, why the Arctic?" inquired Chenglei, squinting with a critical eye.

Thor took a deliberate glug of mead, delaying his answer.

"We wanted," interjected Astrid, "to go to a place where we could get lost, where nobody could find us."

"I see." Chenglei nodded with curious scepticism.

"We'd grown weary of being poor," Astrid went on, leaning over the table to assert her authenticity. "We had nothing to lose. We were so poor that I was selling my eggs to IVF clinics"—she gestured to her ovaries—"to earn a living. Like a hen, I gave up my eggs; but even a hen is at least fed properly every day. I was lesser than livestock."

"Things were bad after the markets crashed, weren't they?" said Chenglei, sympathetically. Then his face altered to one of suspicion. "But why did you really come?"

Before Astrid or Thor could respond, something very rare occurred. The local drunkard swapped his timeworn stool at the bar for a seat on the hard floor beside them. He was hardly ever seen to vacate his perch, nor did he ever offer any words other than "barum bum-bum". Yet he and his ugly head wobbled over to them. He had a terribly oily face and a grotesque excess of earwax; and having slipped a sharp fingernail into the cavern of his ear, he mined from it a sizable golden nugget. After a moment of appreciating its enormity, he pocketed the rancid lump for safekeeping. His ears now unplugged, the drunkard listened to their conversation intently (though he continued his ignoble mining of gems from the deep recesses of his body and was later seen to dig out an emerald or two from his favourite nostril).

Other foragers looked on in surprise at the drunkard, since a brimming flagon ranked above all other of life's pleasures to such a person; it was a strange occurrence to see that something else diverted his attention. Whatever it was, it must've been of supreme interest. So, like the drunkard, other punters gathered by the fireside. Silence befell them, and they all turned in their ears like cats do when they hear the faintest snicker of prey among the tangled undergrowth.

This unwanted attention caused the blood to rise up Thor's face like a volcano on the brink of eruption.

"Insignificant people caused us significant harm," said Thor. Astrid nodded with vehemence.

The foragers in the crowd were rubbing thick strips of tobacco between their fingers and dropping pinches in the chambers of their pipes. Once lit, they puffed away and blew smoke rings into the air like a brood of dragons. They'd come for a story, not a sentence.

"Thoughts of suicide got me through dark times," added Thor. Foragers gasped, and some mothers covered the ears of their younglings. "On days when I felt powerless, knowing I could terminate my life and end the pain was the most empowering thought."

The drunkard ran to fetch his drinking horn, which he'd left at the bar. Then he came back with it, said "Barum bum-bum," and handed it to Thor in what was probably the single most generous donation to occur on the planet that day.

"Erling Battlehorn, good health to you," said Thor, leaning over to give a polite headbutt. The drunkard was delighted that his name was known to the Magnussons. Thor glugged down his golden draught to honour the gesture.

"What did your parents and siblings say when you told them you were running away?" asked Chenglei, stroking his smooth chin with a slender finger.

"I haven't any siblings," said Astrid, staring longingly into the fire in a state of reminiscence; "but my parents ... we had our differences. Though I miss them, and I feel guilty for abandoning them."

"What about you, Thorsten? Do you have siblings?"

Thor pretended to take a drink from his horn, which was already empty.

"Thorsten?"

There was a kicking of shins beneath the table between Astrid and Thor.

"Sorry, Cheng; I'm one of three brothers—nuh, I *was* one of three brothers. My twin, Karsten—he's dead to me; and I am to him. Sigsten is the eldest; I loved him, though he ran away from home when he was a teen. He went abroad, but I don't know where. He never came home. Being much older, Sigsten was more of a parent to Karsten and me than our actual parents. My parents ... I'm ashamed to call them so."

"Ashamed?" said Chenglei, being naïve to his intrusion.

Something about Thor's mood changed. Chenglei and the foragers around the room averted their eyes for fear of meeting his leaf-green eyes. Even the drunkard reinserted the golden nugget into his ear out of respect and returned to his stool at the bar. Mining, it seemed, wasn't his only profession; he was also disposed to farming, and he sat on his stool for the rest of the evening harvesting a family of marrowfat peas from his nostrils, then moulding them together to create a pea of monstrous proportions.

"I've said as much as I'm willing to say," said Thor, leaning forward and cradling his bowels. Astrid heard the rumbling and squelching of his anxiety passing through him. He got like that when pressed about his past, and if ever questioned about his cramps, he'd lie about them, saying only that he was hungry and hadn't eaten recently. Little known to Astrid was anything of Thor prior to their courting, though she was certain that he withheld a particular secret, a dark secret that she was unlikely to ever discover—perhaps for her own sake. But that was his choice, and she respected it.

"I'm sorry, Thorsten," pleaded Chenglei. "I shouldn't have asked personal questions. That's your business. I'm too nosy for my own good, aren't I? It's just that you're both remarkable people, and I've learnt so much from listening to you. I've not been lucky enough to call many people friends during my life. And to think that here I am now making enemies of you. I'm such an idiot."

"Cheng, nuh," said Astrid, reaching out for his hands, which were the soft, dainty hands of one acquainted with the keyboard. "You're too kind. Please don't say sorry. You weren't to know." Judging by the slight rise of his Adam's apple, some minor relief overcame Chenglei, but she supposed those same words would've been more profound had they come from Thor. But Thor slumped in his chair, and in holding his crinkled face towards the fire he tried to dry the mist from his eyes. He was too proud to use a sleeve to absorb the welling at his tear ducts: that would've confirmed his sadness to all. He'd be overthinking it now, wanting to wipe his eyes but abstaining in case he drew someone's attention. She knew all this about him: all his quirks, tendencies, loves, hates, preferences, peeves; but this *childhood haunting*, whatever it was that was on his mind, this shame of his parents, she'd never gained so much as an inkling about and had been shunned at every effort to do so. He said only that to reveal his secret would be to infect her with the same plague of the mind and that no possible good could come from the sharing of such a disease since there would be two sufferers and twice the suffering. But hearing that only doubled her desire to know.

Above the low hum of civil chatter there burst an uproar like thunder announcing a storm. Rushing into the entrance of Isbjørn Huset was a man padded in layers so thick he appeared like a marshmallow with limbs, featureless save for the great trumpet lips protruding from under his hood. Svalbard etiquette concerning the wearing of shoes indoors had been violated, and the storekeeper, foaming at his mouth, looked upon his floor in horror at the dishonour done to it. Like a pinball, the troublemaker bounded from table to table in search of something—or someone. He trumpeted the name Magnusson at each table, after which a forager's arm reached out from across the room and pointed towards Astrid and Thor. Thor drew himself up to his full height and clenched his cubic hands; his chest huffed out into a solid square; and he buried his menacing brow halfway down his face.

The dwindling murmurs ceased.

"Thorsten, is that you?" said the troublemaker, wringing his woollen hat in his hands—conscious of all the glaring eyes. "Ah, it is you; and you must be Astrid. I've been in every tavern on this road looking for you. May I speak with you both alone … in private?"

"Why should we trust a mainlander like you?" said Thor. "Tell us why you're here, and be quick about it."

"Sorry, I can't do this," the stranger said, veiling his face with both hands.

"Do what?"

"Your boy, Ulrik … he—"

Thor took him by his collar and looked in danger of roasting the marshmallow-man over the fire.

"What about him?" said Astrid, her bones shaking in anticipation of a dark revelation.

After much stammering, the man told them he was employed by mountain rescue, and he held up his official lanyard as proof of his occupation. He'd been called out to a scene of two boys who'd fallen through ice—an accident concerning their son. "I'm sorry," cowering now like a dog does when caught by its master carrying out some gross mischief, "your son fell beneath some ice. A lake on the edge of Nordenskjold."

When Thor and Astrid first heard this, a wave of relief washed over them. That would be Ulrik just going about his usual swim … But severe lineaments occupied their faces when they remembered Ulrik was supposed to be resting with his arm up in a sling.

"What lake?" asked Thor, massaging his temples as though to awaken his memory. "I don't recall there being a lake there. I don't believe it. I won't believe it. Who's putting you up to this, you shameless worm?"

"Yah, you've got the wrong person," said Astrid. "My son is at home resting."

"Nobody is putting me up to this, I swear. There is a lake. I almost crashed under myself. But we got your son out, the Englishman and I."

"I'm really sorry, but I'm afraid he's right," said Chenglei; his Adam's apple shrank to the size of a raisin as he swallowed hard. "There *are* new lakes on Svalbard. It's because of the precipitous summers we've seen in recent years. Warmer summers produces greater humidity, which produces greater rainfall. I've studied endorheic basins and glaciation at length, and I've seen these new lakes form over summers and ice over in winter, including the one at Nordenskjold. I know the region well."

"Then where is he now?" said Thor.

"I took him to hospital."

"To hospital," echoed Astrid.

"He wasn't … responding."

The words ricocheted about her skull. Her legs gave way like a hamstrung horse, and she collapsed to her knees. For a moment, she forgot who she was. In straining her eyes, a vivid galaxy of nebulae dazzled her vision—splotches of purple and green—the likes of which are seen when staring for too long into bright lights. When the cosmic foreground fizzled away, she saw in front of her the face of a pleasant forager, snapping her fingers and clapping her hands, although there was no sound. Astrid noticed that her own chin was being held in another forager's hands, as though she were some delicate book whose binding and pages might fall apart if not held together in such a way. Such good people they were to be helping her with … whatever it was she needed help with. Had she fallen? Rising to her feet, she neither saw nor felt injury. It was only when she saw Thor being poorly restrained by a handful of thinner folk that she remembered.

"Let's be going, then," said Thor, unhanding the man and suddenly mellowing at the realisation.

"What of Ivar?" said Astrid, smacking her mouth. "There was another boy with my son."

Marshmallow-man's eyes fell to the ground and he shook his bereaved head, implying that he knew nothing of Ivar's fate. "The only person still out there is the Englishman. If somebody doesn't get to him soon, we'll have another casualty on our hands. He sacrificed many layers to keep your son warm."

"I'll go," said Chenglei, without hesitation. "I've had no alcohol, so I'm legal to drive, and I know the way. Is there anyone who can loan me a snowmobile?"

"You can take my Snowrover, Chenglei," said a mature lady, who said she knew him through a mutual connection from work. She told him to swing by her home next week for coffee and return the keys to her in person. Though he kindly said he'd post them through the letterbox so as not to be a pest.

Marshmallow-man told how he could only escort one passenger: Astrid or Thor, but not both. He asked if anyone else could take one of them, but most were too drunk and in no fit state to drive.

"I'll take one," said the tavern master, "preferably the lady here, she being of a lighter build—meaning no offence, Thorsten, sir. I've had some drink, but the law doesn't forbid me from riding in my dog-sled. My huskies are quick, and their bellies are full. We'll be right behind you."

Thus the transport was settled. Snowmobiles, dog-sleds, reindeer-sleighs, sparks, and skis bolted in all directions; some to the hospital, others to Nordenskjold to rescue the Englishman, one as the dreaded messenger to Ivar's parents, and many headed home at once to squeeze their younglings who were sound asleep beneath their bedsheets and not a sheet of ice. The storekeeper, having taken up stewardship of Isbjørn Huset in the tavern master's absence, jostled the stragglers out, some without their belongings. "Out!" he cried. "We're closed—as a mark of respect." (From then on, Isbjørn Huset was always closed on that day, a day which later become known to foragers as Ivar's Day.)

Astrid and Thor alighted from their transport at the entrance of Longyearbyen Hospital and pelted inside past scores of bodies lingering in the lobby. Astrid charged through so hard that she almost knocked an unsuspecting nurse to the ground, and had she connected, she would've been certain to have made a patient of them both. She beat on the triage window, begging for the attention of the secretary who was busy filing away documents of no importance.

The secretary looked over the rim of her ruby spectacles, and when she shook her head, her marble earrings shook with equal disdain. She gave a grouchy, sour look, as though she'd spent the entire evening eating her way through a sack of onions. And having her routine disturbed, Joy (as her name tag read, ironically) recoiled as though she was in danger of contracting leprosy from the other side of the glass. Then, with a shrill tone, she cawed in a voice that sounded as though her nose was being pinched: "Security!"

CHAPTER NINE

UNEXPLAINED PHENOMENON

"Security!" squawked the secretary.

Thorsten pivoted on his heel to see the secretary flapping her wings in a great rage. Her crooked beak seemed to grow, as though in a mutinous attempt to abscond from her face so that it might go forth and be free to carry out, without hindrance, a lifetime of incessant pecking at those who dare to disagree with its owner.

This secretary was a proud custodian of the unofficial ban imposed on foragers visiting public institutions: a prohibition which was all but written in law. Some rumoured that it was in the interest of patient safety to keep foragers away since many were unvaccinated (vaccines didn't exist a thousand years ago). Others rumoured that the foragers' lavatory etiquette, or lack thereof, made them suitable hosts and carriers for invisible diseases. But perhaps the truth was that ordinary folk subscribed to the collective opinion that foragers were a clan of ill-mannered scroungers who, having paid nothing into the system, didn't deserve to occupy the least bit of temporary territory under any municipal roof until their fair dues had been settled and their equal taxes paid.

Behind the secretary, a figure scurried into view, who, in his black jacket, looked akin to a fat beetle: a security guard in uniform. Then there were two, then four, then eight; and the guards seemed to go on multiplying like spores of mould in a petri dish.

"We're not looking for trouble," said Astrid, advancing with dainty hands held up in surrender. "We're looking for our son, Ulrik Magnus—"

But no sooner had she begun speaking than both their hands were bound and spit hoods resembling plastic bags were dragged over their weary heads, presumably because of the misconception that foragers were a people liable to spray phlegm.

"Visiting hours are over," said one guard.

"If you wanted to visit someone," said another guard, "harassing our staff and causing a scene at the entrance wasn't the smartest move. This way now, foragers. Move. Quickly now. You're only delaying things for yourself. I get paid for this, so I can wait all day …"

A molten mood frothed at Thorsten's core, and his hot face turned the colour of a ripe tomato, owing to the livid pulse snaking throughout his temples when heaving in vast gulps of air, and somehow the pressure in the room seemed to deplete in correlation with the expansion of his lungs.

"Do as they say, Thor," said Astrid, through gritted teeth, "and we'll get to Ulrik sooner."

Just this once he found himself heeding Astrid's advice. She was right, so he kept his tongue knotted in case he hindered proceedings with his offensive language.

They were led into a cold grey stairwell and thereafter ascended two or three storeys. After stepping out onto an upper wing, they passed numerous overhead signs and tried to make sense of where they were heading—where Ulrik might be. But medical language reads to the layman like a language of the ancients: only those who've studied it at length can decipher its meaning. Coronary this, endoscopy that, and innumerable *ologies*: ophthalmology, neurology, oncology. How was anyone without a medical baccalaureate supposed to navigate these labyrinths?

Down the corridor and turning left they entered another ward, where they saw, through the windows they passed, many patients looking like victims of vengeful voodoo, with pins, tubes, and rods attached to their various body parts. Sad eyes looked back at them from the other side of the windowpanes. Even so, Thorsten hoped to see Ulrik among them—as proof of him being alive. But there was no sign of him ... only sombre whispers of his name on the corridors.

The foragers were detained in a spacious room, or rather cell, where the security guards removed their cuffs and spit hoods before departing. Little was said to them before they did, except that they were told someone would be around to speak with them soon.

It was an odd cell. Its floor, ceiling, and walls were tiled with high-definition screens, and not a seam was visible to the naked eye. Overhead, on the digital ceiling, a sun that looked not dissimilar to a juicy apricot rolled at leisure across a fuchsia sky. The concave walls were a digital panorama depicting a languid seaside; looking westward they saw striped marsupials with gnarled ivory horns grazing on a stockpile of white plums and blue mangos under the shade of luminescent palm trees. Beneath their own feet, the floor panels appeared to be composed of golden sand, and wherever they stepped, deep footprints were imprinted. Like babies suspended in silent awe by the sight of a rotating mobile, their eyes flitted hither and thither. It was a sensory asylum for those of unstable mind—all designed to distract. A progressive prison of sorts.

Astrid's face was awash with icy dread, and her chin crumpled like the craterous surface of the moon as she tried to suppress her tears. But from the bottom of her lungs came a grievous, gravelly cry; a cry which only a mourning mother can summon.

Had the sand been real, Thorsten might've buried himself in a shallow grave. Instead, he lay flat with limbs outstretched as though he was being drawn apart by a medieval rack. His imagination was fraught with images of Ulrik on the ice; falling—suffering—dying. Each haunting vision was like another crank of the ratchet, pulling his limbs further and further apart. Through clenched teeth he sucked the air in and out, spitting as he did so as the slow torture intensified.

Eventually, it was an acidic smell that disturbed him from his delirium. Jets of bile streamed from Astrid's orifices; mouth, nostrils, and seemingly her eyes and ears. Chunks of heart lay strewn across the pseudo-sand—the heart of the venison they'd eaten for supper at Isbjørn Huset. Astrid heaved and retched till all the contents of her stomach bespattered the floor.

"Eugh-urgh," she groaned. Then, with her throat badly burnt from vomiting, she cried out in a hoarse voice, "I don't even know if my son is alive or dead!" Then she collapsed in a heap of inanimate bones in the corner.

Upon hearing such dread, Thorsten grappled with his face, his muck-engrained fingers molesting his view for several dark moments. "My son ... dead? We don't know that yet, Astrid. Don't say that."

At once, his attention was drawn to the silvery screech of metal whetting metal. He noticed that the door to this room had a hatch resembling a letterbox, through which they were being watched by a pair of black eyes, so searching that they appeared to be reaching into the room like antennae. Then, when Thorsten locked eyes with them, the antennae seemed to retract, and the hatch slammed shut.

"Wait, please," he begged, crawling to the door on his knees like a cripple.

No answer.

Thorsten stood up and slammed his fist on the door, the gong of which threatened to wake the sleepy hospital. Still no answer. Then, with a seismic effort, he used his body as a battering ram and tried to bring the door to ruin. But it was forged of some durable alloy and looked akin to the entrance of a bomb shelter.

Somehow, the room and its digital walls, floors, and ceiling took notice of the current ambience, for the weather seemed to change spontaneously; a cooling breeze tickled the fronds of the trees, the bright hue of the sky dimmed, and the roaring surf against the shore softened. All of these subliminal distractions were, no doubt, effective in reducing a lunatic's stress levels.

When he calmed, the hatch slid open. "Thorsten," said the guard, "believe me, I'm on your side. But if you continue to ram the door you'll only prolong your time in there. Help me to help you."

"Are we arrested?" croaked Astrid, her throat so hoarse that the guard mistook it for Thorsten's voice.

"Well, Thorsten, not in the legal sense. But think of yourself under *citizen's arrest*."

"For what crime? We came only to see our son."

"For causing a public disturbance. For causing a commotion at a time like this—in a hospital. I've lost count of the number of hospitals across DRUE which have been targets of Saifullah terrorist attacks. It's poor timing to be running around hospitals causing a scene. Everywhere and everyone is on high alert, you know. We don't take any chances."

Gong.

"*Timing*? Should we be timing the death of our son better? Is that what you're saying?"

An inquiring squint arose on the guard's face, and his black eyes dilated so much that they appeared like black holes threatening to engulf his entire face. "You have me confused. Your son's death … Ivar is your son, then?"

"Nuh, not Ivar," said Astrid, rising with hope in her eyes and vomit in her hair. "Ulrik Magnusson is our son," pressing herself up to the door.

Heated whispers were exchanged on the other side. It sounded as though another guard was in receipt of a professional scolding. The chief guard pinched the bridge of his nose, looked down, and released a regretful sigh. "Foragers, I'm sorry if at any point you've been led to believe your child Ulrik passed away. He is very much alive."

Astrid had him repeat that sentence no fewer than nine times before accepting any word of it as truth. Even when satisfied with the account, neither Thorsten nor Astrid could allow themselves to be merry having learnt of Ivar's harrowing end. All that initial despair which they themselves had now escaped was being felt somewhere else by Ivar's parents.

Astrid insisted upon seeing Ulrik and made terrible threats should her demands not be met swiftly.

"Soon. But first, Dr Freyja Lyngstad needs to explain a few important things to you."

"Important things?" said Astrid, going up on her tiptoes in order to align her eyes with the hatch. "What like? Ulrik is well, isn't he?"

"I ... I don't know. I only said that he was alive."

"But alive and well?" interrogated Astrid.

"I'm not in a position to say; but only because I know no more than you do."

"You have me worried. Is my son conscious? Is he breathing? Oh, please, nuh. Nuh, nuh, nuh. Is he brain damaged? Tell me."

The hatch slid shut again, this time with slow, respectful courtesy.

Gong. Gong. Gong. Thorsten's knuckles became scarlet and swollen from his assault on the door.

"Thor, what if something terrible has happened to Ulrik? What if he's ... different? What if he's no longer the Ulrik we know? Something isn't right. I just feel it. A mamma knows these things. I wish I were wrong, but—but—"

"If something isn't right, Astrid, I'm hoping that whatever it is, it doesn't prevent him from swimming. Nothing could be worse for him."

"That's if he's fortunate enough to remember what swimming is," she said, burying her head in his midriff, where she shed a few private tears. "That'd be horrible."

There was no way of telling what time it was in that progressive prison and no precise way of judging how long it'd been since their conversation with the guard, but at mealtimes many dishes had been posted through a food hatch by the shaky hands of a porter. Breakfast and lunch had come and gone, but having no appetite for warmed-up dinners from the hospital scullery, they left their plates untouched. Instead, to absorb time, they made good use of the en suite bathroom; and for the first time in almost two decades, they performed their ablutions with running hot water and conducted their toilet without moss or snow.

Later, there came a nuclear knock at the bomb shelter door: gong—gong. It swung open, and in came a lady wearing turquoise scrubs. Her uniform was so unkempt and slovenly that it looked as though she'd got dressed that morning in total darkness for the very first time in her life. Her wonky fringe was rudely chopped into the profile of a comb (the irony being that it looked as though a comb had never been run through it). Yet she seemed little concerned with her outward appearance and spoke with such a fervent burst of self-assurance despite the speech impediment that warped her use of her r's.

"Astwid, Thorsten, I'm Dr Lyngstad," she said. Then she gave a gentle bow as though half wanting to honour the usual forager ceremony of a headbutt, but she retracted her neck when she saw the sheer profile of Thorsten's menacing skull.

"Dr Lyngstad," said Astrid, her ashen face utterly drained of blood and tears, "Dr Lyngstad, our son, is he—how to say it—in a 'vegetative' state? Is my son brain damaged?"

"Heck, no. Who's been telling you this? Welax. Here; dwink some water. Now, we *do* have some unusual learnings which need to be discussed, but please be at ease: Ulwik is in a vewy stable condition."

Hearing this from the doctor was a great relief, and Thorsten and Astrid squeezed each other, never fully letting go of one another for the remainder of their conversation.

"Sorwy I couldn't get here sooner. Ooo, that feels good." Dr Lyngstad's eyes glazed over for a moment as she slipped off her sneakers and aired her bunions. "Oh,"—suddenly remembering she was in company—"you don't mind me putting my feet up, do you? It's the first time I've sat down since my shift began fourteen hours ago."

The foragers shrugged their shoulders. All three of them were seated on a beanbag each.

"Bwilliant, thank you. Now, I understand you want answers. Soon everwything will become clear. I'll twy to be as bwief as possible since I know you'll be weddy to see him. But please understand, there are some questions that even I don't know the answers to at this stage."

"This stage?" said Astrid, almost lunging out of her seat. "What's happened to my son?"

"Astwid, please, in time. It would be easiest if I were to explain things first; then, when I've finished, you can ask me any question you like."

Thorsten massaged Astrid's spine with gentle pressure. It calmed her, if only for a short while—a reminder that cooperation with Dr Lyngstad was necessary if they wanted to be with Ulrik.

"Thank you," continued Dr Lyngstad. "Before I begin, I have to ask you about a discwepancy on your personal wecords. We have you, Thorsten, down as father to Embla Magnusson: a female wegistered as twenty years old. Embla is showing as your only child. Is Embla a child of yours fwom a pwevious welationship?"

"Embla?" said Astrid, turning towards him, her eyes silently hissing at him. "Who's this Embla?"

"Woah, you have the wrong person," said Thorsten, with feigned laughter. The air in the room seemed to diminish, and the weather on the digital walls overcompensated for it with a rush of refreshing wind— the blast of which issued from the air conditioning. "Ulrik is my only child—*our* only child." He grasped Astrid's hand, but she flung it away playfully and crossed her arms in jest. He'd been in trouble like this before when she'd dreamt of him having lain with another woman: for some reason he had to apologise for that, too.

"How stwange. There's no wecord of Ulwik being your child. In fact, there's no wecord altogether. Where did you have him wegistered?"

"We're foragers," said Astrid, "we believe registering a child's birth to be an unnatural affair."

"As I thought," said Dr Lyngstad, making a greater mess of her hair in her confusion. "It's a stwange misunderstanding, this Embla Magnusson anomaly. I've never known the archive to be incorwect. But perwaps the system has you confused with another Thorsten Magnusson. Stwanger things have happened, I guess. Whatever the cause, I'm sure we'll find out in due course. It just makes it hard to vewify you as the legal parwents of Ulwik without the corwect documentation."

"That's your problem," said Astrid, her patience already withered like a pile of autumn leaves. "Enough about your system and all its misunderstandings about who we are—and who our children are. I need to hear about my son …"

"Sorwy, yes. One moment, please."

Dr Lyngstad gave one last wiggle of her toes before slipping on her sneakers again and rising to her feet. She poked her head around the bomb shelter door, issued an order of dismissal, and the guards scurried away. When Dr Lyngstad was satisfied that nobody was eavesdropping, she said, "Ulwik came to us in what ought to have been a vewy fwail condition, to say the least—having entered an extweme stage of hypothermia. Did you know the human body temperwature is awound 37°C? It'll surpwise you, then, to learn that the men who wescued Ulwik wecorded his temperwature at only 13°C."

"This is unheard of, Doctor?"

"Unheard of, yes, Thorsten. Ulwik ought to be—well, dead. It's wemarkable. The Medical Ministwy classifies such occurwences as *unexplained phenomena*."

"He's been swimming these frozen shores for years," said Thorsten. "Obviously, we were mad when he first told us about that, but he came out without injury. And since he's always hot and bothered with all that body hair of his, he took to swimming as his way of cooling off."

Dr Lyngstad ran her fingers through her frowzy fringe in disbelief. At length, Thorsten spoke with glowing pride about Ulrik's affinity for swimming in Arctic waters.

"Interwesting," shivering while Thorsten told his splendid tales. "Oh, that weminds me, before we continue, I'm obliged to tell you about the care we've given Ulwik durwing his time here. Despite him showing signs of wecoverwy, we performed a woutine pwocedure on him: an EMCO. Don't wurwy about the meaning. It's a pwocedure in which we pump warm oxygenated blood awound a body to help fibwillate the heart."

"Fibwillate?" said Thorsten. "What's that?"

"No-no, fibwillate."

"Fib-rill-ate, she means," said Astrid, pinching Thorsten's triceps.

"That's what I said: fibwillate. Anyway, the EMCO was a success.

Though as a pwecaution, we sedated him to give him a pwoper wrest. It's likely he'll be sleeping when I escort you to him. But don't be concerned. Oh, he also came to us with a fwactured collarbone and a badly bwoozed eye, which I'm told he'd suffered beforehand in an unwelated incident. Oh, and he's got a gash on his arm—but nothing too sewious. We've pwescwibed him some pain welief to help with the collarbone."

"This is all sounding very good," said Astrid, gliding one of her braids along her tongue in a way that an archer might do to the flight of an arrow when preparing it to fire, "but I saw you telling those guards to stand down. Why in such serious tones? Why the secrecy? What aren't you telling us, Dr Lyngstad?"

"Nothing gets past you, does it, Astwid? Well, it's no secwet we're puzzled by your son. By wights, he should be dead. His body has a stwange ability to wesist the cold. So we've wun a few pweliminarwy tests on him that have weturned some interwesting wesults."

The foragers exchanged a look of concern.

"This might sound stwange because it does to us doctors: when examining his blood we found a high concentwation of antifweeze pwoteins." At once, the atmosphere of the digital room seemed to suspend; all sound was swallowed up, all movement halted. The leaves of the palms stopped rustling; the sun was apprehended at its exact meridian; the ocean surf ceased its lapping, and there appeared an endless pond without ripple or tide; and the marsupials froze upright, turning their attention, it seemed, towards the sound of Dr Lyngstad's voice.

"You found what in his blood?"

"Sorwy, Astwid, my speech impediment pwevents me fwom pwonouncing it pwoperly: antifweeze pwoteins."

"Antifreeze proteins?" echoed Astrid.

"Yes, that's it," said the unoffendable Dr Lyngstad, who'd probably suffered a lifetime of being misunderstood. "We see these antifweeze pwoteins mainly in the blood of Arctic fish. It's a defence mechanism that pwevents them fwom fweezing solid."

"Bah! Fish, you say?" said Thorsten.

"Yes; and there's the occasional example in the plant kingdom known to synthesise antifweeze pwoteins, too. But no known cases have ever been wecorded in humans."

"So he's a tough boy."

"Oh, he's more than that," said Dr Lyngstad, with sceptical passion. "But only a scientific explanation will do."

"What's the scientific explanation, then?"

"I don't have one. Not yet. As I said earlier, in our line of work this is categorwised as an unexplained phenomenon. Now, I'm twying to find a polite way of saying something else, but I fear I may have to be wude."

"Speak freely, Dr Lyngstad."

"Vewy well. Ulwik is a stwange child to look at. His gwoath hormone levels are high, which would explain his chiselled features, his height, and his surplus body hair. An early bloomer, I expect. Cwazy. My nephew is sixteen years old, and there's barely a whisker on him. Sorwy, I digwess. Have you ever noticed anything else stwange about Ulwik?"

"For sure," said Astrid. "There are a few things I can recall. He was a pre-mature birth, but he wasn't underdeveloped in the way you might expect."

"Pwemature, wow—and not underdeveloped, you say? Anything else?"

"Well, he has hard skin. It's always dry; I'm thinking, from being exposed to the cold. You can pinch or scratch him, and he hardly feels it. He says it's like having elbow skin stretched across his whole body. Oh, and something else: he eats as if he's about to go into hibernation. He eats all day, yet he never gets fat. He just grows upwards like a pine, never outwards like a yew."

"Interwesting. A hyperwactive metabolism. This might've helped wegulate his temperwature. Fuel for the furnace, if you catch my dwift."

"And," interjected Thorsten, holding his hands out flat, as though steadying his balance for the revelation to come, "in the dark of winter, I take him hunting with me. Even on nights without starlight or moon-light, he can spot our prey a mile off—long before I can. His vision is no better than ours during the day … but at night nothing escapes his attention; I'll bet it's as sharp as any nocturnal creature's."

"I see," making furious scribbles on paper. "And what can you tell me about the hair on his body, face, and forewhed? Does anybody else in the family have that kind of charwacterwistic?"

"Nuh, he's the only one."

"Cuwious, indeed. There'll be many more questions to come, but for now I ought to answer one of yours. Astwid, you asked why I was speaking in such sewious tones. It's because under JOEL I'm obligated to weport instances of unexplained phenomena to the Medical Ministwy of the Dem400000cwatic Wepublic of United Euwope."

"Bah! DRUE ... JOEL; who's coming up with these names?" said Thorsten.

"Dr Lyngstad, ignore my husband," said Astrid. "So, you're obliged to report unexplained phenomena. What's this mean for us, exactly?"

"Ulwik is being wefewred to the mainland for further analysis." When she said this, an ochreous sea fog rolled in on the digital screens—clouding the horizon.

"After what he's been through," said Astrid, "you think I'm going to be letting you send my son away? His friend has died, Dr Lyngstad. This is our time to mourn and grieve. Have a heart."

"I know. Don't shoot the messenger. If it was up to me—"

"You can't take him away," said Thorsten. "You're not going to. He needs to stay here, on Svalbard. Where he's safe."

"It's not me that's taking him away. But the law compels it. I don't agwee with it; I'm on your side. And I know the news of Ivar will be difficult for him to compwehend, but maybe the time away may serve as a distwaction. And Ulwik will be given the gweatest care and attention. See it as a good thing—an adventure. A chance to welax for a month or two."

"A month or two?" Astrid's hand latched onto Thorsten's knee with the force and dexterity of a crustacean's pincer.

"We refuse," said Thorsten, narrowing his eyes and puffing out his chest. The digital clouds above them burst like piñatas, and the sky rained rose-gold glitter. Perhaps the word "refuse" had triggered the mellowing distraction, and perhaps many other signs of protest throughout their conversation had been detected by clever algorithms and responded to with subtle sensory influences.

"I'm sorwy, but we're bound by JOEL. The only choice you have as parwents is whether to accompany Ulwik or wemain behind. Should you decide to go, you will, of course, be given generwous bursarwies to cover your time and expenses. If Ulwik's condition wemains stable, you'll have a day to pwepare for the departure to the mainland. I'll leave you to think about that. But I should also make you aware of one last thing: you could be in sewious twouble with the law considerwing you left a child alone without a guardian. If you cooperwate now, the Governor has suggested he'll make that pwoblem go away. He alweddy knows about it since I spoke to him about the unexplained phenomenon before coming down here. I had to. It's the law."

"The Governor already knows?" said Thorsten, scratching away at his sweaty palms. The thought of returning to the mainland sent acid rising up his gullet, which he quenched by swallowing, with considerable effort. "What's he got to do with—"

"Understood; we'll cooperate," said Astrid, squeezing Thorsten's wrist and towing him towards the bomb shelter door. "Now, to see our son …"

"Vewy well," chaperoning them out of the progressive prison. "It's vewy exciting, isn't it? This unexplained phenomenon? Never in all my years have I heard of a case of antifweeze pwoteins in humans. I expect one day you might look back on this—despite it being a vewy sad day in many wespects—as a day when your lives changed forwever."

The disturbing suggestion of their lives changing awoke an anxiety within Thorsten, and Astrid was sure to have heard his digestive system protesting from end to end, for her linking her arm through his was her silent way of telling him that whatever should come to pass, as long as they had each other, everything would be okay.

Chapter Ten

FOR VALOUR

Ulrik's eyelids hung like curtains of chain mail over his grass-green eyes. Separating them required the intervention of a vigorous finger to rub away the liquid gold adhesive glueing them fast. At first, the effulgent white light overwhelmed him, and it took a few moments for his pupils to orientate. He sniffed at the warm, stale air, and even before his vision was restored, he supposed, given the smell of festering germs, that he was in a hospital.

When propped upright, he noticed many wires connected to his body, and he imagined himself a puppet caught up in a hopeless tangle beyond salvage. There were bleeping monitors to the left of his bed and a visitor's chair to his right, surrounding all of which was a privacy curtain patterned with an ugly mosaic designed to hide the many stains that bespattered it. He thought about getting up to haul the curtain aside, but his collarbone (which was now in a proper sling) had him wincing at the slightest rotation. Fortunately, affixed to the rail of the bed was a digital panel displaying six icons: bed, lightbulb, fan, thermometer, curtain, and nurse. He'd heard about Tech, though he'd never used it. Prod—tap—tap. His primitive thumbs slipped, and he found the reading lamp behind him to be in a state of disco. Eventually, having accidentally altered the height of his bed and its inclination, having dimmed and brightened the lights, and having sent a whirlwind forth from the fan overhead, he drew back the bed curtain and fancied himself the most advanced human being that ever lived.

At the farthest end of the room stood a clean-shaven patient with cold, menacing eyes, dressed in a hospital gown and analysing his bed, busy smoothing out the faintest creases in the sheets. There wasn't a single stray hair on his shiny head or chin; only a strong band of eyebrow had escaped his compulsive razorblade. Nor was there likely to be a single stray hair, fibre, or filament of any kind lingering on his bed; his attention to detail was such that he took his time obsessing over the symmetry of pillows and devoting himself to the tucking in of bedsheet corners. To Ulrik, it looked as though the bed-making was finished, and it seemed as unspoiled as freshly fallen snow. Yet, when squatting low and running his eyes along the surface, the man seemed dissatisfied with the upper-most stratum of quilt, so he stripped away the bedding and started over from scratch.

Ulrik counted six additional vacant beds which had all been prepared to the exact same standard.

The man was so engrossed in his work that he hadn't seen Ulrik spying on him. When he finished making the beds, he made a start on polishing his boots; timeworn boots that looked as though they'd had quite enough already of been buffed. Despite their stupendous shine, their ears drooped, their tongues lolled loose, and their laces were frayed and greyed like braids of brittle hair.

Delicate footsteps clicked on the floor tiles, but they weren't his. Someone else was approaching. At once, Ulrik pretended to be asleep. He held fast his eyes and feigned a light snore. A presence drew near; someone loomed over him, watched him, and assessed him before departing. When it was safe to do so, he peered through a tiny slit in his right eye.

"Mr Nightingale," said a nurse, speaking to the bald man, "excuse me ... ahem."

"Less of that formal talk. Call me Tristan."

"Well, Tristan, I see Ulrik's bed curtain has been drawn. Has he been awake this morning?"

"Has it, now? I've not heard a single peep from him, ma'am," said the patient, not relinquishing his gaze from his boot polishing while there was still work to be done. "The lad must've rolled over in his sleep and elbowed the panelTech by accident. Keep doing that myself—knocking the lights on. It's like the Blackpool illuminations in here."

"Still sleeping, is he? I was hoping his medication would've worn off by now. The whole hospital wants an update on his recovery. Ah, I'm so sorry, Tristan; I meant to ask: how are *you* this morning?"

"Thought you'd never ask. But since you're so concerned, I'm as well as a recently rogered rabbit's rectum," placing down his gleaming boots and giving a sprightly salute with a bandaged hand.

"Go steady with that frostbitten hand of yours. You're lucky we're not amputating it. Now, there's no need for you to be up at this hour. Please, get into bed, will you?"

"I'm sorry," his keen eyes a-glow at her suggestion, "I don't mix business with pleasure."

Blushing with faint rose upon her cheeks and rolling her fair eyes, the nurse said, "You know that's not what I mean, Tristan. I'm very busy, so is there anything I can get you to make you feel less like a—how did you put it—recently rogered rabbit's rectum?"

"I'd murder a bacon sarny."

"I'm not sure what this 'sarny' is you're referring to and why you'd murder it, but we don't serve bacon of any kind. There's no pork on the menu."

"What a sad day—no pork!"

"Don't shoot the messenger. It's not me who makes these laws."

"Laws, eh? This another one of those laws introduced by the Holy Shepherd? I'm from England, you see; JOEL doesn't apply to us there. Lucky for us."

"The Bible prohibits the consumption of pork; so, yes, it's now written in law. Now, will you be wanting anything else, or can I go back to caring for my other patients?"

"Right, I'll settle for a cup o' tea, but don't be serving me any of that Earl Grey shite—excuse my French, ma'am. Please. Oh, and some toast, if you'd be so kind. I like mine properly burnt, thank you."

"I'll have the porter bring you some. In the meantime, you are to call me at the first sign of Ulrik waking. We're extremely low on staff today, so I can't get around as often as I'd like. It's really important you do this for me, please."

"All right, all right, I will," he called, as she glided out of the room and down the corridor to carry on with her life-saving errands. When the nurse was out of earshot, he stared forlornly into the abyss and muttered aloud to himself, "Ma'am, I'd drag my testicles through a trench of rusty shrapnel just to drink your dirty bathwater."

Ulrik broke out in a muffled laughter. Tristan's vulgar words reminded him of something Pappa would say.

"Suppose it's no wonder I've been single all my life, eh, mate?" said Tristan, noticing Ulrik stirring. "How you feeling?"

It was only when Ulrik was asked that he attempted to recall the events that led to his being here. Much of it was a blur, a curtain of amnesia veiling his memory.

"Ulrik," added Tristan, waving at him with his bandaged arm, "want me to call the nurses?"

"Nuh, I'm not ready for that kind of fuss," he said, shuffling himself upright. Even then, his legs were too long for this hospital bed of ordinary dimensions. "How long have I been sleeping? Where's my friend Ivar? You're the one who saved us, aren't you? It's coming back to me now. I remember your face."

"Ulrik, brave young Ulrik,"—a shadow seemed to pass over Tristan's face—"you are young and ..." Tristan prattled on at length, but Ulrik heeded no further words while stricken by the vivid memory of the drenching and the dragging and the drowning in that icy hell.

"It's coming back to me," he whispered. "He can't be ... Ivar can't be ..." With silent stealth, Tristan drew the bed curtain around them both and took the seat beside Ulrik's bed. "Ivar is tough. He'll pull through, won't he? He's a forager like me. We're survivors. If I can make it, so can he. He's tougher than I am. He must be receiving care elsewhere in this hospital."

There was a long pause. Only the melody of bleeping machines could be heard.

"Your name—it's Tristan, isn't it?" added Ulrik. "I'm right about you being the one who saved me, aren't I?"

"I seem to be adept at keeping others from danger, but not myself," gesturing to his bandaged wrist.

"How did you come by your injuries?"

Tristan went on to tell him about how, from the mountaintop, he saw a polar bear spring upon a group of boys and how he fired several shots at her before she fled. Later, after seeing the two boys fall through a sheet of ice, he hastened full pelt down the mountainside. "Then I came across the ice at the speed of a thousand gazelles and dragged you away from the weakest part of the lake. I wrapped you up, sparing what layers I could, and there we waited for mountain rescue." Tristan then spoke about how the emergency responder had come with space on his snowmobile for only one passenger and how he was abandoned in the wilderness, alone save for the prowling polar bear. When she pounced, he spent his last few rounds of ammo, and a lucky hat-trick of bullets ended her life. But being unable to find his way through the snowstorm, he had no choice but to stay put, so he plucked out Ivar's knife, which was lodged in the bear's frozen breast. "I reckon it was harder drawing that dagger from her bones than it was for King Arthur when drawing Excalibur from the stone." Then he gave an account of how he used the knife to open up her belly. "After climbing inside her bloody carcase, I made a makeshift tent out of her and lay there freezing to death, until Chenglei—one of the soundest blokes you could ever meet—found me shivering my raisins off. Anyway, the rest is history."

Tristan had been careful to omit the fate of Ivar in his tale, but Ulrik wasn't satisfied with the hole in his account. So, when Ulrik pressed him for confirmation, Tristan told him, without censorship and with a dispassionate numbness to the business of death. It was unusual to hear an adult speak so honestly among children. Younglings everywhere are accustomed to hearing "I'll tell you when you're older" or sentiments to that effect, but there was no skirting the issue when Tristan said, "Aye, lad, your friend Ivar didn't make it."

Upon remembering the truth, Ulrik tried to vacate his bed but got himself trapped and tangled in the wires like a floundering fly in the silky gossamer of an arachnid. Unable to move, he slumped where he was and smothered his face with a pillow. Throughout his anguish, Pappa's voice seemed to narrate inside his skull: "You must never let anybody see you cry. Don't you dare cry." His head felt as though it might combust, but somehow he stifled his emotions and kept his eyes dry.

"I've been there too, mate," said Tristan, with calm indifference, as though he was the Knocker himself; the Knocker who, with his regimental cap curled up in one hand, comes uninvited during the night to the family home to deliver news of the loss of a loved one. Well-practised was Tristan in the business of delivering harrowing news. "I've lost friends. Seen 'em die. Seen 'em bleed out right in front of me when there wasn't a single thing I could do to save 'em."

"But I *was* able," said Ulrik, his voice muffled by the pillow. "If anybody could've saved Ivar, it was me. Arctic water doesn't scare me. I go swimming about the fjords for fun in all seasons. But I couldn't take his weight—my collarbone. I couldn't. I was too weak." The cadence of his voice ran into a decline when he said, "My only friend—gone."

"Nothing can prepare you for it, mate. Look, I reckon it's best I leave you to grieve alone. I know that's what I'd want if I were in your shoes. If I can do anything for you, and I mean anything, just let me know."

"Nuh, stay," said Ulrik, snatching the pillow away from his face as if someone other than himself had been suffocating him. "I don't want to be on my own anymore. I've been alone all my life. Stay with me, Tristan."

"All right, mate. If that's what you ..." Tristan dropped his voice to a whisper. "Wait ... shh ... I think the porters are coming with the food cart—with my toast and tea. Let me send 'em on their way. Don't want 'em coming down here, finding out you're awake, and alerting the nurses, do we, eh? I'll bet you're starving, mate. I'll grab you a bite to eat. There's no friggin' bacon, though. Will you be all right for a few minutes on your own? Good lad."

Tristan vanished behind the mosaic bed curtain. Not long after, Ulrik heard raised voices from some way off. It sounded as though Tristan was complaining (presumably to the porters) about the state of the "rotten rations being served up in the cookhouse". Then there was silence for a few moments; Tristan must've gone wandering elsewhere. He came back later carrying in the kangaroo pouch of his hospital gown a bunch of fruit, a bowl of nuts, and a basket of pastries. In his unbandaged hand were two mugs brimming with tea and in his teeth were two triangles of buttered toast. Together, their scoffing and slurping sounded like several snaffling warthogs stricken with swollen sinuses.

Content with a full stomach, Tristan scraped the chair along the floor and drew himself in close beside Ulrik again. He told him about how he'd heard his name mentioned on almost every corridor and in every waiting room. When Ulrik asked what the people were saying, Tristan said only that he'd heard all kinds of wild rumours, though he hadn't hung around long enough to gather any reliable intel.

"It's got me wondering about what they're wondering," said Tristan, sucking at the leftover sugar on his thumb and forefinger, a delicious remnant of a cinnamon swirl. "Though I know this much: they think you're some kind of enigma. You're a mystery to them, lad."

"Well, I'm thinking there's a greater mystery about you, Tristan."

"Oh, you reckon so, do you, eh? Don't you be casting aspersions about me. What you see is what you get with me, Ulrik."

"I want to ask you a question," said Ulrik, dismissing Tristan's unconvincing pitch, "if you'll allow me."

"Fire away." Tristan rose, then patted away the flakes of pastry that had settled on his knees. Free from crumbs, he sat down again, poised with hands interlocked as if ready for an interview. "But if I'm to stay, we need to whisper. Otherwise, our voices will alert any nurses passing by."

"You're a soldier, aren't you?" said Ulrik.

Tristan seemed taken aback by the question and slurped his tea as though deliberating whether to deny it. "So, that's what you think, eh?" He reclined a little and crossed his ankle over his opposite knee.

"Yah, you said you'd seen friends die." Ulrik leant forward, almost forgetting about the pain in his collarbone. "I'm thinking you meant on the battlefield. And the way you were making your bed and polishing your boots ... I've heard they teach that kind of discipline in the military. Not only that, but when you were rescuing me on the ice—it's coming back to me now—I think I heard you saying to the other man you'd been to a place called Badgag."

"I think 'Baghdad' is the word you're looking for."

"And I might never have been to school to study joglaffy, but I don't think Baghdad is a fun place to be going."

"Joglaffy? Oh, haha, you mean *geography*." Tristan had a private chuckle to himself. "Baghdad, then; you heard me say that? I'd no idea you were still conscious at that point."

"Tell me, am I right?"

"No, but you're not far off the mark. See, I *was* a soldier. What I am now, who I am now, is a thing even I struggle to understand."

"So, you no longer serve?"

"Not for the British Army, no. I would if they still existed. But that's a long story. Anyway, enough questions. When I was your age, I'd little extra capacity in my noggin for anything else other than girls and sport, so—"

"If your army no longer exists, does that mean they were defeated?"

"Sort of, but not in battle. You've heard of DRUE, haven't you? Right, to cut a long story short, we Brits voted to leave the Democratic Republic of United Europe; we voted to become an independent nation again—to make our own laws, control our own borders, conduct our own trade, repatriate our parliamentary powers, blahdy-blahdy-blah, you get the picture. But in return for our independence, we paid a heavy price: the sacrifice of our Ministry of Defence. Since then, the European

Defence Consortium has had complete control of our armed forces. A long time ago, new recruits swore an oath of allegiance to the Crown. Now they attest to the Holy Shepherd—the Chancellor of DRUE. Gets me riled up just thinking about it. I'd never serve under that bastard flag or stand for its bastard anthems or salute that bastard Holy Shepherd."

"Tristan, what did you do in the military?"

"So that's your first question, is it?"

"My first question? Yah, why?"

"Well, when most people learn I'm a soldier, the first thing they ask me is if I've ever killed anyone."

"That's nobody's business but yours. Besides, it takes much more courage to save a life than to take one. I care only to know about those you've saved."

"You sound like my good mate Spider. Hmm. Strange young lad, aren't you, Ulrik? Not like anybody I've ever met before ... Now, as for your question, I was in the Paras (the Parachute Regiment). Me and my 'orrible lot, we jumped out of quadcopters and planes. Did airborne assaults, compound raids, counter-terrorism strikes, stealth ops in the dead of night, urban espionage, that sort of thing."

"Sounds impressive."

"Yeah, those were good times," said Tristan, dragging up his sleeve.

As Tristan itched his elbow, a little too aggressively, Ulrik noticed some curious marks rising up his arm and spreading like a sleeve of cobalt flame. These patterns weren't so different to Pappa's knotwork carved on all the furniture throughout Thrudheim, though Tristan's tribal swirls were filled with azure ink, their edges stencilled in silver. Ulrik craned his neck to get a better view.

"Oh, you saw that, eh? My Celtic tattoo." Tristan yanked down his sleeve and started scratching the nape of his neck.

"What's Celtic?"

"Well, the Celts were the people of ancient Britain—the place where I'm from. They painted themselves before battle with a blue dye from the woad plant. They wore their warpaint to frighten the Romans. You've heard of them, I'll bet? No? Never mind, mate. Anyway, Britain gets its name from a much older word, 'Pretani', which means 'painted people'. At least, that's what Colonel always told me."

"I've heard of Britain. Pappa says the Vikings sailed there. At first to Lindisfarne, I think. Then they settled later in York. Jorvik, I think they called it."

"They did indeed, lad," said Tristan, seeming impressed by his knowledge on the matter. He sat rubbing his monkish head and appeared to be meditating over him; very soon it looked as though his head was in danger of catching a shine like that of his polished boots.

"Your tattoo … I'm thinking it's more than just warpaint to you." A faint curve arose on Tristan's lips, but in becoming aware of his emergent grin he tightened his mouth, then cupped a hand to it, reckoning to cough. "What made you get a tattoo like this?"

"I like art, that's all."

"If it's art you like, you could hang your favourite picture on the wall. That way, if you grow to dislike it, you can take it down. Yet you have a permanent tattoo, something you can never erase. I'm thinking this Celtic tribal pattern is a reminder of something. Let me see it again."

Tristan loosened his gown while drawing in a reluctant sigh. Seeing the tattoo in its entirety, Ulrik noticed that it spread across his chest, over his shoulder blade, and down to his elbow. It looked, in an abstract sort of way, like a tailor-made pauldron—a plate of armour shielding his heart.

"Why get a tattoo—a big tattoo—if only to keep it hidden?" added Ulrik. "Maybe it means a great deal to you, and yet maybe it's something you don't want others to know about, so you keep it hidden. Something personal to you. Am I right?"

There was conflict in Tristan's furrowed aspect, as though he were resisting the discovery of his deepest secrets. He pinched his eyes to buy himself a few moments away from eye contact. "Keep your voice down, will you, mate?" he whispered, looking over to his right and left as though he were umpiring a rapid match of tennis. "Right, some things I'm about to tell you, not even my mother has a clue about, so I'm trusting you not to repeat it. Understand?"

Ulrik took that as a sinister warning: repeat, and you'll suffer some agonising consequence. Who'd dare tempt those cold, menacing eyes? Their rapid flitting zigzagged from all corners of their field of vision and seemed to be capturing an accurate inventory of all the matter in between, including Ulrik and his innermost intentions. This symptom of war—this hypervigilance—was a thing to be both envied and pitied; it was a resourceful detriment to be perpetually disturbed; never resting, yet always on high alert in anticipation of anything and nothing. Not a particle of fluff escaped the racing, pacing eyes of this veteran.

"You can trust me, Tristan," said Ulrik, thudding his hollow sternum to assert his honesty.

Upon giving his word, Tristan produced a brass tin from his pocket, the likes of which are used for the secreting of family heirlooms. It surprised Ulrik when it was offered to him, and for a moment he dared not take it, knowing his cumbersome hands weren't well suited to handling precious artefacts. But curiosity got the better of him, and he snatched it in a fit of excitement.

When he opened the brass tin, he saw, set in a black velvet cushion, a dull medal wrought into the shape of a fat cross with a short wine-red ribbon attached. With a fingernail, Ulrik prised the medal from its cushion. At the centre of the cross stood a proud lion mounted upon a regal crown, and below it read the words "For Valour".

"This is my Victoria Cross (or VC)," said Tristan. "I call her Vicky. Now, Vicky is—or was—the most prestigious military award for valour in the British Army. She was given only to the bravest of the brave for valour in the presence of overwhelming enemies. She might not glitter, glimmer, or glow—after all, she was forged from the ingots of an old cannon—but in her own way she's beautiful, isn't she?"

"For valour," whispering the words to himself. "And this is yours?"

"Well, I didn't steal her, mate, if that's what you're suggesting. She's a rare lass is Vicky. But there are other Vickys out there, you know."

"You have more?"

"Not me, but I know a few that have one. Remember when I said earlier the British Army is no more?"

"Yah ..."

Being paranoid about eavesdroppers, Tristan peeked through an opening in the bed curtain to check that nobody was lurking nearby. He then retracted his head back inside like a turtle does within its shell when in the vicinity of aerial predators.

"Well," continued Tristan, "I belong to a small fellowship of veterans. We're the last of the living Victoria Cross winners, and we gather in secret and hold council about ... certain things. We might not be the strongest, or the fastest, and we certainly aren't the youngest, but we VC veterans are among the bravest; and that's what unites us."

"Why do you meet in secret? Bravery isn't something to be ashamed of. Unless you're in danger. But danger from what? Or who? What kind of council do you hold? What does the council actually do?"

So many questions, and all went unanswered. Footsteps drew closer from the other side of the bed curtain. Tristan ducked as though taking cover from a mortar strike, but not without first scooping up his medal and brass tin. He whispered that he'd be back soon, placed an index finger over his lips, crept beneath the far side of the bed curtain, then vanished.

Ulrik held fast his eyes, and, for many long moments, his breath too. The bed curtain flapped, and it sounded as though a flock of physicians had descended upon him. They spoke in loud, clear voices across his bed to one another, perhaps in a purposeful attempt to disturb him from slumber. Most of what they spoke was about him—some kind of *unexplained phenomenon* was the subject of their prattle. There was a great deal of ambiguous prophesying about him; and if even only the most conservative of their claims were true, then he could fancy himself as having won some kind of lottery of life. But he felt no such luck, nor did he share in their glee: how could he raise a smile when his closest friend had ... ? The bed curtain flapped again, and the voices slowly died away.

Soon after, the curtain rippled again, like a half-mast flag in a gentle breeze. This time, Tristan stole under it like a burglar through a window. It suited him very much, the profession of burglary, owing to his roguish aspect. Had the forces not ironed out the crinkles of his ways, it's likely that he would've made an excellent thief.

"You're the talk of the hospital, lad. I've never seen such a fuss made by grown adults. All the medics are cutting about like kids on Christmas Eve."

"I'm not interested in what they're saying about me. They'll probably be making fun of how I look. Please, Tristan; I know you've done much for me already, but I'd like to hear more about you. Your stories have kept me in good spirits: they're the best medicine."

"I hear you, mate," said Tristan. "Stories have been the best form of distraction for me in my darkest days. And isn't that their purpose? For us to binge and get so badly drunk on stories that we divert our attention from our own sober reality? We forget the hourglass of mortality—forget that we're all slowly dying and escape into worlds of greater possibility. Hmm, how poetic of me ... Speaking of poetry, I've got a poem here with me that I penned, if you want to hear it?"

"Yah, for sure."

"Don't get your hopes up, mate. It mightn't be to your liking."

"My pappa—he writes poems. So, I'm sure it'll be to my liking. I'm a keen listener."

"Very well," said Tristan, unfolding a crumpled page of yellowed paper that he took from the brass tin. "It's only a short one. But you might find it an insight into who I am." In a slow, melancholy manner Tristan read:

"Listen in, then;

> I once pledged an oath to white graves of no name
> That I would defend their cause and repay their souls no shame
> For if alive today afore their eyes

They'd see their kinsmen in their demise
Their greatest sorrow would be the sin
That their descendants' hearts surrendered their win
And upon the stroke of the Eleventh Hour they all would wave
Goodbye to the Europe they'd died to save

Yet in my sacrifice a debt shall be paid
To join the Unnamed; my oath never strayed
Upon my lid shall the poppy wreath be laid
Wrought from the Cannon, a new medal be made
An emblem of gallantry long after bones fade
For Valour; may it inspire man in his courageous crusade

As you were."

Suddenly, Ulrik became aware of all the places he had hair. Each stood on end as though to attention, about to march out to war in their polar ranks.

"We owe so much," said Tristan, "to our ancestors who fought for the freedoms we enjoy today. But now the baton has been passed on. It's up to us now to honour their sacrifice."

"When you say 'us', do you mean the council of Victoria Cross winners?"

"Right, I tell you what: before I say anything else, I'll do you a fair deal. I'll tell you what you want to know about me if you tell me what I want to know about you."

"Seems fair; although you may be disappointed to learn nothing exciting about me in exchange for your tales."

"We'll see about that. Do we have a deal?"

Ulrik nodded. "So, tell me about the council."

"We call ourselves CIGMa. Nobody else apart from you knows we exist."

"CIGMa? What does such a name mean?"

"It's an acronym: it stands for Celtic Iceni Guild Masters; we, the Victoria Cross winners, are the masters."

"Celtic—Iceni—Guild—Masters," repeated Ulrik, having never heard such a bizarre string of alien words. "I'm not sure what any of that means."

"Well, the Iceni were a Celtic tribe of Britannia who rebelled against the invading Roman Empire. Just as the Iceni did, we stand to defend our nation against the imperialist, ideological bullies who enforce their rule upon us—DRUE."

"But I'm still not sure what CIGMa do, exactly."

"That's because I haven't told you. And I can't say too much—only that we are an *invisible influence*."

More mystery enshrouded Tristan now than ever. Each question answered gave rise to ten more riddles. It was clear he was more than just a soldier.

"Invisible influence? That's not an answer; that's just another riddle."

"It'll have to do. If I give you specifics, it could endanger us both. However, let me finish by clearing up a thing or two. Remember when I told you earlier about how the British Army has merged with DRUE's army? Well, there's one man who's in total control of it all: the Chancellor of DRUE, known by his devout followers as the Holy Shepherd."

Without realising, Ulrik held onto the side of the bed as though he were flowing down turbulent river rapids in a rickety boat without a paddle.

Tristan added, "The Holy Shepherd is the architect of it all. His European army—it's a danger to continental peace. It's too much power. So, at CIGMa we're committed to bringing down the Holy Shepherd's regime."

There was a bitterness in Tristan's words. His way of life had been taken away—his career, his identity, everything. He and his friends, he suggested, had been abandoned.

"I won't press you any further about CIGMa's invisible influence," said Ulrik, "though I do have one last question about your tattoo. What's the significance of it?"

"Well, mate, you were on the right lines earlier when you were guessing. We masters each have a tattoo like this. It's a symbol of our permanent commitment to our common promise. Like the painted Celtic people, we rebel against the tyrants who seek dominion over us. Take this, for example: in my country I'm free to get a tattoo, yet it's illegal for citizens of DRUE countries to get one."

"Illegal? Why?"

"Because religion prohibits it. I don't want to get into all that right now. It'll just piss me the fuck off—excuse my French. But ever since the House of Abraham formed, pork, tattoos, and working on Sunday (the Sabbath) among other things have been outlawed because of what a couple of desert novels said centuries ago. Anyway, like I said, your laws in DRUE don't reach out to us in Britain anymore. Though I suppose here in the Arctic you're in your own little world and see little of all that anyway. So, now that I've satisfied all your questions—some of which were bloody personal—I'll expect the same courtesy from you."

"Of course, we had a deal. Tell me what you want to know."

"I'm gonna be blunt here, mate: you stick out like a racing dog's bollocks. I've never seen anybody with blond hair all over their body like you. You look … different. And I sneaked a peek at your hospital notes earlier. Apparently, you're only fourteen years old. That's got to be a mistake."

"It's not. I am fourteen."

"You're as tall as any man I've ever clapped eyes on, let alone any fourteen-year-old."

"I'm just like my pappa. I'm almost as big as him."

"Right … and did you say earlier you swim in the fjords for fun? Because if so, that's not bloody normal that, mate."

"What's wrong with swimming? It's my passion. It's what I love to do more than anything. It's my ferrapy."

"Nothing wrong with swimming. But swimming in the Arctic Ocean? Friggin' dangerous that, you utter nutter. Why not swim in a pool?"

"My parents don't want me around other younglings. But I dream of swimming in a real pool one day. Taking lessons. Winning competitions.

When I sleep at night, I dream about winning a medal of my own; people standing up out of their seats, chanting my name, stamping their feet, clapping."

"Well, to be able to swim in icy waters, you must be … I dunno … impervious to the cold."

"I'm just me."

"I trust that you believe that, but if I'm honest, I don't."

"Brynolf Grimstad says I look like a Neanderthal. Whatever that is. I'm guessing it's not a very nice thing to be."

Tristan scowled and seemed offended on Ulrik's behalf. His face had the aspect of one who'd served a lifelong prison sentence. "And is Brynolf Grimstad that fat little fucker who was giving you grief before the bear sent 'em packing? I saw 'em; the heartless scumbags left you for dead. Give him a good hiding the next time you see him." With his bandaged hand strapped up like a white boxing glove, Tristan shadow-boxed thin air.

"It's because of Brynolf that my friend Ivar is—I can't say it. We lost our way, crossed the ice, and—"

"Ulrik, look at me." A bandaged hand propped up his chin. "Hey, you are here. You made it out. You have to keep living life to its fullest. That's what your mate Ivar would've wanted."

"What if I don't want to keep living? What if I'd rather be dead at the bottom of that lake?"

Without explanation, Tristan rose and revealed his bare back; blotted and blemished with pink skin it was, as though he'd been dragged through a patch of brambles tethered to a charging horse. "These aren't shrapnel scars, Ulrik … I was bullied, too."

"You? How did you come by those?"

Tristan's lips underwent a slight downward curvature. "A story for another time, mate. You of all people will know these things aren't easy to talk about. But what I will say is this: fear to a person is like a whetstone to a blunt sword; acquaint yourself with fear, and it'll sharpen you."

"I'll be sure to remember it. Thank you."

"The next time Brynolf Grimstad comes at you, hit him so hard and so fast that he thinks he's surrounded."

The two of them yammered long into midday like two Svalbardian huskies. Tristan spoke of his experiences of war: mortars and maps; vanguards and vantages; claymores and close protection; parades and parachutes; and bayonets and battles. Ulrik spoke of hunting, carving, kneading, trekking, fishing, and most of all, swimming. It enthused him to find someone so interested in him, and by slow degrees he felt his spine extend so he was no longer slouched in bed.

"Here they come for you, mate," said Tristan. "I think we got a bit excited and they overheard us."

Abrupt clicks of footsteps. The curtains flapped open. Mamma and Pappa were here alongside a host of doctors and nurses. Mamma flung her arms about him; her tickling hive of hair was all up in his face, and she forgot all about his fractured collarbone until he yelped like a hound when its tail is accidentally trodden on.

"Thank the Holy Shepherd, you're awake," said a nurse, almost enraptured by her own excitement, who seemed now to levitate an inch or two off the ground when tiptoeing.

Scowling, Ulrik said, "It's not because of the Holy Shepherd that I'm safe. Tristan is the hero. You should be thanking him."

Mamma and Pappa paid Tristan great compliments and wished him good health, but Tristan dismissed the praise. Shrugging and surrendering his hands, he cast his humble eyes low. He then stroked his chin with his bandaged hand and seemed for a moment to be in deep contemplation, nodding as though the last of some specific criteria had been met. He rummaged around surreptitiously in the pocket of his gown—click-clank, click-clank.

"Our short time is up, Ulrik Magnusson. It's been my pleasure to meet you, young man."

Already, the physicians were wheeling him elsewhere in his hospital bed. "Wait, what? Tristan, won't I be seeing you when I—Stop wheeling the bed. Stop. Where are you taking me?"

Tristan followed for a few paces; and reaching out for one another, they clasped hands, bringing the bed's wheels to a halt. Ulrik insisted they headbutt in the forager custom, though regretted it thereafter since bashing Tristan's head was akin to doing so against bare rock. As Tristan pulled away, Ulrik heard the click-clank of the brass tin.

"Thank you, Tristan. I hope your hand heals well. Good luck with—" Tristan cocked his head discreetly, "—with whatever mountain you decide to climb next."

"About-turn, lad, keep your eyes forward, and get gone at the speed of a thousand gazelles." Tristan winked, passed among the gathering crowd of physicians, and vanished.

"A thousand gazelles ..." remarked Astrid. "What a strange thing to say."

Ulrik made no reply. His mind was overwhelmed with ideas about CIGMa. He'd hoped to ask Tristan about how he'd acquired his medal, his scars, the Guild's invisible influence, and their assaults on the Holy Shepherd's regime. But he'd gone. Too soon. All his life, Ulrik had believed southerners were fickle and friendless; born of privilege, but not of handicap; rich of purse, but not of tale; hard of wants, but not of work; miners of data, but not of dirt. Pappa was wrong.

In hasty transit, they passed down the corridors, all the while the eyes of the nurses and doctors twinkling with strange foresight. Though now there was a growing rumbling of discontent, the likes of which can be heard prior to a lashing of thunderbolts.

"You haven't told us where we're going," said Pappa, striding to keep up with the hospital bed.

"It's all there in the information pack," said an officious-looking pen-pusher. "Can't you foragers read?"

"You're going," said another, "to the Norwegian University of Science and Technology in Trondheim. Your flight departs tomorrow evening. Now, we're already behind schedule. We need to run a few diagnostics on your son. Sir, please step out of the way."

Already, without knowing what was happening, Ulrik felt an

enormous gravity surrounding him, and amid this ruckus his eyes began to prickle—though not long enough for tears to leak. When placing one hand somewhat accidentally on his hip, his fingertips met with something unexpected in the pocket of his gown—click-clank: a cool metal box was pressing against his thigh.

"I need to relieve myself," he said at once, attempting to alight from the moving bed while trying hard to prevent the object from rattling in his pocket. "It's my bowels. Show me to the nearest toilet. Quick!"

It was no small amount of trouble for the medics to unplug all the wires from him—catheter, drip, heart-rate monitor, and all. He knew, by the looks on all their faces, the medics were silently fearful of the hygiene of foragers and were as motivated as he to find the nearest toilet.

Alone, and not knowing how to be correctly seated on a toilet, he sat upon the cold porcelain of the rim. Then he took the stowaway gift from his pocket. As he'd suspected, it was Tristan's brass tin. He dared not imagine that something so precious as Vicky could be under his stewardship. Perhaps inside the tin was the sheet with the poem only. Or if the medal was inside, more likely it was that it'd fallen into his pocket by accident, and he supposed he'd better be quick in returning it to its master. But then, something so precious couldn't be misplaced by Tristan; nothing escaped those veteran's eyes. After drawing his finger along the edge, he gave it a gentle shake and heard something rattle inside. Opening the tin by slow degrees, he saw, nestled in its black velvet cushion, the Victoria Cross looking as regal as any museum artefact; and he drew in a short involuntary gasp when brushing a thumb over the words "For Valour".

"Is everything okay in there, Ulrik?" called a nurse, knocking and trying thereafter to gain entry.

"I'll be out soon," he said, looking down at an accompanying note. On the underside of Tristan's poem was another message written in handwriting so terrible that it was likely scribed by his non-dominant hand (the one uninjured by frostbite). He held the dull medallion in his hand alongside the note and took his time to make sense of it (reading being something that came unnaturally to him), and he silently mouthed these words:

keep Vicky for now, and at all times keep her secret.
Until we meet again ...

For Valour,
Tristan.

Chapter Eleven

GLASS TOWERS AND
HOT SHOWERS

Ulrik bade farewell—as younglings often do when leaving behind a beloved place—all the objects in his view. Goodbye, fjords; goodbye, mountains; goodbye, colourful cabins; goodbye, boats on the shore; goodbye, howling huskies; goodbye, auroras of the sky; goodbye, anything and everything as small as a pebble and as large as the moon.

Against a bitter headwind, a hulking bodyguard chaperoned Dr Lyngstad and the foragers from the hospital to a landing strip by the sea. He was an odd beast, this guard assigned to them; he rarely spoke and instead issued only a few stock grunts when leading them this way and that. From the outset he'd said that his English was poor, but Ulrik knew well this clever tactic to avoid idle chatter with foragers.

Drawing near the coastline, they trod a path between fluorescent orange glow lamps, a path which, owing to the number of inbound tourists that day, was churned up so dreadfully that the snow had thawed into a strip of brown slush. Deeper they trod through this melting mire, feeling, with each step, more and more as though they were wading through an open slop of sewage. Ulrik supposed they were not so different, the slush and he, being both in their short lifetime so excessively trampled upon.

Their path terminated a short distance from the runway, where there was parked a stark black aircraft which gave off such a sheen that it would've rivalled that of Tristan's army boots; it was buffed and waxed like polished obsidian, and drenched now in milky moonlight it seemed surrounded by an effulgence similar to those intangible wreaths of light that crown the heads of angels. If only Ulrik had known of those privileged passengers who'd taken to the skies in this quadcopter before him—monarchs, politicians, billionaires, superstars—he might've dared to reckon his own exclusivity and indulge himself in dreams of his coming into equivalent fame ... or even surpassing theirs.

At once, four propellers gyrated, whipping up hostile winds and scattering the snow up into the air.

"This is our pwivate quadcopter," boomed Dr Lyngstad, over the whooshing blades. "We secured it at short notice, what with Ulwik being a case of unexplained phenomenon. Eeek! Super-exciting, isn't it?"

Pappa scowled. This was all too much for him.

After stepping up into the aircraft, the co-pilot assigned them their seats, but not before first bestowing on them some headTech; headTech that looked like a centurion's helm, albeit with a transparent visor veiling the eyes and without the red plumes of horsehair arching over the crown. There must've been some audioTech built in to them, for it was calming to hear one another's voices again after such deafening attacks on the eardrums by the aircraft's propellers.

The co-pilot slammed the passenger door shut and delivered a swift safety brief through the speakers of their headTech.

Nervous about take-off, Ulrik buckled himself in, with some intervention from Mamma, for his collarbone and arm were still strapped up in a sling. With little else to do but wait, he gazed out of the window while his hands underwent a terrible episode of fidgeting. After enduring many moments with his fingers, legs, and toes locked in a rheumatic twist (to prevent his fidgeting), suddenly the ground shifted. Jolting upright with his eyes stricken wide, he seized the armrests as one would if poised on an electric chair. As the aircraft began its vertical ascent up into the ether, all his anxiety abated, and for a moment he felt weightless. Never in his most far-fetched fancies had he imagined himself an heir of such fortune. A tingle ran riot throughout the fibres of his breast and spread throughout the conduit of every sinew and tendon until it reached his extremities. From the window, Svalbard appeared to grow smaller and smaller, so much so that the twinkling diamond and ruby lights of Longyearbyen shone like a cluster of faraway stars and planets.

"I feel like Julenisse riding through the sky on Juletide Eve," said Ulrik, looking across to his parents. Pappa was scowling down out of the window, and in his current mood seemed to be entertaining the idea of throwing himself out of it.

"You know," said Mamma, leaning forward, "the little fledglings on the mainland are calling Julenisse 'Santa Claus' these days, and they call Juletide 'Christmas'."

"Well, no gift has he ever brought me that amounts to the happiness of this. To me, flying is like swimming through the sky."

"I'll tell him you said so."

"Bah, Mamma, you know I stopped believing in him years ago."

Ulrik had pressed his nose to the window for so long that it had fogged up under the closeness of his breath. After many moments of unblinking focus, his eyes dried over, so he allowed himself some respite from the window. He drew his gaze down to his feet, and only then did it occur to him that the deck was entirely transparent—an entire floor of glass; and it appeared as though their legs were dangling in mid-air. At this sensation, Dr Lyngstad was in a general state of fluster and appeared to be eating away at her oxygen mask. Pappa's golden belly-laughter filled the aircraft while he parried Mamma's feisty hands; her nipping nails were making for his triceps—to punish his rudeness.

Just before Svalbard passed from view, Ulrik beheld it one last time. Anywhere he'd ever been, anyone he'd ever known, anything he'd ever done—his whole life had happened right there. Until now, it had been his entire universe. And then, after passing through a stratum of thick cloud, it vanished.

An ocean of white foam lay before them. It appeared as though they were in some kind of vessel surfing atop woolly waves and navigating like the sailors of old with the aid of glittering starlight. Never has there been a more dependable map.

By now, Ulrik had got so used to wearing headTech that he'd forgotten he was wearing it altogether. Until, on the inside of his visor, there flashed up a vivid digital display. Despite the display appearing in the foreground, everything in the background remained somewhat visible—he could see Mamma sleeping on Pappa's shoulder, jaw agape, and drooling down his arm. Then, all at once, the start-up menu dominating the foreground faded, and there appeared a hologram of a man levitating in mid-air. He seemed not of the ethereal but a person who Ulrik could reach out to and exchange a handshake with—or headbutt. He was a wizard-looking man, whose snow-white tresses ran past his shoulder blades, and in his grasp was a beautifully warped white wooden crook.

Ulrik extended his snow-shovel hand and brushed aside the hologram as though he were performing his most aggressive breast stroke. But his hand passed through the man's body. After a while, it was impossible to distinguish between that which was genuine and that which wasn't, so convincing was the overlapping dimension of the foreground of this pre-recorded message.

When the wizard spoke, Ulrik supposed him to be casting some sort of spell. "Hosanna, shalom, salaam, and hello," he said, genuflecting with peaceful reverence. "My name is Emmanuel Saint-Pierre, and as the Chancellor and Holy Shepherd of DRUE,"—he gestured with the crook in his hand—"it's my greatest pleasure to receive your company in mainland DRUE." Behind the Holy Shepherd rippled a purple banner emblazoned with a golden sword at its centre. A faint choir of angelic voices played in the background. "It's my duty to ensure that at all times during your stay in DRUE you're made to feel at home. Here you'll receive the warmest welcome, and so, as with all our citizens, I want to start by offering to you your own personal gift: the headTech you're wearing. Consider it yours; you own it. Why? Because in DRUE we believe Tech is a basic human right—as important as food, water, shelter, and clothing. It's my hope that through it you'll learn to see the world through clearer eyes—that you'll find the way, the truth, and the light. We gladly open our hearts to you; I only ask that in return you open your heart to us. The Lord be with you."

The hologram genuflected, then faded.

It occurred to Ulrik that this man was the Holy Shepherd—the man against whom Tristan and CIGMa worked together as an invisible influence to bring down his regime. Ulrik reached for the brass tin in his inner breast pocket and pressed it firmly to his heart. He thought it a great betrayal of Tristan to have so absently listened to the Holy Shepherd, no matter how generous and vulnerable the old man seemed. Free headTech or not, Ulrik's loyalty wasn't for sale, and any enemy of Tristan's was an enemy of his. The livid veins about his temples grew hot and swelled; and when the hologram reappeared with a new message, he was in danger of bursting a blood vessel.

"Here's your *daily bread*," announced the Holy Shepherd. "Before you can access all the latest content on your Tech, you must first listen to a short reading from the *New Continental Bible*. Because you're very busy, I've collated the most salient excerpts. They're short, they're insightful, and they won't demand any longer than a minute of your attention each day. Then, upon completion of the reading, all the content of your device becomes available. Are you ready for your daily bread? Nod for 'Yes', shake for 'Not right now'."

Curious and indeed hungry for bread, Ulrik nodded, and the Holy Shepherd went on to say: "Matthew 10:34: Jesus said, 'Do not suppose that I have come to bring peace on the earth, but a sword. For I have come to turn a man against his father, a daughter against her mother, and a daughter-in-law against her mother-in-law—a man's enemies will be the members of his own house.'"

A man's enemies will be the members of his own house? What did that even mean? For a moment, Ulrik looked pityingly upon Mamma and Pappa, who were both sound asleep, and pondered the sinister sentiment about his being turned against them. With a corrugated frown, he glanced back towards the Holy Shepherd, whose hologram had now retreated following the delivery of his daily bread. It was a disappointment that there wasn't any actual bread, for he was hungry for food, not philosophy. Though, as promised, all the content of his headTech became unlocked, and a message popped up in a window: "Need help getting started?"

Ulrik nodded. Instructions and tutorials were presented to him for all the free content: Abraham TV, Abraham Music, Abraham Books, Abraham Marketplace, Abraham News, Abraham Gaming, Abraham Scholar, AbraGram (an application in which one could hologram anywhere with friends in virtual reality), and Congregation (a social media platform). All of this overwhelmed him; and being cynical after what Tristan had told him, Ulrik placed the sophisticated Tech in standby mode and felt sober for lifting his visor and seeing the world through his own clear eyes again.

He turned his eyes back to the window and stared longingly into the black of night. The night was mild, and their passage was calm through the sky. Several hours had elapsed since their departure from Svalbard, yet in a matter of moments they were making a sudden, vertical descent into Trondheim. From high above, those faraway grains of light on the ground were tiny twinkles, but hovering among them now, the streetlamps seemed to orbit the quadcopter like a system of moons. After the pilots conducted their final checks, they lowered the aircraft down onto a patch of greensward surrounded by a coordinated jumble of stone buildings and glass towers. As the aircraft grounded, it groaned in response to its uneven landing, and the momentum of the propellers abated.

Ulrik felt himself a stranger from another planet, his surroundings being so alien to him. He checked to see if the visor of his headTech was up, for he looked upon the urban architecture, half expecting it to be some illusion of the Tech. But it was all real. There were buildings that seemed hewn out of bare rock, and the towers of glass looked as though they'd been sculpted out of icebergs. Here, not all houses were made of timber and had turf roofs.

"Look, Pappa, trees," he said, thrusting out his index finger at the speed of an arrow. "Real trees."

Pappa ignored him and continued to glare out of the window as though the land to which they'd come was cursed.

"Real trees ... I wonder what they look like in the other seasons." Many were bereft of blossom and berry, denuded by winter's pillage, yet they seemed the happiest wooden skeletons, for their majestic boughs waved at them in concert, swaying like an audience of sprightly limbs. "And what about those over there? Are those leaves? They look like green feathers to me."

"Those ahead which look like tall green arrows? Pines, they are," said Mamma."

Ulrik assumed all trees would look the same, yet they were so different in appearance, and, like people, they seemed dressed in different attire and wore varying hairstyles. He referred to the evergreens as clothed and those which were deciduous as naked, and he said he hoped to be around to see the naked trees getting dressed in spring.

It amused Dr Lyngstad, the pilots, and the bodyguard to learn of a person who'd reached the age of fourteen without ever having seen a tree. But when Ulrik's vine-green eyes throbbed in his skull in response to their amusement, the subject was dropped and all laughing ceased.

"We have arwived," said Dr Lyngstad, "at the Norwegian University of Science and Technology. We'll be staying at the edge of Twondheim campus."

"It looks a lot different since the last time we came, Thor," said Mamma, lifting off her headTech.

"Last time?" said Ulrik.

A sharp hiss announced the cockpit's opening, and the pilots alighted from the vehicle. A few yards away, a small force of border police received them. They entered into lengthy discourse and handed over official paperwork for validation.

"Astwid, you've been here before, you say? To study?"

"Not to study," replied Mamma, "but I have been here before. I took part in some research. After the markets crashed, I struggled to find work, so when a friend told me Trondheim University was looking for egg donors and were paying good money for donations, I signed up to the programme."

"Eggs? You were selling eggs?" said Ulrik, his thoughts turning to hens and geese.

"Not eggs like you're thinking, Ulrik. My own eggs—from my ovaries." Mamma told him she'd explain it to him later.

"Ovum," said Dr Lyngstad, "is the scientific term. And I wemember that pwogwamme vewy well. They had the IVF laborwatorwy here. It was incwedibly successful. See," turning to educate Ulrik, "back then it was perfectly legal to take a mother's egg and a father's sperm and fertilise their baby under lab conditions: a pwocess known in its abbweviated form as IVF. It was a pwetty standard pwocedure; quite a common thing for parwents who stwuggled to conceive a child. But here they were more advanced: they could fertilise a mother's egg without—yes, without—a sperm donation fwom the father."

Confused by Dr Lyngstad's words and more so by her unfortunate impediment, her lecture was lost on Ulrik.

"So," said Mamma, "how did they fertilise an egg, if not with sperm?"

"Well, they had to cweate it—the sperm, that is."

"Create? Surely, you can't—"

"You *can*," asserted Dr Lyngstad, removing her headTech in the manner of a warrior who removes their helm when willing to fight without their armour. "And they did. They extwacted DNA fwom skin and hair cells fwom the father. A specific type of cell known as somatic cells."

"And what did they do with those—how do you say—somatic cells?"

"They turned them into *induced pluripotent stem cells*, which are sort of like master cells since they can be used to pwoduce almost evewy cell and tissue type in the body, be it eye, tooth, heart, or sperm. It just so happened the market for sperm was, at the time, the most lucwative. It was life-changing for parwents who stwuggled to conceive a baby natur-wally. Until, for better or worse, IVF was deemed a *blasphemy* by the Holy Shepherd and outlawed ..."

All hesitated to offer any further opinion on the Holy Shepherd, and they observed an awkward silence. But the way in which Dr Lyngstad ended her last sentence, with a strong serpentine hiss of the word "blasphemy", revealed her attitude towards him.

At long last, the pilots returned and gave the passengers permission to exit the quadcopter. Ulrik lunged forward and was the first to disembark. He removed his headTech and, caring little for the sharp twang of his collarbone, fell to the frosted silver-green grass, where he stretched out the knots in his spine like some restless cat.

The sighting of a quadcopter aroused the curiosity of nocturnal scholars, and Ulrik noticed that many were pointing towards him; and that some were now following him. At this, Pappa told everyone to hurry and gather their things, for the attention was too much for his liking. And no sooner were the companions out of one vehicle than they were escorted to another that was parked on a nearby strip of asphalt.

When settled in the back seat of this car, Ulrik realised the legroom in the quadcopter had, in fact, been generous. The headroom in here was worse, too, and he and Pappa spent the rest of the journey crouched and with their necks retracted into their shoulders.

According to Dr Lyngstad, it was now only a short journey to their lodgings, where she assured them they'd be able to relieve their aches of travel and gorge on their choice of food and drink. Upon hearing this, the foragers and the bodyguard buckled up and sat like expectant children on their best behaviour in anticipation of sugary snacks. Dr Lyngstad tapped at the panelTech on the dashboard, keying in their destination. Without notice, the driverless car rolled forward, turning and acceler-ating of its own accord, requiring no further human influence over its locomotion.

"Anyway," insisted Ulrik, "back to the egg story. You said this place used to be some kind of farm for babies. I don't pretend to understand all that's been said, but, Mamma, if you gave up your eggs, does that mean I'm not your only child?"

"You *are* my only child, Ulrik," she said, reaching across Pappa (who was sitting in the middle seat) to clasp his hand.

"Stop lying to me," retracting his arm up his sleeve and pressing his face to the window.

"Technically,"—she conceded a sigh—"there's a chance there could be another child, yah, Ulrik. But not my child. They'd have parents of their own. I haven't raised them, lived with them, or loved them. I wouldn't be their mother; you wouldn't be their brother."

"And," said Dr Lyngstad, "IVF wasn't gawanteed to work everwy time. There's a chance your mamma's eggs were never conceived—born a child, that is. But we can never know for sure. That information isn't available to egg donors—to pwotect the child's identity."

"Trust me," said Pappa, in a tone of reminiscence, "it takes more than blood to make a family. Put down the thought, Ulrik; relax your frown, and don't be asking your mamma again. We did what we had to—to survive. Let it go."

For some time, he was livid that such a secret had been withheld from him. Somewhere out there he could have a brother or sister, who, like him, was oblivious of the other. A sulking silence dominated the journey until they substituted the subject for another.

"Look, Thor: the flags."

Flagpoles lined the campus avenues. Here, they were as common as streetlamps. The fluttering flags at their tips were red with a blue cross to the fore.

"Haven't seen the Norwegian flag in a long time," said Pappa, squinting.

"Look closer ... the crest in the corner."

The national flag was emblazoned with an unusual crest in its top-right quadrant.

"The Sword of Abwaham," said Dr Lyngstad. "It's the insignia of the

House of Abwaham. You'll notice it on the flag of all member states of the Democwatic Wepublic of United Euwope."

"I'd thought it a stain at first," said Astrid. "I do still now."

"I would choose your words more carefully, fwends." Dr Lyngstad's eyes flared wide in friendly warning. Dr Lyngstad wasn't patronising them; she was looking out for them. Educating them. Protecting them. "You don't want to wisk bweaching blasphemy laws."

Instant silence befell them again. But there was a mutual disdain among the companions for the flag and the symbol molesting it.

Not caring, and still irritated by Mamma's secrets, Ulrik craned his neck beyond ninety degrees, looking for something else past his own reflection in the window to divert his attention. His eyes met with a group of lairy scholars who were stumbling about the walkways. It was hard to make out any of their features since most were immersed in their headTech, but he could make out, by the tresses of free-flowing hair and curvier profiles, by their fluffy boots and tight-fitting coats, the girls among them. Many had painted their lips with neon lipstick which gave off an alluring luminescence; some of the boys had much of the same substance smudged over their lips, albeit unintentionally, although no doubt through very intentional kisses. And Ulrik supposed that he shouldn't mind if one day the same accident should befall him.

"Ahem, Ulwik, your attention for one moment, please," said Dr Lyngstad, snapping her fingers. They'd been trying to catch his attention for a while. "A word about the plan for tomorwoah. Are you with us? Good. Awound noon there'll be a sewious meeting—the first of many, I expect—in which severwal leading scientists and theologians will partake in a discussion about your case of unexplained phenomenon. You don't need to pwepare anything. Nor do you need to contwibute in the meeting. But you must bwing your headTech because you'll need to pay attention thwoughout, so twy to get some sleep tonight—although I know I'll be too excited to do anything of the sort.

"I have a stwange feeling in my heart that I can't wemember ever having expewienced before in my life. I don't mean to build your hopes up, but I just know this is going to be something extwaordinawy; and being a scientist, it's not generwally in my nature to be so pwesumptuous. Okay, so, do you have any questions? Or are you thinking of food only? Well, you're in luck because we've arwived at our lodgings."

The driverless car rolled to a halt. Stepping out, they were greeted with a strange hum overhead. All about were flying postal drones that looked not dissimilar to miniature quadcopters. Ulrik had seen one or two in his time, when tourists had come to the beaches to shoot footage of the fjords, but he'd never seen such a condensed covey of them, all with parcels in their talons and dispatching deliveries at all hours, wheeling about at high speed like bats in the night. Each time one whizzed overhead, he ducked and unleashed a swift swatting hand in their direction, though they never ventured within striking distance. When seeing that Dr Lyngstad, the bodyguard, and even Mamma and Pappa were unfazed by their presence, he no longer viewed them as a danger, and soon after he learnt to appreciate the sophistication of technology.

"Your lodging has won many awards for its design," said Dr Lyngstad, nodding to the skyscraper ahead. It had the semblance of a glass beehive, oval in structure with hexagonal golden windowpanes; and when lit up at night, the vast honeycomb skyscraper appeared edible. "You'll be staying at the vewy top where the wooms are weserved for the most esteemed guests."

"Woah," said Ulrik. When standing in its golden shadow, he appeared to glow like a lustrous statue.

"Scum," grumbled Pappa, who'd developed a habit of referring to any modern design with contempt.

For a good while, they loitered in the lobby while Dr Lyngstad took care of the formalities with the concierge. During this, parties of drunken students staggered by, unconscious of the hubbub they were making, yet they were conscious enough to come to a deliberate halt under the shadow of an enormous portrait, and at once they appeared sober, as though some spell had been lifted—or cast upon them. They stiffened like military personnel on parade, then with delicate hands they each produced a sign of the cross and genuflected beneath the portrait, before stumbling away to their luxury dormitories.

In the portrait, the Holy Shepherd's proud head was so far inclined that his gaze seemed fixed on an upward trajectory towards the highest tier of heaven. His congruent lips were perfectly parallel, as though to smile was a characteristic of the most common customer, something practised by those far removed from the serious business of statecraft, and not at all the behaviour seen in those whose affairs in this world carry great influence, eminence, and consequence. Beneath the portrait was a gold plaque into which was engraved:

> *Trust in the Lord with all your heart and lean not on your*
> *own understanding; in all your ways submit to him, and he*
> *will straighten your path.*
> — Proverbs 3:5–6 —

Even the hulk of a bodyguard fell to his knees in subservience, muttering "Amen." Dr Lyngstad was next, but her eyebrows formed a begrudging crease in her face as she lowered herself to the ground. It troubled her deeply when the foragers refused to kneel, and she suggested they do so, for their own sake, in case someone had seen and were to report them. Mamma and Pappa laughed at the suggestion, and Ulrik claimed exemption due to his collarbone being in a sling, so she ushered them from sight before any witnesses noticed the apparent violation. Little else was said about the portrait of the Holy Shepherd, but Ulrik couldn't lay the thought aside.

His mind became overcrowded with questions. Even when riding a glass elevator for the first time, he was too preoccupied with mystery to derive any pleasure from the breathtaking views of Trondheim. After alighting from the elevator at the uppermost storey, they headed down a corridor where stationed at equal intervals on the wall were even more portraits of the Holy Shepherd. In the eyes of his people, he was decorated a hero. What had he done to command such reverence?

When standing outside their lodgings, Dr Lyngstad bade them good evening; in return, they bade her good health. And when Dr Lyngstad told Ulrik she'd arranged for him his very own suite, all the fibres in his breast tingled with delight. She'd gone to great lengths to enhance their comfort and had done things that were outside her remit, not least demonstrating with her headTech how to order food to their rooms with simple voice commands. After this, she turned to Ulrik and told him not to worry about the bodyguard who'd be posted outside his room at all times.

"Why?" said Pappa, wringing his nervous hands as though he were warming them by some invisible log fire.

"It's just a pwecaution. Weporters have been seen lurking about, and they'll do anything to catch you alone and at your most vulnerwable. So, Ulwik, Thorsten, Astwid, don't go anywhere without consulting me. If you need me, you can hologwam me diwectly via your headTech."

Pretending to be interested, Ulrik gave his most convincing nod. After Dr Lyngstad gave her final farewell, and after Mamma bade her a last good health, Ulrik turned into his room when, quite abruptly, he was shepherded back by Pappa's hand.

"Don't be getting too ahead of yourself, son," he said, the ridge of his eyebrow casting a shadow over his face. "While we're here, you need to keep your head low and your mouth shut. If you do, we can all go home a lot sooner and mourn the loss of Ivar. You trust me, don't you, Ulrik? These people don't care about you; I do. Don't listen to them; listen to me. Understand? I need you to act normal. If you don't, they might never let us leave this place."

Ulrik nodded fearfully and recoiled an inch or two. Then Pappa released his grasp and bade him good health. After the reprimand, Ulrik fled inside his own room. When there, he dropped his baggage and looked around in silent awe, forgetting all about Pappa's paranoia.

At the far end of the room, long damask curtains fell from the high ceiling to the carpet like locks of navy-blue hair; these were parted so that through the hexagonal pane of a golden window his view stretched out beyond the coast of Trondheim and even as far as the other side of the fjord. Standing at the centre of the room, he felt for the first time in his life like a dwarf living in a giant's chambers.

He went for a look around and on his tour found many articles that intrigued: royal chandeliers, majestic mirrors, giant wardrobes carpentered out of dark, expensive heartwood; their handles were golden, as were all the door handles, light switches, plug sockets, tabletops, chair legs, wineglasses, ornaments, plant pots, and paintings; even the bathtub and taps glimmered to the same effect, so that when he ran the water it flowed like a brook of honey. And almost everything was operable by Tech.

His most immediate urge was to take his first ever hot shower, after which he plunged himself into the overflowing bathtub and disappeared behind a cloud of thick steam and rising bubbles. By the time he'd got out, his fingers and feet were wrinkled like sun-dried produce, he smelt of coconut shampoo, and all the muck engrained beneath his skin had been obliterated.

After slipping into a cotton dressing gown, he quitted the bathroom and let the soles of his feet sink into the thick pile of the carpet, where half his toes disappeared; a welcome change from the scratch of splintered wood underfoot.

A short while later a postal drone landed on his balcony, depositing there a package of hot food. He'd paid little attention to Dr Lyngstad's instructions on how to order food using his headTech and ordered, quite accidentally, an excessive quantity: sushi, tagine, and zucchini linguine; then chilli, tapas, and tandoori sea bass; then risotto, milkshake, and tomahawk steak; then tofu, noodles, and apricot strudel; and pizza, tagliatelle, and cherry-cola jelly. And having gorged on it all, he settled on the idea that the luxury life was the life for him. No more foraging for food.

Bed, it seemed, was calling him, so he climbed up onto it and sank into a mound of cashmere duvet. He'd thought about jumping around on it and trying, as children do when trampolining, to bounce up to the ceiling. But the nasty pain in his collarbone served as a deterrent against his frolicsome impulse. When reports of noise came from the adjacent room, he suspected Mamma and Pappa were enjoying a bounce on their bed, for there was a great rush of muffled excitement, heavy panting, light screaming, and no small amount of swearing. But that didn't last long … so it didn't keep him from sleeping. His current bed was the only one he'd ever lain in where his limbs hadn't hung over the edges, a bed he supposed to be the most comfortable in the world.

It'd been a long day, and he'd run himself into exhaustion having experienced more in the last fourteen hours than he had in the last fourteen years: glass towers, hot showers, flying quadcopters, driverless cars, elevators, postal drones, trees of exquisite profile, comfy carpets, and sightings of girl scholars—and their luminous lipstick. There was a determination in him now never to return to his previous life, and he hoped that whatever this "unexplained phenomenon" was, it would enable new adventures.

He was about to drift off into a slumber when his headTech flashed blue like the lights of an emergency vehicle—it was some sort of notification. Reaching over to his bedside table, he swiped the headTech, donned it on his head, and pulled down the visor to see the contents of the alert. Bah, daily bread again. How so, when it was only a few hours since the last sermon? But, of course, midnight had passed, and they were into a new day. So the Holy Shepherd had come at his earliest opportunity to say:

"Isaiah 1:19–20: 'If you are willing and obedient, you shall eat the good of the land; but if you refuse and rebel, you shall be eaten by the sword; for the mouth of the Lord has spoken.'"

The Holy Shepherd vanished.

All this about the Holy Shepherd and the House of Abraham excited his curiosity, but to those who lived here it was their normal routine of life: bowing to portraits of their supreme leader, listening to daily bread, and being zombified by Tech. Yet it didn't trouble him in the way that it did Mamma and Pappa. If anything, it was now his chief interest, and he desired to know more. Except now the day's excitement got the better of him, and his eyelids eclipsed his eyes.

Early into dawn, his dreams were infiltrated by what he thought to be the serene whisperings of the Holy Shepherd's voice reciting daily bread. But being too comfy in his headTech, and too tired to remove it, he drifted back into a deep sleep, all the while the words of the gospel playing on repeat to his subconscious.

The next day, Ulrik awoke knowing other Bible verses, yet he had no recollection of ever having learnt them.

CHAPTER TWELVE

THE CONCLAVE

Drum-drum-drum, rat-tat-tat. Above the mad rapping of fists at the door, Mamma's desperate voice begged him to hasten on out.

Grumbling while stumbling out of bed, Ulrik fastened his dressing gown (as best as he could with one arm up in his sling) in an attempt to dignify himself. When he opened the door, the intrusive flash of several cameras jaded his vision; and for some time after, his eyesight seemed molested by a galaxy of dancing blotches—which were present even when closing his eyes. Upon reopening them, he saw a band of reporters being routed by Mamma, Pappa, a shield wall of bodyguards, and, heading up the vanguard, a berserk Dr Freyja Lyngstad. Ulrik drove the door into the frame with his shoulder and retreated to the safety of his room, where he got dressed in his tunic and trousers—with Tristan's medal secreted in his trouser pocket.

"Hurry, Ulrik," called Mamma. "We can't hold them all day."

"And don't forget your headTech," added Dr Lyngstad.

"Ready," said Ulrik, stepping out into the fray and donning his headTech as though it were a chieftain's war helm.

"Follow me," said Dr Lyngstad. "We'll have to take the stairs. Nobody speak; not to each other, not to anybody. You give these weporters an inch, they take a mile. Understand?"

All agreed.

They burst through into the stairwell, where hordes of reporters stood waiting in ambush; some hung from the stair rails, others mounted windowsills, and most formed part of an impassable phalanx, their telescopic microphones reaching out into the foragers' faces like black spears.

"Ulrik, in your own words, tell us what happened that day on the ice."

"Some say it's a miracle you're alive. Do you believe in miracles, Ulrik?"

"At nearly seven foot tall, is it true you're only fourteen years old?"

"Ulrik, a few words: what would you like to say to your fans out there?"

"Fans?" he replied, eyes glistening like uncut emeralds at the suggestion.

"Ulwik," said Dr Lyngstad, cupping his mouth with a forceful hand, "for your own sake, not another word."

"But," he said, fending her away, "I should tell them all they need to know so they aren't getting the wrong story. Nobody has ever been interested in me like this. Not ever."

"You have to twust me, Ulwik; they're interwested only in selling your storwy—and pwobably a false one at that."

"But they think I'm special ... I have fans ... I just want to talk ..." His eyes flitted from Dr Lyngstad to the reporters, and his jaw cranked open like a portcullis—a gateway to dialogue. He stalled, and while deciding on whether or not to rebel against Dr Lyngstad's unwelcome advice, the rabble of reporters closed in. But as they did, a stocky bodyguard with no regard for his own safety leapt up and bowled himself down the stairs, toppling the foremost contingent of reporters like skittles. The remaining reporters broke ranks and fled like critters amid a great bushfire.

"Let's go," said Dr Lyngstad, towing Ulrik away by the elbow for the first few steps before he shrugged her off. "It's answers we need, Ulwik, not questions. This way now."

Ulrik followed, begrudgingly, and the companions looped around and down the stairwell and passed into a narrow corridor where at the farthest end was a conference chamber. Two guards with a surplus of testosterone coursing about their bulging biceps flung open the doors, granting them immediate entry. When they were in, two other guards on the inside barred the doors behind them.

Right before them, almost filling the entire room, there was a white marble table which had Roman columns for legs; and sitting around it there seemed a senate of Roman noses drawn up; and on the outskirts of the room, the Roman blinds were drawn down over the windows. Heavy were the critical eyes of the intellectual elite, examining the foragers from behind the visors of their headTech. Beards, it seemed, were the fashion for middle-aged mainland men.

As Ulrik entered this den of bearded patriarchy, he was unsurprised to see a life-sized portrait of the Holy Shepherd dominating the farthest wall, a portrait in which his philosophical hand was stroking his chin while his other grasped the hilt of a sword—the Sword of Abraham. Beneath the portrait was a gold plaque into which was engraved:

May the praise of God be in their mouths and a
double-edged sword in their hands.
— Psalm 149:6 —

Heading up matters was a chairman not yet sporting any headTech and who instead seemed perfectly content with his crooked eyeTech spectacles. Stepping forward, he pushed them to the summit of his nose to gain a clearer view of Ulrik, and his eyes seemed to magnify when he did so.

"Pwofessor Solomon Gweenberg," said Dr Lyngstad, with an exaggerated huff, trying to catch her breath, "my apologies. We were delayed."

"Hush, Dr Lyngstad. It's not held against you. Besides, you weren't the only ones who were delayed."

To all external appearances, Professor Greenberg had that unhinged outward visage that seemed a prerequisite of professorship. Most of his hair had receded, and all that remained was a fuzz of steely wool at the crest of his head and two wisps of the same fluff hanging above his ears, clinging on like moss does on a cliffside. He was dressed in the colours of root vegetables—beige, brown, and green—and looked as though he'd been dug up that very morning from the university allotment.

"Pwofessor, this is—"

"Ah," he said, removing his eyeTech spectacles, "the boy needs no introduction, Dr Lyngstad. After all, the whole of DRUE is talking about him. Well, you're much taller than I expected, Ulrik. Much, much taller. Why they suggested you needed a bodyguard, I'll never know. I'll bet there's not a man in DRUE who'd willingly arm-wrestle you—except, perhaps, your father." It seemed a bizarre thing to do for the professor to remove his spectacles, only to put them back on again; then, in the next moment, he slid them down again and balanced them on the end of his nose. A second or two later they were off again, dangling over his chest on a spectacle chain. It was as though the entire time he had Ulrik under a microscope and was adjusting his focus to optimise his viewing accuracy. "Never in my career …" muttered the professor, scratching the wire wool on the top of his head.

Formal introductions were made between the foragers and the regents—for that was the title of the members of that conclave who were sitting around the table. Judging by the sounds of their titles, most were clerics and clergymen. It was their responsibility to ensure that any research undertaken was done ethically and lawfully. Only Dr Lyngstad and Professor Greenberg had academic credentials worthy of announcement.

At once, the niceties were interrupted when one of the bearded regents brought to the conclave's attention something of immediate importance: "What's that thing around the boy's neck?"

Professor Greenberg's eyes fell upon Ulrik's necklace. He reached up with one inquisitive hand and, making no apology, took possession of it, turning it over in his hand while it was still about his neck as though he were on some kind of leash. "Not a crucifix?" said Professor Greenberg, donning his eyeTech spectacles again.

"It's Thor's hammer, Mjolnir," said Ulrik proudly, as though he was of direct descent from the Viking god; and his pride visibly impressed Pappa.

"Ulrik,"—removing his spectacles—"you ought to know that symbols of this nature are offensive in DRUE. Not only are they offensive, but they're a symbol of blasphemy, too."

"What's a blast-fairy?" he replied, imagining a tiny winged creature wielding a rocket launcher of sorts.

"A *blasphemy* is an offence to the Lord our God."

"Do foragers not understand that blasphemy is hate speech?" said Beard VIII. "That symbol is no more welcome here than a swastika."

Outrage broke out around the table, but Professor Greenberg was swift in coming to the defence of the foragers. Balancing his spectacles on the end of his nose, he looked down and around at his peers with the terrible frown of a headmaster when condemning mischievous children to silence during detention.

"I won't tolerate derogatory slurs such as 'heretic', 'gentile', and 'kafir' from around this table. If I hear any more language of that nature, I'll be certain to put forward a motion to suspend the regency of those responsible. Blasphemy *is* a sin, but a greater evil is this mockery you lower yourselves to when in the company of those you don't understand. Ulrik, Thorsten, and Astrid have travelled with little sleep—and, I hasten to add, against their own will. You cannot imagine what they've been through in the last two days alone, so I expect you to show them nothing but the highest courtesy. Foragers, it's a privilege to have you here with us today."

The rancour abated, but the subject of the necklace remained alive: "Nevertheless, Professor Greenberg," said Beard IV, who had the wispy beard growth of a pubescent teen, "on the matter of blasphemy and *illegal* symbols under JOEL, surely you understand that such an offensive article ought to be confiscated? Otherwise, I'm not sure any meaningful discussion can take place here today."

"Ulwik," said Dr Lyngstad, feigning a desperate smile, "if you wouldn't mind, the customs on mainland DWUE may seem stwange to you, but—"

"Dr Lyngstad," said Professor Greenberg, with a venerable twinkle in his eye, "that won't be necessary." His stance when facing the conclave was one of confrontation, and he told them that anyone who felt an inanimate necklace to be a cause of great upset would do better to never, under any circumstances, leave the house again; and he said it was a great wonder that a person so terribly injured by the mere sighting of a historical artefact should have survived such a debilitating syndrome of psychosis and not have perished from offence-related stress a long time ago.

At this, six of the regents left the meeting, their faces puckering as though resting on each of their tongues was a sour pastille made from crushed-up nettle and wasp sting.

With a sanctimonious spirit, the last of the escaping regents turned to Ulrik and said, "'Every knee will bow, and every tongue will confess to the glory of God the Father' (Philippians 2:10–11)." Mustering all their available testosterone, the guards slammed the door behind him.

"Which god does he mean, Pappa?" whispered Ulrik.

Pappa gave no answer. Instead, he drew himself up to his full height and stomped around the table. Deep breaths were drawn in and held by the regents as he passed behind their chairs; the air in the room seemed to deplete as they did so.

"This isn't a board of regents," said Pappa, his eyebrow thickening with fury. "It's a board of religions." In orientating his body towards the portrait, he stood for a moment with his hand resting on his chin as though mimicking the posture of the Holy Shepherd. Then, with his bare hands, he seized the gilded frame and, to the horror of the regents, carried it away beneath his armpit. He wandered over to the coffee station, where, laying the portrait flat, he converted it into a serving tray. There he helped himself to a teapot, cured meats, cheeses, and buttered pastries. Having loaded up his tray, he sat at the table and ate at his leisure, caring little for the spillages tarnishing the lacquer of the painting (the heaven-white hair of the Holy Shepherd had been anointed with black coffee so that he was now a brunette). Then, to the visible annoyance of his immediate neighbour, Pappa girded his dominant arm over the shoulder of his chair—and nothing was said about that.

All eyes fell on Professor Greenberg, and a silent, shared expectation was wrought into the regents' expression: such an act must call for immediate expulsion. But the professor simply removed his eyeTech spectacles, fogged up the lenses with his breath, and wiped away the condensation with a handkerchief. After putting them on again, he claimed ignorance of the prior drama and explained how his eyesight was so poor that a degenerate could rob the shirt off his back and he wouldn't know a thing about it until he read about it in the news. The professor's rising cheeks betrayed a hint of a nascent grin, which he suppressed (out of politeness), yet little could be done to extinguish the twinkle of honest mischief in his eyes.

"Accuse me," said Ulrik, looking around for a suitable place to sit. "My legs are weary, and I want to sit."

"Accuse you? I don't accuse you of—oh, you mean *excuse*," said the professor, who was beside himself with the warmest of chuckles. "Ulrik, as the most important person here today, it would be remiss of me not to offer you my seat at the head of the table."

Delighted by the professor's offer, Ulrik took him up on it. The swivel chair was a thing of novelty to him, and taking a few spins in it was a temptation too great to resist. Though, a short while later, his stomach gave a clear warning that too much swivelling might bring about the regurgitation of last night's supper. So he curbed his joy and brought himself to a halt.

When the conclave sat, the professor instructed all lights to be dimmed and all headTech to be donned, before entering AbraGram (the virtual reality hologram application). Until now, there had been a few vacant spaces around the marble table, but holograms of other regents who couldn't be there in physical attendance now occupied them, in a metaphysical sort of way.

Of the twenty or so regents, there was only one who stood out among the crowd of beards: a person in the farthest corner veiled from head to toe in a loose-fitting black gown. Not a hand, not a cheek, not an ankle, not a strand of hair was visible, nor was a single word uttered; so it came as a surprise to Ulrik when the professor referred to this person as "she" (given that all the other regents were male). At first, Ulrik supposed her to have got the wrong address for a funeral service, being clad in such a morose colour and her entire face being hidden—convenient for the hiding of tears, he suspected. But for reasons he didn't understand, this was the outfit of her culture. Behind the facial veil he could just about make out two olive eyes that seemed deliberately fixed on him. He was used to people staring him out, but here he sensed himself to be the subject of an extreme obsession.

"Professor, shall we pray before we begin?" said Beard XII, who was adjusting golden cufflinks that were tempered into the shape of the Sword of Abraham. "It is right to give thanks and praise."

"If it is," said Professor Greenberg, straightening his crooked eyeTech spectacles, "if it is the will of the conclave, we will accommodate. But let's offer our prayers up for the boy Ivar, and let us pray also for our forager friends that they might find the strength to endure what remains a dark time for them."

Ulrik thought it a pleasant thing to be prayed for. It was a sentiment not too dissimilar to a forager bidding a person good health. Both were pleasant to say and hear, yet neither actually contributed anything of any tangible worth.

Prayers commenced, and the regents took to their own rituals; some joined their own hands around rosary beads; others removed their shoes, washed their feet, rolled out rugs, and knelt upon them facing south-east (towards Mecca); Professor Greenberg covered his face with his hands and faced the wall (towards Jerusalem); others left the room for privacy; some holograms logged out for a time; throughout all of which, the foragers yawned and twiddled their thumbs. Dr Lyngstad joined her hands together and closed her eyes; and after peeking through her eyelids and seeing that those in the room were preoccupied, she took out a pocket-sized bottle of hand sanitiser beneath the table and squirted a dollop into her hands, working the lotion into her palms thoroughly as though to cleanse her hands of the act of enforced prayer. When prayers had finished, they all took their seats again and donned their headTech.

"If everyone is ready, I suggest we make a start," said Professor

Greenberg, looking down at his watchTech and shaking his head. "Welcome, brothers and sisters; and a special welcome to you, Thorsten, Ulrik, and Astrid. We all know why we're here. So, without wanting to waste any more time, I'll skip the formalities and hand over now to Dr Lyngstad, who will outline her proposal for research. Dr Lyngstad, if you please ..."

From the farthest corner of the room, Ulrik was aware of the omniscient eyes of the woman in black watching him as she subtly perched over the table, like a patient raven on a branch ready to swoop down for its prey at any moment, yet prepared to wait.

Dr Lyngstad rose and made her way to the corner of the room where there was a raised lectern of sorts, behind which she stood now, gathering her notes, ready to present to the conclave. Her first action was to draw everyone's attention to a vial in her hand; the fluid inside had the properties of liquid gold.

"What's that?" asked Beard xiv, lifting the visor of his headTech.

"This," said Dr Lyngstad, "is Ulwik's plasma—a substance separwated fwom his blood. To the naked eye, his plasma is no differwent to yours or mine." She paused for melodramatic effect. "But at the molecular level, we see that within it are pwoteins that not you, nor I, nor his parwents, nor any human being has ever been known to possess: antifweeze glycopwoteins."

"Antifreeze glycoproteins ..." repeated Beard xx, like a parakeet that mimics sounds without any comprehension of the words' meaning.

"Ulwik survived his accident because of the large concentwation of antifweeze glycopwoteins in his bloodstweam."

"Then it must be a miracle?" suggested Beard xvi. "It must be, if it's not hereditary—since we know Thorsten and Astrid don't exhibit these traits."

"But," said Dr Lyngstad, holding up the stiff finger of a lecturer while pacing back and forth, "humans, or any other living organism for that matter, are not just necessarwily pwoducts of our parwents; we're pwoducts of our enviwonment, too."

"Ah," said Beard VII, stroking his sea-foam beard doubtfully, "I already see where this is going. You'd have us believe Ulrik is a product of his environment and not, I suggest, the laboratory. We'll not be falling for this pantomime of unexplained phenomenon, not when there is no medical record of Ulrik having ever been born. Convenient, don't you think, regents?" The entire congregation of pious heads nodded with conviction, while Mamma and Pappa snorted at such an absurd accusation; but rather than correct them and explain to them that foragers keep no records, they seemed interested to see what madness would spill out next. "The truth, I'll bet, has been buried, along with any evidence of Ulrik having been tampered with."

"What fools do you take us for, Lyngstad?" said Beard III.

"This is a shameful infringement of JOEL," said Beard XVII.

"You've no right to play God," said Beard V. "Genetic experiments were outlawed by the Holy Shepherd years ago."

"Wait—what? No. That's not what—no, no, no." Dr Lyngstad turned to the professor, who was resting a finger over his lips, as though denying himself the impulse of speech. After a few moments of consideration, he removed his finger and said, "The absence of birth records raises many questions, but it's lazy logic to reach a conclusion without evidence to substantiate the claim. Regardless, regent-of-whose-name-I've-forgotten, you're correct that genetic *experiments* are illegal, but genetic *research* per se is not. I've read Dr Lyngstad's proposal at length, and—correct me if I'm wrong, Doctor—the aim of the proposal is to conduct research: to understand how Ulrik is capable of synthesising antifreeze glycoproteins." Professor Greenberg's eyes twinkled like diamonds.

"You're corwect, Pwofessor," said Dr Lyngstad, reflecting the same twinkle. "We need to understand how Ulwik's body wegulates temperwature compared to that of ordinawy humans—to study the pwocess of thermogenesis acting within him."

Beard XIX let loose an almighty tut. "We need to stop talking about thermogenesis and start talking about Genesis."

A chorus of parliamentary cheers and jeers erupted around the table.

Only the woman in black remained silent, her eyes still burning with intent into Ulrik like two solar orbs on a cloudless day in some binary star system.

"It will please you, regents," said the professor, "to learn that, since the scientific method is to be employed, Dr Lyngstad will actually set about trying to *disprove* her own hypothesis."

"Yes, yes, I will," said Dr Lyngstad, who would've seconded any announcement made by the venerable professor.

"Evidence-based research will lead us to the truth," added the professor. "So, if Ulrik should be the product of an earlier experiment, this would surface in our findings."

"Professor," said Beard IX, "you don't need me to remind you that a breach of JOEL pays a heavy penalty ..."

"Then why remind me?" said Professor Greenberg, sliding out of his chair and cracking his hips, which had grown weary with inertia. The steel wool on the crest of his head was damp with anxiety, and he mopped it with a handkerchief. Turning to Ulrik, he said, "Ulrik Magnusson, I'm excited for what this could mean for you. You appear attuned to your environment; do you really like to swim among the ice floes? Fascinating." The professor now took up a piece of handTech, and in poring over Dr Lyngstad's written proposal he seemed to peck at the page as though each word was a seed and each sentence a delicious trail of seeds. It was a wonder that his eyeTech remained on his head throughout the incessant page-stabbing of his nose. "And, Ulrik, I believe this condition of yours not to be exclusive to this single phenomenon of antifreeze glycoproteins: there's more to you than we even dare guess. Hence, contrary to the conclave's opinion, I think it would be a sort of blasphemy *not* to pursue further research."

As he said this, the regents seemed to foam at the mouth, hissing, spitting, and spluttering words in redundant languages.

Even with the aid of his enchanting spectacles, the professor couldn't have foreseen the consequences of his next decision, and he couldn't have known, even for his minor part in this story, that at that singular point in time he was the most influential person in the world.

"I grant the research," said the professor.

Little could the regents do to overturn the decision. The process of appeal—according to the professor—was lengthy, and would be likely to exceed the duration of the research. Beard II submitted the last of the challenges: "What, then, will be the value in learning the truth? It's a scandal that public funds are being put to such frivolous uses when there's still so much to be done in tackling the rise of blasphemy and hate speech across the Continent."

With a fragile hand, Professor Greenberg scooped off his crooked spectacles—the harbinger of some profound wisdom—and said, "When William Herschel discovered infrared radiation (an invisible form of light), he couldn't have known this knowledge would be used to develop the night vision in our headTech, or be used to convert heat for methods of cooking, or be used as a method of communication, or be used in astronomy to detect celestial bodies. I can't imagine what profit will be realised from our initial findings, but I know our early profits will one day seem a mere trifle when compared to that which is discovered thereafter."

Ulrik sank into his swivel chair, drumming his fingers on the armrest, poised like a king on his throne contemplating the riches of his kingdom. But his present smugness diminished when he noticed the woman in black in his periphery. She was no less absorbed in him now than when they'd first met an hour or so ago. Had he the means right now, he would've drawn a similar veil of black over himself to put an end to this unwanted attention.

The professor rose and concluded matters in his bedtime story voice: "Brothers and sisters, we shall meet again in eight weeks to consolidate the findings of the research. I grant you the funding."

All at once the regents gave thanks and praise to the Lord in their own custom:

"Baruch HaShem."

"Allahu akbar."

"Gloria, in excelsis Deo."

The conclave being dismissed, the regents dispersed with haste—all except one. For a while, the woman in black lingered, her obstinate focus still on Ulrik. By now she ought to have catalogued his every trait and mannerism. She was privy to so much about him, yet if he were to pass her in the street without her black garb he wouldn't have known it. But suddenly, unaware of her mistake, a hand emerged from underneath her garment; it was a broad, venous, white wrinkled hand, the thumb and forefinger of which appeared to be moulding an invisible ball of plasticine, as though a new miniature world was in the process of creation. Then, noticing the error a second later, the hand slipped back under the black garment. For the first time, the gaze of those spying olive eyes dropped to the ground and flitted about fretfully. At once, the person in black vanished—the harassing hologram was gone.

The rest were too engrossed in senseless prattle to notice what Ulrik just had. He wanted to tell them, but decided against it, fearing the offence caused if he were found to be mistaken; it could jeopardise the research! But in his heart he was as sure as the Svalbard sunrise that the hand belonged to a man of advanced age and that those olive eyes belonged to a man of advanced intellect.

CHAPTER THIRTEEN

FIRE AND BRIMSTONE

Weeks of intensive assessments and tests flashed by. The research was concluded, and tomorrow Dr Lyngstad was to explain the unexplained. Until then, the whole campus, and indeed the whole continent, remained suspended in anticipation.

Astrid perched beside the hexagonal window of her skyscraper apartment; there she sat overlooking Trondheim, running a hairbrush through her barley-blonde hair and harvesting away the knots. Even when the tangles were untangled, she continued to rake away, the rhythm of the therapeutic brush being a calming influence on her, and with every stroke she seemed to enter deeper into a mindful stupor.

For as far as her view stretched, rows of glass towers protruded like overgrown crops from concrete fields, where colonies of life scuttled around their urban agriculture, ploughing their means and pleasing their masters; reaping with the sickle of Tech, their output crunched by the millstone of algorithm. Somewhere out there, in a city not unlike this, her parents would still likely be employed in such a strenuous profession and working far beyond the pensionable age.

It was a failing, she thought, for a daughter not to know the whereabouts of her mamma and pappa. But when she'd made initial enquiries and searches, the regents blocked her Tech so she could place no outbound calls and had, at the very outset, coerced the foragers into signing non-disclosure agreements regarding their business here. Her thoughts now turned to Ulrik, and an aching sadness seemed to contract her heart. What if one day he were to do what she had—run away from a former life, cutting family ties forever—never to see her again?

In a lapse of concentration, Astrid looked down at her hairbrush in which was collected a thick bundle of hair about the bristles, all of which had come out in that one episode of brushing. There was enough perhaps to spin some yarn, and continuing at that rate she'd have enough to weave a tapestry of golden lace before the week was through. Life's stresses always manifested in her hair's tresses: when she was full of spirit, her hair was as hardy as jute or twine; when she was fragile, it was brittle and thin. And as the weeks went by, she discovered occasional strands in the bathtub, or strewn across her pillow, or even in her breakfast spooled about her spoon, or commingled with Thor's beard.

"Astrid," said Thor, approaching from behind and massaging her shoulders, "you seem quiet this evening."

"It's worrying me, Thor; all this attention. I feel like we're in the middle of something much bigger than us. Something dangerous."

"You sound like you know something I don't …"

Fidgeting with her hair, she said, "Well, I've learnt how to operate this handTech to understand what they've been saying about us. Hey, don't look at me like that."

He rubbed his forehead as though he were subject to a sudden migraine.

"What's your problem, Thor? It's not as if I've bought the Tech. Don't you want to know what they're saying about us in the news?"

"Go on … tell me what they're saying."

"I think there's a rat in the conclave, Thor. One of the regents must have been leaking information to the public. And their findings—whatever they are—are the source of great interest across DRUE."

"Show me," said Thor, poised with his arms hugged tight across his chest, as though bracing himself for impact.

Sitting on the edge of the bed, Astrid took up the piece of handTech, flicking and swiping with dextrous fingers at the touchscreen tablet. Article after article, the unassuming faces of the foragers were pictured alongside headlines often featuring the buzzwords: *kaleidoscopic genome.*

"Kaleidoscopic genome … what's that mean?" said Thor, taking a seat beside her on the bed.

"Science babble," nibbling the ends of her hair. "I'm not clever enough to understand. But the articles are suggesting Ulrik is some kind of lab experiment. Not born but spawned—not unlike that mammoth back home."

"So, those regents have been spreading lies about our son … I can't say I'm greatly surprised. We need to get out of here."

"But why would they think Ulrik was an experiment? I'd like to show them the floorboards where I birthed him in Thrudheim—where the bloodstains remain to this day. Fools."

"Well, maybe they've seen on your record that you once donated your eggs to fertility laboratories; that's suspicious as far as they're concerned. Then there's the matter of Ulrik having no record of his birth—again, suspicious to those who don't know us."

"And don't forget about what Dr Lyngstad said in Longyearbyen hospital: apparently your records show you have a daughter. I forget the name she used."

"Oh, yah, was it Elin, or Embla, or Erika?" smoothing the creases of his furrowed forehead. "None of this is making any sense."

"I know. Anyway, whatever Dr Lyngstad claims to have discovered— this kaleidoscopic genome—it's something the conclave aren't looking upon favourably. They're suggesting Ulrik is unnatural and are trying to shut us down by slandering us with conspiracies. Oh, and you won't believe what I came across earlier. Let me see if I can find it. Wait a minute—ah, found it."

Tapping at the handTech, Astrid zoomed in on one particular article: an interview with the Holy Shepherd, Chancellor Emmanuel Saint-Pierre. There was a short clip of him passing judgement in response to the widespread coverage of the case of unexplained phenomenon. Astrid hit play on the footage: "The creation of life is solely, unequivocally, indisputably, the charge of God," said the Holy Shepherd, brandishing his beautifully warped white crook. "Beware the work of scientists and their quest for biological supremacy, for theirs is the work of the Antichrist; and I'm certain that this boy Ulrik Magnusson has been spawned in some lab."

"I know he's an old man," said Thor, "but I'd love to smash his skull with that wonky branch of his."

"Thor, I can't believe this news has gained such coverage that even the Holy Shepherd knows of it, and he seems deeply troubled by it. Don't you see? This case of a kaleidoscopic genome must be some kind of threat to him."

"I see that, but it has me worried. We'd do better to stay out of state business. The most important thing right now is to protect Ulrik. We do that by keeping him out of the public eye. I don't care if he hates us for doing so; his safety comes first. Astrid, just think of the way people have been treating him in a small society like Svalbard. I fear the things they'll be saying on an international scale. I don't want to—nuh—I *won't* hear any more about it."

"You're right. I haven't come across a single article that looks upon us foragers favourably."

"Then put away the Tech, and never switch it on again. This is dangerous business." He yawned, interlocked his fingers behind his head, and reclined on the bed, staring blankly at the ceiling. It was getting late. "In a way, I'm glad these regents are sabotaging the research. Otherwise,"—yawn—"it could mean we'll be trapped here doing more and more research for longer and longer."

After switching off the Tech, Astrid sprang up from the bed and drew the curtains across the windows, closing off the wretched world.

"I wish Cheng was here. He'd know more about this, Thor."

No reply.

"Thor … ?"

Snore.

It annoyed her how he could fall asleep in a matter of seconds. Especially when there were important things to discuss.

"I don't even care anymore," she said, sighing emphatically. But that was a routine lie generally voiced at times when she cared the most, hoping it might arouse in him some care about her uncaring. But her reverse psychology failed this time, for he slept soundly. Fine. Time to tidy. Noisily.

She carried out unnecessary nocturnal chores in the noisiest, most deliberate manner. Every clumsy clank was calculated and purposeful; cushions were thrown; bags were dropped; wrappers were crinkled; light switches were punched; the lavatory was flushed; doors were slammed, yet he still slept without a care. So she got herself worked up further and spoke directly into his ear canal with a horrendous hiss, startling him so he flew upright at ninety degrees.

"Eight weeks on this campus. Trapped. Not guests. Prisoners. And all I wanted was to see my mamma and pappa again. They're getting old, Thor. If we go back to Svalbard tomorrow, I'll know I'll never be seeing them again."

She knelt on the bed beside him, her eyes assuming the acutest squint.

"What do you want me to do about it, Astrid? You know we can't leave this campus. Dr Lyngstad said so, and it's not safe."

"Since when did you care about rules?"

"I care for our safety. If the Holy Shepherd, of all people, knows we're here, don't you think Karsten will know we've returned, too?"

A severe knock at the door. At first, she thought—because he was at the forefront of her mind—it was Karsten, hammering away with his cubic fist.

"Mamma, Pappa, it's me, Ulrik."

Her heart resumed its thudding.

"Bah," groaned Thor, rising and facing the door, "if you've wet the bed again, Ulrik, you best be cleaning it yourself. Your mamma and I are arguing. Leave us be!"

Feet skittered away from behind the door, and the footsteps died away.

"Karsten will be watching us, Astrid, and if you think otherwise, then you're stupider than I thought."

"If you think this is about you and that twin of yours, you're stupid. This is about me and my family—Ulrik's family."

"Me and Ulrik *are* your family." His sledgehammer fist collided with the dressing table; its legs shook with terror, and all the tubes of complimentary shampoos and cosmetics dived for cover.

She caught a sideways glimpse of herself in the mirror; her eyes were suffused with dark dew; her kohl eyeshadow was smeared with tears. "This isn't your choice."

"It's a father's duty to keep his family safe; so, it *is* my choice. When we return to Svalbard, trust me, we'll never be coming back here again." His arm reached about her shoulder.

"Don't touch me," she said, recoiling. "If I want to see my parents again, you won't stop me."

"And if we run into Karsten, what then? Astrid, when he found out about us being together, the man tried to set fire to our house while we slept. Don't be thinking that twenty years will have mellowed his temper. You don't know him like I do. He's not all there." Thor thrust his finger towards his brain so swiftly that he might've penetrated his own skull had he not diverted its course at the last moment.

"Doesn't matter what I say anymore. You never listen to me." She faced the door. It pleased her to imagine walking out of it. Turning to face him, she saw how he reddened with the hue of terrible sunburn. His chest inflated, his eyes expanded, and his nostrils flared as though he were about to unleash a breath of fire.

"Go, then. I see you looking for your escape. Walk out; see if I care."

When she got halfway to the door, she heard a crack of thunder followed by the groaning of wood. It sounded like lightning striking a tree, though this was a mortal vandal. Others would've flinched in fright, but she'd weathered these storms before. At no point did she hazard a glance back until it'd passed. Eventually it did. Pivoting on her heels, she saw Thor lying marooned among a wreckage of wood: the bedframe was battered, the slats were splintered, and the duvet was torn like a sundered sail.

"Done?" she asked with indifference, twisting her wedding band around, unscrewing it in contemplation.

"Done," blinking vacantly. In a low-spirited voice he murmured that he was sorry.

With harsh palms he kneaded his face, as if he were attempting to sculpt himself a new profile out of clay, so that upon his next visit to the mirror there'd no longer be looking back the identity of a shameful vagabond who was so easily reddened by rage. After the sculpting, he buried his face under the duvet, though he couldn't hide his incessant hiccupping.

Was he … crying?

Sigh. Astrid dropped the notion of walking out. She'd lived her whole life like this, a life dedicated to the cares of others. After slumping beside him, she drew his sweaty head into her bosom. "Here; I'm here."

Just then, shuffling feet appeared outside the door again.

"Mamma, Pappa—"

"Ulrik, back to your room," said Thor, roughening his voice and dabbing his eyes, then summoning a corrugated frown so as to eliminate any trace of sadness. "Don't make me come out there."

"You're scaring him, Thor."

But Ulrik continued to beat on their door with desperation.

Astrid groped at the broken bedframe and rose. "Whether it's Karsten or the Holy Shepherd, we can't live our lives in fear of those who pit themselves against us, Thor."

"But we can, Astrid. Fear keeps us from danger." There was a stubborn light in his eyes that warned she could never reason with him.

"You may choose that life for yourself, and as your wife I'll go wherever you go. But as for Ulrik, he'll decide his own path." She took his solemn head in her hands, squashed her lips on his, then backed away to the door.

When she twisted the handle, the door flew open.

"What's all this abo—"

"Mamma, look!" exclaimed Ulrik, storming through the room, hurdling the wreckage as though it was of no concern and heading straight to the window.

Astrid peeked out into the hallway and glanced left and right. All was quiet. A draught stole over her, and the hairs on her neck prickled her skin. Not a single bodyguard was present. Odd: they'd been like statues, ever watchful and ever present since their arrival. The only company in the corridor was those omniscient portraits of the Holy Shepherd. She slammed the door and sought refuge inside.

"Look!" said Ulrik, hauling the curtains open, granting thoroughfare to a wild orange glow.

"Gah! A fire," said Thor, pressing his nose to the window.

Some hundred yards away, a rampant blaze was going strong on the greensward below. There were no firefighters in sight, though, and there seemed no panic at the scene. Had it been mindless arson, there would've been disorder among the spectators, but the throng of folk clad in pointed white hoods gathered about the bonfire and spoiled themselves in its warmth.

"Who are those weird-looking worms?" said Thor. "They look as though they're wearing pillowcases on their heads."

"Students, maybe?" said Ulrik.

"Not students," said Astrid. "I've been reading about them—the Whitehoods. They're demonstrating. It's a protest."

"A protest for what, Mamma?"

"Where are security?" said Thor. "We haven't been able to piss alone for the last eight weeks without them spying on us. It's convenient that they disappear when these lunatics are running around torching the campus."

All at once, a long kite of sorts trailed past their window. Upon closer inspection, it was in fact a banner being towed along by drones; drones which were now suspended in an aerial hover so that the message on the banner could easily be read:

> *The cowardly, the unbelieving ... those who PRACTISE*
> *MAGIC ARTS. They will swim in the lake that burns*
> *with fire and brimstone.*
> — Revelation 21:8 —

"Magic arts?" said Thor. "What's this about? Is that supposed to be aimed at us?"

"I told you," said Astrid. "They think we're part of some experiment."

"Mamma, my English isn't so good. Tell me what it says."

Thor pinched Ulrik by both shoulders (whose fractured collarbone had all but healed in these past eight weeks, and so he'd unslung his sling) and in a stern voice said, "Ulrik, these obsessive worms think you've been spawned in some laboratory. Whatever this condition of yours is, they don't believe it to be natural. It's dangerous for us all here. We're not welcome."

"Agh, they're watching us," said Astrid, who was swift in hitting the light switches, plunging them into total darkness (so they could see without being seen).

Ulrik gave report of something far off in the thick of night that at present was visible only to his keen eyes. "Shapes," he said, "not unlike more drones. Yah, in fact they are drones. Three of them. Each one airlifting a person. Nuh, they're too stiff to be actual people. Dolls, they're dolls dangling on the end of rope."

Then, coming their way at speed, the three drones and their cargo were made visible by firelight, rising one hundred—two hundred—three hundred feet into the air. Arriving at the foragers' window, they saw, dangling on the end of the rope and tethered to the drones' metallic talons, three straw effigies—man, woman, and boy—clad in the fur and leather garb of foragers.

A sudden silence befell them.

At once, the drones sped away on some predetermined course, drawing close to the bonfire like moths to a flame. Steering lower and lower into the tendrils of fire, the ankles of the straw effigies went up in a blaze.

"Back, both of you," said Astrid, clawing at the curtains with the frenzy of a feline.

The livid hue of sunburn returned to Thor's face, and within seconds his cloak and boots were on and he was striding for the door.

"Thor, where are you going? Nuh, don't be a fool. They're trying to draw us out. That's what the Whitehoods want." She flung herself in front of the door, making a spindly barricade of her limbs. But he picked her up beneath her armpits and put her back down again as if she were a youngling.

"Pappa, where are you going?"

"To confront them."

"You're mad, Pappa: there must be fifty of them."

"They're ugly little folk, Ulrik—about to be made uglier. Watch how one wolf can scatter a flock of sheep."

The door slammed behind him.

"Stay here and lock the door, Ulrik," said Astrid, squeezing his hands. "I'll be back soon with your pappa."

In times like this Ulrik was as untameable as Thor, and he followed her out anyway. They took the elevator to the ground floor, passed into the lobby, and darted through the revolving doors at the entrance of the honeycomb skyscraper.

Some way off in the distance, Thor was confronting the clan of Whitehoods.

"Harass me and my family, would you?" he cried, with his lead foot forward and his cubic hands clenched. "And now you see me, you're suddenly mute."

No answer.

"Why don't you submit your leader so we can get to know each other?"

No answer.

"Take off your hoods, cowards; or if you prefer, I can unmask you myself."

When arriving at his side, Astrid and Ulrik stood close under his protection.

The fire made known its intolerance of the newcomers: logs of enormous girth crackled, spat, and hissed. And in altering its direction, the wind cast nefarious plumes of smoke their way, which carried a batch of glowing ash into their faces. Thor drew up his giant cloak like an enormous wing and shielded Astrid and Ulrik like two newly hatched fledglings. When the wind abated, Thor lowered his cloak, and they saw the leader of the Whitehoods advancing from behind the smokescreen.

"At last," said Thor, closing down the space between him and the Whitehood leader. "So, this gathering, is it some kind of threat?"

"Not a threat," said the Whitehood leader, drumming his nimble fingers together, "but more of a reminder; a reminder that we're all sinners. We want to help steer sinners away from hellfire, Thorsten."

"You know my name."

"Anybody who's been watching Abraham News will know your name." The Whitehood leader cocked his head to the left. "Ah, hello, Ulrik. You're almost as tall as your father, aren't you? Exceptionally tall for a fourteen-year-old."

Thor turned towards Astrid and Ulrik. A look of volcanic violence bubbled away in his eyes. "Go back inside, Astrid. You shouldn't have brought him here. Do as I ask."

"Perhaps," said the Whitehood leader, "it would be better if you went back also … to where you belong. All of you."

"Is that why you're here? You mean to scare us so we never return to DRUE? Then you must feel threatened by my son's presence." Thor lunged forward. "Why is that, exactly?"

The Whitehood leader joined him at the centre of the pitch, and they stood like two captains before a coin toss. He gestured below at Thor's glowing club-fist, which was shaking with adrenaline. "You mean to strike me, Thorsten? I know you will. You see, violence is acceptable to those who know not the Lord our God. Without God, you think it's okay to do as you please without consequence. That's the way of animals."

"Thor!" screamed Astrid, as she saw a sweeping hand draw back and then the blur of an arm lunge forward.

It wasn't a punch that struck the Whitehood leader about his cheek but a humiliating slap. When sprawled on the floor, he appeared dead, save for the faint rise and fall of his chest. Not a single Whitehood prepared for retaliation, nor did they come to the aid of their leader; they simply hummed a prayer in Latin. Then, when the Whitehood leader stirred, spluttering and coughing as he did so, he lay supine, staring up into the blackness of the heavens, his robes all greened with grass stains. Few victims of the club-fists of Thor got up so suddenly, but the Whitehood leader seemed to draw some strength from the prayers of his fellowship and rose calmly to his feet as though he was the Resurrection.

"Fight me!" demanded Thor. "Or be gone from this place."

Astrid wedged herself between Thor and the Whitehood leader, acting like a referee, keeping them both at arm's length to diffuse the tension.

"I forgive you, Thorsten," said the Whitehood leader.

"What?" said Thor, reclining his head.

"That's right; I forgive you. Peace be with you." The Whitehood leader extended his nimble hand for the shaking.

"Don't listen to him, Thor." Astrid slapped down the scheming hand, and her eyes searched for Thor's; their cooling effect dampened his temper. Though his chest heaved and his shoulders rose and fell with great exaggeration. "Thor, please, listen to me." She took his face in her fingers, and they exchanged a look of concern. "Thor, they have cameras and Tech everywhere. Stop the violence, or this will be the ruin of our family."

The Whitehoods had them surrounded; turrets of Tech were pointing, aiming, and shooting, as it were, in their direction. And now all the firepower of their technological artillery was concentrated on Ulrik.

"Stay away from my son." Thor burst free from Astrid's hold, taking great offence to one Whitehood who, having snuck up on Ulrik, appeared to be narrating in the style of a parodical documentary. With patronising exaggeration in his voice, the Whitehood alluded to the "humanoid" as being a creature not unlike a yeti, Bigfoot, or Sasquatch; and he went on to say, "This aboriginal northern thing—tall, broad, and forested with white-blond hair—ought to be more aptly acknowledged as the Abominable Snowman of the Arctic."

It was no great effort on Thor's part to wrestle the Tech from the Whitehood's infantile grasp. And he would have spanked the Whitehood with his own device, had Astrid not intervened with a shrill plea.

"You're making things worse," she said, wresting the Tech from Thor's hand and passing it back to the Whitehood.

"It's too late now," said the Whitehood leader, gesturing to the several cameras still taking aim and shooting footage. "We have all the evidence we need to have you arrested and charged with assault."

"*You*, silence," said Astrid, addressing the Whitehood leader. "*You*," pointing to Thor, "if you want me to fix this mess, then leave; and leave quickly and quietly, with Ulrik."

It wasn't in his nature to accept orders, and he resisted the idea for a short while, if only to salvage a little dignity. But when she whispered a promise in his ear, she won his cooperation: it was a promise which would see him get everything he desired—at the expense of Ulrik. Thor girded his arm over Ulrik's shoulder, and together they sought asylum in the lobby of the honeycomb skyscraper. Thence they looked on, their faces wrung with worry.

When they were beyond sight, Astrid turned to the Whitehood leader, lowered her voice, and asked to speak with him in private. The leader gave a gentle bow, and the clan of Whitehoods returned to the fire to resume their humming and praying.

"Please, that footage of my husband—"

"You are to leave this place tomorrow," said the Whitehood leader, "never to return. You are to take part in no more research—no more experiments. They can't force you to remain here any longer. Decline to take part in anything further, and let the secrets of *Homo nova* remain just that—secrets."

"*Homo nova*? I don't understand. What secrets?"

"I've said too much. Though I suppose you'll hear more of that tomorrow. But our deal is to be done tonight …"

"If we leave, I want assurances that you'll destroy the footage of my husband and drop any assault charges."

The Whitehood leader joined his hands and with pious sincerity said, "As well as those who practise magic arts, the liars, too, will swim in the lake that burns with fire and brimstone. The Lord as my witness, I'm no liar, Astrid; we'll destroy every piece of footage."

"Your word. How can I be trusting—"

"Because I shall have the footage destroyed before your own eyes. Will you bargain with me if I do?"

Before she could commit to an answer, he spun around and entered into talks with his clan. He must've promised them a seat in heaven because without question, one by one, the Whitehoods disposed of all their Tech into the fire. The pile of melting plastic squealed in collective anguish.

"Good. Now be gone," she said, backing away. "After tomorrow, you'll never see us again."

"The Lord be with you, Astrid; and may He deliver you from evil."

She strutted back to the honeycomb skyscraper with a feigned confidence, and there she saw Ulrik watching from the lobby. He'd been so content in these few short weeks abroad—the most content he'd ever been. A pang of guilt snatched at her conscience, and she scrunched her face, resisting a flood of tears. When she passed through the revolving door, Ulrik was first to embrace her. He told her he loved her; thanked her; hugged her; kissed her—happily unconscious of her betrayal. Whatever was to become of tomorrow, whatever "*Homo nova*" meant, whatever this kaleidoscopic genome was, it would make little difference now. The deal was done, and they were going back to Svalbard to live in much the same conditions as they always had.

"You're too clever a negotiator, Astrid," said Thor, attempting to collect her in his arms to save her weary legs from further walking. But she declined, choosing instead her independence. "How did you convince them to throw their Tech into the fire?"

"Because," she said, fending off Thor at the chest, "in buying their silence, I may have just cast our future into the fire ..."

She sped up the stairwell, not wanting to enter into any further discussion on the subject. On some lower level of the stairwell, she overheard Thor mutter, "Women, huh?" to Ulrik, and the pair of them jested about all that had taken place.

That night, Thor would find himself locked out of their room and so would sleep either with Ulrik or out in the corridor with the portraits. She didn't care where.

Unable to sleep, and with nowhere to sleep after Thor's earlier vandalism, Astrid perched beside the window of her room in darkness, watching the dying embers of the bonfire while running a hairbrush through her barley-blonde hair, the rhythm of the therapeutic brush a calming influence on her. Some while later, she noticed that another clump of hair had been lost to the bristles of the brush and had wound about them like yellow thread around a bobbin. Though she was unfazed about that right now. All her concern was with Ulrik.

She knew, through her motherly intuition, that in less than a few hours they'd be privy to the secrets of *Homo nova*, this kaleidoscopic genome, and whatever this unexplained phenomenon was; yet she worried herself with the suspicion that her bargain with the Whitehoods was the most frivolous forfeiture of fortune in the history of mankind, not unlike the accidental throwing away of a winning lottery ticket.

CHAPTER FOURTEEN

REVELATION

"When we enter," said Astrid, in a private whisper, "if there's any talking to be done, you leave that to me. Remember, there's a rat among the regents; don't be giving them any more excuses to slander us in the news."

Ulrik and Thor rolled their eyes but agreed to her reasonable demands. With their headTech on and their daily bread heeded, they made for the conference room, outside of which were garrisoned two bodyguards; and in their expression, Astrid saw a reluctance to return her gaze, their treacherous eyes searching at all times for the floor, for they'd abandoned their posts during the night, allowing the Whitehoods free rein on the campus. As the foragers passed, the guards stepped aside and shrank against the wall.

Inside, the conclave resumed their seats around the white marble table; some were present in hologram form, most were there in the flesh. Assembled at either side were two long lines of beards, the only exceptions being herself, Dr Freyja Lyngstad, and, presumably, the woman in black, who never uttered so much as a breath.

Astrid had given little thought to the woman in black at their first meeting, but the trouble with the Whitehoods last night had affected her with a newfound paranoia when in the company of those who veiled their identity. Growing up on the mainland, she'd seen a handful of burka-clad women in her time and had heard folk remark that such clothing was a symbol of oppression forced on Muslim women by their culture; but then, upon closer inspection, Astrid saw a definite lure in the idea of going about unseen: maybe these weren't cowls of oppression but cloaks of invisibility.

After much hesitation, and having warmed to the idea of what she'd once misjudged to be radical raiment, Astrid took the seat beside the woman in black. Upon being seated, she paid her a compliment or two on her outfit—as is common in the female fraternity—but she was ignored. So Astrid knotted her arms and orientated her body away from her. For the rest of the meeting, she maintained her frosty attitude and neither made any further attempt to converse.

Professor Greenberg stood to address the room; his slovenly shirt, as usual, was untucked at the rear, and he seemed to be wearing the same clothes that he had at their first meeting. Yet there was some marked change in him, as if something troubled him: the warm twinkle in his eye had vanished; his throat seemed parched, and he tried to remedy it by consuming water from the fountain at the rate of an elephant at a watering hole; and at almost every juncture in his address, his eyes traced the room for those of the woman in black—as though seeking permission to proceed. Though she never offered a verbal response. In sitting to her immediate left, Astrid soon became privy to their system of communing: the woman in black had two distinct coughs; one being a light cough of approval and the other being an asthmatic cough of disapproval. Strange.

When the professor mentioned the midnight disturbances caused by the Whitehood clan, a raspy cough of disapproval shook the room, causing him to flinch so that his eyeTech spectacles fell—though luckily they dangled about his neck by his spectacle chain. At once, the professor changed the subject and proposed that prayers begin, at which the woman in black offered a sweet cough of consent.

It was some time before they made any progress. When the pleasantries, or rather unpleasantries were over, Dr Lyngstad ejected herself from her seat and took herself to the lectern in the corner to present her findings.

She waved a piece of handTech and instructed the regents to each collect the tablet device which lay in front of them. They had each been pre-loaded with a document showing the subheading "Abstract".

"Wead it, digest it, then we'll discuss it," said Dr Lyngstad, now fanning herself with the handTech, becoming visibly humid with the anxiety of public speaking.

Upon reading the last sentence of the abstract, the professor seemed to transform into a human ventilator, sucking in dreadful quantities of air. Removing his spectacles, he said, "You're suggesting Ulrik is a new species of man—*Homo nova*?"

The woman in black spluttered a cough of disapproval. Thor was taking a gulp of water from a glass when the surprise of the news caused a geyser to burst forth through the dam of his lips. Astrid might've been embarrassed on Thor's behalf, had a sense of overriding guilt not dominated her thoughts. She looked at Ulrik—who was oblivious to the contents of the digital journal—and pinched her face in self-reproach. In doing her deal with the Whitehoods, and in promising to leave the mainland, she'd robbed him of the rarest privilege. A new species of man!

"Dr Lyngstad, you insult our intelligence," said Beard XI, whose facial hair had the appearance of rice noodles dangling from his chin. "You can't be serious."

"I'm being deadly sewious," blowing her frowzy fringe upward to allow some air to her crimson forehead. "Ulwik Magnusson is not the same species as you or me. *Homo nova*—it's Latin for 'new man'."

"Dr Lyngstad," said the professor, "until you offer some kind of explanation, it'll be impossible for the conclave to take you seriously."

"Understandable, Pwofessor Gweenberg. Please wefer to the journal in fwont of you on your handTech, and I'll—"

"Tell us, what's this nonsense about a *kaleidoscopic genome*?" interrupted Beard III. "I see here that you suggest it's the world's first diagnosis of its kind? Sounds like science fiction to me, Lyngstad."

"Or maybe science *fact*," she said, elongating her neck and tiptoeing to appear a few inches taller behind the lectern. "To answer your question about the nature of Ulwik's kaleidoscopic genome, think of it like this: imagine you're looking down into a kaleidoscope where you can see a mosaic of vibwant colours; then, when you twist the lens, count-less awangements of unique patterns emerge despite all the owiginal components wemaining the same. Well, this is stwikingly analogous to how Ulwik's genome operwates: at first, we observe the static mosaic of his genome—his DNA; then, twisted by his interwaction with nature, it undergoes fantastical permutations so that the varwiable, observable manifestations we see are an alternative pwojection of the same ingwedients we started with."

Dr Lyngstad went on to speak with such fervour that she failed to pause for sufficient breath when lecturing on the rudiments of the science of epigenetics.

"Beautiful, just beautiful," said Beard xvii, commencing a slow, sarcastic clap.

"Mankind is on the verge of a biological wevolution, and—"

"Biological revolution? There it is, regents; the heresy we've long been expecting," said Beard iv. "Lyngstad is about to advocate the theory of evolution."

"Evolution *is* just a theory, is it not?" remarked Beard vii, enraptured with his own certainty.

The woman in black submitted an amiable cough of support, and an obnoxious chorus of parliamentary cheers and jeers broke out from the jaws around the table. Professor Greenberg dispatched a glare about the room, instilling a silence that would be the envy of Benedictine monks.

"It would," said the professor, putting on his eyeTech spectacles again and sliding them up the bridge of his nose for better viewing, "be to your advantage now, Dr Lyngstad, while we have silence, if you could substan-tiate your claim. Explain how you've arrived at the understanding that Ulrik is of a different species."

"The evidence we have shows that Ulwik Magnusson—I can't believe I'm saying this—is a species of hominid like us *Homo sapiens*, but not the same as us."

Another cough of disapproval. Astrid wondered whether the woman in black's costume was the chief instigator of the cough, the fabric perhaps being an allergen responsible for a ticklish irritation. But then, the nasty cough always seemed acutely timed in response to Dr Lyngstad, the cough always seconding the conclave's challenges.

"Evolution," added Dr Lyngstad, "as you and I know, Pwofessor, generwally happens over millennia. Genes mutate for a vawiety of wandom weasons, and this wandomness is the catalyst for the varwiation and biodiversity we see across the plant and animal kingdom."

"I don't disagree."

"But at pwesent we scientists use several models to classify species; often we classify based on *genotype* (an organism's genetic constitution), which is essentially a biological barcode. Now, Ulwik's genotype is identical to other humans' in almost everwy way; he has no abnormal mutations and has the same number of chwomosomes. But his *phenotype*—that is, his physical charwacterwistics—is observably differwent, and it's deserving of special wecognition ..."

All glared at Ulrik now as though noticing his visible differences for the first time.

"Which bwings me on to methylation ..." added Dr Lyngstad.

"Did she say 'meth'?" said Beard ix.

Mockery broke out from around the table. Some laughed at what she said, many at how she said it.

"Please rewind for a moment, Dr Lyngstad," said Professor Greenberg, holding out his clenched fist in a demand for silence. "You're saying Ulrik has the same constitution of genes as *Homo sapiens* ... yet is somehow a different species?"

"Yes, it's the *expwession* of Ulwik's genes that's the most vital factor in his varwiation." When lecturing, Dr Lyngstad made use of her exasperated hands and looked as though she were directing the flow of heavy traffic, pointing down this lane, gesturing to the street ahead, bending into this avenue, turning onto that road, and halting here and there whenever she came to a cul-de-sac in her sentences. "Ulwik's kaleidoscopic genome is powered by episodic bouts of hyper- and hypomethylation. Methylation is a pwocess in which methyl gwoups bind to genes and instwuct them. It's how a cell *knows* whether—"

"To grow into a tooth or eyeball," interrupted the professor, reclining his head a little and pondering the ceiling.

"Yes, and in Ulwik's case, this methylation, his hypermethylation, can be so twemendous as to instwuct genes to switch on or off—ancestwal genes, genes of our ancestors, which are dormant, or on standby. Understand? Methylation acts as a kind of master switch."

"Correct me if I'm wrong, Dr Lyngstad,"—his eyeTech spectacles flew off again—"but you're suggesting methylation is responsible for switching on a sequence of genes which produce antifreeze glycoproteins and that this is some kind of bodily response to Ulrik's environment?"

"Pwecisely. After all, he swims for—how many hours per day in icy water, Ulwik?"

"Uh, about three hours, but sometimes I spend a whole day in there," he said, his cheeks swelling with pride.

"Thank you, Ulwik." Dr Lyngstad threw him a thumbs-up from behind the lectern. "Arctic waters are perfect conditions for the synthesis of antifweeze glycopwoteins."

Professor Greenberg nodded, but the coughing in the background caused him to develop a frown and reconsider.

"Dr Lyngstad thinks," said Beard xiii, "she can confuse us into believing her lies with these made-up words about some kaleidoscopic ancestral homo genes."

"Not at all. Ancestwal genes simply means those genes which we've inherwited fwom our ancestors. Think of our genome as an archive of our ancestors. One of our ancestors must've had a sequence of genes which allowed for the synthesis of antifweeze glycopwoteins. And we've discovered (in Ulwik's case) that these dormant genes had been sleeping for generwations until hypermethylation awoke them fwom their slumber."

"This sounds like laboratory mischief," said Beard ii.

A cough like gunfire almost caused Astrid to fall back over her chair; her grip remained locked on the armrests until her heartrate slowed some minutes later.

"Dr Lyngstad," said Beard xix, "I'm reading your journal, and it says that today there are really only species of fish, insects, and plants that synthesise antifreeze glycoproteins."

"That we *know* of; yes, that's corwect."

"So which ancestor passed on this trait to humans, then? A fish?"

"A question beyond the wrealms of this wesearch, I'm afwaid. Theorwetically, it could be any of our ancestors since the first organisms appeared about 3.8 billion years ago. It'd be like twying to find a needle in an evolutionarwy haystack. Armies of the most learned taxonomists have attempted to map out the genealogy of man, but to no avail."

"Convenient," said Beard xii.

"Think about it this way: we've all pwobably watched or heard documentarwies about babies been born with vestigial tails, webbed feet, scaly skin, and the like. Our wesearch tells us these are the indelible stamps of evolution—where ancestwal genes have been switched on because of hypermethylation."

"Nonsense;" said Beard xii, "experiments gone wrong, I'll wager."

A cough of unwavering support from the woman in black.

"Dr Lyngstad," said the professor, wiping the lenses of his eyeTech spectacles with his handkerchief, "in those examples you cite of unexplained phenomena (of webbed feet, tails, scales, et cetera), wouldn't those children, according to your argument, be classified as different species?"

"Indeed no; because no evidence fwom our wesearch points towards any of those other cases as having a kaleidoscopic genome."

"It seems nothing could convince you otherwise, Dr Lyngstad," said Beard v.

"I think this doctor needs a doctor," said Beard x.

A spontaneous guffawing filled the room, and, falling victim to the foul comedy, Dr Lyngstad became overrun with dark-grey patches of sweat. The back of her shirt now had the look of an atlas, sporting abstract areas of dry land amid a watery expanse which comprised two thirds ocean.

"What's so funny? Fwom which cwooked institute did you godlings gwaduate? You're supposed to be scholars of biology, not men of the cloth."

Being chairperson, it was within Professor Greenberg's gift to mute those holograms who annoyed him; and tapping at his eyeTech spectacles, he put a curfew of five minutes upon Beard x, disabling him from any further mockery. "Given that most of you here are present in the flesh," said the professor, "and not remotely like the hologram just silenced, you'll probably suppose yourself safe from a temporary gagging. But our friends standing by the door"—gesturing to the guards—"will resort to physical evictions, if necessary. Proceed, Dr Lyngstad."

"Thank you, Pwofessor. I was about to explain something that might help contextualise what I mean by ancestwal genes: we each of us have within our DNA awound 20,000 genes which encode for pwoteins (known as the exome). That may sound a lot of genes, but the exome accounts for less than two per cent of our entire genome. Why, then, do we possess so much DNA when so little of it is weadable or useful? Well, maybe the wemaining 98 per cent isn't excess baggage as pweviously supposed but untapped potential. What if the wemaining 98 per cent of the genome are the twaces of ancient DNA handed down fwom pwimordial ancestors? Not junk DNA but DNA that can be switched back on under certain conditions? Think of our genome as a supercomputer where the exome (the functional two per cent) is a catalogue of the most wecent files, the wemaining 98 per cent being the back-up memorwy of files inherwited fwom our ancestors—and in Ulwik's case those files are still accessible!"

"Wonderful analogies, Dr Lyngstad … Still, evolution happens in tiny gradations over millions of years; and since modern humans only emerged around 200,000 years ago, not enough time could have passed for another species to emerge. If I we're to argue that a person could run a lap of the equator before the close of the hour, you'd say that such a feat is impossible. Time is the vital ingredient—time. Are you attempting to supplant 200 years of Darwinian science?"

"Not at all, Pwofessor. But evolution happens out of necessity, not because time passes. Conflict, Pwofessor, conflict; it's evolution's vital ingwedient; whether that's social pwessure, geogwaphic isolation, or enviwonmental changes. No other human has ever been known to possess a kaleidoscopic genome."

"You make several assertions without substance; and I make no apologies for stating that your theories are incompatible with the Darwinian school of thought."

"You're wrong, Pwofessor. My theorwies *are* compatible with Darwinian logic; just not the Church's, or the Mosque's, or the Synagogue's. This is naturwal selection: Ulwik survived because his body was fit enough to adapt to his surwoundings. And Darwin himself wrote at length about genetic weversion—"

"Genetic reversion?"

"Yes, genetic weversion: the phenomenon whereby a charwacterwistic fwom wemote ancestors weappears in organisms whose more immediate ancestors lack the charwacterwistic."

"Dr Lyngstad," said Beard IV, "you've bandied some clever words around. Your conviction in the way you speak, it's … admirable. But you stand before us on a lectern today attempting to preach to us that Ulrik has switched on genes inherited from his great-great-grandfather the fish."

"Haven't you listened to a word I've said? I didn't say he inherwited the genes fwom a fish. We're welatives, meaning we have a common ancestor. Ugh, just because we share DNA with bananas it doesn't mean we're their descendants."

"On this point, Dr Lyngstad, I agree in part," said Beard XX. "I happen to think you the closest relative of the banana."

At this quip, Thor couldn't contain a thunderous laugh, and he smacked his belly in boisterous hysterics. A nip on his triceps from Astrid soon brought an end to his disrespect.

"I see I'm wasting my time here," said Dr Lyngstad.

"So far, you've wasted ours," said the professor, who was seconded by an immediate cough. "You talk of a kaleidoscopic genome as though there were more to Ulrik than this single phenomenon of antifreeze glycoproteins. Some other empirical examples would be helpful."

"Of course. I wanted to discuss photopsins—the photoweceptor pwoteins in Ulwik's eyes ..."

"Photoreceptor proteins, what about them?" straightening his spectacles and sitting upright.

The woman in black launched a vigorous volley of coughs. Astrid couldn't help but shield her face from the coughing, even though the woman was present as an intangible hologram. A good job too, for she supposed there would otherwise now be a pestilential smog of germs circulating like invisible clouds about the room.

"Dr Lyngstad, you were saying?" said Professor Greenberg, tapping at his eyeTech spectacles and lowering the volume of the coughing hologram. If only Astrid had known how, she would've muted her and every other regent through her headTech.

"I'll twy my best to pwonounce this one pwoperly to avoid confusion, but I do stwuggle: w-w-rhodopsin."

"Rhodopsin;" said Professor Greenberg, tickling his beard, "it's a chromoprotein found in our eyes."

"Yes, Pwofessor. Ulwik has an incweased photosensitivity in dark enviwonments due to an abundance of rhodopsin. Again, we find methylation to be wesponsible for the amplification of the genes that govern their pwoduction. It takes us *Homo sapiens* about forty-five minutes for our eyes to adjust to the dark, but in Ulwik's case it takes less than two minutes. I wish I'd had more time to wesearch this. I do, I do."

"You mean," said Beard VIII, gardening his creeping beard with his forked fingers, "you wish you'd had more time to get your diabolical story together. Learned colleagues, Lyngstad is now suggesting the boy has night vision. Expect her to tell us soon that he's some relative of the nighthawk."

"Well, that's true: we're all welatives of all living cweatures."

Until now, Thor had kept his vow of silence to Astrid, but he seemed to take pity on Dr Lyngstad, who'd done admirably throughout all the coughing and criticism. He said, "I don't know about rhodopsin, but for the naysayers here, it's true Ulrik's eyes are keen in the dark. I've taken him hunting with me since he was a little fledgling, and he can skewer a ptarmigan with an arrow from fifty yards away without the aid of starlight or moonlight. I used to put it down to my vision being poor, but I'm thinking now that this is an extraordinary ability of his."

"Thank you, Thorsten," said Dr Lyngstad, clasping her hands together and beaming with delight. "It's entirely logical: Ulwik lives in the Arctic, where for almost thwee whole months of the year the sun doesn't wise. In wesponse to his enviwonment, Ulwik's body has switched on a sequence of ancestwal genes which enable the overloading and swift wegenerwation of rhodopsin. Therefore, there must have lived a nocturnal ancestor of ours who had similar faculties for night vision."

The conclave was stunned; whether stunned in disbelief, though, or stunned because of a mass genocide of their brain cells, it was impossible to tell.

"You want to know the cwazy part? We wouldn't be talking about antifweeze pwoteins or rhodopsin if Ulwik lived elsewhere in the world. Imagine the gene expwession we'd see if he wesided in a diffewent habitat. Would he, if living in the Himalayas, switch on genes to enable better bweathing at a higher altitude? Would he, if living on a herbivorwous diet in the Amazon wainfowest, switch on genes to allow for the digestion of gwass and herbs? Would he, if living in the Saudi Awabian desert, switch on genes that enable the gwoath of long eyelashes to shield his eyes from blowing sand?—if, indeed, we had ancestors with any such charwacterwistics."

"Well, Dr Lyngstad," said Beard vi, "I find the more I listen to you the lower my IQ plummets. I think we've heard quite enough."

"You hear me, but you're not listening. DNA isn't a static pwedetermined pwogramme. It's not hardware but software; and it's software which, in Ulwik's case, continues to upgwade of its own accord."

By now, many of the regents had developed a cough similar to that of the woman in black; it was a contagious cough, not in a bacterial sense but in the behavioural sense much like a yawn.

"Still, Doctor," said the professor, "those are but two examples. If your hypothesis is true, he ought to exhibit other obvious symptoms of a kaleidoscopic genome."

"Look at him!" Dr Lyngstad hit a shrill note which caused Astrid's ears to ring for almost a minute thereafter, and in her hellish wrath nobody dared to interrupt her. "There's so much we've been unable to explore: his heightened gwoath hormone levels; his skin is like a hide—thick and leatherwy—which we think is to pwevent body heat escaping; and his polar-white body hair acts as a good insulator. His lactate thweshold is such that his muscles hardly tire; we had to intervene in his endurwance test where he swam for hours without stopping to west."

"I could swim for a full day—maybe longer," said Ulrik, as though surprised to hear that exercise was a strenuous affair for others. "I didn't know you people tired so easily."

"See; Ulwik's physiology lends itself to all kinds of athletics."

"Lately," said Ulrik, lifting the visor of his Tech and revealing the magic in his eyes, "I've been thinking I could compete in a real swimming pool. I never thought I'd be able to, but maybe now I can if we stay here a little longer. Pappa, if you'll allow it?"

"I-I don't think—" Thor stammered.

"A boy like you must!" said Dr Lyngstad, grasping both sides of the lectern and appearing to reach her gawky body over its edge in dangerous enthusiasm.

"Imagine ... me, a swimmer. What if I could compete at the Wholeimpics? Imagine."

"Olympics?"

"Yah, Wholeimpics."

"Wish? Oh no, you don't need to wish: who needs a magic genie to gwant you a wish when you have magic genes?" She winked at him, then turned to the regents: "I'm not suggesting we have all the answers.

Though I'm confident if we had the means to conduct further wesearch, we'd discover the secwets."

"Blasphemy," said Beard xiv, submitting thereafter a cough like a hound when having eaten too much grass. "Shut this hoax down, Professor Greenberg."

"Do you people," said Dr Lyngstad, "play the blasphemy card whenever something is an inconvenience to you? You people would find your own shadow a blasphemy."

Professor Greenberg mopped away the beads of sweat clinging to the fuzz of his hair with a handkerchief. He balanced his eyeTech spectacles on the end of his nose and said, "You're getting carried away, Dr Lyngstad. You're suggesting Ulrik is a new species and that characteristics can somehow be unlocked on a whim—that Ulrik can somehow mutate genes on and off within his lifetime."

"This isn't about the *mutation* of genes, it's about the *methylation* of genes—which is vewy differwent and arguably more important. Ulwik alweddy has the genes—as do we all. Yet, in Ulwik, certain genes can be switched on and off due to hyperactive methylation. For God's sake, look at him." Intense simultaneous gasps. "If methylation has the power to cause such significant gene expwession, shouldn't we also consider methylation when determining species? Shouldn't we consider the epigenome? You say 'no', I say 'yes'; let's agwee to work together to understand the twuth. Further wesearch must be gwanted, Pwofessor, if only to dispwove my hypothesis ..."

"Yes, he looks distinctive; I agree. But it's far too abstract an idea to think of methylation as a factor in species classification. And I think a woman of your intellect already knows that, Dr Lyngstad. You see, I think what you're trying to do here is to win a few headlines in the news. Though I don't believe you to be an ambitious woman, so the reason escapes me ..."

Dr Lyngstad neither confirmed nor denied it. In Astrid's mind, that was silent confirmation that some calculated ploy of Dr Lyngstad's was under way.

"Okay, don't get tied up in the semantics of naming," said Dr Lyngstad. "Wegardless of whether you agwee with my hypothesis of Ulwik being *Homo nova*, he stands before us today observably distinct from you or I."

"Because he's been tampered with, Lyngstad, and you know it," said Beard XVIII, with a dismissive swish of the hand as though shooing away a swarm of midges. "This pretend discovery is a mockery. You've resurrected some kind of genetic experiment like that devilish mammoth on Svalbard. It's not natural; evolution isn't natural; *he's* not natural."

Ulrik cast the regent a sharp look beneath his jutting eyebrow, and he had the imposing look of his pappa when he did so. If at fourteen years old he frightened grown men without having to raise a fist, what fear might he strike into their hearts upon reaching maturity?

"I wemember," said Dr Lyngstad, amid a chorus of reproachful coughing and groaning, "I wemember a time when the Church accepted evolution … before the Holy Shepherd came along: a time when the world believed Sapiens weren't the climax of cweation but a twansitional animal; a time when the world believed evolution was a force constantly acting upon us."

"Professor Greenberg," said Beard VIII, "I'm of the sudden opinion we should make public the results of this erroneous research and humiliate Dr Lyngstad forthwith."

"Yes, please, please, expose it for all to see," said Dr Lyngstad, her eyes aflame with opportunity. "And let's go one step further and assemble a team of the most cwitical scientists so they can peer-weview my work. (And when I say 'scientists', I mean weal scientists; those who are qualified in their fields, not conspiwacy theorwists.)"

The temptation among the regents was to publicly disgrace Dr Lyngstad and make an example of her blasphemy. But judging by the smirk on her lips, she seemed content with that plan. The only objection came in the form of a negative cough from the woman in black.

"I will say this," said Professor Greenberg, turning to Ulrik and removing his eyeTech spectacles for the last time, "we have only ordinary evidence for extraordinary claims. But that doesn't mean I think you're ordinary, Ulrik. Though the powers that be"—his eyes unconsciously flitted to the woman in black—"may mean we never come to understand the truth about your kaleidoscopic genome." The professor took a glass of sparkling water in his hand and remedied his parched throat with its contents. Hidden in the contours of his face were traces of an internal battle going on between angels and demons; and when he next spoke, it was clear the demon had bested the angel: "But the evidence we have is inconclusive: no funding for further research is to be granted, and no research here is to be published. All traces of this blasphemy are to be destroyed. The foragers have our leave to return home."

"Baruch HaShem."

"Allahu akbar."

"Gloria, in excelsis Deo."

A roaring medley of cheers and jeers filled the room, as though it were now a stadium that was home to a major sporting event and as though a disgraced Dr Lyngstad had been sent off with a metaphorical red card.

There was hate in Ulrik's eyes. Unforgiving hate. The kind of hate Astrid had hitherto seen only in Thor's twin, Karsten. His face was brought to a boil; she could hear his heart boxing against his chest and his teeth grinding with painful pressure. Yet a selfish relief overcame her: in his decision, Professor Greenberg had saved her the trouble of acting the villain; no longer would Ulrik put the blame on her for their returning home—as had been agreed last night with the Whitehood leader.

"You might," said Dr Lyngstad, stepping down from the lectern and collecting her belongings, "you might think I'm surpwised by your decision, Solomon Gweenberg. But I understand why you did what you did." Her eyes narrowed as she cast a look at the woman in black. "I don't blame you, Pwofessor."

Professor Greenberg's regretful lips trembled, and he plugged a finger into his tear duct to prevent its leaking. Then he mouthed, "Thank you, Freyja."

"No, no, thank you. All of you. The outcome for Ulwik and myself is favourwable. My work here is done."

All at once the regents ceased their breathing and turned their ears in. "How is this favourable, Dr Lyngstad?" retorted Beard XI, suddenly finding his manners now that he was desperate for a swift explanation.

"Ah, I see you're not laughing now, are you?" said Dr Lyngstad, with a victorious air about her, smug eyes half closed, a creeping, crescentic smile opening wider. "You don't wealise what you've done, do you? And I'm of a mind not to tell you. But since we're such good fwends, I don't mind letting you in on this one. Psst, psst,"—in a mocking whisper, with her hand curled about her mouth—"who here has heard of the Stweisand effect?"

"The Streisand effect?" said Professor Greenberg. "You mean the social phenomenon?"

"Yes, the Stweisand effect. Do you know, Pwofessor?" By now she was at the door, halfway to freedom.

"It's where," said the professor, very slowly as if turning the definition over in his own mind, "it's where an attempt to hide or censor information has the unintended consequence of boosting publicity."

"Corwect, Pwofessor: you censor the twuth, and the appetite of the laity becomes insatiable. So you may have gagged us (having forced us to sign non-disclosure agweements), but our inability to answer the weporters' questions twuthfully will only excite their cuwiosity. They will sniff out the twuth of all that's gone on here, and when the laity fathom out that you've burwied the wesearch, the people of DWUE will descend upon Mont-Saint-Michel demanding answers." A high-pitched squeak of celebration. "The chwonicle of *Homo nova* is about to garner more publicity than you could possibly imagine, and there's not a thing you can do to silence us.

"Ulwik," said Dr Lyngstad, turning now to him, "this conclave here wants you to be invisible to the world, but a boy with a genome as special as yours can never be invisible. Wemember what we talked about in pwivate? Dweam big. If you weally want to swim, do so on the world stage in fwont of millions chanting your name. Aim for the Olympics. Pwove to these ordinawy bearded men that you're extwaordinawy; the world needs to know who you weally are. Twain hard, and who knows what ancestwal genes you might awaken on the way."

His grass-green eyes sparkled with belief and at the same time narrowed with intent. He looked as though he were daydreaming; as though he could hear the sound of applause and see the strobe of flash photography. Then his eyes darkened a shade or two and turned bloodshot like a venous network of red lightning bolts. There was a ferocity in them, and he seemed imbued with a rebellious determination. "You can't keep me hidden from the world," he said, through clenched teeth while eyeing the conclave—and Thor thereafter. "This is my legacy, and my life will never be the same again. There's nothing you can do to stop that. Just you wait."

Saying nothing, Dr Lyngstad leant back and nodded in admiration. Her work here being done, she scuttled out of the room and played no further part in the events that unfolded.

A graveyard silence stole over the room. When it was broken, it was done so only by a cough from the woman in black; not the binary cough of approval or disapproval, but a new, third type of cough: one of profound regret.

CHAPTER FIFTEEN

ONYX

The season of perpetual sun set in motion the melting of glaciers. The last remnants of frost thawed, and the turf rooves, laden with seedlings newly sprouted, had in the space of a few days gone from brown to yellow to green like the colours of the homes they flourished upon. And so winter's debt was repaid in full by summer: months of unceasing sunshine compensated for months of bleak blackness. Like a newly minted golden coin that had fallen from the galaxy's treasury of loose change, the midnight sun rolled across the horizon, occasionally accompanied by the silver token of a full moon.

Being on the edge of the North Pole, summers on Svalbard were not without a sharp nip; only Ulrik could be found cooling himself off in the sea and sunbathing on the pebbly beaches. But summer was a fine time for forager gatherings; a time when day and night meld into one.

Owing to their terrible timekeeping (since foragers refused to wear wristwatches given that they didn't exist a thousand years ago), it wasn't uncommon to see large gatherings at midnight, feasting on banquets of meat and drinking barrels of mead; dancing around fires in their furs to the beat of goatskin drums; singing songs and telling sagas; and at hours past their bedtime, giddy golden-haired younglings refusing to sleep until they'd heard just one more folk tale of the Kraken, the Nattmara, or the Huldra.

Thorsten, Astrid, and Ulrik kept a low profile that summer. Since returning from the mainland, many wanderers had come snooping around Thrudheim; some even dared to venture past the trench of bear traps (which Thorsten had newly laid) and came knocking at their door with cameras and questions: "Is this where Homo Nova lives?" they inquired, among many other things. It was just as Dr Lyngstad had predicted: the appetite to know about Ulrik had become insatiable, so much so that the skies became infested with surveillance drones at all hours. The foragers had little idea as to who watched them, nor were they privy to the magnitude of their audience.

On one particular morning, on the veranda at Thrudheim, Astrid and Thorsten were playing their fourth game of hnefatafl (Viking chess) while Ulrik strung his bow for target practice. He didn't have to wait long for a flock of drones to swoop into view. With dextrous hands, Ulrik nocked a goose-feathered arrow and drew back his bow; eyes narrowing, aiming for the thickest cluster of the flock. Then he let the arrow fly with fatal precision. The barb shattered its mark, and the shrieking scrap of metal spiralled down and crash-landed in a bear trap, where it was gobbled up by the appreciative snap of rusty teeth. Sensing danger, the other drones wheeled round and migrated back to their urban roosts as if they were pre-programmed to do so.

"Bah! Down with the metal bats," said Pappa, shaking his cubic fist at the sky.

Ulrik retrieved the arrow from the electronic carcase and inserted it back into his quiver for another victim on another day. Then he unpicked the wreckage from the jaws of the bear trap, slung it on the drone scrapheap, and said, "I make that seventy-three now, Pappa."

"We're going to need more arrows. I'll see the fletcher on the market tomorrow. Whatever the price to replenish our stocks, I'll pay it."

At once, Astrid shot up from her seat and squinted at the horizon. She made a visor with her hand to shade her eyes from the sun.

"What is it, Astrid? More drones? Ulrik, ready that arrow."

She didn't answer, but her beaming smile suggested it was friend, not foe. She skipped down the steps of the veranda, hurdled the bear trap trench, and there waited for the oncoming mountain cyclist to arrive. Chenglei! He'd been here often of late and had come with a regular supply of news from the outside world. Never had a person been welcomed so openly into Thrudheim as he; never had a guest so much as eaten under their roof, let alone lodge with them as he'd done on recent occasions. Throughout their troubles, he'd been exceptionally charitable to them; in their absence he'd kept their home tidy and made a repair or two to some broken cladding, and since their return he'd run all kinds of errands on their behalf to save them the grief of encountering general society. It might've seemed odd to anyone else that a person like Chenglei, with so little in common to external appearances, could have such a profound connection with the foragers, but their similarities were indeed deep-rooted: all of them knew well what it meant to live alone, in isolation, without access to any friends or family.

When Chenglei dismounted his mountain bike, he removed his crash helmet and flattened his badger-hair, though he could never stick it down fully. Mamma threw her arms about him before he could do anything else, and one by one the foragers traded a soft headbutt with him and bade him good health.

"Sorry, sorry," said Chenglei, holding up surrendering hands, "I know you don't appreciate unannounced visits, but this will be a short one."

"Shh, Cheng," said Mamma, the gold of the sun illuminating her face, "it gladdens us to be seeing you again. You're always welcome in Thrudheim."

"What a pleasant thing to say, Astrid; I can't remember ever feeling more welcome anywhere," he said, his happy Adam's apple elevating to the uppermost storey of his neck. "But I can't stay long. I'm in a rush." He stepped back to get a full view of Ulrik when speaking to him: "Ulrik, I remember the day I met your mamma and pappa, and we talked about you for a long, long time, in Isbjørn Huset. They told me you've always wanted to see Onyx up close, the white woolly mammoth at the Arctic Sanctuary. Well, as you know, I work at the Sanctuary, so I asked the zookeeper if you could volunteer and work alongside me. He said he'd be glad to have you on the team."

"Me?" Ulrik dropped his bow and quiver. "I'd get to be seeing Onyx? Does that mean I'd have a job? What would I be doing?"

"Cleaning, tidying, feeding, and lots and lots of playing. If you want to, that is?"

Pappa's head reddened. When his hair blew in the wind, his head had the visage of a burning candlewick.

"He'd love to, wouldn't you, Ulrik?" said Mamma, nodding at him with imploring eyes stretched wide. There seemed to be some unspoken scheme at hand, which Pappa, until now, was unaware of.

"When will I be starting, Cheng?" said Ulrik, tiptoeing with anticipation, feeling as though he were about to float off.

"Today! If you're ready …"

"He *is* ready; aren't you, Ulrik?" said Mamma, her eyes turning bloodshot with strain.

"I-I-I—yah, I think so, yah. Do I need to bring anything?"

"Oh, only the two things you should take with you anywhere and everywhere: a curious mind and a willingness to learn," reaching up and knuckling Ulrik on the head as though the act might crack open a doorway to a realm of intellect. "Now, let's be going." Cheng donned his crash helmet and handed a spare to Ulrik; it was a size that would fit an ordinary fourteen-year-old, but not him, for when he balanced it atop his crown it had little more coverage than a priest's skullcap.

"Ready, Ulrik?" Cheng mounted his bike and beckoned the boy to join him. "I'll stand; you sit behind me here on the saddle and piggyback. Hey, don't look so frightened. I might not be as agile as I once was, but my joints are well oiled, and,"—patting his heart—"the engine room still runs impeccably."

Ulrik clung to Chenglei as an infant chimpanzee does when riding upon its mother's back, and he brought his knees right the way up to his ears to keep his gangly legs from trailing on the ground. After bidding their farewells, Chenglei got them off to a wobbly start and peddled in a state of considerable imbalance before gaining enough momentum to stabilise. As they passed over the threshold, Ulrik chanced one last look over his shoulder and saw Pappa striding about Thrudheim with his sun-burnt expression, jabbing his red cuboid finger in Mamma's direction, and no doubt accidentally spitting while shouting something like: "A job? Meddling with mainland scum is an invitation to trouble." Then Pappa fell to his knees and let loose a flurry of meteors on the ground with his flaming fists. Mamma spun around, her braids lashing the air as she did so, and she made off into the wilderness, where she'd likely spend the rest of the day away from him. She always came back with the sorest eyes and blamed it on the wind being fiercer on higher ground.

"How about you keep your eyes on the fjords ahead, Ulrik?" said Chenglei. "Hold on tight now."

"Argh, Cheng," pressing his cheek into Chenglei's shoulder and squeezing his eyelids as they flew downhill. Only upon sensing that they were now in flat country did Ulrik dare to peep open his eyes and there-after relax as they slowed to a comfortable pace. Even when Chenglei stopped peddling, their momentum kept them going for a long while after. Then, his stomach having settled, Ulrik struck up a conversation: "I've been meaning to ask you something, since you know about science things. But I haven't had the chance because Pappa is always around, and he says I'm not allowed to be mentioning 'Homo nova'."

"Sure. What is it you want to ask?"

"Dr Lyngstad said I have genies that I can switch on from my ancestors, right?"

"Genies ... aha, yes. It's true that it's possible for you to switch on dormant *genes*."

"Yah, genes. I want to know—since swimming is my favourite thing to do—if we have any ancestors who were good at swimming."

"Aquatic ancestors, oh yes. So, I'm presuming you want to know if it's possible to switch on genes that make you a better swimmer? Hmm, well, from memory, I think the *Tiktaalik* is one of our most recent aquatic ancestors."

"Recent? How recent?"

"Oh, about 400 million years ago. So, while it's *possible* you share some genetics, I'm not sure how *probable* it could be for you to switch any genes on—given how divergent our anatomies are."

"Oh, sorry, am I being stupid?"

"N-n-n-n-no; you're not stupid, Ulrik. You have a curious mind."

"Thanks, Cheng; you're always making me feel better."

"I mean it. It's a curious idea in itself—wanting to know if you can become a better swimmer by switching certain genes on. Hmm."

"You think I could?"

"I'm not sure. Hypothetically, yes. Maybe. Maybe not. Hmm. It's worthy of further research, that much I know."

"So, you *do* believe it—that I am *Homo nova*?"

"Ah, well, that's a complicated matter, Ulrik," applying the brakes, the back tyre skidding out as they came to a halt. They hadn't yet arrived at the Sanctuary and were still some way off, but this quiet part of the country was as good a place as any to hold private council. The only beings snooping about were a small herd of reindeer, champing away at the tundra moss, filling their stomachs with the all-you-can-eat salad, and minding their own business as long as other creatures went about minding theirs. "Not long after you returned home," added Chenglei, "someone hacked the university's network and leaked Dr Lyngstad's journal far and wide. So, I've been able to study her findings—critique them, even. And I've spoken at length with your mamma about my own interpretations."

"And what's your take on this?"

"Well, Dr Lyngstad overestimated many things in her research—on purpose, I believe." Chenglei's face shone bright like baby skin, and Ulrik supposed him never to have frowned in his life, for why else would a single wrinkle not occupy the forehead of a man of his age? His only wrinkles were those pronounced paper fans at the corner of his eyes, formed, most likely, over years of excessive smiling.

"Am I *Homo nova*, Cheng? Speak plainly."

"No, I don't believe you to be another species of man. Also, I don't believe Dr Lyngstad ever supposed you to be, either. I think it was a ruse of hers to embellish the facts. She knew, somehow, that methylation wasn't a subject that would gain the attention of the masses. I mean, most people have never heard of it. But a newly discovered species of mankind? Such a controversial idea was certain to generate powerful intrigue across the Continent. I think she knew it'd be doubly controversial if the research should be buried—as it was. So, thanks to Dr Lyngstad, the genetics debate has reopened. Everybody is talking about it—about you, Ulrik. People are asking questions, demanding a public inquiry, and behind closed doors people whisper about the resurrection of dormant genes. You see, whether or not you're a new species, this is still an affront to the Holy Shepherd since it's evidence of evolution; evidence which rejects the idea that humans descended from Adam and Eve because it demonstrates that we have non-human ancestors. She's a clever lady, that Dr Lyngstad."

"She's a scheming liar for convincing me I'm *Homo nova*." Every aspect of his face sank, and all the hope in his heart evaporated. "I wanted to be special—more than anything."

"Hey, hey, listen here;" Chenglei knuckled Ulrik's crash helmet. "I didn't say Ulrik Magnusson wasn't special. In fact, Ulrik Magnusson is the only person in the world to possess a kaleidoscopic genome. So I'm afraid the name has stuck, and it's become a sort of unofficial term to describe your genetic constitution of having this kaleidoscopic genome. Whether you like it or not, you'll be known as Homo Nova for the rest of your life. You should own your new status."

"I'm not sure what to believe anymore. They say I've been engineered, Cheng. Everyone is saying I'm a fake. A genetic experiment. Even the Holy Shepherd has been telling lies about me. He says I'm the work of the Devil."

"Ulrik, my big friend with the big heart, only those with the lowest standard of proof say you've been engineered. You are special, Ulrik Magnusson. You are Homo Nova. You are the first."

"Bah! What good is being special when I'm stuck here, unable to show the people who I am? I'm only special if other people believe it, too. See, it's like being a millionaire but not being able to spend money or tell anyone you're a millionaire. What good is that? Might as well be poor like a stinking forager, or better still, dead. Nuh, Cheng, while I'm stuck here, I'll always be a nobody. That's why I can't stay. I'd rather die than endure this frozen torment for the rest of my life. I have to prove to the world I'm special."

"Well, maybe that's about to change very soon ..."

"Change? Why would it? What do you mean, Cheng?"

"You asked me earlier about swimming, didn't you? You want to become a better swimmer?"

"The *best*. More than anything! Ever since I was a youngling, it's all I've dreamed of doing. Though I always supposed they were just that—dreams. Never did I believe I could. But Dr Lyngstad says she believes I have the talent to go all the way to the Olympics. That much I do believe, of all her claims. Nuh, I *know* it. And this is my life now, and I won't let anyone force me to act a certain way—to be somebody I'm not. Not Pappa, not those bearded regents, not those crazy Whitehoods. They want to keep me here, keep me hidden, keep me silent, close me off from the real world. Going to mainland DRUE was my chance to become something—to be a someone; and they tried to rob me of my ambition. I never chose the life of a forager. I want to show the world who I am—what I can do. Show them I'm special ... Did I mention that Dr Lyngstad said I have the talent to go to the Olympics?"

"You did." Cheng chuckled. "And what if I told you it was possible for an ex-professional swimmer to coach you?"

"Who?"

"Someone who once competed at the Olympics."

"You think such a person would willingly coach me? Why, when I have no money to offer in wages?"

"Not everybody is motivated by money, Ulrik. Being a forager, you of all people should know that." Chenglei knuckled him on the head, the paper fan crinkles of his eyes deepening as his grin grew. "Vladimir Lukashenko is an old friend of mine who has, let's say, a lot of unfinished business."

"What kind of business?"

"Well, Vlad won a silver medal at the Moscow Olympics in a long-distance freestyle event when he was only fifteen. Pundits tipped him to be the next biggest sensation—an icon—a superstar."

"But?" said Ulrik, with his inquiring neck outstretched.

"Well, Vlad suffered a nasty injury at home when chopping down a tree in his own yard. It toppled the wrong way, fell on him, and crushed his spine. He was in rehab for several months and had to learn to walk again. Hey, don't look so concerned; it was years ago, and he made a full recovery. Though he could never swim competitively again."

"That's worse than dying," massaging his own spine empathetically, as though he felt a phantom pain there. "To be born with such talent and yet to have the opportunity taken from you. Anyway, how did you come to know Vlad?"

"I met Vlad a decade after his accident. You see, we met when studying a master's degree at St Petersburg University. I always thought it a bizarre career change to go from professional swimming into academia, but I later realised that it was the most obvious choice for him. His dream had always been to win a gold medal at the Olympics. He never lost sight of that—even after his accident. So he gave himself over to the study of marine creatures and educated himself on underwater locomotion, a field he referred to as aquadynamics (in the same way aeronauts are experts in the ways of aerodynamics). Vlad became an extraordinary stroke technician, and ever since, he's sought extraordinary students to coach; students who show the potential to win a gold medal on his behalf."

"And has he?"

"Has he what?"

"Has he ever coached a swimmer to win a gold medal?"

"Not yet," seizing Ulrik by the shoulders. "Even at his age, he's as dogged as a dragon in his pursuit of gold."

"So tell me, what do I have to do to convince this Vladimir Lukashenko to coach me?"

"Aha! I'm glad you asked. Well, here's the thing:" Cheng dropped his voice into an excited whisper, "Vlad knew of Homo Nova before Homo Nova knew of Vlad. He's been following you on a drone of his, although he tells me you've shot down three of his bots."

"I have? Agh. He must be thinking I'm some kind of savage. Please tell him I'm sorry. Wait—did you say you'd already been speaking to him about me?"

"*He* reached out to me, knowing I live on Svalbard, and he's told me that to coach you would be his last chance of fulfilling his dreams. You'd be his project, if you're up to the challenge ..."

"Whoa ..." Ulrik grappled his own face with both hands; his open mouth elongated to its fullest. "You think he'd agree to coach me?"

"It depends on one thing, Ulrik: how badly you want this. There'll be sacrifices, the least of which being that you must live elsewhere, some place far away from here without—"

"Cheng," Ulrik dropped to his knees, pleading with hands interlaced, "this life on Svalbard is making me miserable. I can't be living here forever like some caged bird."

"—without your mamma and pappa. You'd be going somewhere without them." Cheng helped Ulrik to his feet again.

"Without my parents? Oh. Where exactly?"

"*If*, Ulrik, *if* you were to be going, you'd be living in Russia."

"Russia?"

"Yes, Russia. You'd be living in hiding for a time. Somewhere outside of DRUE, somewhere safe. Away from drones, news reporters, and all that extra pressure and stress. And it's convenient because Vlad lives a life that's not so different to yours, though not as extreme. You see, he lives in a cabin in a forest, and he goes hunting, fishing, and foraging. Though he's not quite so stoic as to deny himself Tech and other comforts just because they didn't exist a thousand years ago."

"But my parents would never let me go to Russia."

"And you're sure about that?"

He stammered and stalled, then eyed Cheng in confusion.

"Your mamma has been confiding in me, Ulrik. She knows you're feeling trapped here and wants you to have your new adventure. This, she knows, could be the beginning of something extraordinary. Because *you* and your kaleidoscopic genome are extraordinary."

"She knows about Vlad and Russia? What about Pappa? He wouldn't want this for me."

Suddenly, sensing a hum of electricity in the air, the reindeers ceased their munching of moss and trotted for cover behind the hills. A single drone floated across the sky, but neither Chenglei nor Ulrik saw it.

"Ulrik, this isn't about what anybody else wants; it's about what *you* want." Chenglei gripped the bike's handlebars and patted the saddle. "Come; on you get. We need to be going."

"I'm desperate, Cheng." Ulrik knotted his arms in defiance. Not until Chenglei recognised his seriousness would Ulrik get back on the saddle—even if it made them late for work. "Here on Svalbard, I'm just Ulrik the forager, or Troggler (as Brynolf calls me). Elsewhere, I have a chance to be Homo Nova. I want to be out there showing the world I'm special."

The drone hovered above them like a stalking kestrel hunting field mice, appearing, as it were, suspended in space-time.

"Then be clear about what you want me to do, Ulrik, so I can arrange it."

"I want Vladimir Lukashenko to coach me," he said, with a great spirit of conviction. "I want to go to Russia."

"Lower your voice, Ulrik. We have company," looking at the drone with his scrutinous eyebrows scrunched. "As for swimming, I need to make one more thing clear: a scholarship—which is what you'd be taking part in—is a contract of sorts. Think of a contract like an official promise. When taking out a contract, you promise to do certain things for a designated period. It's not something you can easily walk away from, and nor could Vlad either. In a way, you'd be sworn to each other. So be certain this is what you want."

"Cheng, all my life I've loved swimming. I want to win a gold medal and become an Olympic champion. I'll enter into this scholarship contract if that's what it takes, and I'll do so gladly, without hesitation. What do I have to lose? Nothing. This is it: my chance to show the world who Homo Nova is. Please, Cheng, you have to help me."

"Then I'll do all I can to arrange the scholarship for you, although these things can take a while. In the meantime, say nothing to your pappa. Your mamma made me promise not to say anything to him. It's for her alone to approach him in her own time. Now, off we go. Come."

Ulrik gave Chenglei his word and sealed his promise with a kind headbutt. Then he mounted the saddle, and the two of them sped away on the mountain bike, the solitary drone stalking them all the way to the Arctic Sanctuary. Had Ulrik brought his bow, he would've shot the black bot from the sky. But then he soon wondered about the drone's pilot, and he became convinced thereafter that Vladimir Lukashenko captained it and was watching him all the way from Russia.

After arriving at the Arctic Sanctuary, Chenglei padlocked his bicycle at the bike station while Ulrik stood in the shadow of a great arena, looking up in wonder. How had he passed it so many times and never ventured close enough to notice the details of the Stone-Age-style stadium? The front entrance had the aspect of a cave entrance, with a round stone door that rolled to one side when Chenglei swiped his keycard.

"Here we are," said Cheng, girding his arm over Ulrik's shoulder in the manner of a sage guide. "Interesting fact: the Arctic Sanctuary is the biggest draw of tourism to Svalbard. No, let me rephrase: *Onyx* is the biggest draw of tourism to Svalbard. Hundreds of thousands of people travel from across the world to see him every year because he's the only one of his kind in the entire world—a bit like you, I guess. And because of that, he's worth millions to the Svalbard economy. But do you want to know a sad fact? Some animals that live in captivity have a much shorter lifespan than those that live in the wild. An elephant—which is Onyx's closest cousin—would be lucky to make it to their eighteenth birthday when bred in captivity, whereas in the wild they can expect to live for three times that."

"That *is* a sad fact, Cheng. It must break their hearts to be trapped and alone. I know how that feels ... Now I'm afraid to ask you how old Onyx is."

"Then perhaps it's better you don't."

"I don't want to be hearing any more sad facts."

"How about a weird fact, then? Did you know they feed Onyx a diet rich in coffee beans, and when he poops, the zookeeper collects his dung, which is then ground and turned into—well ... mammoth dung coffee? You wouldn't believe how much elite professionals pay to drink this shit. Some people are so fucking stupid."

"Cheng, I don't think I've ever heard you swear before."

"Oops, sorry, sorry. Did I swear? It's rare that I do. It's not that I dislike stupid people, just those who are both rich *and* stupid ... like pastors and preachers. I find it an insufferable combination."

When they passed through, they came out into an open belt of parkland with several forks of path cutting through it. At every juncture stood enormous menhirs (standing stones) upon which were inscribed cave paintings—symbols, arrows, and charcoal silhouettes of stick-men and beasts, signposting the many exhibitions and attractions.

After a brief wait, they were greeted by a zookeeper who wore a seal hide parka (the garb of rangers). Ulrik lunged forward to headbutt him before Chenglei hauled him back and reminded him that shaking hands was the custom of ordinary folk. But the zookeeper said he knew the custom of foragers, and so they connected foreheads.

Before the Sanctuary opened to the public, the zookeeper insisted on giving them a guided tour as part of Ulrik's induction. On their way around, Ulrik saw reindeers locking antlers, bear cubs sparring, foxes chasing their tails, wolves harmonising their howls, Icelandic horses whinnying, musk ox grazing on grain, lynxes spying and surveying, hares madly mating; and in SeaPark he watched narwhal fencing with their ivory spears and trained walruses clapping for cod. Then, over to the far north-west, at the end of all the paths, stood the exhibition of all exhibitions: a huge amphitheatre encircled by a great henge of standing stones.

The zookeeper led them down a narrow precinct where they found themselves backstage and making their way into the upper terraces of the amphitheatre. Then, looking out over a balcony and down at the centre of the pen, they saw the colossal beast under his shaggy snow-white fur, and his trunk had the aspect of an albino anaconda; but perhaps the starkest feature was that which his name derived from: his eyes. Two of the most arresting onyx eyes bejewelled his head, and these shiny black stones seemed to absorb all the surrounding light and yet seemed, paradoxically, a source of black light.

Having spent a few moments watching him, it became apparent to Ulrik that Onyx was the second glummest creature in existence (himself being the first). Onyx stood motionless with his domed head bowed, huffing and sighing and staring into nothingness. Ulrik knew well the feeling of being held in captivity for the appeasement of others and neutered of his desire to run, play, and explore, for he often sat in silence in his own room, staring at length at a knot in the wooden wall when there was little else to busy the mind. This theatre was no sanctuary for Onyx, just as Thrudheim was no sanctuary for him.

Down they went into the arena to meet him, where Ulrik tiptoed around balls of steaming elephantine dung. There was, as Chenglei pointed out, a fragrance of coffee about these moist, turgid orbs. A strange breed of folk, he thought to himself, are those who sip on coffee derived from those soiled beans and think of themselves as privileged. Eugh!

As they drew near, Onyx dipped his trunk into a play-pool and drank through his tubular nostrils. Then the beast raised his head, straightened his hose-nose, turned it on Ulrik, and blasted him with all the force of a firefighter putting out flames.

"Bad Onyx," said the zookeeper, wagging a finger.

Ulrik's sodden furs rained about his feet. Being so wet, there was little reason not to go for a swim now. At once, he leapt into the pool fully clothed.

"Be careful, Ulrik!" cried Chenglei. "Believe me, you do not want to offend Onyx."

The mammoth stomped to the poolside; his eyes now had the aspect of black holes that might swallow up everything in close proximity.

"Woah, woah, hey! Easy now, Onyx," said the zookeeper, in a calming, persuasive tone. "It's all right. This is Ulrik. Say hello, Onyx."

"He's no harm," said Ulrik, paddling and splashing about in the water. "He just wants to play."

Onyx looked upon him with a certain curiosity; a curiosity generally exclusive to children who have experienced so little of this world that they are impressed by everyday happenings. The mammoth dipped his albino-anaconda trunk into the water again. Sensing a second blasting, Ulrik ducked under the water, but he didn't catch a full breath so didn't last long submerged. When he resurfaced, Onyx unleashed his water cannon, blasting Ulrik in his face; and Onyx tossed his floppy trunk this way and that as though in self-congratulation.

"Ah, I think he likes you, Ulrik," said the zookeeper, mopping the beads of sweaty relief from his forehead.

"Good health, Onyx; I'm Ulrik," he said, swimming to the poolside.

Onyx unfurled his trunk into the water. This time he blew a few amiable bubbles. Ulrik reached out slowly. At first, he mimed the motion of a pat and a rub, then, growing in confidence, he placed his hand on the trunk and gave it a stroke and a tickle, at which the beast made low trumpeting sounds and bass rumbles of approval.

There was an instant kinship between him and the beast, what with both being a kind of genetic phenomenon and being the only one of their kind in the world. No sibling or cousin did either of them have with whom to relate.

"Isn't this just the most spectacular thing you've ever seen?" said Chenglei, running a hand through his badger-hair in disbelief, eyes a-glisten with tears.

When Ulrik asked later in the day why Chenglei had seemed so moved, he apologised and said, "I don't know why I'm so prone to tears. You see, to look up in wonder at the stars or across a vast vista of canyon; to hear the rip of ocean tide at dawn or the melodies of birdsong at dusk; to feel the touch of fine sand or the soft prickle of grass; to smell the fragrance of fresh ginger or the warm earth when it rains; to sample the sweetness of wild fruits or the tingle of a hot chilli pepper—I don't know why, Ulrik, but in the presence of nature's greatest bounties, I sometimes get a bit overwhelmed."

After that day, Ulrik saw much less of Chenglei, at least for a while. Few really knew what sudden and urgent business occupied Cheng, but he flew to and from the mainland on several occasions. Where, he never said, but Ulrik thought he'd overheard one of the Sanctuary rangers using the words "Chenglei" and "Russia" in the same sentence—or had she said "rushing"? Perhaps his mind was playing cruel tricks on him and his ears were betraying him.

Onyx loved Ulrik, the boy who gave extra apples, extra pats, and extra playtime, so much so that he trusted him to ride upon his back without a saddle. One day, some sleuthing park guest captured footage of the spectacle on their Tech—despite video footage being strictly prohibited. Within thirty minutes, it was the most talked about footage on AbraGram; and by the end of the day, millions across the world had seen it, leading to a sudden surge in interest and a sudden surge in Sanctuary ticket sales. By the end of the week, the summer event calendar had sold out.

On the following Monday, Ulrik was ushered into the zookeeper's office and was delighted to hear that he'd been promoted. A stage director of exotic nationality, whom he'd never seen before, presented his vision for a production in which Ulrik and Onyx were the stars. "You'll get to play the lead part—an ancient forager. You needn't memorise a script. All you have to do is grunt a few times, and the show will last about fifteen minutes. We'll perform it once a day—to begin with. No trouble for a brave kid like you. See, I knew you'd be happy about it. Let's get to work, then!"

In less than a day, scaffolding was erected within the amphitheatre and decorated with faux foliage and cables of counterfeit creepers to make them look like trees. Stage lights were installed, props were positioned, and rehearsals got under way. But the rehearsals were long and exhausting, and Ulrik found he had little time or energy thereafter to swim.

On the evening of his first show, Ulrik found himself needing to relieve his bladder every few minutes. A feverish convulsion shook his bones, and his bowels gave him malodorous reminders of his anxiety. He'd have vomited if there were anything in his stomach to expel, but he hadn't eaten all day. And when he confessed to the stage director that he'd barely slept in the past two days, he tutted and replied, "Ugh, there's plenty of time for sleeping when you die. But don't die yet; the show must go on."

On the show went, and it went like this: faced with starvation, a prehistoric forager goes on his final hunt, and when a chance sighting of a woolly mammoth presents itself, he stalks it in the shadows. With his flint spear ready, he lunges out and impales the hamstring of the beast. Maimed, and its life almost drained, the beast limps away and thereafter collapses. But when standing over it to deal his final blow, the forager hesitates at the sight of his prey—whimpering cries, contracted breathing, violent shaking. He takes pity on the beast and, with the last reserve of his strength, tends to its wounds and guards it through the night against lurking scavengers. At dawn, the starving forager himself collapses of exhaustion. But he later wakes to find himself being towed along the ground by a hairy trunk, towed under the canopy of an enchanting forest home to a surplus of ripe, ruby-red heartfruit. Here, the two unlikely friends breakfast, lunch, and dine until the full vigour of their health is restored, and thereafter they remain inseparable from one another's company till the end of their days.

Fin.

A deafening chorus of applause sounded throughout the amphitheatre. The entire audience were on their feet, their facial features stretched in wild, tribal excitement, pointing and waving at Ulrik and Onyx, and reaching out to them from their faraway terraces. But the raucous clamour spooked Onyx, and he swayed his head from side to side erratically. This swaying wasn't the humble bow at the curtain call, as the spectators thought. Ulrik knew this shake of the head to be one of disapproval.

"Hey, hey, Onyx," he said, comforting his trunk. "It's all right." He then spoke soothing gibberish like parents do when hushing a baby: "Shh-shh-shh. I've got you, Onyx-x-x-x. Hey, tss-tss-tss." For now, he'd pacified Onyx and brought the threatening sway to a halt.

After the show, Ulrik had planned to go and cool himself off with a swim. But peeping through a gap in the stage curtain, he saw a throng of folk blockading the exit of the amphitheatre. They were waiting, it seemed: queueing to re-enter and have their photograph taken with them backstage for a small fortune. Many wore T-shirts or had in their possession keyrings, coffee mugs, and other merchandise with Ulrik's savage-looking face printed on them. When news of a new souvenir shop reached him, his arms rattled with adrenaline and sweat trickled down the nape of his neck like a volcanic brook. So much money, yet little more than a tractor tyre was divvied out in wages to Onyx for all those rehearsals. And where was his cut?

Ulrik wanted fame, but not like this—not through performing in some Arctic circus. Not in a show that represented him as some prehistoric savage. If Chenglei were here, he'd help him undo all this. But he'd gone—to Russia, or *rushing* somewhere else—and it was up to him alone to make things better for Onyx.

"We need to be getting you out of here," muttered Ulrik, while alone backstage with Onyx. While everyone else was hurtling about—the director, the stage crew, and the technicians—Ulrik rummaged about in his cloak pocket and took Tristan's Victoria Cross from its brass tin, keeping it secreted at all times beneath his cloak in case someone should be spying on him from the shadows. Just holding it and feeling it was enough to connect with his old friend, and when he rubbed his thumb over the words "For Valour", he adopted that same patriotic stare of Tristan's and became resolute and absolute in his own convictions. "Onyx, we're getting you out, even if it's just for a stroll. Curse all those who are using us for money and treating us like this just because we're different."

The sun made several loops around the sky by the time he'd planned Onyx's breakout. It was to happen on Sunday, or the Sabbath, as the mainlanders called it. The Governor had prohibited working on the Sabbath for all except a few key workers. On any given Sunday, the only such key worker present at the Arctic Sanctuary was a solitary park ranger, whose only task other than his infrequent patrolling was to test the fire alarm at the exact same time every week. The perfect cover for a breakout.

On one particular Sabbath, Ulrik gained entry to the Sanctuary about midday, and when arriving at the entrance, he told the park ranger he'd left a few belongings behind after last night's show. The park ranger granted him entry, in return for a photograph with Homo Nova. Once inside, he made his way to the amphitheatre, where he hid inside a tractor tyre and waited, and waited, and waited.

At 8 p.m., the fire alarm test rang shrill throughout the Sanctuary for ten pulsing seconds, during which Ulrik snuck out of the tractor tyre and dragged it to an enormous green iron door—the fire escape. He removed the iron bars barricading the exit and drove his shoulder against the door, which he then wedged open with the tyre. Elsewhere, the park ranger overrode the fire alarm. Then there was silence, save for the hammering heart in Ulrik's breast. The fire escape gaped open. They only had to pass through and freedom was theirs.

Ulrik waved fragrant roots and leaves about Onyx's nostrils, but he needed no coercing outside. The mammoth barged through the fire escape and out into direct sunlight, where all of nature seemed at peace: no drones, no vehicles, no tourists, no markets. Everyone was at home, absorbed, most likely, in their Tech and televisions. But perhaps the greatest fortune was the Sanctuary being situated at the edge of town, for nowhere during their escape would they stumble past a house, home, shack, or shelter.

Onyx lowered himself to the ground, and Ulrik scaled his haunches, grappling his shaggy white coat to aid his ascent. They set out along the shore and headed north for a couple of miles to the abandoned camp at Hiorthhamn before heading back again the same way. That was all for their first breakout, since Onyx's legs were unaccustomed to carrying the weight of his colossal body, let alone a rider, too, for more than the occasional lap of his pen.

Each Sabbath, Ulrik and Onyx snuck out with the same stealth, and they roamed the wilderness together. They went on many adventures; sometimes they got up to mischief like chasing herds of reindeer, but often they did good deeds, like the time they cleaned up a margin of beach of the plastic that had washed ashore (foragers hate plastic since it didn't exist a thousand years ago). As summer came to a close, and as the first snows returned and the darkness closed in, Ulrik risked other journeys that would've been foolish to undertake in broad sunlight.

One Sabbath evening, Onyx looked particularly subdued, so Ulrik decided they should venture south and inland, thinking a walk among the more rugged land would do his legs some good. They arrived at a place of spiritual humbling: a forager crematorium of sorts, where instead of plaques and gravestones there were piles of rock (or cairns) honouring the dead. "Onyx, I want you to meet Ivar, my other best friend," said Ulrik, dismounting the mammoth and standing over one cairn where the smooth stones were piled the highest and out of which blossomed hardy clusters of purple saxifrage. Each stone was a token from the forager families who occupied the region of Bjørnland (western Svalbard), upon which were carved their household emblems. Among the stones were those belonging to the Forkbeards and Finehairs, the Firebanes and Frostmanes, the Hammerfists and Hornfoots, the Ironbones and Ironsides, the Bloodaxes and Bluetooths, the Battlehorns and Cattlehorns, the Serpenteyes and Stonecloaks, the Ravenrunes,

Ragnarsons, and Magnussons—Thor's hammer, Mjolnir, being the emblem of the Magnussons.

Ulrik took a knee and leant his cheek into the purple flowers as though to commune with the spirit of Ivar, while Onyx lay on a couch of snow. It was rare for Onyx to lie prone out of choice, and Ulrik supposed the uphill journey had sapped him. At least the journey back to the Sanctuary was downhill and would be less trouble. Besides, they'd climbed steeper slopes with much less fuss; Onyx was probably looking for attention. But now wasn't the time for play. It'd been too long since he'd last visited Ivar's cairn.

"Ivar, you were the strongest person I knew. You faced down Brynolf when he was armed and you weren't. You protected me. But when the moment came for me to protect you, I couldn't. I was too weak." He tapped his collarbone; memories of the incident under the ice came flooding back. "I should've been stronger—fought harder through the pain to save you. Never surrendered. So today I'm promising you I won't ever be so weak again. Soon, I'm going to be swimming a lot more—in Russia, I think. Chenglei is going to help me get a coach: a man called Vladimir Lukashenko. I want to be the best swimmer in the world, Ivar. The people are calling me Homo Nova because I have this thing called a kaleidoscopic genome. But there are those who deny my claim. I have to prove myself to the world. So, I'm going to the Olympics. I'm going to be the strongest swimmer the world has ever seen. I won't let you down again. I promise."

A sudden strange gurgling interrupted him. It sounded like ground movement or failing engines—or both at once. It was Onyx.

"Why are you sulking?" drawing himself away from Ivar's cairn. "You want to go back to the Sanctuary? Fine. Let's go."

Gurgling groan.

"Onyx?"

A trumpeting cry echoed throughout the sky. There seemed to be a storm happening inside Onyx's organs: an attack on the heart or fluid on the lungs. No amount of poking, prodding, or patting motivated him to rise.

"What? Are you sick?" Ulrik patted and stroked his hairy hide. "Well, you can't be sleeping out here. We've got to get you back, or we'll be in big trouble."

At once, Onyx panted as one who'd come to the end of a long sprint, and he heaved out dense mists of breath. He girded his trunk about Ulrik's body, hugging him tight like a teddy bear. The mammoth's body ballooned then shrank with each rapid breath. Then, suddenly, the trunk, which was coiled around Ulrik, fell limp, and the production of mist ceased. All the weight of Onyx's head fell onto his sweeping tusk, which cracked and snapped off with as much ease as a dead branch. His black eyes faded to a shade of raincloud and were onyx no more.

"Onyx, wake up. Please! Bad Onyx," Ulrik shouted, wagging his finger. Then he smacked him on his buttocks to shock some life into him. "Bad, bad, bad—oh, your poor tusk. I'm sorry, Onyx. This is my fault." Crouching, he collected the splintered tusk in both arms. "I'll try to fix it for you. Be still while I …" He unbuckled his leather belt and attempted to strap the shattered ends of broken tusk together, but it hung and swung and was flung off by a moderate breeze. "Onyx, why won't you wake up? Please, I need you." The evening freeze stole any remaining warmth from Onyx, and he froze over so that he became rock-hard to the touch. The woolly mammoth was extinct once more.

Ulrik's chest tightened; his gullet contracted to the width of a straw. Despite dragging air inward, he was unable to exhale thereafter. His lungs filled and expanded in a way that felt like he was drowning in air—like an aquatic creature out of water. "I c-c-can't—can't breathe." Talking was no use. Nor was coughing. The only way to expel air was to pound his chest like a gorilla, and picking up two cairn stones—those belonging to the Firebanes and the Ravenrunes (stones shaped, ironically, like lungs)—he bashed at his ribcage until he overcame the suffocation.

For a while, he lay supine staring at the black clouds, heaving in and out while his senses returned to the present. By now, Onyx's eyes had frosted over so that they looked like swollen pearls. Ulrik turned away. Then he stood up, paced about, sat down, shook his head, rumpled his hair, chewed his lips, plucked his beard, pulled his ears, smacked his forehead, scratched his elbows, headbutted the ground, and bit his knuckles bloody. What to do—what to do—what, what, what?

It was dangerous to remain. If found here grieving, there could be no denying his involvement. So he abandoned the cairn-ground as fast as his legs would carry him, but he came to an abrupt halt halfway down the hill when a sudden thought struck him like an invisible wall: the place of Onyx's death would be an obvious clue—Ivar's cairn. Everyone would know it was him. So he dashed all the way back.

What to do now that he was here again?

He thought he heard an engine approach. "Sorry, Onyx," he whispered. "I have to be leaving you again, or they'll catch me." He dashed away; his forehead crinkled, his nostrils flared, his lips curled, and his eyes watered and froze over in an instant.

Before entering Thrudheim, he mopped his brow and waited a while for his crimson face to return to its normal colour, so as not to arouse any suspicion. But then another disturbing thought took root in his mind: prowling polar bears. Visions of Onyx being clawed to pieces tormented him. If the bears got him, nothing would be left of him. What kind of person would he be to allow his friend's body to be dishonoured in such a way? He hastened all the way back to the cairn-ground again.

Arriving there, his thoughts betrayed him for the last time, supposing that if bears were to come and leave no trace of the mammoth ... all blame on him might disappear. "Nuh," grappling his face. "What am I thinking? Nuh, nuh, nuh!" But he removed his hands from his face and groomed his beard in contemplation. "How, then, to lure a bear? Blood. The scent. But I have no knife with me. A sharp rock? Nuh. Mammoth hide is too thick. A tusk. Yah. A sharp tusk ... Nuh, nuh, nuh. What am I thinking?" He shook his head and slapped his face. There had to be a better way. Maybe he could bury Onyx. But then, it'd take far less time to bury himself ...

A moment of sinister tranquillity took hold of him, and he fell into a dark envy of Ivar. He sat staring at those cairn rocks and fantasised about piling the earth over him, all the while a haunting voice in his head persuading him it was better to kill himself today than to suffer the sorrows of tomorrow: "You've ruined your chances of ever becoming anyone special. The people will hate you; they'll want you dead. Don't give them the satisfaction of watching you suffer. Take your own life. The world doesn't deserve you. Be brave. Just this once. You can do it. Snuff out the candle, and be at peace forever. You've nothing left worth living for."

But he'd seen enough of death for one day and fought back at the voice with a combination of blows to his temple. "Shut up, shut up, shut up!"

Chapter Sixteen

ARROGANT AMBITIONS: ADMIRABLE ASPIRATIONS

Longyearbyen's new contemporary stave church had become the office of municipal affairs while the Governor's Chamber of Law underwent renovation. A fitting place was God's house for the dealing out of judgment.

A tide of foragers ebbed and flowed against the church steps, armed with glinting spears at their sides, bows on their backs, and axes strapped to their belts. Though their coming armed wasn't a cause for immediate concern, for even ordinary folk carried rifles at all times on Svalbard (since it was *illegal* not to do so, owing to the threat of the numerous polar bears). But before the day was over, many of their wooden weapons would be put to extreme use.

When the church doors flew open, a flood of foragers burst through, shouldering past one another to secure their seats among the pews, or rather gallery. Burning incense would've filled the air with sweet perfumes had it not been smothered by the reek of the black draught which the foragers passed about in their goatskin flasks, and their sulphuric, eggy breath which they exhaled having consumed it. Not until a few days later would their collective pungency be aerated from the furniture of that house. There were, however, at least some foragers who practised basic hygiene; some of the Finehairs took it upon themselves to scrub their unhallowed hands in a marble basin, until Father Eggert, Governor of Svalbard, emerged with the deepest shade of plum in his face and shooed them away from his baptismal font.

Few adored Father Eggert, and even fewer now since the rumours of him hosting the Holy Shepherd had begun to pass about the tongues of foragers. The Holy Shepherd, according to these rumours, had taken a special interest in Svalbard of late, and his quadcopter had been sighted two or three times throughout summer, and two or three times this very week—in the run-up to the trial. What business he had here, nobody except the Governor knew.

In an upper tier of the church (the dock), overlooking the gallery, sat the accused. Astrid sat between Thor and Ulrik; her arms interlocked with each of theirs as though they were the sinewy threads keeping her family together. To her left, Thor looked in danger of gnawing his thumbnail down to the bone; to her right, Ulrik shivered, and the hairs of his arms stood on end like toothpicks. She looked out across the gallery, but she couldn't see Chenglei among the turnout of foragers. Where was he? He had promised her he'd be here.

Before the sentencing took place, Father Eggert took to the pulpit with the *New Continental Bible* in his hand and conducted prayers. Throughout this, the foragers of the gallery grumbled and groaned and whispered and moaned, and they showed a particular disdain for the purple tapestry hanging over the altar: the Republic's coat of arms—the Sword of Abraham.

When Father Eggert finished, he gave way to the judge, a squat lady wearing an official black robe, who, apart from her pinched face, had no other discernible feature owing to the headTech smothering her head. She craned her neck towards the dock where the accused sat and said, "Ladies, gentlemen, and foragers of the court, please rise."

There! As the gallery rose, Astrid saw the top of Chenglei's head, and when he gestured to her with a deliberate nod, her heart bounded about her breast. Everything was going to be okay.

221

"I hope he knows what he's doing," said Thor, massaging his temples. Astrid grabbed his hand to stop him from fidgeting. Holding hands also stopped her biting the ends of her hair, the greasy tresses of which had since lost their golden luminosity and appeared now to be many shades darker than her natural colour. Under a certain light, she was brunette.

"As I made you aware at the start of the trial," said the judge, tapping a sheaf of papers so the edges were flush, "since Ulrik is fourteen years old and therefore a minor, it would not be lawful for me to sentence him for his part in the crimes here mentioned. But I'll explain what is to happen to Ulrik in due course. To be clear, Thorsten and Astrid, this sentencing applies wholly to you."

"Does that mean I'm free?" said Ulrik, tiptoeing as though he were about to levitate with glee.

"Shh," whispered Astrid. "I don't know for certain yet."

"Over the last few days," added the judge, "we've heard evidence from all parties. The jury found the accused guilty on the count of *child neglect*, which, although indirectly, gave rise to the later events in which two other offences were committed: one being the *theft of corporate property*, and the other being *animal cruelty resulting in death*—the mammoth Onyx being the stolen and deceased."

Unhappy with their own legal literacy, the front row, back row, and every row of foragers in between bobbed in unrest like a current of stormy waves.

"Thorsten and Astrid, you have also been found guilty," continued the judge, "on another count of *child neglect*: that being the incident earlier this year on the ice which led to Ulrik being hospitalised. So you're being sentenced on four counts here mentioned."

Thor's sweaty hand released Astrid's. He launched himself forward, puffed out his chest, and shouted, "It seems, Your Honour, that you're more afraid to pass this sentence than I am to hear it. We know why we're here. We've heard rumours of meddling politicians. Get on with it."

The judge reclined her head and looked down her sharp nose inquiringly at him. Astrid yanked his arm, drawing him back as an owner does to a hound on a leash when it strays from the right path. "Thor, sit," she said, in a hoarse whisper. "Now isn't the time for any of your silly stunts." She raised her voice. "Please proceed, Your Honour. My husband will now be silent."

The judge dispensed a severe pout, then carried on: "To settle the damages to the state, a fine amounting to €1.2 million is owed to recover partial losses of the tourism and tax revenues that would otherwise have accrued throughout the remainder of Onyx's life."

The tide of foragers foamed and frothed with ugly passion.

"Rest of Onyx's life?" spluttered a forager. "And just how long were you supposing him to live?"

"That ill-looking mammoth was lucky to have lived as long as he did," spat another.

"Beasts of his sort don't even live this long in captivity," said another, sending forth an ocean spray from his lips as he did so.

The judge dismissed the rallying cries from the foragers. "Luckily for you, Astrid and Thorsten," she said, in a tone that suggested that what she was about to say next promised no such good fortune, "your legal status as foragers affords you an alternative. In order to settle the damages, you can pay your fine in hours worked, that is, working in a community correction programme."

"A slave camp for foragers, she's meaning," shouted a forager. "This is all the Governor's doing. He wants to put us foragers to slavery in the mines because he hates the faithless. The Republic hates nonbelievers!"

"I might remind the foragers of the gallery," said the judge, blinking with surprise and disgust, "not all ordinary citizens would have the luxury of this second option. Had the accused *not* been foragers, the other alternative at this stage would've been to hand Thorsten and Astrid an extreme prison sentence and repossess their home. That still remains a possibility ..."

Outrage flowed throughout the gallery. Invisible hands clutched hatchet handles and hunting spears.

"It's a sham trial."

"A kangaroo court."

"Where's the legal defence for us foragers?"

"Yah!" the gallery cried out, their fierce black eyes darkening with hidden intentions. As the sun passed across a window, a shaft of light sped through the glass and illuminated the dust motes floating about the air; dust motes that were so alike to foragers in their insignificance that it was easy to overlook them and forget their existence until a chance ray beamed upon them, revealing how they glowed with savage intent on never settling.

"I politely remind you," said the judge, lifting the visor of her headTech as if to impart her greatest sympathies, "that since foragers aren't taxpayers, legal aid is, unfortunately, not provided. As for the figure of €1.2 million, I can assure you this is at the lowest end of the chargeable fine."

The foragers of the gallery bared their acrid teeth and shook their dirty fists. They spent their lives in poor hygiene, but they slept with a clean conscience, for they suffered the concerns of their brethren above their own.

"So," said Thor, leaning over the balustrade, "for what length of time will we be serving in this correction programme?"

"In order to settle the €1.2 million fine, each of you, Astrid and Thorsten, will serve a total of 22,500 hours in the mines of Sveagruva. Based on the minimum continental hourly wage (€26.67 per hour), you will work forty-eight hours per week, every week of the year for the next nine years. You are to begin work next week and continue till the close of your sentence *or*, if by some extraordinary luck, your fine be paid."

Thor's head and hands seemed to vibrate; then Astrid noticed everything else about him shook, too. But when he turned to her and clasped her face in his steady palms, the seismic shaking abated. "I've got you, Astrid," he said, bringing her head to his chest. Was it she who was shaking, then? It was only when his hot hands pressed against her face that she realised her chilliness, and she drew her arms across her bosoms as though she were naked and exposed.

"As for Ulrik," said the judge, "given that you, Thorsten and Astrid, have been found guilty of two counts of child neglect, under the Journal of European Law, the Court rules that you are in no position to retain custody of your son. He must therefore be brought into the custody of the state and its system of social care."

Roaring waves of hatred dashed about the gallery.

"You mean," said Thor, in such a low key that his quivering voice was barely discernible, "you mean to be putting Ulrik into some sort of orphanage? He's my boy. A forager. You can't."

"Cheng," shouted Astrid. "Tell them they can't, Cheng!"

"That's right, you can't," announced Chenglei, waving a thick file of papers in his hand. He was dressed in brand-new clothes for the occasion: a stylish blue suit with a colourful tie depicting galactic matter and nebulae; his belt buckle was Saturn, and the strap around his waist looked like the planet's beige rings. He'd even gone to great lengths to flatten his badger-hair for the occasion (but had done so with a little too much wax). "Mrs Magnusson is correct, Your Honour. The state can't take custody of Ulrik because custody has already been granted to another guardian."

The judge was surprised to see anyone but a forager in the gallery. She gave him a slanting stare as he advanced, then beckoned him forward with an impatient hand.

"Mamma, what's he doing?" said Ulrik, tapping her arm.

"Shh, you'll see."

Eyeing the file, the judge muttered aloud to herself, "Hmm, legal guardian ... an official stamp and case reference number. Oh, a scholarship? I see. Okay ... so an application ... and granted, I take it? Yes. But in Russia? Odd choice. Swimming ... a professional coach. Lucky for some. And signatures—let me see ... here, here, and here." She cleared her throat. "Ahem, well, this is a peculiar turn of events. This will require a team of experts to verify, but if this documentation proves to be of an authentic origin, and if the legal guardian of Ulrik is indeed this Mr Vladimir Lukashenko, then the Court will rescind its decision to rehome Ulrik."

"What does that mean, Mamma?" said Ulrik, tugging at her tunic.

"It means they can't stop you going to Russia. They can't stop you pursuing your scholarship. Unlike us, you're free."

Thor's eyes sprang open with both surprise and relief.

There was a great deal of legal prattle before they drew the case to a close. When the judge stepped aside, Father Eggert came to the pulpit to deliver a closing prayer. He tilted his head to heaven and spoke in the spirit of victory: "Psalm 17:13: 'Rise up, Lord, confront them, bring them down; with your sword rescue me from the wicked.'" Then he made a sign of the cross and sang, "In the name of the Father, and of the Son, and of the Holy Gho-ooo-oooost." Then he licked his forefinger and pinched the wick of a candle as though, by some divine power invested in him, he was immune to the fiery sting of Satan.

Devils of another kind were present, it seemed. The strike of hooves on the ground sounded throughout when the foragers of the gallery rose in unison, their red faces glowing, horns a-blowing—battle-horns they were, blasting out hellish booms. And those without such horns commenced a satanic screaming. The only law enforcement officer on duty fled after saying he didn't get paid enough to risk his life.

The foragers showed him mercy. They were here to cause no violence, only vandalism.

"Impertinent, pertinacious, and obstinate heretics," said Father Eggert, crouching behind the altar and clutching the crucifix at his breast.

First to be ravaged by the foragers' ravenous hands were the purple banners of the House of Abraham; they were badly rent, then taken outside, where they were torched and cast into the wind like flaming kites. Then came the violating of the altars and toppling of statues. Stones were catapulted through the stained-glass panes, benches were scarred with spears, posts were hacked with axes, and sacred texts were corrupted with vulgar bodily fluids.

Father Eggert prayed and prayed, but no divine intervention prevented the ransacking of the Lord's own church that day.

When Ulrik, Astrid, and Thorsten escaped the fray, they found themselves alone in Father Eggert's guest lounge—where they'd spent a good deal of time waiting during every adjournment of the proceedings. It was dotted with antiques and other curious oddments: oil paintings, tapestries, leather-bound books, quills, wax stamps, tobacco pipes, cigars, and century-old red wines. From these lavish quarters, they could still hear the thud of axes, the ringing of steel, and the tunes of horror playing out on the pipe organ as two foragers fornicated wildly over it—changing position often, so it sounded.

Lying supine on the polar bear rug, Ulrik had the look of one who'd washed up dead on some sandy shore, while Thor paced about from wall to wall repeating, "What do we do?"

"We keep going," said Astrid, folding her arms and hugging herself. "We have no other choice."

"Shut up! For once, woman, say nothing. I can't tolerate your voice when I need to think."

Her blood burned as though it were viscous magma flowing through her veins. The words of retort died away on her tongue. Not that it mattered. He never listened anyway.

For three entire days Thor hadn't set eyes on Ulrik; it was as though to look at his own son was equal to the damage done when gazing directly at the sun. When he finally turned to him, with his copper head glowing hot and buzzing like some industrial lightbulb, he said, "Do you realise what you've done? You've broken our family!"

"You may think," said Astrid, reaching out with a sharp finger, "that it's okay to be speaking to me like that, Thor, but I won't let you speak to my son like that."

Ulrik shrank into the furthest armchair of the room and there hugged a cushion.

"Astrid, in stealing that mammoth, he's sentenced us to nine years of hard labour. Nine years. He's ruined our lives. Ruined." His strained eyes were like those of a killer, but his desperate demeanour was that of a victim.

"I didn't *steal* Onyx," said Ulrik, flinging the cushion, which toppled a stack of hymn books. "I set him free, but I wouldn't expect you to be knowing the difference."

"Yah, you set him free … and killed him in doing so."

"Better that than to be living a life stuck in prison."

"Stuck … like you, living here on Svalbard?"

"Nuh, stuck like you working in the mines. Now you're going to learn how it feels to be held captive."

Thor's head turned red as though it was about to detonate: "Don't you speak to me like that, you little—"

"Lucky for you, Pappa, I'm going to be earning the money to pay your fine and set you free."

"Oh, *my* fine? Bah-hah! Tell me, how do you hope to be earning €1.2 million? Selling photographs and T-shirts with your picture on them? Nightclub appearances, maybe? The famous Homo Nova in the circus? Nuh, boy, these are arrogant ambitions."

Through gritted teeth: "I'm going to do what I've always wanted: I'm going to swim in a real pool—at the Olympics. If I win gold, nuh, *when* I win gold, there'll be prize money, which I'll use to set you free."

"Ah, these dreams of yours. There are no guarantees you'll even qualify to go to the Olympics. You haven't even raced competitively. And you're thinking you'll win gold and set us free? I've let you run with this dream of yours because I thought it would give you something to distract you from Brynolf and the bullies; to distract you from Ivar's death. But it's time you knew the truth: you're a forager, and you'll never be good enough."

"I'm not a stinking forager; I'm Homo Nova," deepening his voice by a noticeable degree, as if he were trying hard to become a man. "And what would you know about my dreams? You wouldn't know how hard I've been training or how much I've suffered. Where were you when I swam through the night? You don't know me. Ever since Dr Lyngstad said I could be Homo Nova, you've hated the idea. I have a chance to be living a better life, and you want to trap me in Thrudheim. But I'm not like you;

you're afraid of being different or doing anything different or meeting anybody different. You want to know what I fear the most? An ordinary life. This isn't living, it's surviving. I hate being a stinking forager, but not as much as I hate being your son."

"The gods will not like this, Ulrik," said Thor, his voice becoming froggy.

"I don't believe in your stupid gods. I never have." Ulrik snapped the hammer necklace from around his neck, slung it across the room, and yelled, "I only ever pretended I did to make you proud."

Thor bent low to the ground and scooped the necklace up. He cupped it in his hand, and when he'd finished rubbing his thumb over it, he stowed it away in his pocket. "Ulrik, I'm sorry you turned out the way you did. Go now, and be a disappointment to me no more."

"Get out," said Astrid, her stiff arm pointing to the door.

Thor made for the door and would've crashed through it had Chenglei not entered at the same time.

"Oh, hello, Thorsten," said Cheng, slackening his cosmic tie knot and loosening his Saturn belt. "Heading out?"

Thor towered over him, bared his square teeth, and growled so that Chenglei backed himself up to the wall. "You,"—prodding his hollow, bony chest—"this is all your fault. If you hadn't taken my son to the Sanctuary in the first place, none of this would've happened."

Chenglei feigned a smile, but his bottom lip quivered the harder he tried. After Thor slammed the door and fled, Chenglei took himself to the window where he cupped his own fragile hands and looked out at the mountains in silence.

As the sun retired westward, the room seemed wrapped in a grey haze, and everything within it seemed bereft of warmth and life.

"Give him time, Cheng," said Astrid, taking his hands in hers and quelling the tremor. "He's not himself."

"Yah, he is," said Ulrik, the black kohl around his eyes smudged from crying. "He's always like this."

"Ulrik," she said, "you know nothing about what shadows his past.

There are things which even I don't know about him. Your pappa is ... troubled."

"That's no excuse for treating us the way he does. Anyway, enough about him; he's gone now, and I hope to never be seeing him again. I mean it this time. I do. You know I do, don't you?"

"He might not say it," said Chenglei, stepping away from the window and trying his best to smile, "but your pappa loves you, Ulrik. Behind his worst actions are the best intentions."

Ulrik came forward and embraced Chenglei like a grandfather or uncle, and he thanked and praised him for arranging the scholarship with Vladimir Lukashenko. "Cheng, I thought that after what I did with Onyx you'd be angry at me."

"I've been very upset. What you did was very irresponsible ... but it was also very brave and, I might add,"—winking—"quite crafty, using the fire alarm for cover. I can't be mad, Ulrik. Onyx was at his happiest with you, and I'm grateful for the love you showed him. Let me now apologise for abandoning you when I had to fly to and from the mainland. Arrangements were a little more complicated than expected."

"Is everything ready?" said Astrid.

"Everything, as promised. Our flight tickets are for open travel, which means that if you wanted to, we could catch the next one ... today." Chenglei handed Ulrik his very own DRUE passport; it was purple, and gilded with a Sword of Abraham at its centre.

A look of astonishment flashed on Ulrik's face as he traded a glance with his mother then Chenglei. "You're serious ..."

"I am."

Astrid watched his pupils reduce to the size of pinpricks while considering his options. "You don't need to worry about Pappa, Ulrik," pressing the passport to his heart. "This is about you."

"Will I get to say goodbye?"

She let slip a heavy sigh. "You know he'd talk you out of it, and we don't want him to be doing that, do we? Ulrik, I don't know much about swimming, but I know that to be the best at anything you have to be willing to do things others are unwilling to do. Leaving Thrudheim today is one of those things. During my life I've come to learn that if ever a road is painful, you should continue on that road, for greater strength comes from a greater share of life's sufferings. So be brave and take the path of most resistance because it's only there that pain will forge a champion of you."

When he blinked, she perceived a subtle yet radical shift in his eyes; her words emboldened him so he now seemed a sleeping giant awoken: his outlook was now one of belief and aspiration. She grabbed him, kissed him, and gave him a parting headbutt. Then, being careful not to overwhelm him with love and emotion—since too much sympathy might invoke in him a desire to stay—she turned her shoulder and looked solemnly out of the window.

"We'll be seeing you soon, then," said Chenglei, the door creaking as he made his exit.

"Cheng, wait," said Astrid, blowing her nose on a linen handkerchief. "I need to speak with you alone. Ulrik, wait for Cheng outside. Remember everything I've said to you, won't you?"

"I will, Mamma. And remember, one way or another, I'm going to rid our family of this debt. I know Pappa doesn't believe me, but this is my promise. You believe me, don't you?"

"I do," she lied. "With all my heart."

The door clicked shut, and she heard Ulrik's cumbersome footsteps fading away. Springs emerged from her eyes and streams ran down her cheeks.

She clutched her breast. "What k-kind"—heavy pant—"of mamma is she"—heavy pant—"who is allowing"—heavy pant—"her fledgling to fly away before he can flap his wings?"

"You've done the right thing," said Chenglei. "He's been shut up here like an insect in amber. Here, take some of this water." He handed her a bottle from which she slurped every drop. Then she drew her forearm across her face to dab away the spillages on her chin.

"I just hope it works out for him, Cheng. All this methylation, switching genes on, kaleidoscopic genome, the fame, everything. I hope he's ready for it."

"Astrid, at this stage we just don't know the transcriptional potential of his genome. As I've said from the very beginning, it's *possible* that he could switch on a gene to better his swimming, but not *probable*. But I'll tell you what is more than probable: under Vlad's stewardship, Homo Nova or not, Ulrik will receive world-class training."

"Just promise me he'll be safe, Cheng. I've heard terrible things; terrible things about the attacks at the last Olympics."

"You mean the Saifullah terrorist attacks? I understand your concern, but there's a military presence at all major events these days. Try not to worry about the *what ifs*, silly." He knocked on her crown with a sharp tap of his knuckles.

"Hah-ouch," rubbing her head. "Is that supposed to reassure me?"

"Well, take comfort in this: the Munich Olympics this summer weren't so bad."

"So bad?"

"Yeah, every single plot was foiled. These days, military security is just the new norm. So put that out of your mind, otherwise you'll go crazy before these next four years are over."

"Go, then, before I do go crazy." She reached out her arms; not for a headbutt but a parting hug. Then she pressed her lips to his squidgy cheek. "Cheng, thank you ... for everything."

He placed a hand on each of her shoulders, gave her the softest headbutt, the paper fan wrinkles at the corner of his eyes deepening as he smiled, and bade her good health. "I'll see you soon, Astrid."

"Very soon, I'm hoping."

When Chenglei disappeared, Astrid remained behind and pilfered the reserves of Father Eggert's wine from the mahogany rack. She filled her bloody glass to the brim and found company in those portraits on the walls. Standing at the centre of the lounge, she entered into a contest of stares with one particular portrait of the Holy Shepherd. His heaven-white locks rested on his shoulders like snow on the boughs of a slender elm. In this image, he toiled in an armoury about an anvil, tempering the Sword of Abraham. Beneath the portrait was a gold plaque into which was engraved:

When I sharpen my flashing sword and my hand grasps it in judgment, I will take vengeance on my adversaries and repay those who hate me.
— Deuteronomy 32:41 —

In like preparation, without breaking her gaze or blinking, Astrid whetted her fingernails with a coarse pebble (a forager nail file of sorts, which she kept in her upper breast pocket). Then she blew away the debris and held them out like ten spangled spears; and when she remembered what the Holy Shepherd had said in an interview about Ulrik, she wanted to claw them through the canvas. "What is it you were saying about my son?" she said, aloud to the portrait. "'Beware the work of scientists,' you said, 'for theirs is the work of the Antichrist; and likely it is that this boy Ulrik has been spawned in some lab.'" The strain in her eyes caused them to twitch. "You must feel threatened by my son to be speaking about him in such a way." She blinked and forfeited the contest of stares.

At least Ulrik would be safe in Russia. Despite the rumours and reports people conjured about the place, it was a country unaffiliated with DRUE and one of the last bastions of Europe not under the jurisdiction of the Holy Shepherd. No Holy Shepherd; no Whitehoods; no Saifullah; no House of Abraham.

The sun set for the last time that year on Svalbard, and the Arctic moved back to the dark side of the world. The long black days had come.

CHAPTER SEVENTEEN

THE PHIAL OF BLOOD

The black veil of winter was drawn over the Arctic. Blacker still it was underground when toiling away in the mines of Sveagruva. Anyone who went into those underground manufactories came out covered in the sootiest film, and, in similar aspect to the raven, not a single tinge of another colour could be detected in their plumage. Such is how the foragers came to know their station as Ravensvik (Ravens' Bay).

Their wild nature made the foragers effective and profitable workers, being, as they were, so disposed to physical labour and the frequent risking of their lives. No breed of folk was better suited to that frightening line of work than those whose fear is routinely checked by the perilous Arctic. They were the best of slaves.

In the belly of the earth a cage ascended the mineshaft, the screech of unoiled axles piercing the ears of those waiting to begin their shift. Among those waiting was Astrid, who fixed her hair under her helmet and did so with much less trouble than before when it'd flowed freely about her haunches in the thickest lengths of twine. As the mine cage approached the platform, it gave one almighty screech, and its angry brakes sparked in protest.

Out poured the miscreants with blackened faces, who always came out coughing up and sneezing out black nasal syrups, for deposits of grit lined their airways. Most no longer donned their strong beards or virile locks as before. Being shorn of their hair like a lamb is of its wool, they seemed a good deal skinnier. Perhaps they were skinnier because of the insoluble grit of coal they ingested throughout their daily toil; perhaps their appetites were tricked in much the same way as the famished gull whose belly brims with ocean plastic.

The foragers swapped their hard hats for woollen hats and their luminous jackets for fur pelts, though they might have been better suited to striped pyjamas of blue and grey, since many were destined to die in that camp. Before they quit the mines and marked their shifts as complete, they each genuflected to a portrait of the Holy Shepherd, who in this painting had his silver brow raised to the crest of his forehead, as though he was on the lookout for any soul who refused to pay their respects to his intelligent designs. And below this was a gold plaque engraved with the verse:

> *Slaves, obey your earthly masters with respect and*
> *fear and sincerity of heart.*
> — Ephesians 6:5 —

Where was Thor? Astrid tapped her feet, chewed the ends of her hair, and leant over the guardrail with her neck outstretched. He was harder to spot these days, for he no longer appeared above the tops of the others' heads with his usual height difference, and his back was hunched from the strain of life's burdens. But then, not so far away, she heard a sneeze. Not an ordinary sneeze.

"Tchoo—tchow—tchee—tchar—tchah."

There he was, sneezing away and looking like some woodpecker pecking away at a thick bough as he did so.

"Over here, Thor!" She waved frantically at him, and when she caught his attention, she saw how he extended his spine and how his plant-green eyes lit up again with the hue of spring.

As he passed through the exit lane, and as she passed through the entry lane, they each kissed their own fingertips. With their wet hands, they reached across the lane separating them, their fingertips latching onto one another's for less than a second before the current of foragers heading both ways dragged them apart, and Astrid was swept into the mine cage before she could tell him she loved him. Here, she pressed her lips to her fingertips, having had his kiss transferred to them.

That brief glimpse at their bittersweet tryst was all they saw of each other on their working days. She knew they'd been separated on purpose; kept apart to grind them down.

The rattling cage plunged down the mineshaft. It was so densely packed with foragers that she could feel hands pressed up against her and moist breath tickling her neck. Lower and lower they descended, all the while the air thickening and the heat rising, bringing an attack of sweat to every forehead. They were almost two miles closer to the earth's core, where magma oceans flow and, as legends have it, the Devil governs. Bound for hell, unless they repent and convert, or so they were always told by those in authority.

The mine cage groaned before grinding to the severest halt, and the foragers went their separate ways to their stations. Astrid was one of the few nimbler foragers whose job was to crawl down a branch of burrows and there take up sapper duties.

So began her daily drilling where she bored conduits through the heart of the earth for the running of cables. Here, in the acoustic confinements of those airless tunnels, did the shrill ring of her drill perforate her eardrums. Then, at required intervals, she buttressed the conduit walls to prevent them from collapsing in on her. Her crawlspace was so narrow that she could hardly stray an elbow left or right. Turning around was impossible, except maybe for a youngling. To head out, she had to crawl backwards. Still, at least there was room only for one in here. It was a place of solitude—something she'd never had.

After a while, the air grew close and clammy. Normal breathing was difficult to maintain. Dizzying blotches appeared in her vision like a colourful cosmos. Now a throbbing headache. Off with her helmet. Then, wriggling in her compartment, she tore off her clothes, save her undergarments. Exhausted, she lay there for a while and made a pillow out of dirt where she rested her head, promising herself she'd get back to work in just a few moments. But the stifling heat demanded that her eyes close, and she dozed off, drooling.

An hour passed. Then two. Then ten. A siren rang out. The end of the shift!

As Astrid came to her senses, she dressed herself and wormed her body backwards in haste, grazing the skin of her knees and elbows as she did so.

When arriving at the mineshaft, she saw nobody else around—except the abject creature operating the shaft. As her head torch panned over him, his eyes, for a moment, had a red hue about them, like that of vermin that delve into sewers and there find themselves in their most comfortable habitat.

"We haff a straggler, I see," said the forager, who housed not a single tooth in his bleeding gums. As she approached, he unbuttoned the collar of his shirt down to his sternum; his grey chest hair was bedraggled with sweat.

"Ah, I know you. You're Eirik the Ruthless, aren't you? You were one of the first foragers who settled on Svalbard." He was once a man of reputation, though his reputation was now that of a traitor.

"Bah-hah!" He let out a wheezy, whistling laugh, and his chest seemed to rattle when he coughed. "Eirik va Toofless vey are calling me now 'cause I got no teefs; see ..."

"Very nice, Eirik. Now, tell me, am I too late?" with a flirtatious flick of her hair, cringing all the while inside. "I think I was so busy with my loud drilling that I didn't hear the siren."

"It's a good job for you vat today I'm delayed; else you'd be spending va Sabbaff down here. And you know what va punishment is for working on va Sabbaff, don't you, naughty woman?"

"Yah, yah, I do," giving him a playful tap on the elbow, at which she sensed him shudder: the kind of shudder that affects a man who hasn't felt a woman's warmth in many winters. "Sorry, Eirik, I was so lost in my work—and my love for the Republic. You love the Republic, don't you? Thank you for waiting for me, you sweet, sweet man. It's true that not all gentlemen wear ties." She fanned her eyelashes at him.

The fickle creature licked his bleeding gums and tapped the bill of his hard hat. Her grovelling delighted him. "All right, but only 'cause it's you. In you go."

He cranked a rusty lever, and the doors of the mine cage trapped her inside. Safe and alone. The carriage hauled her out of the depths of the underworld. She shuddered, paranoid with the belief that she'd contracted some disease during her contact with Toothless. She scoured her hand against the ridged soles of her boots to rid it of any lingering germs. "Eugh, if I were ever to lose even a single tooth, I don't think I'd ever show my face in public again. Ever, ever, ever."

When alighting from the mine cage at the top, an eerie silence struck her like a chill. There wasn't a soul about. But of course: hers was the last shift of the week, tomorrow being the Sabbath. All the miners and supervisors had left.

After swapping her overalls for her furs, she made her escape; and in passing through, she halted at the portrait of the Holy Shepherd. Ordinarily, she'd pay her respects with a genuflection, but with nobody else around, she considered breaking the commandment. She checked over both shoulders. Still alone. Nobody would know. Her feet faced the exit, but her body remained orientated towards the portrait. For a while she stood in a state of twisted hesitation. What if there was a hidden camera behind those all-seeing eyes about to capture evidence of her dissent? Not wanting to spend weeks haunted by the paranoia, she submitted a reverent bow to the Holy Shepherd and burst outside before she burst into tears.

It was too cold to cry out here. Having spent the day sweltering in the mines, the freezing air came as a welcome regulator; and when she sucked in a tremendous gust of breath, it felt as though a frost formed on the back of her throat and glazed her tonsils with ice. Tonight, the sky was one of jewellery: the platinum gleam of the moon, the twinkling diamond stars, the ruby of Mars. It saddened her to think that of all the mineable rocks, coal was the one she slaved over.

While basking under the starlight, two giant mittens came from behind and smothered her face, albeit unthreateningly. "Guess who," said a voice, squeaking to disguise its usual ruggedness.

"Oh, let me see ... mittens with terrible holes ... hands smelling like fish ... hmm. You've got me wondering. Which of my husbands could it be?"

She backed her haunches into Thor and drew his arms across her chest. His arms felt sharper about the elbows and wrists. He was lighter and thinner for their lack of wholesome, hearty meals, since, after a day at the mine and the terrible commute there and back, they had little energy left for hunting. After Ulrik had gone abroad, their supply of crabs and krill had ceased overnight. Their poor diet had a lesser effect on her, being of a dainty build, but for Thor, his muscles seemed to soften. They no longer felt like tough meat, and he came out in bruises at the slightest knock, like a perished apple. But that didn't matter to her: he still pressed his kisses with the same affection.

"I've been waiting for you, Astrid,"—they squashed lips—"but when I couldn't find you, you had me worrying."

"Sorry," she said, nuzzling her face under his arm. "I fell asleep. Couldn't keep my eyes open. Not even through the sleepless nights when Ulrik was a tiny fledgling have I been so tired. So tired, Thor. I can't keep doing this."

"Here, let's get you home." He swept her up in his arms, but she pushed off his chest and planted her feet firmly in the snow.

"Nuh, I prefer to walk off my aches," she lied, supposing him too weak for the task.

"Why walk? I've repaired our kicksleds, and I've even made a custom modification to them."

"Amazing." She drew in a deep, calm breath and held it in for a prolonged moment. She felt a buoyancy in her body again—inner happiness at the news. Then, when she exhaled, she reacquainted herself with her kicksled. Without delay, she hopped on, and from Ravensvik the two of them sped across miles of snowy hills, bound for Thrudheim.

"Anyway," she said, "what was so important that you came to meet me after work? You've never done that before."

"Gah, I almost forgot to say. A letter has come. Delivered by postal drone."

"From Ulrik?"

Thor nodded. "Well, the address on the envelope is written in Cheng's handwriting."

"Show it to me," driving her heel into the ground and bringing her kicksled to a halt.

"I left it at Thrudheim. The wind being fierce tonight, I didn't want to risk bringing it out and losing it."

"Haven't you read it?"

"Call me what you will, but I'm no sneak. I wouldn't read it without you."

Without a word, she sped on at such a dogged pace that he struggled to keep up with her for most of the journey. A favourable wind being at their backs, they drew off their cloaks and attached them to a sort of mast which Thor had newly modified (a single baton of vertical timber affixed to the frame of the kicksled), forming a makeshift sail; and like windsurfers, they were blown along at the speed of a light jog with no extra effort on their part.

When they arrived at Thrudheim, Thor built a fire in the hearth and lit every available candle; soon the air in the longhouse was toasty—or at least toastier. While Thor poked and stoked the fire, Astrid made a record of her days worked by scratching a tally on a slat of wood with a knife. They'd served over three years in the mines. Neither had the will to see out another six.

She stumbled to the bedroom and collapsed on the straw bed; her weary eyelids clamped shut of their own accord.

"Thor, read me this letter before I fall into an endless sleep."

"All right, all right, give me a chance. I'm here now anyway," he said, crinkling what sounded like an envelope. He tore through the paper with the grace of a hound. "Huh—what's this?"

"What?" shooting bolt upright and prising her eyelids apart with her fingers.

"There's a …" he eyed a peculiar object while holding it up to the candlelight, "a phial of blood. Nuh, wait; there are two phials of blood. Test tubes. But they look different."

Both were red, yet one was of ordinary hue and was labelled 'Typical blood sample'. The other, labelled 'Ulrik's blood sample', was so luminous under the candlelight that it appeared like a neon glow stick. Astrid snatched the vial to get a closer look. Turning it over in her hand, she noticed that, when compared to the watery properties of typical blood, Ulrik's sample had a consistency more akin to a thin red-pepper soup.

"I don't understand," said Thor, thumping the bedside table with his hammer-fist.

"The envelope—was there anything else in there? Here, pass it to me." As he handed it to her, a slip of crinkled paper fell out. They caught it at the same time so that now both pairs of hands held onto a side each. Written on it was a message in Chenglei's handwriting—even shakier than usual and no doubt rushed:

Magnussons,

Excuse my brevity. Ulrik's coach, Vlad, was concerned. So sent me a blood sample from Ulrik. For comparison, I enclose a sample of mine. You'll notice Ulrik's blood is a strong crimson. Not to mention thicker. It's due to a rich concentration of haemoglobin—a red protein which transports oxygen to muscles. But that's not everything. There's another globin: myoglobin. An oxygen-storing protein found in muscles. Whales, otters, beavers, and seals (deep-diving mammals) have myoglobin in abundance. Enables them to hold their breath underwater for long durations. Results show similar concentrations in Ulrik. In short, looks like Ulrik is more effective at transporting and storing oxygen.

Need more time to study, but all evidence so far points to this being genetic reversion … his kaleidoscopic genome has been busy altering the expression of his genes in response to his training. Vlad is trialling some special technique. Won't tell me what, but says it's a feat no swimmer has ever accomplished before. Not competitively. Keeps me awake at night wondering.

P.S. Something even more unbelievable happened just now. Vlad just called me on Tech. Told me Ulrik broke the world record for holding his breath underwater. Unofficially, of course. Said not to tell anyone. But had to tell you.

Good health,
Cheng.

Chapter Eighteen

RUTHLESS PREPARATIONS

"Imagine," said a raspy voice, so badly scoured by the smoking of cigarettes that one could be forgiven for supposing they'd been smoked backwards. "Imagine if you knew that somewhere this morning your rival awoke one hour before you did to train harder and become stronger, to rob you of your gold medal."

"Uhm, wha'?" said Ulrik, halfway between dream world and reality.

"Imagine if," continued the raspy voice, "with only five months to go until the Athens Olympics, I found you sleeping in past your alarm."

Ulrik snorted and shot up. Too much crust in his eyes prevented him from seeing properly, but he knew the hour was early: the birds weren't twittering, and pitch-black enveloped the world. But there was no delay in the arousal of his sense of smell, for Vlad's breath wafted over from a considerable distance; last night's brandy and this morning's breakfast: coffee, cigarette, and spearmint gum.

When Ulrik cleared his eyes, he saw Vlad's silhouette, and at the centre of his face there glowed a tiny orange ember. Puff—smoky vapour filled the air. At once, the duvet was dragged away from him, and the light switch was hit repeatedly to disorientate him. Even before Vlad hit the light switch, Ulrik knew what outfit he'd be wearing. Perhaps the only predictable thing about Vlad was his wearing of the same clothes each day: discoloured blue jeans and a tight black T-shirt, robbed of their original appeal long ago having had their softness steam-ironed into oblivion.

"Agh, sorry, Coach," said Ulrik, pinching his eyes to defend them from the dazzling light. "Are you forgetting today is my eighteenth birthday? I thought I could take an extra hour to rest, and—"

"Oh, you did, did you?" smacking and clacking a pellet of chewing gum about his mouth. "D'ya think Shayne O'Shaughnessy is asleep? Fuck no. Shayne O'Fucking-Shaughnessy swims on Christmas fucking Day, and he's Catholic. Here's my birthday present to you: my time. Now stop wasting it."

Ordinarily, Vlad's face was like a bare rock, grey and rugged, but the rosacea on his nose and cheeks had flared up a monstrous red. The coarse black bristles on his neck and arms seemed to spring out like a porcupine's quills. "Do you sit down to piss?" he said, inserting another pellet of gum.

"Sit down to piss, Coach?"

"Since you're eighteen,"—putting his cigarette out on the sole of his boot—"I thought you'd wake up today a man. But opposite me I see only a little girl. So I ask if you sit down to piss."

"Yah, Coach. I mean nuh, Coach. I don't sit down to piss."

"Well, are you going to grow some balls and tell me why you're not sleeping in the altitude tent?"

"I must've been sleepwalking again."

"Don't give me excuses. Weak people make excuses." Chew, chomp, champ. "Do you realise how important this is? Sleeping in that tent increases your red blood count so your body can deliver more oxygen to your muscles when swimming." He threw up his hands then lit another cigarette, waving it this way and that as though it were a magic wand. "Pssh."

"But I've been getting headaches from holding my breath underwater so much during the day, and sleeping in the altitude tent at night has been making my headaches worse. The air is too thin. It's so hard to breathe."

"That's what an altitude tent is supposed to do. You think I enjoy paying for expensive shit for you not to use?" In one deep drag, the length of his newest cigarette turned to a rod of ash, and he let slip a croaky groan which signified his mellowing. "Anyway, you should know Cheng is visiting later. I've arranged for him to meet us at the pool, where you'll be able to show him what you've learnt."

Cheng! That was welcome news ... but the pool? He hoped it wasn't that grimy pool in that abandoned fishing town. Most of the time Vlad had him training in the lake or racing against the rapids of the River Volga, but every once in a while they travelled for hours to this old abandoned indoor pool. The water was stagnant, and years' worth of accreted scum floated atop in a sticky skin of brown oil. It smelt like a horror scene, especially in the showers, where gruesome drainage was regurgitated through the plugholes as if the sewers themselves thought the waste too putrid to stomach.

Before Vlad turned out of the door, he cocked his head and surveyed Ulrik, his clay-grey face as rugged as ever. "How badly do you want this?"

"More than anything." Ulrik hesitated. "I-I ... I want this more than you could ever know. I owe it to Ivar, Onyx, Mamma, Pappa."

"Who are you trying to convince?" Chew, chomp, champ. "Me or yourself?" Puff—smoke. "Take it from me, silver medals are for those who make excuses—those who don't show up when they're supposed to. A silver medal is as good as no medal because a silver medal isn't a gold medal. Understand?"

Before Ulrik could reply, the door clicked shut. It was only when he was alone that he happened to look down and, to his surprise, saw he was already in his swimming trunks. Sleepwalking—again. He propped up his face with his fist and sang "Happy Birthday" to himself.

Of all the wishes a teen could dream up for an eighteenth birthday, Ulrik desired only to see his mamma and pappa again, if only for an hour. But visions of Mamma scolding him came to the forefront of his imagination: "If ever a road is painful," she said, with her sharp finger inches away from his nose, "then continue on that road, for greater strength comes from a greater share of life's sufferings." He dabbed his shrub-green eyes with a hairy knuckle and inhaled a deep, spirited wind through his nostrils. Then he stood up and creaked his spine, pivoting at the hips and twisting his shoulders this way and that, motivated now for his daily suffering.

"Form," said Vlad, with a chew, chomp, champ. "What have I told you about form? Tighten your shoulders. Stretch those arms to the max." Vlad's commands came to his ears through two waterproof earphones. Somehow, the earTech muffled the croaky garble of his smoker's cords and made him sound much less of a tyrant underwater. "Now turn yourself into the fish kick. Go!"

While underwater, Ulrik turned on his side and stretched his arms over his head, bringing himself into the shape of an arrow as he oscillated this way and that like some lithe eel. He managed this while being fully clothed since Vlad insisted he master the stroke under the constraints of this handicap.

"Hold it. Keep it there. Wait. No. Fuck no. Back. You had it before. Go back. Argh. Stop, stop, stop!"

Having resurfaced, Ulrik swallowed huge volumes of air while striding through the shallow water, his clothes dripping, or rather raining about him as he advanced to the poolside. Vlad was busy scrawling diagrams on a whiteboard; his red pen seemed to squeak in terror under the ferocious drag of his illustrations.

"This is your body now: you're well hinged at your hips and torso,"— hands gesturing—"but your shoulders and knees are too rigid. You're like a stiff dick, but you need to be flaccid. Understand?" Vlad circled his sketch with the pen—squeak—then he underlined it—squeak—after which he drew an exclamation mark beside it—screaming squeak. "You can't swim in a straight line when you're unbalanced. What good is all that power if you can't control your direction down there?"

"Maybe if I could be swimming *without* clothes then I—"

Vlad threw up his arms as though to parry the incoming excuses. "Weak people make excuses. You're not one, so I don't want to hear you speaking like one. You'd do well to remember what your mamma said to you before you came here: 'take the path of most resistance.'"

"You're right, Coach," his thoughts now fixed on rescuing Mamma from that life of slavery. "I'll do better next time. I promise."

"*Better* won't bring us a gold medal home. Today was *better*. Every day you get *better*, but it's not enough. Shayne O'Shaughnessy is a locomotive genius—a hammerhead shark. Where's your killer instinct? I know it's in there. I've seen it once or twice. But where the fuck is it now?"

"Sorry, Coach."

"I don't want you to be sorry. I want you to be angry. Unsatisfied. Fucked off. Get nasty. Stop smiling."

"I'm not smi—"

"Why aren't you fucked off? Where's your inner cunt?" Vlad jumped into the pool fully clothed. Then he waded up to him and prodded his skull. "Set the inner cunt free. Yes, your form is sloppy, but I can fix that. Right now, forget about it being you versus Shayne. It's about you versus yourself." He prodded his skull again. "You're a forager, aren't you? Wild. Primal. This is about survival. It's do or die. You're fighting for your parents' lives. Release the cunt in you." Prod, prod, prod.

"I can win gold," peering through the blond forelocks of his fringe. "I mean, I'm *going to* win gold."

"Again, who are you trying to convince?" with a chew, chomp, champ.

Before Ulrik could reply, there was a sharp, clear tapping at the external window. Outside, there stood a man watching them with his face pressed up to the glass. With the sun rolling behind him, none of his features were discernible; they saw only a black silhouette tapping a key or small stone on the window, and when the stranger had their attention, he waved with the most amiable spirit.

"Ah, Cheng is here," said Vlad, leaping out of the pool. "Stay here and plank at the poolside until I return." He gave a harsh double-clap, which Ulrik interpreted as a direct order to double his speed in getting into position. As Vlad disappeared, Ulrik climbed out. With clothes still sodden to the core, he laid himself down into a prone position, pressed himself up, and held himself aloft under the strain of his aching, shaking limbs.

While planking, he looked on through the window at Vlad greeting Chenglei. At first, they shook hands, then they hugged. It infuriated Ulrik to see Vlad pay him such courtesy, but he supposed he wouldn't like to get within hugging distance of him anyway, owing to his sickening breath. It was a pity for Cheng that he was so polite; anyone else in such close proximity would've turned away to fake a sneeze and catch a fresh supply of clean air when doing so.

A short while later, to the relief of Ulrik's shaking arms, Cheng burst in throwing an excitable wave with both hands. Ulrik collapsed for a while and lay panting like a hound until the burning in his shoulders abated.

"Ulrik Magnusson, well, aren't you just a blond clone of your pappa? You look so alike."

"I hope not," he said, rising; his face screwed up while his breathing returned to normal.

"Body language' ..." said Vlad, reminding him. Ulrik relaxed his face and straightened his spine in the manner of a soldier on parade. "Good, good."

"And such a deep voice since we last met," said Cheng. "You're not the child I remember." They greeted with a headbutt. "And your beard—it's like a lion's mane. Oh,"—knuckling his own forehead—"how rude of me. Happy eighteenth birthday! Shall I sing to you? Come on, Vlad, let's sing to him. One, two, thr—"

"I would hate that," said Ulrik, burying his eyebrows halfway down his face.

"Aha! Such a grump." Cheng knuckled him on the head. "Well, maybe it'll cheer you up to know I have a surprise for you."

"A surprise—for me?"

Cheng winked at him and said he'd have to wait until later to find out what it was. Judging by the sparkle in his eyes, Ulrik supposed the surprise to be excellent.

While Ulrik and Cheng got reacquainted, Vlad scratched his head as furiously as if there were an army of lice attacking his prickly scalp. His impatience got the better of him, and steering the conversation to his own interests, he interrupted: "So, what's your first impression of this place, my friend?"

"Well," said Cheng, turning away from Ulrik to inspect the health of the property, "it's got to be one of the strangest places I've ever been. Not just this pool, but this whole abandoned Soviet town. How did you ever stumble across it?"

"I simply looked for it," said Vlad, standing with his hands tucked beneath his armpits and his chin inclined. "I had only two criteria when seeking such a place: it had to be in a state of dilapidation and also discreet. See, we don't have the funds for wave pools or the latest Tech." Chew, chomp, champ. "We can't even afford cleaners. Good, I say. I wouldn't want any of that crap. As I always say: feed a kid until he's full, and he'll have no room for dessert; but starve a kid—deprive a kid—and when the time comes he'll peck up every crumb, lick every plate clean, and beg for every sliver of success. Desire, my friend—those who've never known hunger have the appetite only for—"

"Silver medals ... I know," said Cheng in a tone suggesting he'd heard the sentence said in excess of a hundred times.

Vlad bitterly hated the colour silver, so much so that when they first took over management of this decaying leisure centre, he had Ulrik daub every chrome balustrade, handrail, piece of furniture, and fixture with black paint.

"Come, my friend," he said now, gesturing around the grungy facility with the pride of a museum curator. "It'd be my pleasure to give you a tour." Ulrik dived back into the pool and swam a few circuits while Vlad and Cheng strolled around. But at all times he kept his earTech connected, curious as to what they might talk about. It was strange to imagine these two people, so wholly dissimilar, having any similarities or mutual interests.

Vlad referred to it as a property with character. Twisted vines had found their way in via a missing roof tile and crept across the conduit overhead; dangling from the same overhead pipework by their nylon laces was a pair of browned sneakers from the days when shoe-tossing was a troublesome sport for terrible teenagers; elsewhere, a pigeon or rat scratched about in the labyrinths of the ventilation; then, when they happened upon the changing rooms, Ulrik knew Cheng was pinching his nose, for his n's sounded like d's and his m's like b's: "Yep, yep, I see how these co'ditiods could botivate Ulrik to wid a gold bedal."

"Look at the state of these," said Vlad. No doubt Vlad was showing Cheng the lockers, which were scarred with profanities.

It's a common yet universal obsession among rebellious teenagers to endow blank surfaces with designs of abstract penises. Of those etched into the lockers, some were short and stubby; others long and thin; some cried, others sighed; many wore hoods, others were hoodless; others had bald, cyclopean heads; all had monstrous veins.

"Savages," said Cheng, still pinching his nose.

To his relief, they moved on, and through his earTech Ulrik could hear the hissing of the lavatory cisterns as they made their way back to the poolside. He resurfaced from the water heaving in and out frenzied breaths. Then he took out the pair of earTech pods. This was the only Tech Ulrik had ever used since being in Russia. Coach Lukashenko had banned Tech of any form to keep him from distractions that he said warped the teenage mind, and, more importantly, to protect him from any rumours and lies he might read about himself in the news.

"Tough conditions," said Cheng.

"I'm glad you think so," said Vlad, resuming his stance of authority with his hands tucked beneath his armpits, chin inclined.

"Here, Cheng, look at this," said Ulrik, leaping out of the pool. He jogged at a brisk pace about the perimeter, his flipper-feet slapping the wet tiles as he went. Then he stopped at a gold plaque on the wall. It was the only shiny fixture in the whole place since Vlad made him polish it before and after every practice session. It read:

A species arises, a type becomes fixed and strong, through protracted struggle against constant unfavourable conditions.
— Friedrich Nietzsche —

Vlad rubbed his forehead as though he were smoothing his permanent frown out of his clay-grey face, and his brows, being elevated now to their natural level, no longer overwhelmed his eyes with shade. Ulrik had always thought his eyes brown, but they appeared now to glisten like sapphires.

"Ulrik,"—double clap—"show Cheng how these unfavourable conditions have made you fixed and strong. Show him your fish kick."

Ulrik slotted in his earTech pods once more, loaded his lungs with oxygen, then entered the water head first like a torpedo. While underwater he turned on his side, stretched his arms over his head, and rippled his body with the grace of a ribbon fluttering in the air. So lithe were his joints that they seemed to undergo a dislocation and relocation at each undulation. After being submerged for an extreme length of time, it felt as though invisible hands were wringing his desperate lungs of every atom of air; his heart burned with every beat, and his throbbing brain felt liable to inflate and burst through his eyes, nose, and ears. Yet under the pain of it all, he remained composed.

"Interesting technique," said Cheng. "Fish kick, you say?"

"Fish kick, yes indeed. It's all about stroke mechanics, my friend. See, swimming *under* the surface is faster than swimming *at* the surface. Why? Because at the surface a swimmer is limited by their hull speed; they can't go faster than the bow wave they create. But below, where the resistance is consistent, a swimmer can glide about because they needn't crash between two distinct elements, air and water, to generate speed."

"Hmm, but if swimming is so easy underwater, why aren't other swimmers doing the fish kick?"

Bubbles escaped from Ulrik's mouth when he heard the word "easy".

"Two reasons why other swimmers don't do the fish kick: first, it's the toughest stroke to learn, and tougher still to master because nobody else can swim for a prolonged period underwater like Ulrik."

"And the second reason?"

"I was getting to that. Second: the fish kick, while not banned per se, is illegal in *most* events because the rules state that an athlete can't swim underwater for further than fifteen metres."

"Most events, you say? What event will Ulrik compete in?"

"A new event: they're calling it the marathon of swimming, and it'll be the first time we've had a long-distance swim in a purpose-built stadium at the Olympics: the 10-kilometre freestyle."

"And judging by your confidence, he's allowed to perform the fish kick in this event?"

"Well, my friend, being a new event, the rules are, shall we say, a work in progress. Right now, there are no rules that refer to a maximum underwater distance like in other events. This minor oversight from the International Swimming Federation is an opportunity—our opportunity to shock the world."

"Ah, so a loophole?"

"Not even a loophole; just a badly written rulebook. But more on that later, Cheng. I've yet to tell you about how he qualified for the Olympics. We'll need to sit down for that—with a bottle of Cognac ... XO."

"I shall look forward to a glass of warm oat milk, if it's all the same to you? I've brought some in a flask with me, you see. But please, rather than keep me in anticipation, answer me this one thing: don't athletes have to compete in heats or championships to qualify?"

"Yes, *normally*; but these aren't normal circumstances."

"True, Vlad. True."

"I'll reveal all to you later, my friend."

At that moment, Ulrik emerged from the water, spluttering from his nostrils like a blue whale does from its blowholes. He drained his lungs of the water he'd swallowed, coughing it out while choking on the air he was trying to replace it with. A throbbing headache spread throughout his brain, but not wanting to appear weak, he made no complaint nor compromised his body language.

"Impressive," said Cheng, his fervent clapping echoing around the walls. He went on clapping for some time and seemed to be humoured by the empty echo of the swimming pool, hollering and whistling as Ulrik swam to the side. After dragging himself onto dry land, he looked up at the yellowed ceiling, feeling like a hero under all this uncommon praise.

"Cheng, I'm so excited. I can't wait to show the world who I am and what I can do."

"What d'ya think you're doing?" Vlad snapped his fingers, the echo of which ricocheted to much sharper effect than Cheng's clap.

"I thought we'd finished, Coach?" said Ulrik, clutching his chest for breath.

Vlad inserted not one, not two, but three pellets of gum into his mouth, and the insufferable clack of his moist chewing was so loud its sonorous echo sounded as though he were surrounded by a dozen Vlads. "You finish when I say you're finished."

Rather than standing up to dive back in, as was the rule here, Ulrik simply flopped back into the water.

"Address that fucking body language!" Ulrik didn't need his earTech to hear that while underwater.

He turned on his side, stretched his arms over his head, and came into his fish kick. But every fibre of muscle was torn from the day's toil, and his tendons felt as though they were being stripped away from their bones. With what little energy he had left, he paddled back to the poolside and, reaching out with his numb fingers, anchored himself to a stair rail.

"Cheng hasn't travelled all this way to see you paddle like a dog." Vlad snapped his fingers in the likeness of a magician, but being in such a state of exhaustion, it worked no magic on Ulrik. There followed a prolonged moment of moist, open-mouthed chewing. "Cheng, my friend, please could you excuse us?"

"Of course. In fact, I've got quite a lot of emails I need to catch up on. So if you need me for anything, I'll be hidden away in some quiet spot."

"Good, good." Vlad's angry lips curled inward.

When the skittering of Cheng's happy feet faded, Ulrik felt a shadow looming over him.

"Out of the pool," demanded the raspy, smoky voice.

"I can't," hanging onto the stair rail by his fingers. "I've nothing left to give."

"Who told you that?" reaching down, yanking his arm, and hauling him out of the water with the strength of a man less than half his age and more than twice his size.

"Argh, Coach, stop. I can't." His body flopped at the poolside, legs still dangling in the water. He pressed himself up an inch or two, but a metallic prickle like pins and needles ran through his hands, numbing them and causing him to collapse onto his face.

"I ask you again, where's your inner cunt?" Ulrik supposed his headache to have returned, but it was Vlad prodding the hotspot of his crown. "You need to stop telling yourself excuses."

"But, Coach, I can't even—" The sound of a familiar jangle stopped him short. Without realising, Ulrik sat bolt upright and sought the origin of the tinkling sound. His heart tried to jab its way out of his ribcage. Tink—tink. Icy sweat trickled down his spine. Tink—tink. So often had Ulrik inspected every surface of that war relic, he knew every way in which it clanked in its brass tin. Tink—tink. Burning bile raged against the lining of his stomach. Tink—tink. There, standing now at the opposite side of the pool, Vlad brandished Tristan's Victoria Cross, striking it on metal surfaces as if he were like some child innocently exploring the sounds of a xylophone—tink, tonk, tunk.

"Give it back!" yelled Ulrik; molten blood snaked about his temples in the likeness of his pappa. He dug his nails into the seams of the tiles and raked himself across the slippery floor.

"Fond of medals, are you? Well, only the veterans of monumental struggle win these—those engaged in constant unfavourable conditions."

"I said give it back," gnarling through his square teeth as he advanced across the floor.

"If you want it, fetch it." Tink, tonk, tunk ... splosh. Ripples in the pool. The medal sank out of view.

A strength surged through his limbs, summoned from some hidden store which he never knew existed. When he rose to his feet, he wobbled as a foal does when taking its first steps. Then, with body straight as a pencil, he plunged into the pool. It was no trouble for him to retrieve his treasure, and when he resurfaced he swam to the poolside and checked the condition of the medal. No marks. If anything, it was cleaner.

"You've suffered enough for today," said Vlad, extending his arm and assisting Ulrik out of the pool. As the sun wheeled past the window, it cast a glowing hue upon Vlad's face, and his eyes appeared to glitter with golden ambition. "I'm sorry I had to do that with the war medal. Perhaps one day you'll understand why."

"I do, Coach," rubbing his thumb over the words "For Valour". "You believed I had more strength within. You were right." He fixed his body language and stood with his spine erect and his shoulders pinned back, assuming the stance of a winner on a podium.

"Ulrik, being almost sixty," nodding his head with certainty, "I've seen all kinds of change, but the graduation from boy to man, the promotion from apprentice to master, the transmutation from a spark to a flame gives me the most satisfaction. I promise that if you struggle like this every time you train from here on in, you'll not struggle to win a gold medal in the aquadrome."

"Make me suffer, Coach. I'm ready for more."

"I wish we could continue, but I intend to keep my promise to Cheng."

"Promise?" Ulrik squinted with intense confusion. "What promise?"

"There's a reason Cheng is here: he's come to take you home to see your mamma and pappa. As a birthday present, I'm giving you the next few days off."

"I'm ... going home?" The news gladdened him, but the greater part of him desired to stay. There was suffering to be had here—*unfavourable conditions.* "But Shayne O'Shaughnessy doesn't take days off. Silver medals are for those who don't show up. Other athletes will be out there suffering while I'm resting. I need to be suffering."

"Well …" lighting a cigarette and puffing away to buy himself some time to respond; "you may find suffering of a more terrible kind back home … I'm sorry; I've said too much."

CHAPTER NINETEEN

EAVESDROPPING

B ack at the cabin, Ulrik wolfed down supper with such terrible accuracy that he looked as though he'd been catapulted in the face with spaghetti Bolognese, for nestled within his noodly yellow beard were remnants of tomato and mince. After snapping up his fifth portion, and having now combed the mess from his beard, he bade Vlad and Cheng good health and limped off to his room, where he readied himself for bed.

When stripping off his day clothes, he noticed that the inside of his underwear was speckled with blood. Of late, his groins and armpits chafed horribly owing to swimming fully clothed, and in some areas the skin was so callused that it'd developed the look of scales and the hardness of lamellar. At one time it'd been sore, but these days, despite the occasional spotting of blood in his undergarments, it was painless to touch. So he troubled himself no more about it—until many months later.

After hitting the lamp switch, he climbed into bed, where he switched on the motor of the altitude tent; then he zipped up the plastic hatch with himself inside. This transparent bubble-pod enveloped his bed, and after a short while the air in it became thinner, exposing him to the extremes of the Himalayas, where oxygen was little more than half the usual concentration. It was common for Ulrik to fall asleep when his head hit the pillow, but an intermittent red blink from some hidden piece of Tech kept him awake.

"Gah," he said, sitting upright, "I must've left my earTech pods switched on." He unzipped the hatch of the altitude tent and crept across the creaky floorboards to the source of the red blinking. Turning over the earTech in his hand, he looked for the power button on the underside, but a sudden fuzz of noise emitted from the speaker. As he brought the earTech closer to his face, the harsh gabble of voices grew louder. Vlad must've left his microphone switched on accidentally, too. Ulrik hit the power switch and silenced the noise. But almost as soon as he powered down the earTech, curiosity pecked away at him, and he wondered what they might be talking about. But then, what would happen if Vlad discovered he'd been spying on him and Cheng? Thoughts of being discovered dominated his imagination; he scratched his elbows, then his neck, tugged his earlobes, yanked his beard, and gnawed his fingernails so that soon his fingers had the aspect of his ugly cubic toes. Then, with his hands grappling his head, he shook himself as one does with a fortune-telling eight-ball, expecting the right answer to surface when the shaking abates. "Do it" were the words which floated uppermost in his mind. A gleam shone over his face as he powered on the earTech and wedged the pods into his ear canals.

"Do you believe he has it?" said Cheng, taking a sip of what Ulrik presumed to be a glass of warm oat milk. "The talent to win?"

"My friend. Talent?" said Vlad, puffing his cigarette—p-p-p-puff. "Don't insult me with such a cheap word. I've seen so-called talented men and women fall complacent." There was a long pause, as if for reflection. "Talent? No, I don't concern myself with such a myth. But if you're asking me if I believe he can win, I'll tell you only that I know him to be the strongest I've ever trained. Not because of his unique genetics but because of his willingness to suffer; he enjoys it, my friend—the suffering. Just imagine … if he's swimming at world-record speeds in training, what might he be capable of when all the build-up and the hype at the

Olympics energises him? Oh, it does, my friend. It's electrifying; the thunderous applause; the flashing lights."

A metallic tingle spread through Ulrik's limbs as he listened to those endearing words.

"And on that subject," said Cheng, "you still haven't told me about qualification."

"Ah, yes, but where to start?" said Vlad, p-p-p-puff. "I suppose I should first explain how qualification for the 10-kilometre freestyle usually works."

"That'd be helpful. You see, my knowledge of sports is erm … well … lacking."

Ulrik crept back into bed and wrapped himself up in his duvet in the profile of a sausage. Then he cranked up the volume.

"Okay. Qualification. So, last year the World Championships were held in Portugal, at which there was a 10-kilometre freestyle swim around a race-course. Those athletes who finished within the top *ten* automatically qualified for this year's Olympics in Athens. Shayne O'Shaughnessy was one of them."

"Yes, yes, I've heard of this Shayne O'Shaughnessy."

"Good. Now, in a couple of months, there'll also be an Olympic qualifier held in Italy where the top *nine* finishers qualify for Athens, too. You with me so far?"

"That's a total of nineteen?"

"Nineteen out of a possible twenty-five. The remaining athletes are representatives from the *five* Global Swimming Federation continents: Africa, Oceania, Asia, Europe, and the Americas. One athlete from each continent is guaranteed a place in the finals. But they can't just select anybody; those who represent those continents are those with the *next* fastest times at the Olympic qualifier in Italy. Understand?"

"So the fastest swimmer from each continent is guaranteed a place, no matter where they finish in the qualifying in Italy?"

"Correct."

"Okay, so ten plus nine plus five—but that still only makes twenty-four athletes. You said there were twenty-five."

"I did." The sound of a sharp scratch, and then a quick fizzing—the striking of a match. P-p-p-puff. "The twenty-fifth place is allocated to the host nation, Greece. They are free to decide which of their athletes will represent them."

"Okay …"

"But there aren't many Greek athletes renowned for long-distance swimming. There was one man, Ajax Iliadis. But he recently broke both his legs, ruling him out of any competition for a while."

"So the only Greek worthy of selection breaks *both* his legs? Suspicious."

"Well, suspicious or not,"—p-p-p-puff—"it occasionally happens that a host nation has no candidate to nominate. And I'm sure you've heard about the Saifullah threats … Many athletes just aren't willing to take the risk … We'll talk about that later. Now, going back to my original point, when a host nation has no candidate to nominate, that position usually gets filled by the athlete with the next fastest qualifying time (regardless of nationality). Instead, Greece has offered that position to Ulrik."

"Ulrik! But how, when the boy is Norwegian and has no Greek ancestry? Don't tell me you've married him off to get him Greek citizenship, Vlad."

"My friend, what do you take me for?" Ulrik sensed there was a temporary smirk occupying Vlad's face when he spoke.

"What, then?"

"Relax that Adam's apple of yours."

"Hilarious. Now fess up."

"All right, all right." By the sounds of it, Vlad's rare smirk had vanished. "If you must know, over a year ago we were paid a visit by a dragonfly drone. How the drone found us I'll never know; all my Tech is encrypted, and I've got blockers on my GPS location. Anyway, the drone came with a message."

"A dragonfly drone? From who, Vlad? Who sent the drone? And why?"

"Those are questions I can't answer. When the drone played its voice message, it didn't tell me who sent it, only that their organisation was called Sigma."

CIGMa! Why hadn't Vlad told him this? Ulrik broke out in a fit of excitable fidgets and thereafter clasped both his hands over his mouth to muffle any noise that might escape.

"Sigma?" said Cheng. "'Sigma' meaning the letter of the Greek alphabet? A Greek organisation, perhaps?"

"Hmm, doubtful. The voice message may have been distorted, but I know a British accent when I hear one. Though I know nothing else about this Sigma or what they're trying to achieve. All I know is they're desperate to see Ulrik competing in the aquadrome."

"So, what did the message say?"

"The drone alluded to a long chain of bribes being paid to have Ulrik take that place in the 10-kilometre freestyle—bribes paid to committees, federations, politicians, et cetera."

"Surely it'll raise a few eyebrows when people hear about Ulrik being selected."

"Well, I did question that, but Sigma told me his place in the final was all but guaranteed—as long as I guarantee he'll compete as an Independent Olympian."

"What ... so not as a Norwegian?"

"Nope. Sigma told me that Team Greece are soon to put out a public statement. Under the guise of diversity and representation, they're to defend their decision and say that the current selection process (that is, having an athlete from each of the five Swimming Federation continents) is discriminatory towards those who don't identify as belonging to any of those continents. And so, since Ulrik is competing as an Independent Olympian, and therefore belongs to no continent or nation, they've allocated that place to him—to ensure fairness and diversity across the roster of athletes."

"Let me get this straight: a British drone shows up out of nowhere and tells you that Ulrik has automatically qualified for the Olympics if he competes as an Independent?" Ulrik imagined Cheng to be presently leaning across the table with his eyes on the verge of popping out.

P-p-p-puff. "Well, his paperwork has been submitted and approved. We can sit back and relax knowing his place in the aquadrome is secure."

"Hmm, makes me wonder … did this Ajax Iliadis really suffer an unfortunate accident? Or was he busted up for refusing to step aside in the aquadrome?"

"It's possible,"—p-p-p-puff—"but I can't know for certain."

Ulrik bit his knuckle, scrunched his face, and shuddered.

"It seems this Sigma will do whatever it takes to see Ulrik compete on the world stage."

"I happen"—p-p-p—"to be"—p-p-p-puff—"okay with that."

"Controversial, though, don't you think?"

"It is. But who am I to complain? I'm not sure what this Sigma's motivation is, but what works for them also works for me. This is what we wanted: to keep a low profile; to take the world by surprise."

"Sigma's motivation—it's exactly that."

"It's what?"

"To be controversial. To cause controversy."

"Why?"

"Don't you see? Whoever is leading this Sigma, I'll bet they're enemies of the Holy Shepherd." Ulrik nodded profusely as though he were sitting opposite Cheng and confirming it to be true. "They're taking aim at the Holy Shepherd."

"You think?"

"Of course. It's no secret the Holy Shepherd has a dislike for anything that rejects the Adam and Eve story of our origin. Remember back when Ulrik's story first hit the news? Intrigue spread across the continent like wildfire; intrigue about evolution and the origin of mankind. At the time, the Holy Shepherd was vociferous about his especial dislike for Ulrik. And so you see, by guaranteeing Ulrik—the poster boy for evolution—a place in the Grand Prix of swimming, Sigma is putting the subject of evolution back in the spotlight, and it'll encourage talk of kaleidoscopic genomes and our genetic origins again. It'll be a reminder to people that DNA is an archive of our ancestry—both human and non-human. As for competing as Independent and *not* under the Norwegian flag, well, that's rubbing salt in the wound. Like most European flags these days, the Norwegian flag bears the Sword of Abraham. And if Ulrik were to win while representing Norway, they'd sing that dreadful continental anthem. Not so if he competes as an Independent Olympian."

"I hadn't thought of it in such detail, but I suppose that makes sense. Brilliant, isn't it?"

"No. It's dangerous, and I can't condone it."

"Why? Chenglei Song is the biggest critic of the Holy Shepherd I've ever met."

"Because I don't want my family getting caught in the crosshairs of the Holy Shepherd, that's why. Ulrik is my family, and I'm not comfortable with him being weaponised and moved about like some pawn against DRUE."

"Yes, I understand, but if we had to qualify through the usual means, everybody would know our strategy—the fish kick. Then it would be a surprise to nobody in the finals. And they'd probably accuse Ulrik of blood doping because he can hold his breath for so long. Or the Global Swimming Federation would probably bring in a last-minute rule change to prevent him doing his underwater technique in the finals in Athens. But now that he's automatically qualified, nobody will be expecting the performance he's about to put on. The surprise will make it one of the greatest sporting spectacles in history."

"It doesn't sit well with me—this Sigma. This whole competing as an Independent Olympian thing will be an affront to DRUE—to the Holy Shepherd. If it didn't involve Ulrik, I'd be in favour of it. But we don't know who's behind this Sigma or if we can trust them. And they must have powerful, wealthy benefactors to be able to pay bribes of that magnitude. No, I don't see this ending well. The whole thing scares me. Are you not concerned, Vlad? You must be."

"Not about the Holy Shepherd, no. But I'll tell you what scares me: Saifullah terror threats."

"Ugh, yes. Don't tell me Ulrik knows about those?"

"Hell no. I want him to stay focused. Being innocent of all of this will be to his advantage in the pool. I don't want him worrying about bomb threats at the aquadrome."

"Bomb threats?" said Ulrik aloud to himself, before smacking a shaky hand over his lips.

"My friend," continued Vlad, "I rarely watch the news these days. When I first heard about Saifullah, I had to research them. They're terrorists from Babylon, aren't they?"

"Yes. Terrorists in much the same way as Al-Qaeda, Boko Haram, ISIS, or Islamic Jihad. The name 'Saifullah' in Arabic means 'Sword of Allah', so I suppose that tells you everything you need to know about their inclination to violence."

"Sword of Allah? What's that about, exactly? Some kind of symbolism in opposition to the Sword of Abraham?"

"Well, yes. It's exactly that. It's a complicated history, but they're essentially Islamist separatists who reject the House of Abraham— the political union between DRUE, New Babylon, and Israel. When Emmanuel Saint-Pierre brokered the Treaty of Zion (the peace treaty between Israel and Palestine), he, along with the Caliph and the Chief Rabbi, created a political union. To cut a long story short, as part of the terms, the Palestinians were forced to give up their homeland and were repatriated to New Babylon. Naturally the Palestinians resented that, and so a faction of extremist rebels was born: Saifullah. And lately they're showing their disdain for the Treaty by attacking high-profile targets in DRUE."

"I don't pretend to know what they're fighting for, but I heard it's got so bad that people in DRUE are afraid to do things like go shopping or to the cinema."

"I've lost count of the incidents: the Stockholm Massacre; the Paris Bombings; the Nuremburg Acid Rains; the Lisbon Cup Final attack; the Arena of Light where Stripes and Fibres were playing in concert; and what about the celebrities they've been abducting? Movie stars, entrepreneurs, musicians ... athletes next?"

"It's fucking outrageous."

Blip-beep. The flashing of Ulrik's earTech intensified. The battery of one of his earpods went dead, and the other was on the verge of expiry. He scrambled about for the charge station but remembered that he'd left it in the lounge.

"Well, you know my opinion," said Cheng. Ulrik imagined his Adam's apple to be struggling up and down his neck and sticking out now like an arrowhead. "It's all outrageous: the Bible, the Quran, the Torah. If you aren't outraged by them, you either haven't read them properly, or you've been radicalised yourself."

"I ... I don't know about that, my friend. You should respect—"

"No, that's right, you don't know because you haven't read them. So you aren't qualified to pass an opinion on them."

"Cheng, like you said, this is your opinion. Remember, you're a man of science; you're not supposed to deal in opinions. Stick to the facts, my friend."

"My opinions are supported by facts, thank you very much."

Blip-beep. The single piece of earTech was struggling on with some last reserve of power. Ulrik lowered the volume, hoping it might survive for a few seconds longer.

"My friend, all I'm suggesting is for you to be careful about being offensive. To slander Saifullah is one thing, but to slander an entire faith is another. You might get away with saying things like that in private, but it'll get you into a lot of trouble if voiced elsewhere. You don't want to find yourself guilty of blasphemy, do you?"

"I'm too old to care about who I offend, Vlad. If I'm guilty of anything, it's telling the truth. I've been silent my entire life, but no more. One day soon, just you wait, I'm going to—"

The earTech died.

Only a few moments ago Ulrik was so tired that he could've slept for a week, but this web of politics which somehow he'd been caught in troubled him; CIGMa and their blatant bribes; then there was the Holy Shepherd and the Caliph and the Chief Rabbi; the Treaty of Zion and the

House of Abraham; and, most frightening of all, Saifullah's intention to bomb the aquadrome. He suddenly felt himself a pawn surrounded by bishops, knights, and rooks, and it was his move next.

CHAPTER TWENTY

THRUDHEIM

Ulrik expected to be greeted with a welcome headbutt the moment he burst through the doors of Thrudheim, but he was met with an icy silence.

"Mamma, Pappa?" he called, the silver vapour of his breath rising about his face. At first, he thought they'd been burgled, for their home was dark and bare. There were no longer any Viking shields or axes on the walls; the pelts and deer hides that had decked the floor were gone; and the ivory narwhal tusk usually mounted above the fireplace had been replaced with a portrait of the Holy Shepherd.

Ulrik's heart raged so aggressively against his ribcage that it felt as though it were beating its way out of its bony prison. Thrudheim, Pappa had always said, meant "world of strength" in the language of Old Norse, but there was only weakness here. What were Mamma and Pappa thinking, mounting such a portrait?

In this portrait the Holy Shepherd was pictured holding the Sword of Abraham in one hand and a neat white cloth in the other. He was wiping his bloody blade with indifference, as a warrior does when battle has been won and there are no further enemies left to slay, and he seemed a holy warlord or a Knights Templar—a vanquisher of heretics and dissenters. As with all these curious depictions, engraved into a gold plaque at the base of the painting's frame was an accompanying verse:

> *But you who forsake the Lord I will destine you for the*
> *sword, and all of you will fall in the slaughter; for I called but*
> *you did not answer, I spoke but you did not listen.*
> — Isaiah 65:12 —

Thanks to Vlad's teaching, Ulrik had no trouble reading English like he once did, but this was a sentence he'd rather have misunderstood, and he wished to erase it from memory. For a while, he stood there in a prolonged contest of stares with the portrait, feeling a strange connection to its subject. He held the Holy Shepherd responsible for the breakdown of his family, and he'd been rumoured to have taken a special interest in Ulrik on the discovery of his kaleidoscopic genome. Reliable accounts came from the forager Runa Finehair, who had spotted the Holy Shepherd speaking with the Governor here on Svalbard around the time of Mamma and Pappa's sentencing. Were it not for Chenglei, Ulrik would now be in the care of the state and living with orphans. He shook his head; his eyes prickled with hate; foam formed on his lips. A portentous mood swept over him, and at once, he was of the definite mind that one day their lives would intercept and that he would stand in the company of the most powerful man in DRUE.

Ulrik strode through the darkness of the hollow house and steered towards Mamma and Pappa's bedroom, where he heard sleepy groans coming from within. When he swung open the door, he saw a batch of yellow eyes watching him. The two recluses whom they belonged to clung to one another's shivering bodies beneath a bear pelt.

"Mamma, Pappa, what is it? Are you sick?"

"Just drained, Ulrik," said Mamma, sitting up and smoothing down her brittle hair. "I'm sorry you have to be seeing us like this."

"My boy—nuh, not a fledgling anymore," said Pappa, rising out of bed, although a little too quickly, for he grimaced and reached around to massage his lower spine. "Happy birthday (for yesterday), and a happy Soldagen to you, too. Hah! The return of the sun yesterday, and the return of my son today: that's a good omen, I say." When Pappa emerged from beneath the pelt blanket, Ulrik hardly recognised him; he seemed shorter due to his having acquired a burdensome hunch; his beard looked rusty and scratchy, whereas before it had the aspect of a powerful flame; and when reaching out, an impoverished wrist emerged from his sleeve. At the sight of it, Ulrik's brain numbed for a few seconds. Pappa's forearm once boasted as much meat as another man's leg, but now there was little more than a thin bandage of flesh about the bone. Yet it was *he* who Pappa stressed had undergone a radical alteration—from boy to man—the fullness of his white-blond mane a symbol of his virility and strength.

"I can't believe it; my baby is a baby no more," said Mamma, sniffling and dabbing her eyes. "We're so glad to be seeing you but so sorry that we have to leave for work."

"Leave? Mamma, you can't. I've only just arrived."

They hugged him, but even when pressing their shivering skeletal bodies against his, he hardly felt their weight. He'd always understood it to be true when Mamma told him that greater strength comes from a greater share of life's sufferings. So why were they weak after all this suffering?

Pappa grabbed him by the shoulders, feigned a smile, and said, "Don't be looking at us with those sad eyes, Ulrik. Today is a happy day."

"I can't help being sad." He felt a fizzing at his nose, like the sensation of swallowing too much soda when it flows up the nostrils and prickles the nasal tubes (this fizzing being the onset of tears). "Look at you. I barely recognise you. What's going on? Where's our stuff?"

"N-n-nuh, don't cry," said Mamma, girding her arm around him. "It's all right. We just had to trade a few of our things for food."

"Why?" shrugging her arm off. "There's food enough out here in the wild. Are you no longer hunting?"

"Nuh," said Pappa, gesturing to his back and massaging his spine. "I can hardly stand without my back feeling as though it's being torn. It's from being bent over in those mines. We giants aren't meant for dwarf work."

"Mamma, you're not hunting either?"

"My knees, Ulrik, I'm in agony with them. They're so worn from crawling about on hard rock, it hurts to walk."

"Then stay here and rest a while." Standing in the doorframe, he blocked their exit. But Mamma pinched his triceps, which awoke every nerve in his breast. "Agh, wait,"—following her into the lounge—"where are you going? Don't go. Say to them you're sick. I came all this way to see you. It's my eighteenth birthday."

"Hey, hey," said Mamma, turning to him with an affectionate glow, then stroking his cheek with her mothering thumb. "We'll be seeing you this evening when we're back. Understand, Ulrik, we can't get out of work today. There was a breakdown last week which means everybody has to work overtime this week. Now, please, no more questions. It's breaking my heart to see you so—"

He interrupted her with another question: "Why is there a portrait of the Holy Shepherd above the fireplace?" He stomped up to it. "It would be better in the fire, if you ask me."

"Nuh!" Pappa threw himself between Ulrik and the portrait as though he were prepared at all costs to defend the Holy Shepherd unto death. "Keep your hands to yourself."

"What are you so afraid of?" shouted Ulrik, his brow thickening so much that it darkened his vision.

"If you bring any harm to it, they'll know," said Mamma, tethering his arm by her side and drawing him back to her. "There are mechanisms behind the frame that can sense when it's been dismounted. Every hour that passes when it's dismounted is an extra hour we incur in working overtime. Don't be condemning us to more work, Ulrik."

"Why is it there in the first place?"

"It's part of the punishment—to remind us whom we serve," said Pappa, now handing Mamma her fur coat and urging her to hasten.

"You can't be going yet. You haven't even had breakfast." Looking around, Ulrik saw that the only edible snack in sight was a piece of leftover bread which, being frozen solid, had the abrasive profile of a pumice stone.

Despite his best efforts, there could be no persuading them to betray their new masters. Before they left Thrudheim for the mines, Pappa gave him one last severe warning not to harm the portrait, after which Mamma begged a promise from him. "The only promise I shall make," he replied, "is this: expect that when you return I'll have plenty of food waiting for you. I'm going on a hunt."

"Nuh, stay here," said Pappa, pointing at him with a cubic finger. "There are too many polar bears roaming the wild of late. Trust me, Ulrik. You'd be the hunted."

They vanished into the darkness before he could protest any more. In their absence he could do as he pleased. At once, he took up his old bow from the weapon rack. Then he nocked an arrow, drew back, and aimed at the Holy Shepherd's breast. Keeping the bow still proved troublesome while his hot hands tremored with adrenaline. Suspending his breathing did little to steady his erratic aim, and doubling his concentration seemed to strengthen the terrible itch that now crawled across his scalp. Such a simple shot was proving tricky, especially now his fingers were wet with sweat. One by one, they betrayed him, and the bowstring slipped from his greasy grip—twang. He closed his eyes. A thud of wood. When he peeped open his eyes, he saw that the portrait was unscathed, though there seemed a smugness now about the Holy Shepherd's expression which he couldn't recall having seen earlier: smug, as though he were untouchable by mortal weapons; smug, as though he were of the belief that, by some divine grace, the arrow had been deflected into the timber of the ceiling. Ulrik stomped outside and sat on the steps of the veranda with his head in his hands.

Out here, the sky was like a black screen of Tech in which the stars were tiny flashing pixels, but the late morning's sunrise soon brushed the heavens with a more idyllic screensaver. After cooling off for a while, he was himself again; but he couldn't sit still while there were errands to run.

His first was to gather several empty netted crates from the outhouse at the back, which he stacked on his old kicksled; and without further delay, he sped off down the snowy slopes and headed for a strip of pebbly beach.

Upon arriving there, he wasted no time in stripping down to his undergarments and strode into the icy waters like a chieftain into battle, slowly yet composed. At first, the temperature shocked him to his core since he'd got so used to swimming in the warmer tributaries of the River Volga and the Caspian Sea. But he shook off its frigid effects and, with a crate in his hands, plunged down and rippled his way along the seabed. As he glided about the transparent waters, he caught spindly snow crabs and krill in his net crate.

When all his crates were brimming with ocean stock, he dried himself and got dressed before lugging his heavy cargo against the sideways wind all the way back up to Thrudheim. He stacked the crates back in the outhouse, where they'd freeze over and keep fresh until their consumption. Yet, after stepping back, he supposed it a meagre inventory. Enough maybe for two weeks? How thin and weak Mamma and Pappa had become. He couldn't abandon them with only light snacks in storage. They needed meat—blood-red meat.

He rested for a short while in the longhouse and there planned his next hunt. But to sit still while the all-seeing eyes of the Holy Shepherd looked down upon him was a feat beyond endurance. "You did this to my family," nostrils flaring, fists shaking, teeth grinding. "I don't know why you're wanting me and my family silenced, but when I get to the Olympics, and when I win the gold medal, the whole world will know about Homo Nova, and you'll hate that, old wizard."

With fleet feet and the fleetest heartbeat, Ulrik quit Thrudheim again, but not before seizing a two-handed axe and a meat cleaver. These, along with some wooden meat crates, were loaded onto his kicksled. This time he made for a different margin of coastline.

By the time he got there, the rose-pink pastel of daylight drenched Svalbard, and the wind had died so much that he could hear the bass grunts of brawling walruses. As he came into view, he saw the bulls fighting among one another in gladiatorial contests, vying for social supremacy; but when one fat scout alerted the rest to the advancing stranger, panic swept over them, and they huddled together in a tight scrummage.

Ulrik crept forward with his axe poised and ready, though he was careful not to make any sudden sounds or rash movements. There were no easy targets, so it required a change of tactics. He taunted them from a distance and hurled rocks at them with cruel force. While under attack, the scrummage of walruses shuffled down the beach, maintaining their formation as they did so. But the more he pelted them, the more they bashed against one another in their retreat. Then, to confuse them, he outflanked them and barked at them in a manner not unlike a sheep-dog when herding sheep. There! A young calf, perhaps a year or two in age. It fell out of rank and tried desperately to return to the scrummage, limping on with a mangled flipper, most likely torn by a tusk in their panic. Time to make a move.

Ulrik checked about him before advancing; there was no sign of a protective mother that might rush to its defence. With the glimmering head of the axe raised high into the air, he lunged forward and swung down, but it missed the creature's skull and cleaved the ugliest chunk out of its shoulder. Guttural shrieks warned the scrum of their fate should they come within reach of the butcher's axe. They shuffled and shouldered and trampled one another as they broke formation and made their escape for the ice floes of Nordfjorden.

After the herd scarpered, Ulrik eviscerated and butchered the carcase, then filled his crates with parcels of meat. Then he hauled his cargo back to Thrudheim, feeling a good deal happier for it and taking delight in the knowledge that he'd guaranteed Mamma and Pappa a hearty supper for many evenings to come.

When arriving at the outhouse, he stored half of the meat inside. He piled the remaining half at the centre of a ring of strategically placed bear traps, hoping the bloody bait would excite the expert snouts nearby. He waited on the veranda, his bow and axe at his side at all times.

No sooner had he reclined and put his feet up than a hungry bear came wandering up to Thrudheim with its nose tracing the ground, drawing ever closer to the meat stack. Ulrik watched with glee as it pitter-pattered across the snow, coming now at a dogged pace having detected its supper. When it passed into the ring of traps, the rusty iron fangs snatched the bear's ankles, whereafter it collapsed in howling helplessness. After falling, it writhed in agony on the ground so that now, locked onto its back, belly, and neck, there were even more jagged fangs puncturing its hide.

Despite the roaring and the howling and the whimpering, Ulrik spectated from his chair on the veranda, stroking his mane in contemplation, deciding it best to keep a safe distance until the bear's life was entirely drained. If he'd wanted to, he could've spared the creature its misery with an arrow or two. But to look upon the creature writhing about felt … good. Watching it struggle for its last breath paled his own sufferings into insignificance. No matter how bad things were in his life, he, at least, wasn't being ravaged to death by metal jaws.

So engrossed was he in the morbid entertainment of watching the bear perish that he hadn't noticed Mamma sneaking up on him. It took him by surprise when she snatched his bow and arrow and took aim. She let fly her compassionate arrow and punctured the bear's heart, whereupon it collapsed, sighed, and died. "Be at peace," she said, shaking now as though stricken by a terrible fever.

"We're going to need bigger storage!" cried Pappa, as he rifled through the outhouse. "Ba-hah! Walrus, krill, snow crab, and bear. I'll get a fire going. Ah, Ulrik, you've made me the proudest pappa alive. You're the best forager there is."

It seemed Mamma disagreed, for when she turned to him, her cold eyes shone like two pale moons, void of warmth. "For how long had you watched the bear suffering like that?"

"Now you ask, I'm not sure. A while, I think. Why?"

"That was cruel of you."

His eyebrow thickened with confusion: "You've always taught me that killing an animal isn't the same as murder. We do what we have to do, to survive. So why are you acting like I've murdered a person? You've eaten bear many times, and you even wear bearskins and sleep under a bear pelt. Many animals have suffered at our hands. I thought you'd be glad I've brought you all this stock."

"I-I am glad." But her top lip curled, and her eyes narrowed as they do when struggling to recognise a person.

"Then why are you pulling that face? You've always taught me it's in our nature to hunt."

She backed away a pace or two and pressed a palm to her nose to hide the look of horror: "But it's not in our nature to kill for pleasure, Ulrik."

CHAPTER TWENTY-ONE

FOR IVAR

Mamma and Pappa slept for most of Sunday—or the Sabbath, as everyone here had taken to calling it. They spent most of their waking hours cooking and feasting—in fact, Pappa only stopped eating to breathe. Both seemed to fatten up noticeably during the day, and by slow degrees a natural colour returned to their cheeks. But those hours in one another's company were fleeting, and the cruel speed at which each new hour succeeded the one before it seemed to make them transition in the time it takes to repeat a blink.

Monday came more swiftly than Ulrik was ready for, and Mamma and Pappa disappeared early as they set out for work again. After scoffing his bear brisket breakfast, he took himself to the beach for the last time, where he swam off the aches that still affected him from the toils of his hunt.

Training naked wasn't something he'd done a great deal of while living in Russia, but given that Vlad was thousands of miles away he could do as he wished without fear of rebuke. So he stripped off, piled a heap of rocks on his furs (to prevent them from blowing away), and strode into the sea. There, he stretched out his arms over his head, turned on his side, and came into his fish kick. So exceptionally light and elastic did he feel when oscillating without the hindrance of clothes that he raced about at a speed he'd never yet attained. At first, he thought he was being carried along by a formidable undercurrent, but there was no such force acting upon him—only his own strength. Never in his life had he felt so … unstoppable.

A blast of tempestuous air struck him when he emerged from the water, and all the droplets clinging to his body hair instantly turned to hoarfrost. Then, unaffected by the chill, he lay down and reclined with his hands interlocked behind his head, basking on the pebbly beach and looking up at the grey sky in search of company. "Tell me, Ivar, is all this for nothing, or will I win gold at the Olympics? I see it; I believe it; I'm ready to receive it; but I want to know it."

All at once nature seemed to respond: there was a certain whispering of the wind, a distinctive keening of gulls, and a temporary suspension of the water.

"Send me a sign, Ivar. Your presence would fan my flames. Watch how brightly I'd burn to know you're with me."

At that precise moment, the sun vaporised the clouds, and against the blue backdrop of the sky there appeared a glinting gold medal. Then, under this shower of torrential light, a rainbow hovered over the water for a few seconds; he'd never seen one before. This was no lottery; it had to be Ivar communing with him from some tier of heaven. Ulrik rushed to his feet, leapt into the air while waving at the sun, and shouted, "I'm glad to know I'm not alone."

"Yeah," crowed a familiar voice from behind, "that's right; you're not alone." Despite its severe deepening since they'd last met, Ulrik knew whom that voice belonged to, for its tone, accent, and inflexion still invaded his dreams. When he turned around, he saw the porky profile of Brynolf Grimstad and a couple of younger brutes he'd apprenticed, eager to carry out their roguery.

"Got nothing better to do than to be spying on me when I'm naked?" said Ulrik.

"There isn't a person alive who'd want to see your ugly body," said Brynolf. "You'll die a virgin, I'm sure."

Ulrik's mind went hollow at hearing the insult. "Uh—"

"Oh wait, he *is* a virgin. Wow. But then, I can't say I'm surprised. Have you looked in the mirror recently, Troggler?"

Ulrik stood fully frontal with his hands on his hips, exposing his trunk dangling between his thighs. At once, Brynolf's swollen cheeks turned crimson, and knowing not where to lay his eyes, he pretended to be engaged with his watchTech for a few moments. In his stead, the thug apprentices commenced their heckling.

"Look, his baby snail has retreated," said the skinniest thug, whose face became a triangle as he grinned, the points of which were two acute cheeks and a sharp jaw.

The freezing air, it seemed, had shrunk Ulrik's gonads back to their crinkly, immature origins: "Ah, is the Kraken asleep?" he said. "Well, since you're unable to take your eyes away, maybe you'd prefer to be taking a photo?"

"You'd like that, wouldn't you, Troggler?" said Brynolf. "Sorry to disappoint you, but you're the only homo here …" When he looked left and right at the younger thugs, they took that as their cue to erupt with fake laughter.

"Homo Nova," corrected Ulrik, through his gritted square teeth.

"Or homo-sexual," said the youngest thug, who, having received a chorus of howling support, puffed out his chest as though he'd secured some kind of social promotion.

"Why are you here?" said Ulrik. A terrible itch crawled across his scalp—the throbbing of his hot, prickly pulse.

"No, why are *you* here, Homo?" said Brynolf. "A lab rat like you shouldn't exist. You've been gene-edited or spliced or something. Everybody knows the scientists tampered with you. They're trying to play God. All this about you having a kaleidoscopic genome is horseshit. It should never have happened. *You* should never have happened. It's not just me who thinks so; there are many people out there who don't think you should be alive."

"What business is my life to strangers?" shrugging his shoulders. "Bah! They must think I'm important."

For Ivar

"You being alive is offensive enough. It's because you think yourself a superior race to us, don't you? You think you're so much better than everybody else, but we know you're a hoax."

"I think I'm better because I *know* I'm better than everybody else. And soon everybody in the world will know it."

"Not if Saifullah bomb the aquadrome with you in it," said Brynolf, crossing his fat forearms in defiance.

"Bah, I don't worry myself about such rumours. If Saifullah wanted me dead, then why would I be alive right now?"

"They're probably waiting for the right time to strike. An event like the Olympics will get them headlines because the whole world will be watching—watching you squirm on live Tech."

The golden medallion of the sun shone down with uncommon warmth. Ivar was with him. He just knew it. And, like a tall plant, Ulrik unconsciously leant towards the energising rays. His clenched fists turned white, and his knuckles protruded like jagged stones. "If you're wanting me dead so much, why don't you take matters into your own hands?"

"Because," said Brynolf, advancing, but not before checking his periphery to make sure the younger thugs followed close behind, "because I'd rather watch Saifullah murder you in the aquadrome. That'll be way more satisfying."

"You mean you're too afraid," said Ulrik, tensing his chest so it appeared pumped and rolling his shoulders as though warming up for some ultimate bout.

"I'm not afraid of you, Troggler. There's nothing you can do to hurt me. Now go before I stomp on your baby snail and make sure that something as repulsive as you can never breed again." The other thugs were in such a state of hysterics that Ulrik could see the little bell clappers wagging at the back of their throats. "And when I'm done with you," continued Brynolf, eyes puffed up with laughter and unaware of Ulrik closing down the space between him, "I'll do the same to your starving pappa. Your mamma? Well, I'll bend her over and give her the best time she's ever had. She's going to beg me for another son—a better son this time. Not another *homo* like you."

It might have been a spear for how swiftly it flew, it might have been a hammer for how heavily it landed, it might have been a dagger for how sharply it struck, but the weapon that smashed Brynolf's cheek was Ulrik's rocky knuckles. A gash appeared in the shape of a squinting red eye, which immediately wept tears of blood. Brynolf toppled backwards like a falling statue, and lying still on his back, his languid eyes rolled about their sockets.

At first, Ulrik thought him dead, but then he murmured something about Saifullah setting homos like him on fire. While mumbling these slurs, he tried to sit up, but his neck was too flaccid to support the weight of his head, and he flopped back to the ground, where he lay on a quilt of snow.

Ulrik turned on the other two thugs; his monstrous eyebrow cast a shadow over his eyes as it jutted out of his skull.

"Stop, please," said one thug, joining his hands together in prayer.

"Mercy! We're younger than you, Homo Nova," said the other.

"Younger, yah," said Ulrik, cocking his head and eyeing them sideways with birdlike focus, "but old enough to be causing trouble."

"We're sorry—we're stupid."

"So, so stupid."

At their begging Ulrik showed them pity, though he spared none for Brynolf. "My argument isn't with you, younglings," he said, before kneeling down and seizing Brynolf's jacket by the collar. "What's my name?" he yelled, frothing at his mouth as he did so.

"Troggler," murmured Brynolf.

"Wrong," said Ulrik, grappling his face and holding his thumbs over his eyes. Pressing lightly: "What's my name?"

"Stop; you'll blind him," begged one thug.

"Maybe I'll stop when he says my name." Ulrik pressed his thumbs deeper into Brynolf's eye sockets and was bent on repaying the same amount of torment he'd suffered over the years.

"Just say it, Brynolf. Say his name."

"Argh, Homo ..."

"Finish it." Ulrik's thumbnails gouged his squishy eyeballs. "Say my name."

"Homo-sexual—argh, stop!"

With the strength of a stag, Ulrik unleashed a wild headbutt: "That's for Mamma ..." and then another, "and that's for Pappa!" Seconds later there arose a hideous lump at the centre of Brynolf's forehead that looked like a golf ball trapped beneath his skin. Not a mumble came from Brynolf, for the headbutt had rendered him unconscious. "Remind me: what did you say to me earlier? You'd stamp on me so that something as disgusting as me could never breed?" Groping about in the snow, Ulrik picked up a fist-sized rock and said, "Well, let's hope something as disgusting as you can never breed, huh, Brynolf Grimstad?" bashing and bludgeoning him between his groins three or four times.

"Enough," said the thug with spindly limbs. "Please."

Ulrik arose while brandishing the rock. "If you tell anybody of this, I'll do the same to you but worse. Believe me, I'll hunt you down and make sure that, like him, you can never breed. Now, swear to keep this a secret ..."

"We swear. We do. We won't tell anyone."

"Get on your knees and beg."

Dropping to their knees, "Please, we swear."

"Swear on ..." Ulrik thought at length, "swear on all you love."

"We swear on our homes—"

"And our snowmobiles—"

"Our Tech—"

"And our pets—"

"Our brothers and sisters—"

"And our mammas and pappas."

"What about Brynolf's life?" said Ulrik, standing now with a boot pressed on Brynolf's windpipe.

"We swear on Brynolf's life. We swear on everything. Nobody will ever know what happened here today."

At once, a bearded seal surfaced from the water and hauled its body up onto dry land. When it saw Ulrik, it stopped and, realising what was unfolding, gave a sideways look that he translated to mean, "Nothing to see here. Good health. Goodbye, humans." Then it crashed back into the sea.

"I'm satisfied with your oaths, though I'm not yet finished," lifting his boot from Brynolf's neck. "I've repaid Brynolf for the evil done to me, but I've yet to avenge Ivar."

When Brynolf, who was a shade of ghostly white, returned to his senses, he shook as though with a fatal fever. Then he reached for his crotch and nursed the savage pain that awoke him. As he sat upright, he discharged a pint or two of curdled vomit down his chest, which glazed over with ice.

"Are you ready?" said Ulrik, indifferent to the stench of bile as he helped him to his feet. Brynolf said nothing and sobbed while cupping his gonads. "Remember when you left us in the mountains alone with that bear? It's because of you, Brynolf, that we got lost and fell through lake ice. So it's time for you to suffer like Ivar did." Ulrik employed himself as a crutch and girded Brynolf's arm about his shoulder. To all outward appearances, he would've seemed a good Samaritan helping the injured, yet, one slow step at a time, he chaperoned him closer to the water's edge.

"No, Ulrik. Please, don't make me go in there. I can't swim."

"He can't swim!" screamed the slender thug.

"This one's so fat," said Ulrik, "he'll float like a boat. Besides, it's not the drowning you should be most afraid of; it's the c-c-cold."

"I'm sorry for everything, Ulrik. Argh, uft, oh, it hurts to walk," still cupping the trauma at his gonads. "Please, I'll die in there."

"You're only sorry that you're hurting, but you're not sorry for Ivar's death." Saying Ivar's name reminded Ulrik of the torment he'd suffered at the end of his life; as the vivid memories flooded back, his pulse and his breathing accelerated. Ivar ... gone ... forever. Then, rumpling his hair and shaking his head, he brought himself back to the present. "This one's for Ivar," shoulder-charging Brynolf into the shallow sea, who yelped as one might if burning alive. Ulrik waded in and towed him out into deeper water.

"Ulrik, let him go. Please."

"You're taking this too far."

Nobody had ever spared him any sympathy. Why should he stop now?

Ulrik dunked Brynolf's head beneath the water, muffling his drastic breathing and pathetic cries. "One, two ..." counting out the seconds as Brynolf thrashed below. When he released him, he scrambled to the surface, his face awash with white shock. The freezing water rendered the brute a voiceless mute: his jaw, lips, and tongue tremored, yet not a murmur was murmured.

"I can hold my breath for almost thirty minutes," said Ulrik, treading water with an effortless swish of his oar-like arms while Brynolf karate-chopped the water to keep himself afloat. "How about you?" Before Ulrik gave him the chance to reply, he clung to his back and anchored him down. At first, Brynolf tried to shake him off, but within seconds he became stiff. When his flailing arms and legs gave up, Ulrik let him scramble to the surface once more.

"You're going to kill him!" screamed the youngest thug from the shoreline.

"I *could* do that ..." said Ulrik, towing Brynolf back to dry land, where he laid him stranded like some beached whale. Within seconds, the Arctic wind froze Brynolf's clothes stiff so that they now had the hardness of sheet metal, and his friends came bearing dry garments to clothe him in. "I could do that, but I want him alive because it's hurting him to know I'm going to be the most famous athlete there ever was. And when he realises this, I'm hoping he'll kill himself and spare me the trouble."

The younger thugs shot one another a look; creases of terror were wrought into their foreheads. When Ulrik dismissed them, they all made haste in their escape. As they mounted their snowmobiles, he overheard the spindly thug ask Brynolf if he needed to go to hospital, to which Brynolf stuttered, "I'll b-be okay. Just g-get me h-h-home. We'll t-t-tell my pappa I had a s-s-snowmobile accident."

A wry smile crept onto Ulrik's face when he heard that, and he looked up at the sky in search of Ivar's presence. But the sun had vanished behind the horizon. There was no transition from daytime to twilight today, and the darkness was swift in enshrouding the world. "Wherever you are, Ivar, I hope I've brought honour on your name today, and I hope you're proud of me. I swear to you, from now on, I'll be treating all my enemies with the same courtesy as I did Brynolf today—without mercy."

Then he plunged back into the icy waters and carried on swimming as though all was at peace in the world.

CHAPTER TWENTY-TWO

PAPAL DISPENSATION

Less than a week had passed since the white smoke billowed from the Sistine Chapel to celebrate the election of the Catholic Church's new leader, Pope Pius XIII.

Easter was coming, and Pope Pius XIII decided that for his first Lent in office he'd go about for forty days and nights not in the usual white garb of the Bishop of Rome but clad instead in worker's overalls and swapping, too, his priestly cap for a denim one. In the disguise of a grounds-keeper, he sauntered through the Vatican Gardens with a gentle breeze at his back and the morning sun beating on his neck, passing fellow workers who went about resurrecting perennial plants and sprinkling and spraying tree blossoms which appeared like galaxies of dainty white stars.

Having carried his toolbox in his weary arm for some time, the Pope stopped for a short rest. He creaked his spine, and as he looked about he noticed a lady donning a headscarf who was struggling to prune the upper branches of an olive tree while standing on the highest rung of her stepladder. At once, he pulled down his denim cap and, daring to stroll across the forbidden greensward, made in her direction. Her face turned to mild outrage, and she checked to see if anyone else had noticed him cutting a path across the lawn, which was out of bounds.

"Bless you," said the Pope. "Bless you for your excellent work on such an excellent morning. What's your name?"

"Miriam," she said promptly, as though answering him with brevity might bring about a premature end to their conversation, perhaps because she feared association with the groundskeeper who'd brazenly trespassed prohibited lawn space.

"Ah, Miriam. A delightful name. The name of our Virgin Mary in Arabic, if I'm not mistaken? And judging by your headscarf, you're a Muslim?"

"Yes, yes," she said with reserve, her modest eyes falling to the floor.

"Rivers, ponds, lakes, and streams, they all have different names, but they all contain water. Just as religions do—they all contain truths."

"Oh, is this a verse from the Bible?" her eyes glowing under the amber sun.

"No, heh-hi-hee-he," slapping his thighs in jest. "It was Ali who said that … you know, the heavyweight-champion boxer."

"Oh," smiling so much her canines became visible.

"May I?" he said, gesturing to the stepladder and the olive tree. As Miriam climbed down, he drew his cap lower to conceal his identity, after which he ascended. With his crooked hands, he reached out and, rather than prune the closest branch, plucked from it a shrivelled black olive, not realising it was a remnant of yesteryear's harvest.

"You can't eat that," shaking the ladder to get his attention.

On hearing this, the Pope climbed down with the olive still in his hand. When he reached the bottom, he lifted his denim cap, mopped his brow, and revealed himself. "Heh-hi-hee," laughing with the vigour of a harmless rascal, "well, if the Pope can't, who can?"

"Your Holiness," averting her modest eyes out of respect, "I didn't know it was you."

Then, as though to prove his point, he put the black olive in his mouth and chewed, but owing to its bitterness his face contorted and seemed to wring out the sweat from his brain; and his coughing only abated after he'd swallowed it, stone and all.

Miriam snickered into the back of her hand and said, "I meant only that you shouldn't eat the olive, Your Holiness: they're bitter when eaten raw, especially when they've perished."

The Pope struck his forehead with his palm. "It might be hard to believe, but that's the first time in my life I've eaten an olive. Well, I suppose there's a first time for everything, right?" He shook his head and rolled his eyes at his own foolishness. "Miriam, will you walk with me? Yes, over the soft grass. Come; eat with me the fruit of the tree; hear with me the song of the thrush and the rushing of the water fountains; let's enjoy the scents of the garden. Not just us, but everybody. Let's open our hearts to the wonders of creation. With our laughter, we shall make this a little patch of paradise—a Garden of Eden."

Miriam followed him and trampled across those manicured lawns. He could sense her reluctance at first, but when he requested a football be brought and invited the other groundskeepers to play, she let down her guard and joined in. He was too fragile to play, but he insisted on refereeing; and for those who couldn't play or preferred not to, he bade them to go about stroking tree bark, picking flowers, harvesting citrus fruit and pressing fresh juices, doing cartwheels and handstands and somersaults, skimming stones, singing hymns, and praying wherever and however they wished (regardless of their faith).

Later, when basking on a couch of grass, Pope Pius XIII was delighted to hear the music of laughter fill the gardens. Miriam, whose knees and elbows were green and brown from a morning of sport, came to him with her cheeks a-glow with glee.

"Your Holiness ..." Her enquiring eyes sought permission to sit with him.

"Of course," gesturing with his hand to the patch beside him.

She knelt beside him with her hands clasped in her lap: "I can't remember the last time I was covered in dirt like this."

"Isn't it wonderful?" crumbling a lump of dry soil in his hands and letting it sift through his fingers as though it was fine warm sand.

"Dirt, Your Holiness?"

"Oh yes, dirt. We avoid getting it on our clothes or skin, and when we do, we're quick to wash it off. But it doesn't hurt us, so why should we be in such a rush to cleanse ourselves? Soil is a magic substance: it's the enabler of life."

"It is?"

"Think, Miriam. Without soil, there'd be few plants or trees, and without vegetation there'd be no air to breathe and no crops to eat. Isn't it odd that all God's creations have some connection in His vast web—from the microscopic to the macrocosmic? It should be the purpose of mankind to explore the Lord's creation, but more importantly, to enjoy its bounties. There is beauty in everything. Even in dirt."

"Your Holiness, the last pope, I served him a long time, but we never spoke like this."

"Served, you say? Oh, there are no servants here except I. Nor are there masters of any kind except He," pointing to the sky. "Down here we're all equal. That's why I dress as you do."

"So it's not because you already want to change careers?" she asked, snickering into the back of her hand.

"Well, I don't think I make a very good groundskeeper," pointing out some decapitated tulips which had lost their heads when the football was blasted at them. "But for now, it gives me perspective—teaches me understanding. You see, I know some people are only nice to me because I'm the Pope. I prefer to see how they treat me as a groundskeeper. Miriam, I firmly, fiercely, and ferociously distrust a person who's disrespectful to a groundskeeper because I know that's how they'd treat me if I was one."

Miriam's face shone at him upon hearing these sentiments.

"Oh, is that the time?" he said, looking down at his watchTech. "I hope you don't mind, but I have some"—pausing for thought—"*other matters in need of cultivation*, heh-hi-hee-he."

"More gardening?"

"Sadly not," gathering himself to his feet and fixing his cap on his head so low that the bill formed a sort of equator at the centre of his face. "An important meeting."

"Good day, Your Holiness." Beaming, she closed her eyes and raised her shoulders to her cheeks in an endearing sort of way. "And thank you."

"Peace be with you, Miriam," bowing and retreating inside.

Pope Pius XIII meandered about the corridors of the Vatican Palace as he waited for his guest to arrive. While waiting, he took it upon himself to roam the unexplored labyrinth of his new home and blessed every single Swiss guard he passed with a "Peace be with you". Thrilled to be acknowledged, they replied, "And also with you, Holy Father."

During his wandering of the halls, he mused about the worth of the Church: "What good is all this treasure gathering dust in these halls? Illustrious paintings as tall as houses; weapons and armour; marble sculptures; antique maps; ornaments; artefacts; palaces; property; estates ..." While tutting to himself, a Bible verse sprang to mind: Matthew 29:14: *Harder it is for a camel to pass through the eye of a needle than for a rich man to enter heaven.* Speaking aloud, he said, "All this wealth— I cannot reconcile. I should put it to auction and use the proceeds to feed the poor, to build new schools and hospitals, to better people's lives." He tapped his upper lip with a slender finger while in deep postulation, but he was interrupted by the patter of footsteps and a rhythmic striking of wood, perhaps that of a walking stick or a staff ... or a crook.

"You there, groundskeeper, my lamb; I'm looking for the Pope, but I can't find him anywhere. Send word to him: tell him the Holy Shepherd has arrived for their meeting."

Pope Pius XIII tugged down the bill of his denim cap before turning to face his guest. The Chancellor of DRUE was advancing towards him with his warped white crook in hand.

"Good morning," said the Pope.

"It's afternoon already, my lamb. So be quick in alerting the Holy Father. I've waited long enough for his counsel."

"Afternoon already?" checking his watchTech. "Indeed. I'll have the Pope come to you at once. But first, can I offer you a drink? Some tea or coffee? Water? Biscuits? We have butter biscuits. How about some lemonade? Croissants?"

"A groundskeeper," said the Holy Shepherd, raising his silver eyebrows and widening his olive eyes, "a groundskeeper would do better to address me by my proper title, as Holy Shepherd."

"Ah, I'm sorry, it's just, my preference is not to address people by their job titles, for that's the custom of strangers."

"It's my preference, *groundskeeper*,"—stabbing the marble floor with the end of his crook—"that you run along now and inform the Pope of my coming before you're stripped of your lowly title and dismissed from employment."

"Ah, well, if you insist on conducting formalities, then you should address me also by my correct titles,"—removing his cap and mopping his brow with it—"for I am Pope Pius XIII, Holy Father, Bishop of Rome, Vicar of Jesus Christ, Successor of the Prince of the Apostles, Supreme Pontiff of the Universal Church, Primate of Italy, Archbishop and Metropolitan of the Roman Province, Sovereign of the State of the Vatican City, and Servant of the Servants of God. Quite a mouthful, isn't it? Heh-hi-hee-he."

"Holy Father, forgive me," said the Holy Shepherd, pinching his eyes and lowering his head in shame.

"There's nothing to forgive, Emmanuel," said Pope Pius XIII, holding out his hand for the shaking, "for I am no judge of man."

"Holy Father," said the Holy Shepherd, examining the filth of the Pope's workman hands, "your hands are …"

"Soiled, yes." The Holy Shepherd clasped his palm begrudgingly. For an uncomfortable duration thereafter, they were trapped in an awkward holding of hands, for the Holy Shepherd seemed motivated to retain the Pope's grip even as he tried to retract his arm. "It's good to see you here again so soon, Manny."

"Did you … did you just call me 'Manny'?" said the Holy Shepherd.

"Oh, I just find 'Emmanuel' a mouthful. You don't mind me calling you 'Manny', do you? Or would you prefer me to call you 'Emmy'?"

"Neither."

"Ah, very well. Anyway, what can I do for the man who was so instrumental in getting me to where I am today?"

"May we go somewhere a little quieter, Holy Father?"

"Do we have to? I prefer the sunlight, and spring is such a glorious season."

"It's ... confidential business, Holy Father," said the Holy Shepherd, gesturing with his crook to the cohort of Swiss guards now marching down the hall with pikes in their hands and pistols at their hips.

"Ah, let's find a room where nobody can disturb us. How about the confessional box, Emmanuel?"

"An apt suggestion. I've much to confess."

—

The Pope's confessional booth was carpentered out of a dark hardwood and had been polished more thoroughly than any other surface in the Vatican. Its bespoke exterior had carved into it a depiction of Saint Michael the Archangel—the general of God's army. His enormous eagle-like wings were spread to their fullest, and he brandished a flaming sword as though he were warding off demons and any other unholy manifestations of sin.

Inside the booth were two separate compartments—one for the priest, one for the confessor—where the two of them sat opposite one another, a partition of latticed wood being all that divided them. The only light in there came from a sconce which cast criss-cross shadows over their faces.

For a moment, they held each other's gaze in silence; silence, that is, save for the periodic buzz of a housefly which had tailgated them into the booth, crawled through the latticework, and flitted from time to time between the Pope's compartment and the Holy Shepherd's. The Holy Shepherd reclined with his dominant leg crossed over the opposite knee and his crook leaning against his shoulder: "Holy Father, the people are fond of your ... personality, what with you going about dressed as you do—as one of them."

"Fond, are they? Well, it's to you I owe my thanks, Emmanuel. I wouldn't be sitting here if you hadn't persuaded the conclave to elect me."

"Holy Father, you're both gracious and kind, but let's give our thanks to the Lord our God," gesturing a sign of the cross with his crook. "It's He to whom we must direct our gratitude."

"Gloria, in excelsis Deo," they both cried.

"Let's begin with a prayer," said the Pope, bowing his head in reverence and closing his eyes. Though, after some time, meditation became impossible owing to the ceaseless buzzing of the intruder. So the Pope swung open his booth door, hoping the housefly would disappear into the effulgence of daylight. But even as he swatted the air, the dextrous pest evaded him with ease and seemed in no hurry to escape. Not wanting to cause it distress, he let the housefly remain and closed the door again, trapping it inside. "Now that we've offered up prayer, Emmanuel, please confess to me your sins so you may make penance with the Lord and so that I may absolve you."

"Holy Father, God enlisted me as his vicegerent, but I have—" He paused at length and hung his head low. The Pope afforded him plenty of time to recover his thoughts. "Holy Father, my people, whom I love so dearly, are losing their faith again. The ideological war of evolution and faith still rages on."

"War of evolution and faith, Emmanuel?"

"Ulrik Magnusson, Holy Father, and all this talk of evolution. Baseless rumours of him having this kaleidoscopic genome. *Homo nova*—a new species of man. Ancestral genes. The faithless believe we're descended from other creatures. Not descendants of Adam and Eve, but creatures and species unknown."

"Ah, the forager from Svalbard? Surely as Chancellor of DRUE you've more pressing issues to worry about? It's an unusual obsession you've developed over one whose popularity is strong only with the fringes of society."

"Fringes of society, you think? Holy Father, not to insult your intelligence, but if you look here on Tech,"—taking out his handTech from inside his cloak and showing an infographic—"you'll see a chart that shows he's the most talked about public figure of the last four years, having overtaken me. Yet he's scarcely been seen in public. Look at the trend, Holy Father: as we draw closer to the Athens Olympics, the people's interest in him has multiplied. And it's not just the faithless who adore him. The journalists obsess over him, too. Every day—more articles. Homo Nova this, Homo Nova that. I'm sick of it. I'm sick of the mainstream media with their liberal bias. Look," swiping the screen of his Tech and scrolling through the innumerable headlines in the search results:

About 88,200,000 results

Top Stories:

1. Homo Nova: Science Fiction or Science Fact?
2. Public Opinion Divided on Homo Nova—Those Who Love and Those Who Loathe
3. Saifullah Vow to Bomb Aquadrome during Homo Nova's Race
4. Ulrik Magnusson's Controversial Qualification for the 10-Kilometre Freestyle Explained
5. A-Listers Demand Algorithm Review as Homo Nova Outranks Social Media Mentions
6. Zion Lion Admits He'll Support Homo Nova at the Olympics: Here's Why You Should Too
7. The Road to Athens: What We Know About Ulrik Magnusson
8. Ex-Olympian Vladimir Lukashenko Rumoured to be Homo Nova's Swimming Coach
9. Ulrik Magnusson and his Kaleidoscopic Genome: What to Expect in the Aquadrome
10. Homo Nova: Infidel or Idol?
11. Spotted in Russia: Rare Footage of Ulrik Magnusson Swimming in the River Volga
12. Whitehoods Plan Anti-Evolution Demonstration in DRUE's Capitals
13. Ulrik Magnusson: The Miracle Everybody is Talking About

Next page >>

"You are the Holy Shepherd, Emmanuel. Don't get drawn into a popularity contest with a teenager."

"I have to because this is, as you astutely point out, a popularity contest between our faith and the pseudoscience of evolution. Don't you see? Ulrik Magnusson is the greatest threat to our religious liberty. If people adopt him as their hero, they'll start asking questions about evolution like before, and they'll start to question their faith. And when they do, they'll demand the teaching of evolution in schools again—the brain-washing of our children. If they succeed, our continent will be one which believes mankind descended from apes and is a cousin of the banana. Remember the lawlessness before my administration? It was a continent of blasphemy and buggery, porn addicts and frivolous masturbators, adulterers and sodomites; sodomites making their liberal demands and parading about with their rainbow flags. Men pretending to be women; women pretending to be men; some freaks pretending to be neither. The people were lost and had no love in their life. Holy Father, if we don't remove the nettle from the garden, our lawn will grow over with weeds again. I want Ulrik Magnusson and his filthy bloodline destroyed."

"Emmanuel, slow down. For a man with an abundance of courage, you have much fear in you. In all matters, you must act out of love, not fear."

"I both love and fear the Lord our God. He's shown me what will become of us if I don't fulfil my duty as the Holy Shepherd." He surveyed the knobbly edge of his crook and, grasping it, drew it into his breast.

"What is it you seek from me, Emmanuel?"

"Holy Father, I seek papal dispensation."

There followed an abrupt period of silence which would've lasted a good deal longer had the angry vibrations of the housefly not disturbed the air like some miniature quadcopter. It flitted liberally between the two compartments, as though taunting the two most influential men in DRUE. "Dispensation, did you say?"

"Holy Father, I seek exemption from canon law."

"I know what it is you're asking: you want my permission to break a commandment."

"Please, Holy Father, I ask for your dispensation to break not one but *two* commandments."

"Two commandments! Which?"

"The first is: Thou shalt not kill. The second is: Thou shalt not bear false witness."

The Pope found his hand groping for his breast, and while there it seized his rosary beads from beneath his shirt and squeezed the crucifix for comfort. "Emmanuel, who do you intend to put an end to?"

"I think you already know."

"Not Ulrik Magnusson?"

The Holy Shepherd nodded while compressing his congruent lips together. "But there'll be some—how should I say—collateral damage. What I mean to say is, Your Holiness, I can't guarantee that others won't die in the attack."

"Goodness, an attack? What sort of attack? … And how, then, is the second commandment to be broken?"

"The attack would be carried out by mercenaries—terrorists belonging to Saifullah. For obvious reasons, the Republic must remain pure in the eyes of the laity. The state cannot be seen to have blood on its hands. So we must, I'm sorry to say, spread falsehoods about the perpetrators of the attack."

"Jesus Christ!" said the Pope, smacking a hand to his lips as though trying to retract his taking of the Lord's name in vain. Many Hail Marys and Our Fathers would he later need to recite to exonerate his foul tongue. He peeled his hand away from his mouth and said, "Emmanuel, I can't believe what I'm hearing. You intend to use Saifullah as mercenaries? As a scapegoat for the attack? Why would you? Another terrorist attack will create tension between DRUE and Babylon—between you and the Caliph. Especially an attack on one so, dare I say, popular."

"There is already tension between DRUE and Babylon …"

"Go on."

"I believe the Caliph has betrayed me. And if so, I don't think it'll be long before the House of Abraham comes tumbling down."

"Betrayed, how?"

"There is, shall I say, an ongoing investigation."

"An investigation into what?"

"I tell you this in the strictest confidence, Holy Father." The Holy Shepherd pressed his face to the latticework. "We've uncovered some intel: Babylon is allegedly manufacturing weapons of mass destruction."

"Nuclear weapons? Then the Caliph is surely in breach of the Treaty of Zion."

"Indeed he is, if the claims are true. I hope it isn't so."

"Babylon has benefited so much from the House of Abraham. Why does the Caliph risk everything?"

"I believe it's his intention to demand complete independence from DRUE."

"Why?"

"For a reason I've long suspected: he wants to recapture Israel from Jewish occupation. He wants to return to his homeland—Palestine."

"How dare he? You worked hard to broker the Treaty and bring peace to the region."

"Thank you, Holy Father. I built this united house because our faiths were fragile. I rebuilt Babylon for the Muslims; Israel, the Promised Land, was given back to the Jews; and Christian Europe has since been born again."

"You brought peace to nations which were riven by war for centuries, and in doing so you saved countless lives."

"Because, Holy Father, I truly believe our God is one and the same—the

God of Abraham. There is more in us that unites us than divides us. Though all this is at risk now because of the treachery of Babylon."

"But disguising an attack on Ulrik Magnusson as Saifullah? Why choose Saifullah as your hitmen? This will only enrage the public ... Or perhaps it's because you *want* to enrage the public? Perhaps because, in enraging the public, you'd gain their support for some kind of retaliation. You'd then appear justified in such a retaliation if you were to deploy troops in Babylon. You'd be able to wipe out Magnusson, then move in for the Caliph? Kill two birds with one stone? Tell me, am I wrong, Emmanuel?"

"I'm not trying to wage a war. I'm trying to arrange the pieces on the board so I may prevent another war in the East."

"And if the rumours of nuclear weapons *are* true?"

"Holy Father, in all things priestcraft, the Lord has placed His trust in you, and in all things statecraft, the Lord has placed His trust in me. Let us invest our trust in one another."

"This is very troubling."

"It *is* troubling, Holy Father. I'm fighting a war on two fronts: foreign and domestic: Babylon and faithlessness. Very soon I fear I'll need to call on every Christian in the Republic to have faith. Which is why I'm here. I cannot invade Babylon without the support and faith of the public. And I need Ulrik Magnusson gone in order to garner the faith and support of the public. But I cannot have Ulrik dispatched without your dispensation ..."

"Emmanuel, if I'm not mistaken, haven't Saifullah already threatened to bomb the aquadrome at the Olympic finals?"

"Yes, they just await the order."

"Order from whom? You? Ah, I see now. It's you who has orchestrated the attack."

"I was hoping Ulrik would withdraw from the competition, but alas, his lack of proper schooling has rendered him ignorant. Besides, my preference is to have all his family together in one place. Ulrik, Thorsten, Astrid. We need them all dead. That way, there can be no perpetuating this *Homo nova* lie, and there'll be no further risk of any of their kind being spawned. But bombing the aquadrome, that was just an empty threat. So I'll have to rethink my intentions on what should happen … Hmm, if he is to compete, I need to do everything within my power to stop him from winning and becoming the Continent's idol. But that's another matter."

"Why not simply have him curfewed or detained?"

"Would that I could. He's somewhere in Russia, and DRUE's relationship with Russia has always been … well, less than cooperative. Besides, it's too late for diplomacy now. The idea of this *Homo nova* has become like a cancerous tumour, and it's up to me to cut it out. For good."

The Pope crossed his arms and exhaled a prolonged sigh. "You look for complex solutions without, but often the simple solution lies within, Emmanuel. Peaceful solutions."

"Not at all. I've sought simple solutions—peaceful solutions. Do you remember Professor Greenberg? At the very outset, I had him reject further research into the *Homo nova* lie. And to be doubly sure the Magnussons would return to Svalbard, I had a clan of Whitehoods harass them at their accommodation when their fame first hit the news. That was their chance to go away. Back to an island with less than a few thousand people living on it, where Ulrik would remain out of sight and out of mind. Forever, I hoped. Never to return. But even then he couldn't stay out of trouble—drawing in tourists, garnering headlines in some circus with that mammoth. Unluckily for him, when that mammoth passed away after he let it loose, I had his parents sentenced to nine years' work in a community correction programme: sentenced on questionable neglect charges; questionable because an autopsy showed that the mammoth died of a lung infection—which apparently is common in animals help in captivity … Anyway, I digress. Your Holiness, I've sought peaceful attempts to keep Ulrik Magnusson out of trouble and suppress his fame, but always the boy seeks to elevate himself above his station. Now he's on a journey to the Olympics. Peaceful solutions are poor solutions. And with nowhere else to turn, I come to you for your dispensation—as a last resort."

"There are better ways to garner the faith of the public than to commit atrocities like a Saifullah attack. Why not pray?"

"I do pray, Holy Father. More than ever. When I do, I'm drawn to scripture," waving now a pocket copy of the *New Continental Bible*. "Though praying alone does nothing if we commit no action thereafter."

"Then let the scripture inspire you, Emmanuel. Don't ignore the teachings of Christ in Matthew 26:52 when he says, 'Put your sword back in its place. All who draw the sword will die by the sword.'"

"Holy Father, I've studied the scripture at length in Latin, Aramaic, and Hebrew; and I have always been inspired by it. Remember Deuteronomy 20:13 in which it says: 'When the Lord your God delivers it into your hand, put to the sword all the men in it.'"

"Don't take the wisdom of the Old Testament out of context for your own bloody gain, Emmanuel."

"Oh, taking it out of context? God is explicit about the *sword*. You, like many, would ask me why I chose the sword as the emblem of the House of Abraham. Why not a dove bearing an olive branch? Because the Lord said in Jeremiah 48:10: 'A curse on him who is lax in doing the Lord's work! A curse on him who keeps his sword from bloodshed.' The sword, Holy Father, it's the sword which we must arm ourselves with when necessary."

"You're dangerously wrong again, Emmanuel Saint-Pierre. The sword is symbolic. You forget that written in Ephesians 6:17 it says, 'And take the helmet of salvation, and the sword of the Spirit, which is the word of God.' The Lord wants us to bring our voice to the heathens' ears, not a sword to their throats."

"Again, Holy Father, it's you who I'm afraid is wrong. I think that's very clear in Ezekiel 21:14: 'So, then, son of man ... let the sword strike twice, even three times. It is a sword for *slaughter*—a sword for great *slaughter*, closing in on them from every side.'"

"Parables, Emmanuel, these are parables. Not to be taken as literal instruction, but to open our eyes."

"No, I don't believe it. They're instructions, not fairy tales. Recall that in Isaiah 1:19 it says, 'If you are willing and obedient, you shall eat the good of the land; but if you refuse and rebel, you shall be eaten by the sword; for—'"

"Enough," said the Pope, holding his fingers up to the latticework like some patient afflicted with vampirism. "It does you no good to harbour violent intentions. To speak in such a way is to be no less radical than Saifullah."

"Holy Father, I understand that the truth is uncomfortable, but these are the fundamentals of our scripture. Remember Proverbs 3:5–6," said the Holy Shepherd, thumbing through the pages of his pocket Bible, "'Trust in the Lord with all your heart and lean not on your own understanding; in all your ways submit to him, and he will straighten your path.'"

"I will not sanction any killing. The Bible doesn't sanction it. God doesn't sanc—" said the Pope, clutching at his rosary beads as his shortened breaths escaped him.

"Holy Father, you have read Deuteronomy and Leviticus, I take it? There are, within those verses, strict instructions for the stoning to death of blasphemers and heathens. Also, hearken back to Psalm 2:8–9 in which it says, 'Ask of Me, and I shall give the heathen for your inheritance; and the uttermost parts of the earth for your possession. You shall break them with a rod of iron; you shall dash them in pieces like a potter's vessel.'"

A silence stole over them, save for the taunting buzz of the housefly which, when it flew near the Pope's ear, sounded like a revving engine.

"Emmanuel, excuse me while I use the restroom. You know how it is for men of our age, heh-hi-hee-he." Before he departed, the Pope left the door ajar, hoping the pesky housefly would escape before he returned.

Gloom befell the corridors now that the sun retired westward, and as the Pope strolled he held his wrists behind his back as though he were handcuffed. He found that he no longer required the restroom, perhaps because he'd been unconsciously pushing down on his bladder through-out the Holy Shepherd's confessions. Still, he was glad for the interlude and strolled a little longer while whispering a verse from Psalm (56:3) over and over again: "When I am afraid, I will put my trust in thee. When I am afraid, I will put my trust in thee. When I am afraid, I will put my trust in thee ..." No fewer than one hundred times had he recited it before he returned to his confessional box feeling replenished with piety, and he trod so lightly that had he been walking across snow or sand, not a single footprint would've been left in his wake. But his gladness soon evaporated, for when arriving back at the confessional box, he saw the housefly zipping about at erratic speed, as though it had, during his absence, gone loopy on a supper of sugar.

"Holy Father, is everything okay?"

"I'm well, thanks, Emman—" A rapid buzzing commenced: zub-zub-zzb. Light legs tickled his arm. Something was crawling on him. "A nuisance is this fly," throwing his arms up in the air to dispense with it. "Do proceed, Emmanuel. Where were we?"

"I await your decision, Your Holiness."

"I can't do it, Emmanuel. I can't pardon murder. I can't grant you dispensation."

Zub-zub-bzz. The Pope's eyes tracked the fly. He'd tolerated it for long enough.

"You're the Bishop of Rome: you *can* do it. Understand this: if this degenerate spawn of Lucifer—if this product of the Antichrist—if Ulrik Magnusson is allowed to roam at will, atheism will spread across the Continent. And if it does, the people will lose faith in my governance. One by one, we'll see DRUE's nations revolt; there'll be more referendums of independence like those traitors in Great Britain and Catalonia. Without a United Europe, Babylon will go unchecked and Israel will be liable to fall."

"These are mere speculations, Emmanuel."

"Not so. He's shown me—the Lord our Father."

Bzzb—zzb. The Pope drummed his impatient fingers on the ledge of wood in front of him. He'd give the fly one last chance.

"Then why has the Lord not shown *me* his plan?"

"Perhaps ... to test your faith in Him, Holy Father."

Zub-zub-zzb. The housefly landed on the armrest and rubbed its forelegs together as though it was hatching a villainous plan. The Pope drew his arm in the air and in the next instant smacked it down on its victim. "Shut up!" Turning over his hand, the Pope saw an unidentifiable mush of moist entrails flattened on his palm. When he flicked it away and scraped it on the latticework in front of him, he returned to his conversation with the Holy Shepherd, whose face was warped with a wry, sly grin.

"Holy Father, thou shalt not kill, remember? The Lord our God didn't say, 'Thou shalt not kill, excluding the housefly'. In this conversation alone, Holy Father, you yourself have broken two commandments, having now killed and having earlier taken the Lord's name in vain. We are mortal sinners, you and I."

It was only when the Holy Shepherd stamped his crook in the manner of one planting a flag into the ground that the Pope returned to the present. He was overcome with vengeful breathing, and he carved divots into the skin on the back of his hand with his fingernails. Eyes twitching, lips chewing. A moment of madness.

"Again, I say to you that which is written in Proverbs 3:5," said the Holy Shepherd, while massaging his thumb and forefinger: "'Trust in the Lord with all your heart and lean not on your own understanding.'"

Pope Pius XIII caressed his gentle hands as though he were washing away his sins with invisible soap. "I pray you know what you're doing, Emmanuel. I fear the outcome of all this, but more do I fear the Lord our Father in heaven, and if it be His plan, then I'll place my humble faith in it. I grant you dispensation and absolution from your sins: take out the heathen Ulrik Magnusson and all those who share his bloodline, in the name of the Father, the Son, and the Holy Spirit."

"Amen," said the Holy Shepherd, raising his crook as though to toast the good news, then striking it on the wooden floor with the authority of a judge who brings down their gavel after a landmark ruling has been decided upon.

CHAPTER TWENTY-THREE

TITAN GARDEN

On the night of the opening ceremony, the black sky and all its celestial objects appeared to have fallen in, for the flash photography about the Olympic Stadium seemed akin to blinking particles of starlight. Here stood Ulrik, queueing in some tunnel, waiting for his call forward. The evening air, it seemed, turned the entire stadium into a sweltering sauna, yet despite sweating, he kept his furs on and his cloak drawn. Somehow, being wrapped up in the garb of his homeland offered him a feeling of safety not unlike that of a suit of armour.

Nation by nation, the athletes paraded around the running track to thunderous chants and electric cheers. Each nation was headed up by cultural mascots: buxom beauties performing capoeira led the way for Brazil; wingless dragons for China; Vikings sailors for Denmark; the Queen's Guard marching in their red jackets and black bearskin caps for Great Britain; Masai warriors for Kenya; floating fairies for Ireland; Romans and gladiators for Italy; enormous sumo wrestlers and samurai swordsmen for Japan; tattooed Māori tribesmen for New Zealand; a caravan of Bedouin nomads for Saudi Arabia; a troupe of flamenco dancers for Spain; and cartwheeling cowboys and acrobatic Amerindians for the USA. Almost every European flag had embroidered into it the Sword of Abraham, and those godly nations received tremendous applause when their banners were raised aloft.

When all the official nations had paraded round the track, it was time for the Independent Olympians to represent themselves. Of those who had no affiliation to any country there was Ulrik and only one other person—a slender girl about his age who was fixing the tresses of hair that had fallen down the right-hand side of her bosom in subtle, shimmering waves of caramel. Her eyes were of a brown hue, yet when a warm light passed over them, they appeared a shade of honey or amber. And she stood now in a lovely little latte-glass pose, with one hand on her hip and her heels brought together. It was only then Ulrik realised she was staring him out ... because he'd been unblinkingly staring at her. He whipped his head to his immediate right to hide the molten reddening of his face. From his periphery, he saw her fanning her face with her hand, cooling her skin, but he suspected this to be a ruse of hers to get his attention, for her swooshing was exaggerated, and there came wafting into Ulrik's twitching nostrils an intense perfume—something reminiscent of a summer flower.

"Independent Olympians ..." boomed the announcer over the stadium speakers.

"We're up," said the girl, seizing her banner. Hers was a flag he didn't recognise, so there was no telling where she was from, nor was there any telling what kind of athlete she was. He'd heard it said that beach volleyballers were pretty; maybe she was one of those. After all, her smooth legs appeared well bronzed, as might well be expected of a regular beachgoer.

After taking up his red raven banner, Ulrik followed her out of the tunnel and onto the running track. They walked side by side, and when they came into view and held aloft their banners, a riot of intolerant jeers erupted from every terrace of the stadium. Frail old ladies, younglings, and every interim generation swore and spat as the two of them paraded round.

"Ria Lorenzo i Lopez—no nation," declared the announcer. When she thrust her flag up high, there followed a series of profane chants, which Ulrik found difficult to understand, although it was easy enough to distinguish words like "traitor" and "treason". It was hard to believe a girl so attractive could produce such an unattractive expression, but such a face as Ria now pulled was warranted under the circumstances.

"Ulrik Magnusson—no nation," declared the announcer to the world. The screams of the crowd turned hostile at the announcement of his name, and he buried his brow halfway down his face in response. Then, with tens of thousands of accusatory fingers thrusting at him from all angles, the crowd chanted, "Lab rat, lab rat, lab rat."

They were hated, both Ria and he. That much they had in common from the outset. A spark, some might say.

"Ssst, look at them," said Ria, turning and walking backwards around the track for a while to impart to those in the southern terraces her defiant glare. "They squawk like harpies."

"I never knew I had so many enemies."

"Having enemies is a good thing; it means we stand for something, right?"

On hearing this, all the strain left Ulrik's brow, and the scrunching of his face relaxed. Until then, he'd been considering whether he should javelin his red raven banner into the crowd, impaling some random skull with it; but he mellowed at Ria's words in the same way that Pappa always did when Mamma appealed to him with tender notions.

Undeterred by the screeches of the crowd, Ulrik and Ria advanced. He never fully looked at her, since her beauty intimidated him, and such a girl was probably weary now of ogling eyes tracking her every step. So it came as a surprise when she offered her hand for him to hold, saying, "Ulrik, walk with me, will you?" He kept his eyes forward while trying to steady his thumping heart and groped about the air until his hand met hers; their fingers were caught up in an awkward tangle before Ria adjusted them to a more comfortable grasp. Her hand wasn't as soft as he'd expected: wrought into her callused palm were traces of hard times—a path of struggle: one of *constant unfavourable conditions*.

The response from the crowd to their hand-holding came to the ears like a dreadful hurricane.

"They hate us even more now because we're holding hands," said Ria. "Good, I say."

At length, Ulrik wondered what Ria had done to warrant such resentment. And his hand grew sweatier as his mind ran wild with speculation. Who exactly was he holding hands with? What kind of scandal was she caught up in? She seemed harmless enough to him.

As they drew to the end of their parade lap, Ulrik was about to turn off the track and onto the field at the centre of the stadium where the rest of the athletes congregated, but Ria stopped on the running track and, being tethered to her hand, so did he. For the first time, he faced her and saw her in her gorgeous entirety, her affectionate bottle-brown eyes looking up at him as she fanned him with her eyelashes.

"Ria, why are you stopping?" tugging at her arm. "We've got to keep moving. We're standing in the middle of the running track."

"Kiss me," she said, tiptoeing, inclining her chin, and parting her lips.

"What?"

"Kiss me, I said. The crowd—they'll hate that even more. Listen, it doesn't mean anything. It's just to bait them. It'll piss them off. Let's have the last laugh."

"You're crazy."

"Quick, quick."

"But everybody is watching, and I've never even—I hardly know you, and, and, and, we foragers normally butt heads to express our liking."

"Headbutt?" She lowered herself from her tiptoes, and her scowling eyes scanned him as she backed away. Then she spun around and flounced off into the throng of Olympians in the centre field, moving at such a speed that her hair flowed behind like tawny tail feathers.

"It's not that I don't want to, Ria;" he called, "it's just—" But she'd gone, leaving a trail of perfume lingering in her wake. He shouldered his way through the throng of athletes after her.

Luckily, their feud had been overlooked, for there seemed to be a great commotion happening elsewhere in the stadium. All heads were now facing east; their eyes were fixed on a man clad in an emerald track-suit emblazoned with a white shamrock on his back. He was jogging at a leisurely pace around the stadium while waving some sort of blazing sceptre—the Olympic torch.

Somewhere close by, yet hidden from view, Ulrik heard Ria's voice over the riotous roaring: "He's gorgeous." Then he saw her with her cute nose scrunched while beaming at the athlete in the emerald tracksuit.

"There's just something about him," said another girl clad in a Team Canada tracksuit.

"I know! He's got a face you just want to lick," said one with an Australian flag draped over her shoulders.

"It's not just his face I want to lick ..." said one with a Danish accent, her mind, no doubt, overrun with sultry passion.

An announcement blurted from the stadium speakers: "Shayne O'Shaughnessy—representing Ireland, DRUE," at which all spectators were out of their seats and waving their hands and screaming his name.

"Shayne O'Fucking-Shaughnessy swims on Christmas fucking day," muttered Ulrik, rehearsing the words of Vlad. His eyes narrowed on his rival; all was dark and shadowed about the fringes of his vision; the only discernible figure was an emerald silhouette. Like a virile demigod, Shayne leapt up a grand flight of stairs, skipping steps throughout his ascent.

"Shh—shh," said Ria to the others, "he's about to begin the countdown."

It was no concern of Ulrik's that Ria was swooning over Shayne. Why should it be? She didn't belong to him. He'd held her hand. Once. That was all. A woman is free to desire whomever she likes. Besides, she was trouble anyway ... Pretty, though—exceptionally pretty. Perhaps he ought to have agreed to chance the kiss. Not that it meant anything.

"Ulrik," she whispered, tugging on his fur sleeves. Looking down, he saw those eyelashes innocently fanning him again. "Lift me onto your shoulders so I can see Shayne."

"What's so special about him?" he said, turning his back to her and muttering to himself: "I'm the only one with a kaleidoscopic genome. It should be me up there. I should be the torchbearer."

"Quit being so mean."

He expressed the sourest scowl as Shayne arrived at the uppermost platform of the grand stairs. There, he winked, blew a kiss, and addressed the world in his colourful accent: "Tha luck of tha Irish be wit' yer!"

A concert of high-pitched screams ensued, most of which belonged to ecstatic teens; and for once it was strange not to see a single person absorbed in Tech and instead paying attention to the present goings-on.

Shayne brandished the torch over the Olympic cauldron which, when alight, would burn for the duration of the games. Then he began a suspenseful countdown: "Tin, noine, aight ..." the entire world begging him to release the inferno, "four, treegh, two, wonn ..." The torch's flame was transferred to the cauldron and thereafter sped along a flammable wire, setting ablaze an enormous beacon of the five Olympic rings. Then, catching Ulrik unawares, a sudden seismic clap of thunder resounded throughout, and the sky flashed orange with fire. A bomb? Stooping down to a normal height, he made himself less visible while searching about for Saifullah terrorists.

Boom—bang—screech—scream—yet all about him ... wonderment and cheer? The sky was a backdrop of purple nightshade; jets of green and gold whizzed about the air; rockets shot high, leaving sparkling trails like tall plant stems, and when they burst, they did so like blooming flowers in spring, all of which, when viewed together, gave the sky the appearance of a midnight garden.

Relieved, Ulrik clutched at his breast. Fireworks. Not terrorists. Though the stray cats and dogs of Athens might've disagreed, for the noise was sure to be a terror to their sensitive ears.

When the world settled and all the shaking hounds in the vicinity had lain down in their kennels again, Shayne readied himself for his address to the world. A unique aura surrounded him; some sort of invisible force field which was best understood in the way in which Chenglei had once described the law of gravity to Ulrik: earth, planets, asteroids, comets, space junk—all rocks big and small revolve around the sun in our solar system. And here was Shayne, a bright star, standing at the centre of the universe with billions of eyes orbiting him from almost every latitude and longitude. A single gesture of his clenched hand was all that was necessary to silence the crowd.

"And now for our continental anthem in honour of tha patron saint of DRUE, Saint Michael tha Archangel," said Shayne. A medley of stringed instruments played, and right on cue Shayne sang solemnly into his microphone:

> Princely commander of the heavenly hosts
> Deliver us from the demon-ghosts
> Hear me now, I vow
> Keep my heart from succumbing
> To the evil that is coming
> See me now, I bow

> When besieged be Heaven by the heathen hordes
> Draw out thy blade, and raise thy shield
> The Lord our Father bids thee to wield
> And declares it's they who shall be eaten by swords
> Be gone unto Hell, Devil and Dissenters
> The Kingdom of Heaven thou shalt not enter

> Princely commander of the heavenly hosts
> Deliver us from the demon-ghosts
> Hear me now, I vow
> Keep my heart from succumbing
> To the evil that is coming
> See me now, I bow

> Be gone unto Hell, Devil and Dissenters
> The Kingdom of Heaven thou shalt not enter
> Thou shalt not enter
> Thou shalt not enter!

The applause rang on long after the hymn ended. All across the world—in tin huts, mud huts, wood huts, stick houses, and brick houses—throats were dry, and eyes were wet with pride.

It was just as well the theatrics were drawing to a close, for Ulrik couldn't take any more of it. To be out here celebrating while Mamma and Pappa were slaving elsewhere was, he thought, a betrayal of their love. So, having jostled his way through the crowd, he dashed out of the stadium and headed back to the convoy of athletes' coaches. Coach eighteen was his, easily remembered because of his age. Luckily, the chaperone was present and allowed him to embark, and he took up his seat towards the back.

Almost another hour passed before the athletes' coach was at full capacity. The only vacant seat was the one to his immediate left (the aisle seat), which for some reason no other athlete wished to occupy. There also seemed a good deal of folk pinching their noses as though everyone except he was suffering with a terrible nosebleed.

"Ulrik, are you okay?" said a soft Mediterranean accent from behind, which belonged to a face poking through the gap between his headrest and the window.

"Huh, wha'?" turning around in surprise. "Oh, you scared me for a second, Ria."

"Where did you go? You left me."

"I didn't know we were together."

"Well, I've been looking for you." Dropping her voice to a whisper, "And I saw you freak at those fireworks. I was worried."

"Ria, forgive me, but I'm not here to be making friends or watching fireworks," drawing his fur hood over his head and looking out of the window. "I'm here to fight Shayne O'Shaughnessy for the gold medal." He watched Ria in the window's reflection; she slumped back against her chair and stroked the tips of her hair meditatively. Then he noticed that she too sat alone. Perhaps he would've sat with her had she not described Shayne as gorgeous. Instead, solitude seemed the most preferable option to him, and having knotted his arms and knitted his brow, he silently resented all those who'd jeered him today. There was a need to get back to his lodgings and abide in darkness for a while, to tear up a few cushions, slam a few doors, headbutt a wall or two.

Without warning, the coach took off and escorted the athletes to Titan Garden—their residential village for the duration of the games.

Later that evening, the athletes were escorted through the armoured gates of the Olympic Village, Titan Garden. A ten-foot boundary wall, rendered a brilliant white, enveloped the entire complex, along the tops of which stood armed sentries who looked out with an air of suspicion on their grizzly faces. Others might've felt safe under their protection, but not Ulrik. After all, defences are generally bolstered like this when an attack is likely and danger is afoot.

When flying into Greece, Ulrik had cursed its stale geography, since from above, every jigsaw piece of farmland appeared arid and brown. But Titan Garden was a patch of paradise made up of stone courtyards and water features and was overrun with vibrant verdure. It was a jungle of creeping tendrils where bright pink bougainvillea crept along the tops of archways and coiled their way down and about pillars and posts in their quest for botanical supremacy.

As he stood contemplating which of the winding paths of the village to take, Ulrik twiddled the room keycard in his hand: room 421. Despite settling in the day before yesterday, he'd yet to fathom out his bearings. Rather than get lost, he decided it best to put himself through the agony of asking a stranger for directions. As it happened, a rowdy crowd of athletes loitered close at hand beneath a wicker gazebo; its roof was thatched with tangles of those same fuchsia flowers as before. Beneath it, there was an uncommon amount of hair-fixing going on; all the colours of autumn—red, gold, and brown—were being brushed, plaited, twiddled, tied up, taken down, swept back, and flicked forth. Then, when towering over the tops of them, Ulrik saw why. Shayne was here. Why Shayne needed sunglasses when the sun had retired long ago was beyond him.

Yet smitten were those vixens in the company of their Irish idol; their sparkling eyes glimmering like rows of precious gemstones.

Suddenly, a path cleared, and Shayne advanced towards Ulrik. "Shayne O'Shaughnessy," said the Irishman, jabbing his thumb at his own chest by way of introduction; "pleased ter meet yer, Ulrik. Woah-ho-hoa, look at tha size of yer! Yaz a real-life giant, aren't yer? Lez get a quick picture of us tergedder. For tha fans?" Not only the fastest swimmer in the world, Shayne was also the fastest talker, it seemed. "Seamus, hurry and take tha photo, yer dirty horse."

Shayne girded his arm around Ulrik, though Ulrik kept his arms rigid by his side and feigned a smile, revealing his square teeth and the gaps between. For a second photograph, Shayne looked directly at the camera and performed his distinguishing wink, but when Ulrik copied him, he looked as though he was attempting to crack open a walnut in his eye socket.

"It'll be tha clash of tha titans. Whaddayer say? Ulrik 'Homo Nova' Magnusson versus Shayne 'tha Shamrock' O'Shaughnessy. Yer know, people are psyched for this event. I tink we're gonna be smashin' records. Tha whole world's gonna be watchin'. We'll give 'em a show, won't we, fella?"

Leering lineaments formed on Ulrik's face.

"Yer don't speak much, do yer? Tha's grand."

It wouldn't have mattered to Ulrik if Shayne rehoused the homeless, helped old ladies cross busy roads, or volunteered at his local donkey sanctuary: Shayne was the enemy.

"I'll be seein' yer around, then?" extending a hand for the shaking.

"I don't shake hands," said Ulrik, in a jovial tone. "Where I'm from, we sniff each other's butts like dogs do to say hello."

"Tha's a weird ting to say." Shayne's smile turned into a smirk as he backed away. All at once, the cluster of heckling vixens moved off with him, and their continued laughter erupted in the distance.

"I was joking," called Ulrik. A silence took over, save for the concert of crickets playing from the verdure.

"Ssst, don't you get it?" said a voice from behind. Turning around, he saw Ria relaxing on a wicker chair with three cats meowing at her ankles. "They don't like us Independent Olympians. We're traitors in their eyes because we don't compete for DRUE. Well, fuck DRUE, fuck the Holy Shepherd, and fuck Shayne O'Shaughnessy."

"I thought," said Ulrik, cocking his head in surprise, "I thought you were a supporter of Shayne? You seemed to be drooling over him at the opening ceremony."

"Ssst, I wasn't drooling. But so what if I was? It's no business of yours who I drool over."

"Nuh, you're right. It isn't any of my business. I shall leave you to the better company of your cats. In the meantime,"—stretching his arms out and yawning—"I'm going to find my lodgings."

"*Lodgings?*" interrupted Ria, smothering her face with her hand to hide her amusement.

"Yah, what about it?"

"Who calls it *lodgings*? Haha."

"I don't see what's so funny. What do you call it?"

Ria was too far gone down the path of hysterics to return any sensible conversation. At the climax of her laughter, she curled over, held her tummy, closed her eyes, and stomped her feet on the ground. As she succumbed to her own hilarity, she became progressively quieter, so that faint squeaks were now the only audible expressions coming from her, until a harsh piggish snort broke the silence.

"It's not that funny, Ria."

"I know, I know, but I can't—" snort. "I can't stop." Streams of tears rolled out, but she was quick to plug her tear ducts with a thumb and finger to protect the integrity of her eye make-up. "I don't know why I'm laughing."

"Fine," he said, striding away. He'd remembered the right way to his dormitory, so he needed no help from her anyway. Muttering to himself: "How can someone so pretty be so annoying?"

The pitter-patter of dainty feet behind him grew louder, and a moment later Ria overtook him. Her hair was now fastened into a ponytail with a frilly black bobble, swishing this way and that while her hips seemed to sway that way and this. It was a composed and collected gait, and the way in which she led with one foot in front of the other reminded him of a lynx he'd seen often at the Arctic Sanctuary: each step one of elegance and, at all times, purposeful.

"Why are you following me?" he said, the entrance to his apartment block now in sight.

"Why would I be following you? My *lodgings* are this way, too. I think everybody is sorted alphabetically. It looks like Lorenzo and Magnusson are on the same wing. Eugh, better not be neighbours …" Then she passed through some automatic double-doors which opened as she approached. When he himself passed through, Ria was waiting by the doors of an elevator and jabbing the buttons repeatedly as though to speed up its transit. Rather than suffer an uncomfortable ride with her, he took the stairs, lunging up them four at a time. Room 421 was his, so he ascended to the fourth floor.

The unmistakable ping of an elevator announced the arrival of another. Out strutted Ria on the fourth floor, glancing this way and that before making in the opposite direction to him.

"You're not on the same corridor as me, are you?" he said.

But she seemed not to hear him and sped away with a subtle stomp which, to his great admiration, emphasised the motion of her hips. At the risk of being discovered, he turned quickly now to room 412, where he waved his keycard over the sensor-panel; then he tried the handle. The door stood fast. He nudged his shoulder into it. The door stood fast. He waved the keycard over the sensor-panel again. The door still stood fast.

"Curse this stupid door. Why—won't—you—open?" he said, bashing his skull on it several times. After one too many headbutts, he took a few paces back and was about to shoulder-charge his way through, but before he could, the door swung open. Standing in the doorway was a squat man in the nude, wearing nothing but a horseshoe moustache; his chest hair looked like a bundle of black wires knotted together; and the hair on his head was up in a chaotic fuzz, as though a frosty wind had frozen it so. Whether he was speaking another language or was simply unintelligible, it was hard to say. But there could be no misunderstanding the universality of his flipping his middle finger and his slamming the door in Ulrik's face thereafter.

Somewhere far off down the hallway, he heard that annoying piggish snort again. Turning, he saw Ria, whose face was crinkled up in a cute, corrugated scrunch, rolling about on the floor and kicking her legs at the ceiling in a silent fit of laughter. "Ria, help me with this stupid thing. The door—it's stuck. And there's some weird Bulgarian-looking guy sleeping in my room."

"And you're sure it's *your* room, are you?"

"Yah, look; it's says here on my keycard, room 421, and—" examining the number under closer scrutiny, "—four, two, one; oh shit."

"And ..."

"This guy's room is 412; mine is 421."

"Here," she said, rolling her eyes and gathering herself to her feet, "pass me your keycard before you start any more fights."

Even though from here on in he knew how to gain entry, he was keen to allow Ria to unlock room 421 on his behalf, for he feared disturbing some other moustachioed man again.

"There's been a change of rules today," she said, arriving at the door of room 421. When standing there, she made a sign of the cross with the keycard over the sensor-panel. "For extra security, you've now got to swipe your keycard in the shape of a crucifix to gain entry to your room."

"Why?"

"Because," joining her hands, "only through Jesus Christ will doors open to you."

"Ugh, Ria, not you, too? Why is everybody in DRUE so obsessed with Jesus?"

Her nose crinkled again. "Did you ... you *did*. You actually believed me. You're literally the most gullible person ever. Ha, I love it!"

"Annoying female," he grumbled, contracting his lips into a tiny, fierce circle.

"Aaaand this is your room," now gesturing with her expressive hands to the most obvious domestic articles as though she were in the business of real estate and selling a property to a creature from another galaxy. "This is a bed where you sleep, these are your wardrobes where you hang clothes, this is the bathtub where you wash, and this is a toilet, but don't get washed in there, forager."

"Don't worry, I won't be going near that. Had to use one once when I was in hospital. Never again."

"What do you mean?" confronting him with her hands on her hips and wearing a look of outrage on her face.

"Why would I want to be sitting naked on a seat where someone else has rubbed their butt?"

"Okay … I'm going to pretend I didn't just hear that."

"Thanks. Now, Ria, if you could leave because … I need to get into my altitude tent. Coach will kill me if he finds out I'm not in it. He's got all kinds of trackers monitoring my sleep pattern."

"Oh, what's an altitude tent? Can I see?" sitting on his bed with her legs crossed at the knees and taking her ponytail out of her frilly black bobble before fixing her hair up with it again.

A girl—on his bed. Don't be weird, Ulrik. Be normal. Act normal. Breathe normal. His pacing eyes sought a distraction. Anything. Just something to avert the impending throb in his pants. Old ladies. Wrinkly old ladies. Wrinkly, old, naked, toothless, hairy ladies—with warts. Such a thought, disturbing as it was, tamed his fancies.

"So, Ria …"

"Yes?"

"The crowd booed me today because of who I am, but what's so special about you?"

"Sit down, and I'll tell you," patting the mattress. He took his seat at the edge of the bed, being careful not to get so close in case it should make her feel uncomfortable. "I'm Catalan, Ulrik."

"You're a what? A catamaran?"

"No, stupid. It's my nationality. I'm from Catalonia."

"That's not a place I know about."

"Most don't recognise us as a country. I'm from Barcelona; you've heard of that, at least?"

"Uh, I always thought Barcelona was in Spain; but I never studied joglaffy because I never went to school, so I could be wrong."

"Barcelona used to be a part of Spain until my people fought for our right to be independent; the right to govern ourselves; the right to make our own laws; the right to conduct our own trade. Until, that is, the Holy Shepherd met us with fire and fury and mobilised his special forces on our streets—the Archangels." Her bottle-brown eyes seemed fixed on a single speck on the wall. "I suppose I can't expect a forager from Svalbard to know this, but my country is one of the few to have taken a stand against DRUE: we're at war with the Holy Shepherd. A civil war. Though you won't hear anything positive said about the rebellion in the news."

"Ria, I'm sorry. I had no idea. It must've been hard for you to focus on your volleyball training with a war going on back home."

"Volleyball? Ssst, who said anything about playing volleyball?"

"I thought you said … ?"

"I'm a shooter."

"Oh, in which sport? Soccer? Basketball? Wait, let me guess … hockey?"

Ria held her arms out as though she were aiming down the barrel of an invisible rifle. Then she reckoned to pull its trigger.

"You shoot guns?" blinking with surprise.

"All my life; and not just for sport in these last few years—sadly."

"You mean to say you've been fighting on the frontline? In the rebellion against DRUE?"

"Uh-hum. That's why I'm here: to represent my people; to show the world we Catalans are unbeatable. Though they wouldn't let me officially represent Catalonia because the Holy Shepherd doesn't recognise our country's claim to independence. So I had no choice but to compete as an Independent Olympian."

"I don't know what to say. I'm speechless."

"You don't have to say anything. It's just nice not to be hated and berated. Everybody always has an opinion, but they don't know shit about me."

"Ria, those people jeering in the crowd tonight—they're cowards. But you're brave. A hero for standing up to the Holy Shepherd."

"And you're cute for thinking so, Ulrik," she said, taking out the frilly black bobble that held up her ponytail and wearing it on her wrist as a temporary bracelet. Their flirting eyes met for a prolonged spell, during which she fanned him with her eyelashes. "Anyway ..." slapping her hips to signal her departure, "it's getting late." As she leant over to him, he thought for a moment that she might kiss him, but she withdrew her face and honked his nose. Then she stood up and made gains towards the door.

"Err, um, well, if I don't see you around then good luck with the beach volleyball ..."

"Hilarious."

He'd hoped after making his joke that she'd tell him he'd see her again soon. But she wished him good luck with a wooden expression.

Do we hug now? he wondered. Nuh. It doesn't look like it.

"Thanks again, Ulrik," she said, fleeing out of the door before things got awkward.

He spied on her as she strutted down the corridor, flaunting her rhythmic waist as she went, her tresses flowing long and loose behind her; and it was as though she knew she was being watched. When arriving at a junction, she turned right and never looked back before vanishing from view.

Ulrik stood for a moment in contemplation, his heart still racing, his eyes dreadfully pacing; and having closed the room door, he wilted like a flower, head bowing, the stem of his spine bending and shrinking. Then he formed a club with his fist and bashed the door six or seven times before backing up into it and relying on it as a means to sink down, reducing himself to a shaggy heap on the floor. He clutched his face in his clammy hands and yanked his head. "That's it, then. You probably won't be seeing her again. But why do you care, Ulrik? You've only just met the girl. You thought she was annoying. So why do you care?" Yet, when he withdrew his hands from his face, he noticed something black and frilly scrunched up in the duvet. A stray odd sock—nuh: Ria's bobble! He crawled over to it and snatched it in the manner of a thief. Then, stretching the fabric across his nostrils and closing his eyes, he surrendered to the sweet perfume emanating from it; and he slipped the bobble over his wrist and wore it as a bracelet as she'd done, not caring about its frilly floral aspect.

This oversight of Ria's (as he thought it) was his golden chance; he had a perfect reason to go tracking her down in the morning without appearing like some stalker. He was determined to get the bobble back to her, if only to witness the cute crinkling of her nose when she smiled one more time.

He hardly slept that night for thinking about her; and only after practising a copious amount of kissing on the back of his hand did he eventually drift off to sleep.

Chapter Twenty-Four

INDOLPHINS

Shivering in a pool of his own sweat, Ulrik lay victim on the bathroom floor to the fever that had struck him the day after the opening ceremony three days ago. So hot and sticky was he that he had to peel his body off the floor tiles when hauling himself upright. As he did, the flannel on his forehead fell into his lap. It had originally soothed him, having been soaked in cold water, but he'd been idle for so long now that it'd dried out like a crusty autumn leaf.

"Everything happens for a reason," croaked Ulrik, hoping to derive some superstitious meaning from the latest miserable hand he'd been dealt. It was just as well this period of sickness should befall him now and not at the time of his event (which was still almost two weeks away). Besides, it was custom for professional swimmers at this stage to remove themselves from the more gruelling aspects of training—this being the science of *tapering*, when exercise is kept to a minimum to repair and prepare the athlete for their ultimate race. "Rest is best," as Coach Lukashenko said whenever the science of tapering was up for discussion.

At once, when sensing a spontaneous feathery tickle some way up in his nostrils, Ulrik seized a sheet of toilet tissue just before a chain of explosive sneezes broke out: "Tchoo—tchow—tchee—tchar—tchah." Such violent sneezing unclogged his nostrils, and he felt a good deal better for expunging a legion of germs that had been leeching the life from him. Then, as he lay back on the cool tiles, he scrunched up the used tissue and tossed it towards the toilet, which it missed and instead joined the growing mound of other tissue balls.

Thud, thud, thud. A knock, or rather an intolerable banging at the door. "Wake up, Magnusson," said a feminine accent of Mediterranean origin.

"Ugh, stop shouting, Ria," he groaned, after which he sat upright and propped up his heavy head with his fingertips.

"Ulrik, it's me," she said, trying the door handle six or seven times with a strength that threatened to devastate the integrity of the handle's ironmongery.

"All right, I'm coming." When standing, it felt as though he was on a vessel being tossed about by waves, for the room seemed to rock from side to side, and he retched at the nauseating sensation. "All right, I'm here. Now please stop shouting."

"I'm not shouting," raising her voice in offence at the accusation; though it was a feigned offence, for a moment later she burst through in all her sprightliness and almost toppled him over. She was a welcome sight to his tired eyes; her caramel waves were fixed up in a ponytail with her frilly black bobble (having earlier returned this to her; his reward being the friendliest of hugs), and her bottle-brown eyes gleamed at him like two ripe chestnuts. "You look better today," she said, smoothing away the wet forelock of hair clinging to his cheek.

"I'm not feeling much better."

"Well, you won't, in this lair. Here, let me open these curtains." She stomped towards the balcony where she drew open the curtains and balcony doors. White light accompanied by a fresh breeze sped into the grungy abode and evicted the stale air. Anyone else would've avoided him, but she, like a nurse whose practice it is to carry on in the face of a pestilential pandemic, was present as often as she could be. Even after her victories today, she'd made it her priority to come and fuss over him and bring him back to health. "Have you had much to drink today?" placing a bottle of water in one of his hands and a kale smoothie in the other. "You need to drink plenty."

"Enough about me, Ria. Today is about you. You were amazing out there."

"Did you see?"

"Did I see? Ria, I saw every shot of every round. I saw everything, including the medal ceremony."

"Oh, I couldn't stop crying. I wish you could've been there to see it. Watching it on TV or Tech is one thing, but being there—I felt more alive than I ever have. But I know how important rest is to you right now. I don't blame you, okay?"

He nodded, but even though he heard her, little did he heed. Both her hands were held suspiciously behind her back, and his ears picked up a distinctive clink-clank at various intervals. His eyes were fixed on her midriff as though he were trying to see directly through her. "What's that you're hiding behind your back? Are those the medals, Ria? Let me see—let me see."

"Close your eyes," her freckled nose crinkling. With his eyes now shut, he mentally readied himself for a kiss—just in case she was to stick one on him. Nuh, it wasn't to be. "Okay, forager, you can open your eyes again."

There, dangling around her neck, were two glinting discs; a sun and a moon—a gold medal and a silver one—and the proudest pout enhanced her face. "Can I touch it? The gold one?" Ulrik's arm drew itself up of its own accord, and before she replied he'd already nudged the silver medal aside and taken hold of the gold one—or perhaps it'd taken hold of him. "Amazing, Ria. They're amazing. I mean, *you're* amazing. I'm so, so happy for you. Proud, even."

"I still can't believe it. Winning me the women's gold final skeet medal," fumbling her words in confused excitement. "I mean, when I won gold in the skeet final. Ugh, what am I even saying? I'm literally just vomiting my words out. Bleurgh. You know what I mean. I can't think straight. I was like that today when shooting. I let the crowd get to me.

I lost my concentration. But after a couple of bad shots, I relaxed. There was nothing to lose after that. So I played for fun. Took some risks. And it paid off! Anyway, that was that. I won gold. But winning a silver medal in the men's skeet final—that has to top everything. I'm one of only a very few women ever to win a medal in a mixed-gender event. Ria Lorenzo i Lopez of Catalonia made history today." She bounced up and down, as did her chest for a moment or two thereafter.

"I know … I've been meaning to ask, how did you come to compete in the men's skeet?"

"You must've heard about those athletes dropping out? So those who scored highest in the women's finals took their place."

"Nuh, I didn't hear about them. Why did they drop out?"

"Seriously? It's all over the news."

"My uncle Cheng—well, he's not my real uncle, but he's like an uncle— he always told me to avoid watching the news. He said the purpose of the news isn't to educate you but to enrage you. That's how they make their money—getting people angry. When people are angry, they don't turn off the news. They become addicted. So tell me, what is it in the news I'm supposed to have missed?"

"Saifullah threats … The authorities have raised the terror threat level to high alert—meaning an attack is highly likely."

"Tell me that's not true, Ria."

"Ulrik, I know you're worried about Saifullah, but the threat levels— they're just a precaution. Back in Catalonia, there's conflict in the capital every day. There's always danger. You have to learn to shut it out, okay?" She reached up and pinched his cheek. "Trust me. Everything will be okay."

"Fine, I'm trusting you this time."

"Good. Now, I have to go. I haven't spoken to my friends back home about me winning yet. But before I go," sidling up to him and linking her arm through his, "I wanted to ask you something."

"Yah … ?"

She drew in a deep breath: "Are you free tonight to celebrate with me?"

"Celebrate? Ah, I'm not sure," breaking out into a fit of sneezes. "I'm not sure if I'm well enough."

"Well," shrugging her shoulders, "the other shooters have asked me to go for some drinks and party with them. Shayne O'Shaughnessy has been invited, so I'd rather not go, but if I have no other options …"

"Shayne?" Suddenly Ulrik's illness departed his body. "What business does he have with shooters?"

"Exactly. I'd rather celebrate with just me and you. But if you want to wallow in self-pity, then that's your choice, I guess."

"Bah, I'm supposed to be meeting with Coach."

"Fuck that guy. Tell him you're still unwell, and meet me instead," fanning her eyelashes at him. "Anyway, if he's concerned about your health, he should let you get some fresh air."

"Just me and you, you say?" scratching his elbow and chewing his bottom lip.

"Yes! So, are you in?" wrapping her arms so tightly about his ribs that she induced in him another burst of rapid sneezes. "Just me and you."

"Where? When?"

"Be ready at six in the lobby, okay?"

"Fine, but before I agree, I've been meaning to ask you a question."

"Shoot …" She looked up at him with shy, expectant eyes veiled behind her tresses of hair.

"What are you thinking of spending your prize money on?"

"Prize money, Ulrik?" Her bottle-brown eyes disappeared as she squinted in confusion.

"For winning a gold and silver medal … your prize money."

"Ssst, silly forager. There's no prize money for Independent Olympians like us, and I know you know that. Don't rub salt in the wound."

A chill ran throughout the network of his bone marrow. "What do you mean?"

"Who'd present us with such a prize? Other athletes get prize money from the countries they represent. Everybody knows that. We don't represent anybody but ourselves, so we get zilch. Surely you know that …"

"I've been training in Russia for the past four years, and I have no access to Tech. How should I know? Bah, I feel stupid now." He ran his hands over his scalp.

"Hey, are you okay? You look pale—like, paler than usual."

"Ah, I'm still feverish, that's all. Ignore me. I'm good. I knew that. I was just teasing you—rubbing salt in the wound, as you say."

"Okay, forager boy. So, shall I see you at six? Meet me in the lobby. Don't you dare think about not showing."

"Lobby at six—lobby at six," he repeated, tapping his skull. "I'll be there."

"Byeeeeeee …" she said, skipping out of the door and prolonging her e's until she disappeared out of earshot, " … eeeee."

"No—prize—money," he mouthed, as he fell to his knees. "Coach Lukashenko. That bastard knew all along and didn't tell me. So that's why he never let me have any Tech of my own … Always telling me it was to protect me … To keep me away from distractions. But all along it was because he knew I'd find out the truth. He's only in this for himself. Bah, I could murder him. Murder him!"

How was he to pay off his debts and free Mamma and Pappa if not by winning some grand prize? Four years of his life he'd spent in training—wasted. There was nothing here for him now, except a friend in Ria. He'd see her tonight; see her lovely face one last time, and go back to Svalbard, never to return.

———

6 p.m. came, then 6:01, then 6:02, and before he knew it, 7 p.m., and Ulrik wondered if he'd got the wrong time and place altogether, for Ria hadn't come.

He'd come dressed for the occasion, having lowered himself to petty knavery: the clothes upon his back had been acquired from lost property by his claiming to be their owner. His khaki shorts and open shirt had been terribly crinkled, though that was no longer an issue, for, owing to their tightness and being a few sizes too small, all the creases vanished when worn. Neither were there any shoes that fitted his flipper-feet, so his only choice was to don a pair of Hawaiian flip-flops. With his hair swept back into a ponytail, his beard plaited, his eyes shadowed in kohl, he loitered in the lobby with a bunch of hyacinths he'd pinched from a verge outside the entrance.

A host of strangers' eyes pried on him. Many folk loitered close by but reckoned to be absorbed in their Tech whenever he cast a glare at them. Such an audience magnified his nerves, and his bowels seemed to growl at their presence. At last, all eyes left him and fell instead on a young woman gliding through the lobby. His hormones leapt into a frenzy at the sight of her, and then he came to understand how, after all these years, Pappa's impatience could subside in a heartbeat and how he mellowed with a sudden forgiveness when he'd spent so long in waiting for Mamma to get ready; for here was Ria, leading with one foot in front of the other like a lynx. She was clad in a golden dress that clung to her shapeliness; the tall black heels she wore pronounced the striations of her lean bronze legs; and the lenses of her sunglasses were like two gold medals accentuating her glowing face. Yet, when she passed through, other women hissed in their envious covens and jibed in their tribes.

"I wouldn't let my daughter go out like *that*," said one.

"I wouldn't let my son go anywhere near *that*," said another.

Ulrik stood erect with rage, though Ria seemed unaffected by the slander. Instead, she dispensed a sour glance and looked down her freckled nose at them before turning away. As she overtook them, she reckoned to spritz water at them with a gesture of her dismissive, sassy hand, at which they flinched and foamed thereafter in silent outrage.

"Hey, gorgeous," she said, resting her sunglasses on her head, linking her arm onto Ulrik's, then casually bashing her hip against his. Compliments were one thing, but her bashing her hip up against his—that was contact he hadn't expected on a first date; and only after they'd passed outside did the redness of his face fade. "By the way, I'm so sorry about being late, Ulrik. It took me longer than expected to get ready. Oh," clutching at her breast, "are those flowers for me?" Tutting amiably, "You didn't need to do that for me. That's too cute. And so is that outfit."

"Thank you." His mouth was too dry to partake in proper conversation, so dry, in fact, that a metallic taste affected his tongue; and his replies were mechanical for a good while afterwards. It was fortunate that within moments their transport arrived: a driverless taxi. As Ulrik made for the passenger side, he noticed Ria eyeing him from the other side with a scrunched expression and her arms knotted.

"Something wrong, Ria?"

"Ssst, aren't you going to open the door for me?"

"Why? Is there something wrong with your arm?"

"No ... it's just polite."

"That's not a custom I'm familiar with."

"Well, it's not hard," grimacing.

"Then why not do it yourself?" grimacing back.

"I should've said that to you when you were wallowing in self-pity these last few days."

They both got into their seats, buckled up, and faced out of their respective windows. Strange customs were these to expect folk to do things for you when a person was indeed capable. Not unless a person's arms had been amputated would he rush to open the door for anyone. Would she expect him to feed her, brush her hair, trim her toenails, flush one of those disgusting toilets on her behalf?

An emotional tug of war played out (as is often the case during the spring of any courtship); neither was willing to concede an inch of battleground in the struggle for dominance. It could be said that a union of personalities such as two Olympians is like the marriage of gunpowder and a naked flame, it being capable of dazzling fireworks but capable also of widespread destruction: the power to bring a blaze both beautiful and bright, but also the power to bring both chaos and plight.

Since there was little conversation to be had, Ulrik pressed his face to the tinted window and watched as the streets of Athens rolled on by. Every pedestrian, it seemed, was fiddling with handTech, eyeTech, or headTech. Even fledglings in pushchairs had their malleable little minds addled by Tech—no doubt with some animated adaptation of daily bread. It was dangerous that faith should be impressed into their minds without their consent; dangerous because, as Chenglei always said, "Of all notions carried by a person, a *truth* which has been handed down in the formative years is the most difficult to expel." In order to get a better look, Ulrik lowered the tinted window and stuck his head out into the wind like a curious dog, but a second later Ria hit the button to elevate the window, trapping his neck. "Ria, agh, let me out. You'll guillotine me if you're not careful."

She snorted and, judging by the sounds of it, was stamping her feet in hysterics. After savouring a few more moments of his suffering, she set him free.

"I'll get you back for that," he said, feeling about his neck to check that he'd not drawn blood. "Just you wait."

"Oh, stop being so dramatic." Before he could retaliate, her hand slid over and grasped his. Under a streak of slanting sunlight, her eyes appeared amber, and her loveliness tamed him.

"Sorry, I don't mean to be so sensitive—or rude in not opening the door for you. It's just ... I've never been on a date like this."

"Neither have I."

"You've never been on a date?"

"Ssst, I've been on too many. Just never been on a date like this. There's usually a lot more kissing ..."

Was that an invitation or an insult? Should he make a move and catch her off guard? Nuh. Fortunately for him, he was spared the embarrassment, for the vehicle came to a halt and announced, "You have arrived at your destination: Port of Piraeus, Athens: a city civilised by the politics of Pericles, enriched by the dramas of Sophocles, and once protected by the walls of Themistocles. Please take your belongings with you."

"Thanks for the history lesson," said Ulrik, at which Ria smirked and said that it was about time he got some schooling.

Not wishing to make the same mistake again, Ulrik quit the cab and sped to Ria's passenger side where he opened the door like a chauffeur. She swung out her bronze legs, slid her golden sunglasses up the bridge of her nose, then arose like one whose station in life had transcended all others, her cheeks being drawn into the tightest pout and her chin inclined as though she were balancing the weight of her own status on the end of it. She gave him her arm to link onto, then led him down a jetty to the seafront where a flotilla of fishing vessels, yachts, and catamarans were moored. Yonder, the ocean shimmered like a sparkling wine, having caught so acutely the warmth of the regressing red sun; golden waves with their silver crests repeated far beyond the horizon; and against the terracotta sky, drones went about in whimsical fashion like a murmuration of starlings.

"How much did you pay for this?" said Ulrik.

"Ssst, it's rude to ask," cocking her head to the sky. "Besides, I wouldn't do it if I didn't like you."

He was suspended for a moment in thought, cherishing her delightful words over and over.

The yacht itself was without a captain in much the same way as those vehicles on land were without drivers. So, when Ria raised the anchor and programmed in their destination, the yacht took off of its own accord and steered them on a coastal journey of the Aegean Sea.

For the first couple of hours, they sat on the upper deck, picnicking on a platter of mezze: breads, olives, cheeses, stuffed peppers, vine leaves, and koftas. As they ate, both unconsciously leant on their elbows across the table and became absorbed in each other's lustful eyes.

When using his cutlery, Ulrik held his knife and fork in the same way he always did—like ski poles pointing down, stabbing and jabbing his way as he slalomed the mound on his plate—and he talked while eating and slurped while drinking and belched when resting. "Oh, this food is excrement," said Ulrik. "I'll tell you one thing: I'm not missing the food on Svalbard. Whatever this is, me like. Me like a lot."

Ria muffled her laughter with a napkin. "What did you say it was?"

"Excrement ... because it is."

Snort, snort, snort. Stamp, stamp, stamp.

"Ugh, what's so funny now?" laying down his ski poles and waiting for her to regain her maturity.

"I think you mean 'excellent'. Excrement is another word for shit."

"Oh, you mean shit like the kind of shit pigs roll around in? Pigs that snort like you, piggy?" he said, trying now to offend her and mimicking her snort. Though it only amplified her amusement.

From there on in there emerged a mutual weirdness, and they were casually horrid to each other, taunting, jibing, insulting, and flirting while familiarising themselves with the deeper details of one another's lives. As the sun rolled over the threshold for its nap, their champagne flutes chinked in salutation of Ria's victory, and they raised a toast to her and her homeland.

Night came on swiftly, and so did their tipsiness.

"So, Ulrik, you probably don't know this, but I recently broke up with my ex. Not that I want to talk about him. I just thought you should know; I'm not looking for anything serious. I'm young; you're young; we should just be out here to have fun, okay?" His hands being beneath the table, he scratched and scraped and scoured his knees. "Anyway, I've been meaning to ask,"—twiddling the cables of her caramel hair—"have you got a girlfriend at home?"

"Nuh, not yet. I'm waiting for the right girl."

"Can I ask you—no. I shouldn't ask that," biting her nails. "It'd be rude."

"I keep no secrets. Ask away."

"Have you ever … you know … *done it*?"

"Kissed a girl?" reclining with his hands interlaced behind his head. "Sure. Many girls. Many times. More than I care to count."

"Right. Kissing … But I've overheard women say other things; things about what they'd do to you. I'm not going to repeat them, so don't ask me to."

"Okay, I won't," he said, taking her in a literal sense and misunderstanding her inquisitive advances. Besides, he'd heard enough derogatory remarks to last him a lifetime. No good would he derive from hearing any such insults about what other women wanted to do to him.

In Ria's smouldering eyes he sensed yet more questions burning, and he supposed they, too, might make him feel awkward when answering. An erratic bout of fidgeting—knee jerking, neck scratching, lip chewing—came over him. He grew hotter by the second, then a sudden urge to cool off struck him: "Ria, excuse me," sliding out of his chair from behind the table. He kicked off his Hawaiian flip-flops, leapt up onto the starboard gunwale, and stood for a moment overlooking the calm black waters. Still clothed, he plunged into the sea.

Darkness. A tranquil darkness swallowed him. A purposeful drowning; his mouth, sinuses, gullet, lungs, his whole respiratory system filled with brine. Then, when he resurfaced, he blew from every orifice, discharging the mucus from his inner engines and pipework so that nasal breathing was made possible again.

"Ulrik, get back here where I can see you," said a faraway voice belonging to a curvaceous silhouette. "You're scaring me."

A flash of rebellion darkened his eyes, and there Ulrik turned on his side, stretched out his oar-arms over his head, and came into his fish kick, oscillating through the water. Although still a little weary from his sickness, his muscles felt a renewed vigour from his surplus sleep of late, and he shook off the dull aches as he thrashed about the water. When arriving at the side of the yacht, he did something he'd never done: a sort of aqueous contemporary dance; turning, stretching, leaping, floating, pirouetting!

"Is it cold?" shouted Ria, while slipping out of her dress. She'd come prepared with a bikini underneath, but Ulrik was too naïve to read this premeditated attack on his desires.

"Nuh, too mild if anything," he said, enjoying the relief of unblocked nostrils with repeated deep breaths.

"Okay, I'm coming in!" tying her hair up in a loose bun. Then she sat on the gunwale and dangled her legs over the side of the boat while tucking her hands beneath her armpits. "Ready? One, two, three ..." Her spindly legs cycled in the air as she crashed into the water. Not even a fish out of water flaps as violently as she did when in the water. "Uh—uh— uft! It's freezing. You tricked me."

Ulrik eddied around her while she kicked about to stay afloat. Her smoky eye make-up had smeared. So, too, had her lip gloss, bronzer, blusher, and all.

"Told you I'd get you back for trapping my head in the window, didn't I?" he taunted.

"Get me out, Ulrik. I can't feel my legs. Uft—uft—oh—oooh!"

"And you say I'm the dramatic one?"

"No, Ulrik. I just don't have antifreeze proteins in my bloodstream like you. Get me out. Quick, quick, quick." She made a lunge for him and dangled herself around his neck, their faces now only a breath's distance away. He could feel her hot panting on his neck and her fretting hands secured on his tense shoulders; and, quite by accident, he found his own hand adjoined to her rear, keeping her suspended above the water. At once, all complaint from Ria quietened. Her wet lips were parted, her chest heaved.

A long pause. Not a move was made on either part. Even the waves seemed still about them.

"Are you touching my ass?" she said.

"Oh, that's what that is?"

"What did you think it was?"

"I don't know. I heard there are jellyfish in these waters."

"You're such a dick."

"Hey, if you want me to let go—"

"No!"

"You want me to keep hold and carry you to the yacht?"

"Uh-huh," she said, nose crinkling and huddling in closer to him for warmth. "There's a jacuzzi on the yacht. Let's get in there where it's nice and warm. Go, go, go."

Ulrik swam over to the stern of the yacht where they both climbed back on board using a ladder. Ria bundled herself into many towels and spent an age fixing her make-up. When she eventually joined him in the jacuzzi, she came bearing two flutes of champagne.

"I've had the best time with you tonight, Ulrik."

Glasses chinked.

"Me too, Ria. I promise, when this is over, I won't ever forget you."

"Over ... It's weird to think there's an end to this—to us. I feel like I've known you my whole life," running a finger around the rim of the champagne flute. "So, what are your plans after the Olympics?"

"I can't lie to you, Ria," letting slip an exasperated sigh. "I've decided to go home tomorrow. I won't be competing in the aquadrome."

"Home?" Her cold eyes demanded an explanation.

"I've made up my mind, and nobody can change it. Not even you."

How she transfigured herself in front of him from princess to hag, as though her moods were configurations to be deployed at times of her choosing. "Fine. It's your life. Do what you want. See if I care. But at least tell me why you're quitting. Don't bullshit me."

"I'm not quitting, Ria. I came to the Olympics to win money; to free my mamma and pappa."

She abandoned eye contact with him and focused instead on the bubbles rising to the top of her champagne; the bubbles of the jacuzzi, too, were rising in like manner. "So because you've discovered there's no prize money, you're just going to throw it all away? Years of training and sacrifice. To go home and live an easy life. Fucking stupidest thing I've heard any boy ever say."

"Being a forager isn't an easy life, Ria. There is danger every day, like not knowing where your next meal will come from or if you're going to have enough fuel to last the winter."

"Don't talk to me about danger. Not even in your nightmares could you imagine what me and my people have been through."

"I'm not saying—"

"I didn't think you were like everybody else—who only care for money."

"You think I care for money? Money is only a means to win my parents' freedom. Tell me, Ria, how else should I be setting them free, huh?"

"You'll find a way. Even if you lose in the aquadrome, your life will never be the same. I've never seen anybody swim like you just did, or hold their breath for so long underwater. You'll probably earn more money from sponsorships. I don't know. I don't have the answer. Join a circus—a freak show. They'd take you in."

"Shut your mouth," he said, gently stubbing her in the ribs with his big toe.

"I'll shut my mouth," sidling up to him and resting her legs over his, "I'll shut my mouth if you agree to stay and show the world who you are. People are counting on you to show up. You going home—that's what the Holy Shepherd wants ... for everybody to forget who you are. Well, if that's what *you* want, go back home and be a nobody."

Of all fates, being forgettable was the cruellest. Small deeds were for small folk, and he wasn't small.

"It's one fucking race," added Ria. "It's not like you have preliminary heats and quarter- and semi-finals to do like I did. One fucking race."

"Yah, because the 10-kilometre freestyle is the marathon of swimming. You don't see marathon runners doing heats. It's a different sport, Ria."

"Not saying it's not tough. Just saying it's one race. The one race everybody is psyched for. Everybody's eyes are on you. Not Shayne O'Shaughnessy. By the end of summer, everybody will have forgotten him. But they won't forget you. Not Homo Nova. So why are you being such a selfish dick?"

That was a sobering sentiment he needed to hear again. "What did you call me?"

"A selfish dick."

"Nuh, nuh, before that. Who am I?"

"Homo Nova." Her eyes appeared to swell when saying so. Then she girded his arm about her and rested her cheek against his body, thereby making a pillow of his chest. Her body was squashed against his, and both her legs coiled about one of his, like vines about a tree trunk. "There's no bullshit with you, Ulrik. You are who you are. You don't pretend to be anybody but yourself. That's why I *love* spending time with you."

"You're right, Ria. And I feel the same about spending time with you. When we're together, I have indolphins."

Ria frowned while processing what he'd said. "You have what?"

"Goodness, we could make candles from the wax in your ears. Didn't you hear me? I said 'in-dol-phins'."

So began her silent hysterics. At the climax of it, she gave a piggish snort. This laugh of hers was sure to be intolerable to strangers, but her weird little ways were now his favourite things.

"Ugh, tell me what's so funny this time ..."

"'Endorphins' is what I think you meant to say, but you said 'indolphins'. Ah, Ulrik, who will I laugh at when you're gone?" squeezing his ribcage, looking up at him with glistening eyes, and curling a pitiable bottom lip outwards. "And what about me? What about us?" breaking away from him momentarily to top up his champagne flute. He found himself more agreeable for having consumed it. "Haven't you had the best time with me tonight?"

"Of course I have, Ria. You didn't have to do this. This was supposed to be *your* celebration."

"I did it because I wanted to be with you tonight. Nobody else."

"Yah, but I wish I could return the favour."

"Exactly. You owe me, forager boy." Ria looked upon him and fanned him with her devious eyelashes. She hauled herself up onto his knee, sat with her spine erect, and interlocked her hands about the back of his neck. "I'll make a deal with you."

"A deal?" He found himself looking to the sky as if the conditions of this deal were to be discovered somewhere up in the ether. Though the chief reason for it was to avert his eyes, for his heart throbbed with untameable lust.

She with the bronze skin, silver tongue, and golden heart made her final move: "I promise," speaking in slow, seductive tones as her wandering hand crept up the inside of his thigh, "I promise that if you win a medal in the aquadrome, I'll give you the best kiss of your life." He thought she was going to kiss him now, but she nuzzled her face into his neck and gently sank her hot teeth into him, causing his body to shudder. He was certain that at some stage she'd licked him, too, though he was careful not to twitch again and show his inexperience, and he abided her advances like a statue. But in pressing her ear to his breast, she was sure to have heard the rampant throb of his heart and have sensed his arousal. "So, Ulrik, do we have a deal?" whispered the amorous, glamorous vixen; pouting, nose crinkling.

"We—" faintly choking on his words, "we have a deal, Ria."

CHAPTER TWENTY-FIVE

INSIDE THE AQUADROME

The coarse black bristles on Vlad's neck, arms, and hands stood to attention as he paced about the changing rooms.

Never had Ulrik seen Vlad so muted. Few words of value had he to offer now, having tutored him on all things swimming and psyche. Besides, the intervals for speech were sparse between his glugging of coffee, dragging of cigarettes, and chewing and chomping and champing of spearmint gum; and under that terrible grinding, the jagged mountain range of his teeth was sure to have eroded to a line of smooth, snowy hills. Not that Ulrik wanted to talk to him anyway. Upon Ria's advice, he'd not yet confronted Coach regarding his deceit about the prize money. All that frustration and anger was to be better channelled in the aquadrome. His mind was fixed now on his race, and here it was. His one shot. Less than an hour to go until the greatest fight of his life.

One by one, the athletes were summoned over the speakers, and the raucous crowd above sent shock waves down to the core of the changing rooms. When in no particular order Shayne O'Shaughnessy was called forth, there was a tectonic rumble as though everyone in the aquadrome, and indeed everyone in DRUE, simultaneously leapt to their feet and screamed his name.

Throughout this violation of the eardrums, Ulrik sat meditatively on a bench, drawing in tempestuous breaths, the scent of chlorine infiltrating his airways. Here he was, clad only in his latex trunks. He wore no goggles, for his eyes saw well enough underwater; and he donned no swimming cap and refused to shave his beard and body hair, unlike the other athletes, who relied too much on the extra millisecond gained from lessening the drag. A weak mindset was that of the shavers, thought he.

To think some of his rivals were earlier complaining about the apparatus here being shabby ... plunge pools, saunas, steam rooms, ice buckets, integrated Tech of all kinds. What might they have said of the rust-eaten establishment he'd been all too familiar with in Russia and of his formative years swimming the frozen fjords? It was thanks to those conditions that Ulrik was desperate; and in nature, it's the desperate beast which levies the most atrocious threat when fighting, having itself the least to lose but the most to gain.

For some time now, Ulrik's sweaty hand familiarised itself with Tristan's Victoria Cross, and he squeezed it in the manner of a Christian who implores a divine favour from a crucifix. When rubbing his thumb over the words "For Valour", he felt a good deal braver, and, imbued with extra courage, he placed the war medal back in the brass tin and stashed his belongings in a locker, thereafter returning to the warm seat on his bench where he awaited his call.

At once, Vlad spun around on his heels and stood before him.

"Coach?" said Ulrik, with the resolute aspect of a soldier bringing himself to attention.

"Ulrik, Ulrik, Ulrik, how to say this?" said Vlad, sighing, the effect of which caused the erect black bristles on his neck to droop like wilting flowers. He seemed to be deciding on whether to say something that troubled him. After much deliberation, he nodded as though he supposed that in this one instance only it would be appropriate to speak with a sober heart. "I'm sorry if you think that, at the last moment, I'd have some wisdom to impart that would spur you on to greatness in the aquadrome. But I've taught you everything I know about this game ... and along the way there's a thing or two you've taught me about the game of life. Ulrik, there's something about me which I should tell you, something I've not been completely honest about." Cracks appeared in his clay-grey face—a sorrowful expression which hinted at some inner regret. At first, Ulrik expected him to confess about the prize money, but he couldn't recall a time in their relationship when he'd ever apologised for anything, so he suspected it was something else. "Swimming has been my life, my whole life, but it'll only be a few chapters of yours. When you walk out of that door, your life is going to change in ways that you, me, and anybody else could never imagine. What I mean to say is—" Vlad faltered and pinched his eyes. "What I mean to say is that to have played a small part in your life, my friend, has been my proudest achievement. I should've been more like you at your age, but in my early success I became arrogant. Got complacent. Failed to show up. Fucked around. Fucked other people around. Fucked up my chances of ever being someone special. I lost everything, and I lost everybody who was special to me. But here I am again; I feel special to have journeyed to the Olympics one last time. And it's because of you." His glassy eyes reddened; his voice shook; his hands tremored. "You saved my life, Ulrik. You did. Believe me, before we met, I almost—it's hard for me to admit ..." Swallowing, he took a long pause. "I tried many times to end it—to take my own life."

"Coach, I never—"

"I'm fine, Ulrik. Don't worry about me. In fact, I've never felt better," dabbing away a joyous tear and clearing his throat. "Sorry to put that on you. I needed to get it off my chest."

There was a knock at the door. A summons for Ulrik Magnusson.

"Looks like you're up, Homo Nova," said Vlad. "Are you ready?"

"Let's do this, Coach," drawing himself to his full height and bouncing on his toes. "I'm bringing you home a gold medal." Arriving at the changing room door, Ulrik halted when he saw he wasn't being followed. "Aren't you coming, Coach?"

"You don't need to call me—" A melancholy inflexion stalled his speech. Recovering, he finished his sentence: "You don't need to call me

Coach anymore. There's nothing more to coach you in. My part in this journey is over. What the champion does next is his concern only."

"You won't be watching me race?" said Ulrik, his swollen eyebrow casting shade over his face.

Incessant knocking at the door: "Magnusson, you're required at the poolside. They're about to announce you over the speakers." Ulrik leant his weight against the door to prevent its opening and told the intruders he was naked and would be out soon.

"I used to think," said Vlad, "that winning a gold medal was everything, but along the way I learnt that results and scores are immaterial. I've seen you practise this race a hundred times. Each time, you succeeded. You succeeded when you begged me to take you to hell and back. I can't be any more impressed by today's race than those I've already seen, and my estimation of you won't change based on the position you finish. In my eyes, you're already a winner."

"So if I come last, you're saying you don't care?" feeling somewhat lighter and liberated of tension.

"I'm sure I'll hear of the result, but when I do, it won't change how I feel. Understand, the only result that ever truly concerned me was that you showed up, that you did everything in your power to take every opportunity to be your best. It wasn't a gold medal I sought, just a warrior who knew what it meant to give their all—something I never did. And I got that, my friend, from you. So, to answer your question: no, it doesn't matter to me if you finish in last place." Vlad rested his hands on Ulrik's shoulders, and Ulrik did the same to him; in the custom of foragers, they exchanged a mild headbutt. "What matters most is that you gave your all."

The last of Vlad's words saw the expulsion of any remaining bitterness Ulrik harboured towards him. Vladimir Lukashenko had sacrificed so much, and without him, he'd still be a forager.

"It's time," said Ulrik, removing his weight from the door, causing an armed rifleman from the other side to come crashing through. A further four Archangels (DRUE's special forces) stood in their camouflage at the ready behind their transparent riot shields, beckoning Ulrik forth with their rifles. Such was the protocol in response to Saifullah threats that athletes were to be chaperoned by a company of guards.

By now, Vlad had turned himself into a corner and fell victim to a faint hiccupping. To save him the dignity of responding in a trembling voice, Ulrik bade him farewell with a determined nod and made haste for the arena.

The Archangels led him down a bleak corridor, taking turns at various junctions, all the while the acoustic commotion of the crowd rising as he drew closer. These corridors were vacant of all but authorised personnel, they being the Archangels. So it came as a surprise when, all at once, a badger-haired trespasser with a protruding Adam's apple sprang upon them.

"Stay back!" ordered the leader of the Archangels, and at once the other soldiers took a knee, placed their backs flat against the wall, and cocked their rifles. "Put your hands where we can see them, and get on your knees."

"Cheng, you old troublemaker," said Ulrik, lunging forward and stepping into the line of fire with no regard for his own safety. "What possessed you to break through security?"

"Shush, silly, there's no time," said Cheng, greeting him with a scrub of his knuckles on his scalp, just like old times. "I came to deliver one thing," hand opening like a flower in the sun, bearing its inner gift. "Your pappa wanted you to have this."

It was a dark, dull pendant attached to a simple piece of twine. "Thor's hammer, Mjolnir," muttered Ulrik, taking it, kissing it, then dressing it over his head. "How did you get through security?"

"How indeed," said the leader of the Archangels, giving Cheng a quick pat down to check he wasn't carrying any explosives.

Before they could exchange any further conversation, they cuffed Cheng and dragged him away in a manner not dissimilar to the way a youngling handles a rag doll. Yet, even when he was out of view, Ulrik could still hear him boasting: "Your parents—they're here, Ulrik. I've brought them to see you. Paid for some of the best seats in the aquadrome. I know you'll make us proud, Homo Nova!" It was doubtful, however, that Cheng would return to his seat and stay within the boundaries of the aquadrome to watch the event, a vehicle with flashing blue lights being the most likely destination for those having breached the tightest security.

Wasting no time, the Archangels led Ulrik on, this time down a more secretive passage where they were joined by a small company of infantrymen. There, at the end of this tunnel, Ulrik saw a rectangle of sunlight—the entrance to the aquadrome. As he approached, he dwelt on the catalogue of events that had led him here and those to whom he owed a debt for his becoming Homo Nova: Mamma, Pappa, Ivar, Dr Lyngstad, Tristan, Onyx, Chenglei, Ria, and Coach Lukashenko.

He squeezed his formidable fists as though pumping up his physique; his lats and obliques broadening like the form of a king cobra when rising before its silent strike. From a side table, he snatched a water bottle, causing the Archangels to flinch as he did so. Then he drank a little and poured the rest over his unwavering, untouchable, unstoppable frame before stepping over the threshold into the aquadrome, where he looked out across the stadium.

Applause turned to noxious screams as drones panned around him, zooming in and broadcasting the offensive pagan symbol of Mjolnir hanging about his neck. In response, he spread his arms as though they were wings, feeling ready to drop from this high nest into the hostile storm awaiting him and yet soar as the mightiest birds do when using a tempest to their advantage as they navigate the skies.

CHAPTER TWENTY-SIX

TO THE LAST BREATH

"I'm Reggie."

"And I'm Saskia."

"And for those of you who are just tuning in, ladies 'n' gen'lemen, hear—that—crowd—roar."

"Yes, yes, yesss. It's a fantastic atmosphere, and I feel blessed to be here right now overlooking the aquadrome. I don't know about you, Reggie, but never in my career as an athlete or commentator have I heard a crowd as wild as this."

"Me neither, Saskia. And it's absolutely stifling out here this evening. Woah-hoa, somebody pass me a fan before I pass out."

"With the air temperature being at 36°C, I dread to think what the temperature of the water is. The athletes need to be careful not to overheat this evening. They need to take on lots of water as they go. Make no mistake, it's going to be a tough one."

"And, Saskia, just for our viewers, tell us: what's it like competing in these conditions?"

"About as harsh as it gets, Reggie. I'd take a freezing cold plunge pool over a sauna like this any day—because that's essentially what this is. The whole idea of this being an evening event was for it to take place when conditions were cooler, but all those glass barriers about the watercourse—sure, they increase visibility for spectators; sure, it gives the place the look of a contemporary aquarium—but it's responsible for the horrendous greenhouse effect going on in here."

"Oho-ho, it'll be tough, but ain't this the one we've all been waiting for, Saskia? A purpose-built stadium for a new event: the 10-kilometre freestyle: the blue riband event of swimming, so they're calling it."

"It's been quite the build-up, Reggie. There's so much to love about swimming: elite athletes, great fans, and this phenomenal stadium—the world's first Olympic aquadrome. What more could you want?"

"Never in the history of the Olympics have we seen a long-distance swim in an arena like this. We've had open-water events, but it just ain't the same as amassing a crowd under one roof. Now, is it just me, or is there a smidge of hostility in the air this evening, or what?"

"I'm feeling it too, Reggie. Sounds to me like it's being directed towards Ulrik Magnusson. No surprises there. Only a few minutes ago, he came into the aquadrome wearing a pagan necklace. They're pretty offended down there."

"Well, he's technically breaking blasphemy laws."

"Doesn't seem to be winning him any friends, does it, Reggie?"

"No, it doesn't. Let's take a closer look."

Ulrik stretched at the poolside, and as the broadcasting drones hazarded a closer view, the screeching of the crowd intensified.

"There he is, Ulrik Magnusson, the one at the centre of so much controversy. And, Saskia, you were saying earlier he's the hairiest swimmer you've ever seen …"

"Yes. It's normal practice for swimmers to shave down before a race. Every millisecond counts in swimming. Not shaving could be a decision Magnusson later comes to regret—like really, really regret."

"Not only that, but I find it bizarre he's opted not to wear goggles."

"Or a swim cap. It makes me wonder what preparation, if any at all, he's put into this race."

"I dunno, Saskia; he's got abs like an ice cube tray and the shoulders of a prize-fighter. But I take your point; Ulrik Magnusson has never even had a competitive race until now. How he's qualified is a mystery to many."

"A scandal, some say, orchestrated by his Russian coach, Vladimir Lukashenko. But I'm sure our viewers out there are well versed in all the conspiracy theories out there."

"Well, whatever your opinion, whether for good or ill, you've gotta admire the fact that Magnusson is thee most talked about athlete of this generation—and, dare I say, in the history of the Olympics."

"And I'm hearing reports that over half a billion—yesss—half a billion people in DRUE alone have tuned in live on Tech."

"Wow. That's gotta be a record."

"The crowd are excited; the people at home are excited; we're all excited. And get this, Reggie …"

"What, Saskia?"

"We have a special guest in the house this evening. Soon we'll have— oh yes, we will—we'll have a guest celebrity who'll be firing the shot to commence the race."

"Who? Let me guess. Is it AfroDisiac? Carmen Ultra? Zion Lion? Oh, come on."

"Don't look at me like that, Reggie. They made me sign a non-disclosure agreement, so I can't say. All I *can* say is the person is hiding right over there, in the crow's nest opposite us."

"Agh, the suspense is killing me. Well, while were waiting to find out, let's take one last look at the watercourse for those who have just joined us on Tech."

Drone footage of the watercourse streamed to millions of spectators around the world. The aquadrome was like a conventional stadium in its oval structure and numerous tiers of high-rise terraces, but it differed in all other aspects. Instead of the usual track and field at the centre, there was a wide watercourse shaped like a figure-of-eight, or rather an infinity loop. Directly beneath the watercourse stood a great host of spectators who looked up in wonder through a glass ceiling as one does when watching sharks glide overhead in an aquarium. Above ground level, at the centre of the infinity loops, were two glass towers that had the semblance of crow's nests protruding from an enormous ship: platforms for 360° viewing. One of these crow's nests housed commentators and broadcasters from across the world; the other housed the VIP guest yet to be revealed.

"Now, in under five minutes, we're going to see these athletes battle it out for ten kilometres around the aquadrome. Each lap is 500 metres, and the swimmers have twenty laps to complete. Analysts expect it'll take around two hours for them to finish."

"And you were saying earlier, Saskia, you think there's potential it could finish sooner?"

"Yesss, and let me tell you why, Reggie: there's a rule which states that if a competitor is lapped, then they're knocked out of the race. There are no second chances in this game. I'll say it again: if you're lapped, the race is over for you. So I'm certain there'll be a few contenders eliminated as the race unfolds, and what I think you'll see is a real struggle as athletes fight to stay in the race—or knock each other out."

"It certainly doesn't suit the swimmer who's used to swimming off pace and hanging towards the back. There ain't no point in reserving energy in this race."

"Nobody wants to be lapped. Mark my words: it'll be intense from the word go."

"And for those tuning in who are unfamiliar with a long-distance swim, this is a freestyle event. Get ready to see a mixture of different strokes throughout. You can expect to see—"

"Sorry to interrupt you there, Reggie, but it looks like the athletes are lining up in the pool."

"There they are, twenty-five of the world's fastest long-distance swimmers readying themselves for their marathon."

"It's looking really rough down there as the athletes jostle their way to the starting line."

"There's bound to be some buffeting of bodies, Saskia. Most of these swimmers will be accustomed to their own space in their own lanes, but they don't have that luxury here. They'll have to adapt quickly to the invasion of space."

"I love the concept of having no lanes—not being protected by boundaries. It gives you more of a sense that this is a real battle. A shark-eat-shark competition. But the athletes need to be really careful not to bash into one another. There are penalties for foul play, and the underwater subdrones will detect any illegal contact."

"Well, here comes one man who seems unfazed by contact. Shayne 'the Shamrock' O'Shaughnessy, muscling his way to the front there. Ain't he just the life and soul of this competition?"

At that very moment, Shayne whipped his hand around and waved to the crowd in a stately fashion, as though he was someone of a noble bloodline.

"He's certainly got one of the more *unusual* personalities, hasn't he, Reggie?"

"He has. And speaking of unusual personalities, what's interesting to see is Magnusson loitering at the right-hand side there. He didn't even try to push himself forward as the athletes lined up. A big engine like that, coming in at over seven foot, ought to have swept the other athletes outta the way."

"Hold that thought, Reggie. Our celebrity guest who's going to commence the race has just appeared. Look to the crow's nest on your left."

"I—I don't believe it, ladies 'n' gen'lemen. I can't—there's me thinking today couldn't get any better. Chancellor Emmanuel Saint-Pierre, the Holy Shepherd, looking as regal as ever, greets the crowd as he takes to a pedestal."

On the highest platform of the crow's nest stood the Holy Shepherd himself, thrusting his warped white crook into the air as though he were about to part water. Right on cue, every tongue wagged to the continental anthem, and mothers and fathers pledged their children in the air; children whose faces were painted in royal purple; children whose cheeks were painted with the golden Sword of Abraham.

"It doesn't get any better than this, Reggie. Trust me, this'll be one event you'll never, ever forget."

"Just close your eyes, and feel that buzz for a moment."

"I'd keep my eyes open if I were you. I wouldn't want to miss a single second of what's about to become Olympic history."

The swimmers were packed together at the starting line like tinned sardines. Goggles were fixed. Latex caps were adjusted. A churchly silence befell the aquadrome.

The Holy Shepherd loaded a round of ammunition into his pistol, then poised himself upright. At first, his regal hand pointed to the ground, in the direction, seemingly, of the athletes; then, by slow degrees, he drew it up in a perfect arc, rising past his line of sight until eventually he aimed at a patch of blood-red sky.

"Here we go," whispered Reggie. "The moment we've all been waiting for."

"Shh," said Saskia.

A pang of gunfire filled the aquadrome.

"The athletes are off, ladies 'n' gen'lemen. They're off! And it's an explosive start from O'Shaughnessy and the Chinaman Wang Ling."

"There are a lot of bodies mingling down there, Reggie."

"Already there's some trouble in the ranks."

"Ruud van Basten—he's lashing out. He's come to a sudden stop. The referee has called him to the poolside."

"Is he now arguing with the referee, Saskia?"

"Looks like it could be all over for the Dutchman."

"Wow. I don't believe it. We're less than ten seconds in, and Ruud van Basten has been given the red flag and disqualified for foul play. 'You have no business swimming in my pool,' says the referee."

"I don't know what went on down there, Reggie, but it looked rough."

"It looked like an intentional clash of arms to me."

"I really don't know what possessed him to behave like that."

"Adrenaline got the better of him during a tussle, I think."

"All those early mornings, all that hard work—gone to waste. The Dutchman's only got himself to blame."

"If you've just joined us, we're already down to twenty-four athletes, and the Chinaman Wang Ling has taken an early lead. He's showing no mercy as he surges on ahead. But he wants to be careful not to burn out too soon. Saskia, you know better than anybody: this is a marathon, not a sprint."

"You've got to pace yourself—make sure there's energy in the tank for the last part. But it's a cunning tactic. Think about it: if the Chinaman laps everybody and knocks them out, the race will be over before the full twenty laps are completed."

"Hmm, I ain't so sure O'Shaughnessy will let him get away with that, though you gotta admire his audacity."

"Looking at the pack, I can see mainly front crawlers. Now hold on just a—what in the world is Magnusson doing?"

"Where are you looking, Saskia? I can't see."

"He's swimming beneath the surface."

"Can we get an underwater subdrone on Magnusson? That's better."

"Is that—oh my. He's performing the fish kick. Just look at his body manoeuvre. I haven't seen that in years. And I've never seen the fish kick used in a competition; it's really only used during training since it's so, so difficult to do for ten metres, let alone ten kilometres."

"Is that even legal? It looks dangerous to me."

"It's illegal in most events since there are strict rules governing the duration an athlete can swim underwater. For obvious reasons, too: lack of oxygen leads to brain damage."

"Well, we're being told Magnusson's fish kick is perfectly legal in this event. Look at him go. He's hardly coming back to the surface for a breath. Has he got an oxygen tank down there with him, Saskia, or what?"

"You'd think so, wouldn't you? But no, he seems to be catching his breath when he resurfaces. Pay attention to the way he gets himself into the backstroke at the surface, catches his breath, replenishes his oxygen, and propels himself down again into his fish kick."

"I've no idea how he's doing it, Saskia. He makes it look like magic."

"Holding your breath is painful enough, but in a high-intensity race like this his body is going to be in critical need of all the oxygen it can get. Oxygen to a swimmer is like fuel to a car—when you run out, you're going to hit a wall. I can't see this stroke being sustainable."

"Still, that's some extraordinary lung power he's got."

"It can't be safe, Reggie; yet for the life of me, I don't want him to stop. It's so addictive to watch. He swims like a merman."

"Watch the way he glides around those bends. Attacking those corners while sideways is helping him master the arcs of the course. Compare his technique with the conventional strokes we're seeing from the others. They seem accustomed to going only in straight lines. Look at how rigid they are when taking on those bends."

"Wang Ling extends his lead. He's really setting the tempo and getting into his rhythm."

"O'Shaughnessy in fourth—looking comfortable. Magnusson in eleventh. No—better make that tenth now."

"Wang Ling is certainly making them work out there. The threat of being lapped is already looming for some."

"I can't believe what we're seeing. We're seven laps in, and Wang Ling is about to overlap the stragglers at the back. There he goes around the outside, and the Olympic dream is over for Miyamoto, Rodriguez, and Peeters. That's three of them lapped at once. Wang Ling sending a powerful message there: get outta here; you ain't welcome in my pool."

"There's no playing for pride this evening, Reggie. Once you've been lapped, you can kiss your Olympic dreams goodbye. It's so, so brutal."

"And it looks like Wang Ling is slowing down to take on some water. He turns into his backstroke; he grabs a bottle from the poolside (it's some kind of electrolyte drink); he drinks from it; and he's off again. That's a perfect drill from the Chinaman. He's hardly lost any time there."

"You can tell that's been well-rehearsed, Reggie. That's one I'm going to enjoy watching again and again later. You don't miss the feed station if you want to win a marathon. There's a misconception that because you're surrounded by water, you don't get thirsty or sweat. In reality, the swimmers are losing so much water as they go."

"O'Shaughnessy has paced himself well. He's vying for second place now—neck and neck with the Samoan, Tangi Leuluai. And it looks like Magnusson is edging his way into eighth."

"Still a long way to go yet, Reggie."

"What's interesting about Magnusson's fish kick is he doesn't have the disadvantage of having to overtake on the outside. He simply dives beneath his opponents and reappears in front."

"He's doing well, but I'm not sure he has the experience to keep up with the veterans as we get further into the race."

"We're about to reach the halfway mark. That's five kilometres down and a further five to go."

"Wang Ling, like a heat-seeking missile, seeks out his next victims."

"Here he comes—Wang Ling. Whoa-hoa-ho, Wang Ling, the destroyer of Olympic dreams, knocks Dragov, Shevchenko, El-Masri, and the esteemed Sir Matthew Davis of Great Britain all outta the race, all at once. I don't think anybody expected a massacre like this."

"They didn't even see him coming. And just like that the Olympic dream is over for them."

"It's a bloodbath down there."

"Someone who isn't giving up just yet is Magnusson, Reggie. He's crept up into sixth place now. But he's going to have to work harder if he wants a medal. Wang Ling has a 200-metre lead on O'Shaughnessy, who's in second."

"Wait—I think there's been some foul play between O'Shaughnessy and the Samoan as they battle it out for second place. It looked as though there was a leg grab from Tangi Leuluai as O'Shaughnessy was about to break away."

"That's really clumsy. See, there's the yellow flag. And that'll be a penalty—so, three seconds added to Tangi Leuluai's time."

"It's easy to get embroiled in the frustrations of it, Saskia. But another offence like that will get the Samoan a fast-track ticket to the changing rooms. It just ain't worth it."

"The clash doesn't seem to have affected O'Shaughnessy, though, does it, Reggie?"

"He's bursting forward now in pursuit of Wang Ling."

"The Samoan tries to stay with him, but it's all in vain."

"O'Shaughnessy closing the gap now on Wang Ling. Wang Ling still on the warpath. He's about to lap another three athletes. And there he goes, sending Bergstrom, Cruz, and Pushkin back to the changing rooms. You can see the sheer fury in their faces as the realisation of what's happened hits them."

"Fourteen athletes remaining."

"Saskia, this could be me, but I've yet to see Magnusson take a drink from the feed station."

"That's right, Reggie. Our subdrones show he's drinking from the pool as he goes."

"Drinking from the pool? Is that even allowed?"

"Apparently so."

"And safe?"

"I'm being informed that it's *not* seawater, though I'm not sure if it's been chemically treated. Still, staying hydrated is one thing, Reggie, but that might not be Magnusson's biggest problem. Lack of air will take its toll. But then, even as we speak, Magnusson is in fourth place now and powering forward."

"It looks like the aggressive pace-setter Wang Ling is tiring somewhat as we head into the fourteenth lap. He's chasing Harris-Taylor of New Zealand. This might well be his last victim. He's got him—he's got him— he's got Harris-Taylor. Harris-Taylor is outta there! Whoa-hoa-ho."

"Wang Ling is as hungry as a Nile crocodile, but I don't see it going this way for much longer, Reggie. I think he's bitten off more than he can chew."

"You're right, Saskia. He's slowing down now, considerably, and Shayne O'Shaughnessy is hot on his tail."

"Here he comes."

"The Shamrock, showing us what he's about—hunting the hunter Wang Ling."

"And there he goes, comfortably, and for the first time in fourteen laps, O'Shaughnessy takes the lead."

"You'd think the entire crowd was Irish with a roar like that, Reggie."

"It's like Saint Patrick's Day all over again. You just wait: if Shayne wins, the whole of DRUE will be wearing shamrocks tonight, and Irish bars across the Continent will be packed to the rafters."

"Everybody loves the Irishman, haha."

"Well, everybody except Levine and Dragomir: O'Shaughnessy is about to overtake his first victims. They're both trying to hold on for as long as they can. Here he comes, storming through a gap between them. The Shamrock sends them packing. It's back to the changing rooms for Levine of Israel and Dragomir of Romania."

"That leaves only eleven athletes remaining as we approach the last quarter of the race."

"Better make that ten, Saskia. Tangi Leuluai has had a nightmare and is pulling up with an injury. Whatever it is, it looks painful."

"A shoulder injury by the looks of it—rotator cuff."

"Ouch, nasty way to go."

"This is going to be the real test now. Those who set off too quickly may struggle in the last part of the race."

"It's not looking good for Wang Ling, either. Billy Robinson of Australia has stolen second place."

"Magnusson powers on. He's about to steal third place from Wang Ling."

"Can you hear that, Saskia? It sounds like there's some chanting over there in the terraces."

"Sounds to me like they're chanting 'Homo Nova'."

"I think young Magnusson has won himself some fans after this performance. He's given us all a surprise, that's for sure.

"Here he comes—Magnusson neck and neck with Wang Ling. Wang Ling—his face says it all. The Chinaman is running out of fuel."

"Magnusson has gone under him."

"This is only going to go one way."

"It's happening, Saskia. Oh-hoa-ho, it's happening."

"And Magnusson, elegant as ever, resurfaces again, leaving Wang Ling in his wake!"

"There's no stopping the eighteen-year-old Svalbardian. Look at the determination in his eyes as he ripples through the water, Saskia. He's leaving nothing in the changing rooms."

"Magnusson's still not satisfied as he sets out for Billy Robinson of Australia and Shayne O'Shaughnessy of Ireland."

"Into lap sixteen of twenty now, and the young Svalbardian records the fastest lap of the race so far."

"He sails past Billy Robinson as though he never existed. He makes it look so, so easy. Robinson's lashing and thrashing through the water, trying to regain second place."

"Magnusson, not content with a silver, hunts down the Irishman. O'Shaughnessy unaware of the deep, deep trouble he's in. He's about to find out the hard way."

"Magnusson ripples under him and is in the process of taking the lead."

"And outta nowhere comes Magnusson. I can't believe it, Saskia. O'Shaughnessy can't believe it."

"The whole crowd is out of their seats. And they're behind him—they're all behind Magnusson. Even the Holy Shepherd is on his feet. That's got to be a tremendous boost for the eighteen-year-old. He'll certainly hear their chanting."

"O'Shaughnessy tries to exert himself, but Magnusson ploughs through the water like a hammerhead. I've never seen a person move like this underwater. Woah-hoa-ho."

"Magnusson takes the lead!"

"He's done the hard work. He just needs to maintain his lead."

"And here he comes ... Magnusson overlapping a cluster at the back now."

"Absolutely brutal. It's back to the changing rooms for Schweinsteiger, Blake-Williams, and Rossi. You can see how much it means to them. It ain't nice seeing the tears of those who've sacrificed so much to get here."

"The titan Giuseppe Rossi departs Olympic waters for the last time. He's one of the most decorated swimmers of all time. His efforts just weren't enough to shake off the young shark this evening, but he can be proud of himself. Look at him. Such a sweetheart—waving and bowing to the crowd like that."

"Don't take your eyes off Magnusson for too long, Saskia; he's approaching his final lap now with a firm lead—at least 75 metres, I'd say. What an experience this has been for the youngster. To come into a sport as an underdog and snatch gold away from the favourites. Think of how unstoppable he's gonna be in another few years. I think we can expect to see a colourful career ahead for him."

"They say Magnusson is another species. I'm starting to believe it, Reggie. I'm really starting to believe it."

"I think the crowd agrees, too."

"Apparently not everyone ..."

"What the—is that a Whitehood?"

"How in the Lord's name has a Whitehood got over the barriers and past security?"

"He's making his way down to the poolside—in the direction of Ulrik Magnusson, it seems. Looks like a bunch of stewards are in pursuit. They're gonna have to hurry up if they're hoping to intercept him. I don't like the look of this one bit, Saskia. Not one bit."

All eyes, and indeed every camera, locked on to the Holy Shepherd who, at the highest point of the crow's nest, peered over the glass balcony with a subtle yet welcome gleam in his widening eyes, though his congruent lips never betrayed him into smiling, not even as the Whitehood outsprinted the brawny stewards who lumbered behind in slow pursuit.

"And for those,"—clears throat—"and for those of you watching at home, we caution that you may find the following footage distressing. A polite reminder that this is a live event."

"We don't yet know the intentions of this unknown person, but it looks as though he's out to disrupt the event. I'm praying those stewards catch up with him quick before he does something truly awful."

As the Whitehood approached the watercourse, he threw down his cloak and hood and held his hands aloft. When seeing that he was carrying no sinister weaponry, the Archangels, who were stationed at various sentry points throughout the stadium, lowered their rifles and stood at ease. Not a terrorist; just a lone prankster with a forgettable face and perhaps an even more forgettable personality—no doubt someone who was aggrieved with a lifetime of being forgotten and was ready now to be remembered, recognised, and perhaps immortalised for making a fearless stand. Then, accelerating his pace, he took a running jump, tucked his knees into his chest while mid-air, and, just as Ulrik rose to the surface for a breath, crashed into the water like a cannonball.

For a short distance, the menace rode Ulrik's back, anchoring him down while he tussled for the surface, before being finally shrugged off with the ceremony of a bucking bronco during a wild rodeo.

"See, that's just cruel. You train for years, dedicate yourself to a craft, and some prankster comes out of nowhere and tries to dash your chances of winning a gold medal. All for a sick, twisted joke."

"Thank the Lord, Magnusson managed to shake him off."

"Magnusson might've shaken him off, but he's lost a few important seconds there."

"Huge credit there to the stewards who are now in the pool. They've detained the culprit and have done a great job of evicting him before he could disrupt the race any further. The troublemaker seems happy with himself; I'm not sure the crowd are happy, though."

"I'm just lost for words, Reggie. Why anyone would do such a shameless thing is beyond me. Never in all my years as an athlete or commentator have I seen anything as despicable as this. I really hope he gets the justice he deserves."

"Well, the Whitehood clearly had only one target, and now Magnusson looks to be in a state of confusion. He's paddling in the wrong direction."

"I can't watch this."

"Magnusson is in big trouble down there."

"It doesn't look good for the Svalbardian. He's looking really disorientated, Reggie."

"And here come the other athletes—about to overtake him. I can't believe what we're witnessing here."

"Wait, Magnusson's realised now, but it could be too late."

"Shayne O'Shaughnessy overtakes a submerged Magnusson and regains the lead. That's tragic for the young forager."

"Magnusson in desperate pursuit."

"O'Shaughnessy and the others breaking away now. They're gonna be counting their lucky stars tonight for their second chance at a gold medal. Surely, only moments ago, before the Whitehood assault, Magnusson had gold in the bag?"

"You would have thought so, Reggie. But now, after almost two hours, Magnusson appears to have given up attempting his fish kick."

"Whoa! He's resurfaced now, and he's turned over into the backstroke. I don't believe what I'm seeing. On his last lap of the race, he's hit a wall."

"Even the backstroke is too much for him. He's lost his technique and has resorted to paddling."

"He doesn't look good down there. I can only think it's because he's deprived of oxygen, Saskia."

"Here come the other athletes on the final straight. O'Shaughnessy leading the pack. It's all to play for."

"Look at the urgency as they dash to the finish line. Look at the foam they're throwing. Just look at the stroke rate. It's hard to believe they can muster the strength for one last burst of energy having spent almost two hours battling it out."

"These athletes won't be able to walk for days after this. They're literally ripping apart every muscle in their bodies."

"O'Shaughnessy—here he comes. In a wicked twist of fate, O'Shaughnessy—about to cross the finish line. O'Shaughnessy ... O'Shaughnessy ... O'Shaughnessy! And there we have it: in a time of 1:48:43, Shayne 'the Shamrock' O'Shaughnessy scoops up his fourth gold medal of the Athens 2076 Olympics."

" ... And Robinson takes the silver."

"It's gonna be neck and neck for the bronze. Kruger, Leblanc, and Papadopoulos giving it their all as they come around the final bend."

"Meanwhile, Magnusson appears to have tethered himself to the poolside and is now catching his breath. He looks utterly, utterly spent. It's so hard to recover from something like that. When your focus is gone, when you lose that meditative mindset, it's nigh on impossible to get back in the zone."

"Papadopoulos takes the bronze in a dramatic photo finish, but all eyes are now on Billy Robinson of Australia, who's heading back. It looks like—yeah, it looks like Robinson's going back to help Magnusson."

"What a heroic display of sportsmanship from the silver medallist. This right here is what the sport is all about, isn't it, Reggie?"

"It sure is. Robinson's hoisting Magnusson over his shoulder and telling him that they're gonna finish this no matter what."

"Well, just listen to that: just under two hours ago, the crowd were lynching him, and now they're giving him a standing ovation. Incredible. Just incredible."

"Whoa-hoa, listen to that crowd ..."

The crowd chanted, "Pierre de Coubertin—Pierre de Coubertin—Pierre de Coubertin!"

"Is that what I think it means, Saskia?"

"Pierre de Coubertin ... yesss. It can only mean one thing: they're calling for Magnusson to be given an honorary medal. It may not be a gold, but the Pierre de Coubertin has been presented on only a handful of occasions. It's a medal awarded to those who show the true spirit of sportsmanship at the Olympics. I'm sure our gracious Holy Shepherd can leverage some influence."

But only those closest to the Holy Shepherd saw him snatch up his warped white crook, draw his cloak about him, and flee inside with the hue of fire and blood in his face.

The crowd thundered like a continuous storm: "Pierre de Coubertin—Pierre de Coubertin—Pierre de Coubertin!"

"Magnusson about to paddle across the finish line. His finishing time won't be ratified; he'll go down as a 'Did Not Finish'; he hasn't won gold, silver, or bronze, but he has won the hearts of the crowd."

"It's been a valiant effort from the young Svalbardian."

"Especially at his age. The world has never seen an athlete like him before, and it's such a shame what happened here today with the Whitehood. Had it not been for that, I'm certain the outcome would've been very different."

"And there we have it, Reggie; the crowd goes wild as Magnusson floats across the finish line. With the help of Billy Robinson, Magnusson is hoisted out of the pool."

"Hold on, Saskia, it's getting hectic down there again."

"Billy Robinson looks distressed. Looks like he's trying to flag down a lifeguard. Magnusson is … he's collapsed at the poolside. He looks to have fainted."

"That was a heavy fall. I heard that from all the way up here."

"The whole aquadrome has suddenly fallen into a horrible hush now, watching on with furrowed brows. This does look serious for young Magnusson. Billy Robinson seems to be checking his pulse—slapping him—shaking him."

"He ain't moving. I can't tell if he's breathing. His lips are blue, his body's turned pale. The medical team are moving in. Let's hope they act quickly and are successful in bringing Magnusson round. Argh, this is tough to watch."

"You can see just how much this means to the fans; anxious faces dotted all around the aquadrome, so many of them with hands joined, so many of them in tears. Praying for Ulrik Magnusson. From faces of celebration only a few moments ago to faces now of alarm. This is truly awful."

"Well, those in the stadium can barely believe what they're witnessing. Ulrik Magnusson still being attended to by the medical team."

"The winning of the competition and medals no longer a concern here now; all that matters is the health of our favourite athlete."

"What promised to be a historic event has been suddenly tainted with an altogether different atmosphere."

"It's been tough conditions for the young Svalbardian: stifling weather; his unorthodox swimming style; the Whitehood assault. These athletes have pushed and pushed themselves to their limits here today, but none more so than Ulrik Magnusson."

"And, I'm sorry, but it looks like we're gonna take a break here in the studio. Live coverage will resume in a few moments. We'll be back soon with the latest updates."

Results — Men's 10-Kilometre Freestyle Aquadrome — Athens 2076

Rank	Swimmer	Nation	Time	Notes & Honours
1	Shayne O'Shaughnessy	Ireland	1:48:43.1	*WR & OR*
2	Billy Robinson	Australia	1:49:01.1	
3	Ares Papadopoulos	Cyprus	1:50:02.3	
4	Theo Leblanc	Canada	1:50:02.4	
5	Johan P. Kruger	South Africa	1:50:06.9	
6	Wang Ling	China	1:50:07.7	
7	Ulrik Magnusson	Independent	DNF	Pierre de Coubertin
8	Giuseppe Rossi	Italy	DNF	KO'd
9	Iwan Blake-Williams	Great Britain	DNF	KO'd
10	Konrad Schweinsteiger	Germany	DNF	KO'd
11	Tangi Leuluai	Samoa	DNF	Injury
12	Grigore Dragomir	Romania	DNF	KO'd
13	Yuri Levine	Israel	DNF	KO'd
14	Brad Harris-Taylor	New Zealand	DNF	KO'd
15	Viktor Pushkin	Russia	DNF	KO'd
16	Elonzo Cruz	Mexico	DNF	KO'd
17	Filip Bergstrom	Sweden	DNF	KO'd
18	Sir Matthew Davis	Great Britain	DNF	KO'd
19	Mustafa El-Masri	Egypt	DNF	KO'd
20	Aleksandr Shevchenko	Ukraine	DNF	KO'd
21	Samuil Dragov	Bulgaria	DNF	KO'd
22	Stefan Peeters	Belgium	DNF	KO'd
23	Marco Rodriguez	Ecuador	DNF	KO'd
24	Hitoshi Miyamoto	Japan	DNF	KO'd
25	Ruud van Basten	Netherlands	DNF	DSQ

CHAPTER TWENTY-SEVEN

THE VISITATION

When Ulrik came to his senses, he found himself lying in a hospital bed with his limbs sprawled out like an octopus. Glancing about his private quarters, and feeling glad about it being occupied by no other patient but himself, suddenly, his sleepy eyes were stricken wide when he noticed a shadowy figure encroaching upon the end of his bed: a spirit of sorts, a dark ghost, a phantom cloaked in a black garment from head to toe. Its only mortal hint was that of a pair of intelligent eyes flitting behind its veil; eyes which, having now locked onto his, seemed to be trespassing on his thoughts and mapping out the pathways of his soul.

"Heurgh," said Ulrik, scrambling upright and backing up against the headboard of his bed. Then he drew out his pillow and braced himself as though it was a shield capable of parrying the sharpest scythe. "Who are you? Am I dead? Step into the light so I can see you."

When the wraith drew itself up to respond, a draught stole under the shroud hanging about its bony shoulders, and the silhouette seemed to levitate. "You've no reason to be afraid, Ulrik, my lamb." The voice that came from within the shroud wasn't the crow of a deathly reaper; it was blessed with the croak of age and wisdom. A man, perhaps, in his sunset years. When the veil drew back, Ulrik saw it was one whom he recognised not from the flesh, but from seeing him in portraits—innumerable portraits.

"So, it's you," studying the profile of the Holy Shepherd's face. His congruent lips at all times remained parallel, never deviating into something so frolicsome as a smile. Lengths of heaven-white hair ran past his shoulders in streams of spider silk. In order to get a better look, Ulrik reached for the lights.

"Don't turn the lights on," said the Holy Shepherd, snatching his hand about the air with the vehemence of an orchestra's conductor. "You shouldn't need to anyway, according to those journals. Aren't chromoproteins more prevalent in your eyes? Don't they enable you to see in the dark? Are your eyes not now adjusted? Quick now, how many fingers am I holding up?"

"Six."

"Huh, the winters on Svalbard must be dark to have trained such keen eyes." After some moments of silent staring, and much to Ulrik's relief, the Holy Shepherd withdrew his wizardly face into his costume again. "Sorry to have frightened you at such an early hour, my lamb. That wasn't my intention. You must understand, men of consequence need to disguise themselves. I wear a burka for my safety since my line of work is dangerous."

"Nuh, I don't believe you."

"What part don't you believe, my lamb?"

"I don't believe the disguise is for your safety. There's no danger here except that which you're bringing. It's a cloak of invisibility for you, spy that you are."

"Perhaps …" The Holy Shepherd withdrew to the window and peered through the blinds. "Perhaps you'll recognise me from Trondheim University, where we sat together on the board of regents and I wore the same attire? At the time, my advisers stressed I had more important matters of state in need of attention. They begged me not to go. But I've long understood the importance of weeding to the gardener; and the idea that a new species of man was on the verge of discovery was the greatest of weeds in God's republic. Heresy, it is, of the highest order."

"So it was you, then! I remember seeing a man's wrinkled hand slip out from that same garment. You didn't fool me."

"That's because you're no fool, my lamb. 'The fool hath said in his heart: there is no God,' so it says in the Bible. You believe in God, don't you?"

"I ... I don't know. My uncle Cheng, he's a scientist and the cleverest person I know; he's always saying there's no evidence of any god."

"I expect, being a scientist, he taught you how the universe came into being? The Big Bang, then cosmic inflation? No, my lamb, these theories leave us only with more riddles. How did they start? Who caused them? Why did they begin? Ask your uncle this: how can something come from nothing? More importantly, ask him: *why* did something come from nothing? He will be unable to answer you; I promise."

"Why did you come here? Not to debate the origin of man with some forager, I expect. What concern is one heathen to the most powerful man in DRUE, huh?"

"The most powerful man"—deep, invigorating sniff—"in the world." Unbeknownst to the Holy Shepherd, his wrinkled hand slipped out of his garment, and his thumb and forefinger underwent a massage as though he were conjuring some dark magic.

"Tell me why the most powerful man in the world has come here in secret at such an hour?"

"To help you, my lamb."

"Why would *you* want to help me? You think me a weed spoiling your garden—the work of the Devil, or so you'd have your flock believe."

The Holy Shepherd dismissed his question with a snatch of his fist and led the conversation back to his own agenda, as the slipperiest of politicians do. Then, taking up the handTech affixed to Ulrik's hospital bed, the Holy Shepherd read aloud his medical report: "Says here, my lamb, that you suffered a stroke. A blood clot cut off the supply of oxygen to your brain. Excessive clotting—caused by hypercoagulability. Exacerbated by high blood viscosity. You gave blood samples as thick as honey due to an abnormally high concentration of haemoglobin. You've been administered blood thinners. Tut-tut-tut. I thought it likely to find you in a vegetative state here today. You're lucky to be alive. Luckier still to show no sign of any lasting injury."

"I'm not afraid of dying."

"Nor am I, and I'm a good deal closer to death than most—having lived for so long. Yet, the Lord Almighty sees fit to prolong my life for some ultimate plan of His. Dying, oh, I'm not afraid of that. It's the hereafter which we should all fear: God's judgement."

There was no reading Saint-Pierre's expression behind his burka, no telling what convoluted desires were closeted in that convoluted mind of his.

"If it's any consolation, my lamb," added the Holy Shepherd, "I consider you a victim in this. They've used you as a guinea pig; a lab rat; a science mutt. Those who've tampered with you—they had no right to play God. They are the worst of men. Worse than thieves; worse than liars; worse than sodomites. They'll burn in eternal hellfire for their sins."

"Believe what you will. I'm weary of all these rumours of me being some sort of Frankenstein. Now tell me, what's so important that you have to sneak up on me in my hospital bed at such an hour?"

"Matters," pivoting on his heels so that he faced Ulrik, "matters concerning the freedom of your parents. I want to make you a deal, my lamb."

"My parents—where are they?"

"In police custody. While you were suffering at the aquadrome poolside, your parents tried to come to your aid, but they breached security and got caught up in a minor tangle with my Archangels. There was a riot; so they were detained."

"Are they in trouble?"

"Serious, serious trouble, my lamb."

Ulrik ran his hands through his hair. "And this deal you speak of, what does it involve?"

"I could have your parents pardoned right now—pardoned of offences both old and new so that they might return to their normal lives, free from their community correction programme in the mines."

"And what price would you have me pay?"

"There's a little something you could do for the Republic, my lamb, if it's not too much trouble."

"Name it, so I can consider it."

"Ulrik, there are a lot of hateful journalists telling lies about you."

"Telling lies?"

"Nasty, deceitful lies. I want to put a stop to their sins. Believe me, I do."

"What lies? Tell me."

"My lamb, have you ever heard of—I believe you must have—the theory of evolution?"

"Yah. My uncle Cheng says life is constantly evolving and natural selection is—"

"You've been lied to, and so, too, has your uncle Cheng. To believe in evolution is to deny the teachings of God. Evolutionists say the world is billions of years old, but we know the earth is about 6,000 years old because the Bible gives an accurate chronology of events. And since the Bible is the word of God, anything else is a rejection of God's love. My lamb, the teaching of evolution is hate speech. We're descendants of Adam and Eve, not primordial fish."

"I don't care. Tell me, what is it you need me to be doing?"

"I need you to sign a declaration. This is the document," demonstrating his handTech and a stylus which he produced from underneath his black gown. "If you sign here, it means I can prosecute those nasty journalists and scientists on your behalf. In representing you, my team will have the power to mount legal proceedings against any libellous content that refers to you as Homo Nova or any other associated terms listed in the glossary on pages seventy-one to seventy-nine. In short: they won't be able to tell their lies anymore."

"So, you'd erase me from the news, huh?"

"My lamb, it's dangerous to tolerate hate speech, whether it be fascism, racism, or, as in this case, blasphemy. I need to protect my people against this media falsehood before it spreads like a virus. You see, this intellectual virus—this theory of evolution—is spreading like a pandemic. But you let me worry about all that. Your only concern right now is your parents' freedom."

A rectangle of effulgent white light shone from his handTech, and Ulrik felt as though the surrounding darkness were the walls of a vast tunnel and that this rectangle of light was the end of it—a route to escape. But then ... no more Homo Nova. In signing this document, he'd be willingly giving up his fame and the world would soon forget who he was. He'd no longer be special.

"Ulrik," continued the Holy Shepherd, "your greatest fear, I know, is irrelevance. But irrelevance can be a noble thing. To come and go unnoticed is perhaps one of the greatest privileges of the common flock. I wish every person who wants to be famous could be me for a day, so they'd see that it's not what they want after all."

"Hmm ..." In freeing Mamma and Pappa, he would've achieved what he set out to do, but to lose his newfound status, his reputation ... this was a wicked bargain. "I want time to think about it."

"As an old man, I have no time to afford you. Give me your answer now, otherwise I'll rescind my offer and look to alternative means of removing you from the public spotlight. I have ... other options."

"Options such as hiring Whitehood mercenaries to do your dirty work?"

"Oh, you think the Whitehood who tackled you in the aquadrome was my doing?"

"I don't really care who plotted it, but please pass my thanks on to whoever did. I'm glad the Whitehood attacked me in the aquadrome. It's because of him that the whole stadium was cheering my name. And maybe, behind their Tech, the whole continent was, too. See, I may have lost the race, but I won the crowd. It's true that many used to hate me, but how many more love me now because of that senseless attack?"

"Don't get too far ahead of yourself," said the Holy Shepherd in a tone that sounded as though every angle of his face sharpened beneath his veil. "It would be very easy for me to have you prosecuted for wearing that blasphemous Viking pendent in the aquadrome. Thrown in jail until the world forgets who you are."

"Then do."

The Holy Shepherd reclined an inch or two and stammered.

"But you won't, will you?" pressed Ulrik. "Because you're afraid the people would disapprove of you; afraid my popularity might outgrow yours; afraid they would take my side. But you need them on your side, don't you? If you lose their support, you become powerless. And you'd hate that."

"Not as much as I hate seeing the lie of evolution perpetuated. I've witnessed the horrors of a faithless world, Ulrik. A world without God is a world without morals. Understand? Before I was the Chancellor of DRUE, the faithless governments allowed scientists to play God with their illegal experiments; they allowed same-sex marriage; and their barbaric regimes allowed the industrial-scale abortion of unborn babies—millions of innocent babies vacuumed out of their mother's womb every year. Not anymore. Millions survive every year because of *me*. It was a continent of sin. Abominable sin everywhere. No. I won't abide the spread of the Devil's fire. Not when I have the power to extinguish it."

"Hmm ..." Ulrik sensed desperation in the Holy Shepherd, and he supposed he'd do whatever it took to silence him, regardless of whether he consented to his scheme. Given the choice, torn as he was, it was Ulrik's preference not to sign. And yet, he supposed, in his shrewd wisdom, he could have it all his way: both winning his family's freedom and retaining his newfound fame. After all, this wasn't the first time he'd been silenced. There was the time when the conclave had forced him into signing a non-disclosure agreement and ruled that no further research would be granted into the case of *Homo nova*. That attempt to silence him backfired and was responsible for his fame spreading across the Continent like wildfire. Fool. The Holy Shepherd had learned nothing.

"So," added Ulrik, "what else would I be agreeing to in this document of yours?"

"As God as my witness, nothing," said the Holy Shepherd, drawing away the handTech and stylus as though in livid offence at the accusation. Then he took out a pocket-sized book from some inner pouch of his black gown, and having now kissed it, he held it aloft, his venous arm reaching skyward like a twisted beanstalk. "I swear on the Holy Bible and all the goodly prophets within."

"So," scratching his forehead, "I sign, and you'll release my parents? We're free to go about as we please?"

The Holy Shepherd nodded.

A long pause ensued.

"Fine; pass it to me."

The Holy Shepherd's arm retreated, and he deposited the Bible back in his gown, close to his heart. His whole silhouette seemed animated now as he shuffled to the bedside, gesturing with his handTech and the stylus. Behind the veil his eyes widened so much that they had the aspect of two full moons as Ulrik readied himself to endow the document with his signature. Not that he had anything like an official signature.

"Just sign here," tapping a slender finger on the Tech. "Press your thumbprint there when instructed."

"Before I sign anything, you ought to know this, Holy Shepherd: it's the custom of foragers to seal a deal with a headbutt. You're welcome to my signature and thumbprint, but my condition is we butt heads also."

The Holy Shepherd seemed to shrivel under his burka at the savage suggestion. "Tut-tut-tut. No, no, no. Me, headbutt a hospital patient? Absurd. I couldn't possibly—you're unwell."

"Then perhaps I'm not well enough to be signing ..."

"Ugh, very well. It's for the good of the Republic. So, how do we ... you know, butt heads?"

"Like this," said Ulrik, creaking his neck this way and that in preparation. "Come closer."

If he'd wished, Ulrik could've thrown the Holy Shepherd some great distance as easily as a bull flings an amateur matador, but a gentle nod was all that was necessary to dent his pride.

"Now, your signature and thumbprint, please," said the Holy Shepherd, holding his temple as though to soothe a sudden migraine.

Ulrik took up the stylus and scribbled, or rather stabbed and jabbed on the dotted line. He wrote his signature in Old Futhark runes and spelt out "Homo Nova" (though the Holy Shepherd didn't know what he'd scribed, for the resemblance of these runes to letters was only slight). Then, after pressing his thumb against the declaration, Ulrik handed the Tech back to him.

"Good," said the Holy Shepherd, secreting the Tech beneath his black gown. "I'll see that your parents are pardoned of offences both recent and historic. Now, I doubt our paths will ever cross again, Ulrik Magnusson. Not in this life, and certainly not in the hereafter."

"Doubt, you say? Have a little faith, Holy Shepherd. I expect we'll be crossing paths again, for you've developed a keen obsession with me."

"My lamb, I say to you as it says in Matthew 24:42: 'Be on the alert, for you do not know which day your Lord is coming.'"

"What's that supposed to be meaning, huh? Am I supposed to be afraid?"

A snicker of amusement came from beneath the veil. With dainty footsteps, the Holy Shepherd made gains towards the door. Before vanishing into the corridor, he stopped and said, "Oh, I almost forgot, Ulrik …"

"Yah, go on."

"Tell nobody about my coming here today. Not even your girlfriend— the Catalan traitor. Otherwise, it might jeopardise our deal."

"What should I say when people ask how my parents were freed?"

"When pressed for answers to questions which I'm not obliged to answer, I always find it's best to respond by saying this: God works in mysterious ways."

The Holy Shepherd moved like a shadow on the wall and fled the room.

Strange was the Holy Shepherd's coming at that hour for the conducting of nocturnal affairs. Even so, it elevated Ulrik's sense of importance, for the Holy Shepherd had come to beg something of him, not the other way around. Now that he'd won his parents' freedom, losing in the aquadrome no longer mattered. Their lives were their own; they could be foragers again. Everything was going to be all right. Except, of course, for the Holy Shepherd's parting words: "Be on the alert, for you do not know which day your Lord is coming." What did he mean? It was a threat, no doubt about that. What sinister plot was he weaving?

The morning drama had rendered Ulrik tired, and to dwell on it any longer was only to rob himself of his much needed rest, so he wrapped himself up in his blankets and thereafter drifted off into a cosy slumber. So tightly had he drawn the covers about him that to move would've been certain to ruin his perfect pitch of quilt. He lay with his arms by his side in the profile of a sarcophagus; and with his drooling mouth agape, he seemed a victim of death. It wasn't long, however, before he rose from the dead, for along came another visitor, making an accidental clatter upon entry—from having stubbed a toe it seemed, for he heard curses being vehemently whispered and the sound of one-legged hopping.

Jaw still agape and his eyelids held fast, he pretended to be asleep. After a moment or two, he felt himself sinking into the mattress, upon which the burden of another person now shuffled, circling the bed in the manner of a hound when inspecting a patch and deciding the most comfortable spot to curl up in. Even before he saw her, he recognised Ria's smell. (It wasn't the smell of perfume, shampoo, or any other cosmetic. It was the zest of the human body, the indescribable essence of which every person has their own unique formula. It can be enjoyed, or it can be reviled, such are its subjective properties, and rumour has it that this pheromonal fragrance can be discovered in sniffing a person's pillow; only then can it be known, by the degree of pleasure, or displeasure, whether a person is vulnerable to its arcane attraction and under the spell of their sweetheart.)

"Stupid, reckless forager," she whispered. "I hope you can hear me when I say you're so, so, so fucking stupid—scaring me like that."

"Heurgh, wha'?" said Ulrik, pretending to be rousing from sleep and stretching his snow-shovel arms high and wide. Turning over, he saw Ria sporting a hideous frown. Then she thumped him on the shoulder with the squishy part of her fist. "Heugh-oof! What's that for, crazy woman?"

She gave no reply. Instead, she rolled off the bed and flounced to the window, where she mounted the sill and sat hugging her knees; her sulking pout uglified her face.

"Why are you mad at me, Ria? Do you expect me to be saying sorry or something?"

"Ssst, of course not. Men are too weak to say sorry when they're wrong."

"I don't understand what I'm supposed to have done or why you're so mad at me."

"Stop saying I'm mad when I'm not, okay!"

"Liar. Your nostrils are flaring like a fire-breathing dragon's. They always do that when you're mad."

She pinched her nose to suppress the throbbing rings, but all the offence in her nostrils diverted to her eyes so that they, too, underwent a psychotic twitching. "If I was angry, you'd know about it, okay. I'm annoyed. There's a difference, you know."

"Nuh, I *didn't* know."

"Well, you should."

"What exactly have I done wrong?"

"You could've died out there—that's what. I've been sick with worry."

"Here I am wishing I had, so I might've got more sympathy from you."

She scowled, then pressed her face to the window: "Stop being so mean." There was a subtle, sad tremor in her voice.

Ulrik clambered out of bed and crept up behind her. When she noticed his proximity to her, she recoiled further into the window; though her reflection betrayed her, for when running his fingers through her hair, he saw the ridges of her frown dissolve and the traces of a smile emerge. As she tilted her head back, her tresses dangled free, and his hands glided through them like the intangible touch of a mellow breeze when passing through the fronds of a willow.

"Your hair stinks nice, Ria."

At once, a farmyard snort erupted and was followed by an episode of unrestrained laughter. "'Stink', Ulrik? I think you mean 'smell'."

"It's the same thing. You do stink nice. Stop it, Ria; stop laughing at me. Fine. That's the last compliment you'll ever get from me."

Her hands eclipsed her face to hide her amusement.

"Why did you come?" he added. "Was it only to laugh at me?"

"No, silly," looking up at him with glowing eyes. "I came to give you this …"

Down she reached into her bra. For a moment his pulse sped in anticipation, and there was a somersaulting within his breast. Panic or thrill, he couldn't tell. To his disappointment, she produced a velvet box which had been stowed rather resourcefully in her bosom (since her outfit lacked any appropriate pocket).

"What's this?" he said, looking down the bridge of his nose at it.

"It's yours."

His hand swooped down and snatched it like a hawk when dive-bombing and seizing its prey in its talons. Opening the box, he saw a platinum disc at its centre, upon which, etched into one side, was a gentleman wearing a stupendous moustache. On the other side were the five Olympic rings.

"The Pierre de Coubertin medal," she said, tiptoeing to get a closer look. "I've been keeping it safe for you."

"Oh, yah, a medal for taking part in the race. How much do you think I could sell this junk for?"

"Junk?" her aspect turning sour. "Ulrik, this is the rarest medal of all. It's given out only to those who show true sportsmanship."

"But it's no gold medal."

"Maybe not, but this is something special. Seeing you out there like that after that Whitehood attacked you, when you collapsed, struggling, fighting for your life, the people fell in love with you. You've won their hearts; you're their champion; your fame—it's soaring off the scale."

"Meaning what, exactly?"

"It means what I said it means."

"Yah, I won a medal, so you should know what that means. I think you're missing the point ..."

"I'm confused."

While holding her gaze, he clasped the velvet box shut and flung it over his shoulder, caring little where it landed and caring more for the prize in front of him. "We had a bargain, Ria, remember? I remember it well. You said: 'I promise that if you win a medal in the aquadrome, I'll give you the best kiss of your life.'"

"Did I say that?" clutching at her heart as though in feigned innocence. "I don't think—"

"Yah, you said so on the yacht."

"Oh, you might've got me a little tipsy that night," fanning her eyelashes at him, "so I can't remember what you had me agree to. Are you sure I said that?" She had a mischievous tone about her, as though she were toying with him. "Maybe I said I'd teach you *how* to kiss, but I don't think I said we'd actually kiss, did I?"

"Best kiss of my life? Bah! Perhaps now you're not so sure you can live up to such a bold claim."

"Okay, okay, I remember. I'm just teasing," she said, coiling her arms about his neck and dangling from him. "But you're too tall for me to reach when standing," backing him up now to his bedside.

Even when he'd sat down on the bed, their height difference made the prospect of exchanging a kiss awkward. So he awaited her direction on how best to transact with their lips.

"It'd be easier if you were to lie down," she added, leaning her weight against his shoulders and urging him backwards. Then, when he'd submitted to her, she swung her legs over his and straddled him, grappling his wrists as she did so and pinning him down like a lioness does her prey; so tight was her grip that the blood supply was cut off to his hands. Her pelvis pressed against his, and he felt a swelling against his groin—no doubt she felt it, too. Her smouldering eyes confirmed it. She responded with a gentle gyration of her hips and said, "I want to get to know you, Ulrik Magnusson; all your weird bits; all your bad bits." The buttons of her blouse no longer seemed fit to hold their goods, her cleavage inflating with each successive pant of breath. "Don't think you can walk out of my life as though I'm some kind of stranger to you. I don't kiss strangers."

"Neither do I."

"So, what are we, then?"

"You're crazy, that's what you are."

"Maybe. But don't you feel what I do? Don't bullshit me, Ulrik. I'm being serious right now."

"I do. But,"—she stroked the inside of his thighs with her bare feet—"but we've only known each other for a few weeks, Ria. Don't you think you're being hasty?"

"Don't you think you're being pathetic?"

"Well, I'm a Svalbardian forager. You're Catalan. I can't give you what you want."

"What is it I want?" fastening her hips to his and grinding away at his trapped pulse below. "To be with you—that's what I want."

"I want that too, Ria. So, so, bad. But I don't belong here. Thrudheim is my home."

"You can't just go home and carry on as though nothing has happened." Her steel grip tightened about his wrists. "You won't ever be able to live a normal life. You're Homo Nova. You are the first."

"Not anymore. I'm just Ulrik now. By next week the world will have forgotten me and have moved on."

"What about me? I won't forget. I can't move on."

"You're a tough girl. The toughest I've ever known."

"Admit it: you're embarrassed about me, aren't you? It's because they call me a traitor to the Republic."

"What? Nuh, it's not that."

"Well, what's the big deal? I could come with you to Svalbard. Just go and I'll follow your lead. Anywhere. Everywhere. Anytime. Every time. Let's at least try. If it doesn't work out, then fine. At least we'd have given it our best shot."

"I …"

"Is it that you need time to consider or that you don't want me to come?" tilting her head like a puppy.

"I need time to think."

"What have you got to think about?" She rested her forehead on his. If only he'd dared to purse his lips, he would've sealed his first kiss. "Imagine waking up on a morning, our bodies huddled together beneath the furs; depending on each other for warmth—for protection against the cold, wintry air."

"Ria, the North is no place for a girl like you. It sounds magical, what with the Northern Lights, the glaciers, fjords, midsummer nights, mountains, and snowfall; but it's a dark place, and when the wind blows it's like having needles blast you in the face. It's too cold for trees of any kind to grow, and there are polar bears. If you were to—" At once, she smothered his mouth with hers, and her wandering tongue stroked against his, so he copied her actions as best as he could. Her frivolous hands became familiar with his chest, and, at her direction, he grasped her by the haunches. Even though he knew he was the victim of raunchy blackmail, it didn't stop him longing for more.

"Think about it," she said, starting a trail of kisses at his lips, then working her way down his neck, chest, past his navel, and stopping an inch or two below his waist. "Promise me you'll think about it. Promise me." She prowled over him, urging her body against his while sinking her hot teeth into his neck.

"I promise," he said, in honest surrender.

Thereafter, they kissed in every occupiable space of the room. Every piece of mountable furniture was stress-tested, and every patch of floor space was rolled over.

"I can die a happy man now."

"Man?" she said, her devilish nose crinkling. "Ssst, you're not a man *yet*." She dismounted him and withdrew to the window, where, under the soft glow of dawn, she powdered her face and reapplied her lip gloss with indifference.

He watched from afar, silently begging her to return for one more kiss, but she continued grooming her caramel waves and seemed more interested now in how best to style her hair. What did she mean when she said he wasn't a man *yet*? A spontaneous insight into the opposite sex struck him, and for a fleeting moment he thought he understood her: it was as though she were suggesting the only route to him becoming a man was through her, and as though she were promising some next round of debauchery on condition that the status of their relationship take some official turn.

Chapter Twenty-Eight

THE LAST CRUMB OF CHEESE

"We started these rumours, Tristan. We cannae fockin' chicken oot now." Her broad Scottish accent was frostier than usual, and in the shadows of the dimly lit war room, her ice-blue eyes panned over him like two searching spotlights.

Tristan sealed the door of the war room behind him, or the dungeon as he took to calling it, for not a strip of daylight entered that underground chamber, and not a particle of air escaped. Upon entering, a prevailing damp musk filled his lungs; and the cobbled walls were in their usual state of perspiration owing to the accumulated moisture which clung to their surface like breath on a mirror.

"Why yae shutting the door?" said Skye, planting her hands on her hips. "We're literally the only fockers aboot for miles."

"I know," said Tristan, itching his neck, "but I just can't shake the idea that someone's listening. Can never be too careful."

"And yae dunnae need to whisper, either," raising her voice, much to his annoyance.

Tristan took up his seat at the Arthurian round table while Skye went from sconce to sconce, lighting candles that were mounted on the cobbled walls. Each of these candles was neighbour to a tapestry; and woven into these tapestries were regimental coats of arms depicting lions, stags, dragons, bugles, harps, swords, castles, crowns, and crosses. These insignias belonged to the fallen: that is, those who were members of that gallant order of Victoria Cross receivers since its conception: Wainwright, Saxon, Penrose, Montgomery, Cleghorn, Haywood, Marshall, Lancaster, Appleyard, Shires, Neville, Percival, Chamberlain, Watson, Wilson, Williamson, Ronson, Bronson, Johnson, and a good many more. Fallen but not forgotten.

Skye saluted them with a thump of her breast and exclaimed, "For valour." Tristan raised his tankard to their names and, having swigged in their honour, wiped the froth from his upper lip with a stroke of his sleeve.

"Now, where was I?" said Skye, taking a seat beside him to close in on him. "Oh, aye. So, I was saying before yae got all paranoid and obsessed with shutting doors that we cannae fockin' chicken oot now. We've come too far to turn back."

"I know, but lying about Babylon having weapons of mass destruction, it just doesn't sit right with me, Skye. Remind me again why leaking this uranium ledger is a good idea."

"'Cause," scraping a stool across the floor and holding it aloft in her wiry arm, "'cause a three-legged stool canny stand on two legs. The Holy Shepherd, the Caliph, the Chief Rabbi—if yae take any of them oot of the equation, the Triumvirate collapses. The Hoose of Abraham collapses."

"Yeah, no, I get that, but what I'm saying is, if our plan works, and let's say the Holy Shepherd buys all this and invades Babylon, countless lives are gonna be caught up in conflict—innocent lives. That'll be on us, Skye. Me and you. There'll be blood on our hands."

"Honestly," cocking her head and tightening her peony-pink lips, "yae knew the risks when we first sat doon and started this. We've been working on this in secret for a long, long time. Not months but years, Tristan. We've forged transcripts, framed images, fabricated recordings, hacked Babylonian systems. We cannae leave a trail withoot any proper evidence at the end of it. This uranium ledger, it's the last crumb on the mousetrap—a big, tasty, irresistible crumb of cheese. If we dunnae lay it, all that hard work'll have been for nothing."

"Maybe, but at least I'd still sleep at night. I dunno. Making the Caliph out to be some sort of villain ... starting a war—" He clutched at his breast as the rising reflux foamed in his gullet and held his breath until the wave of acid subsided. Unquenchable stress had rendered his stomach a magma chamber of late.

"What's the matter with yae?"

"Oh, it's my bloody heartburn. Comes and goes when I've had a drink."

"I'm no' surprised; yae drink too much of that shite."

He shrugged his shoulders, reclined on the rear legs of his chair, and looked up to the ceiling to avoid her hostile eyes.

"Right," continued Skye, fixing her raven hair, "getting back to our wee discussion: what is it yae want, Tristan? 'Cause all this time I thought yae wanted to bring doon Emmanuel Saint-Pierre and his religious regime."

"You know I'll never stop fighting as long as I've got a hole in my arse."

"Then why do yae hesitate?"

He took up a beer mat and fidgeted with it meditatively, folding it, tearing it, and flinging tiny pieces across the round table. Such is the unconscious habit which punters undergo, and the same restless folk are those who, when strolling past a bush, become overwhelmed by the urge to snatch a leaf from its branches, fold it, tear it, and toss it to the wind in an act of bizarre self-therapy. "Because what if this comes back to us? We'd be criminally investigated. Trialled. Charged with treason. Put away for life."

"Have I ever let us doon before, hun? The authorities can never find out 'cause we're no' leaving a single trace. All evidence we're using to frame the Caliph passes their digital forensics tests. Every bit of digital content we've created (files, emails, photographs, footage, purchasing records) and every bit of their DNA (times, dates, coordinates, coding) has been verified using the same system that their central intelligence services use. Look, Tristan, yae'll have to trust me. I was hacking and forging intel long before I joined the Intelligence Corps. So I know my shit. The Holy Shepherd is gownae have an anal prolapse as soon as these latest developments hit the news."

"Such a delightful way with words you have, Skye," he said, screwing his lips up, not wanting to concede a smile.

"At the end of the day, it's all for the greater good. So, it shouldnae be a hard choice, Tristan."

"Yeah, you say that, but what happens if they capture the Caliph and execute him, eh? Then what? You know as well as I do that Sultan bin Ibrahim is the most progressive leader the Middle East has had in decades. What do you think will happen when the caliphate is without a caliph? It'll be ripe for a Saifullah coup to take control. Mark my words, Skye: we'll see someone with a far more extreme agenda rise to power— someone far more deadly."

"Aye," she said, standing up for a moment to stretch her legs. When she sat down again, she did so on the edge of the round table, taking the high ground. "Tha's certainly a possibility, Tristan, but we've already evaluated the risks—time and time again."

"Have we, though?" planting his hands underneath his armpits and turning his head ninety degrees in the manner of an unruly infant. "We haven't even considered the backlash across Europe. Have you forgotten what happened the last time Western governments went to war in the Middle East? Millions marched on Westminster in protest. Millions. Governments didn't listen last time, so don't expect a peaceful demonstration this time. Expect a revolt. Expect violence. Expect casualties."

"Aye, and have yae forgotten why we're here in the first place?" She rolled up her sleeve, exposing her skin where a striking blue Celtic tribal tattoo spiralled up her arm like a cobalt flame. "Have yae forgotten what CIGMa stands for?" She extended a savage finger which, when cutting about the air, appeared like a bayonet owing to the sharpness of her fingernail, pointing, wagging, stabbing, jabbing. "Yae dinnae see the Iceni of Britannia surrendering to the imperial invaders, did yae? Am no' just gownae sit back and watch as DRUE swallows up every fockin' country in its empire. I dunnae wantae see the Hoose of Abraham and its regime worming its way back into British life again; a regime that dictates what people can eat, drink, and wear; a regime that sponsors child genital mutilation; a regime that forbids homosexuality; a regime that teaches that women are lesser than men; a regime that prohibits consenting adults having sex if they're no' married; a regime tha's made contraception illegal, and a regime that tells children they'll suffer in eternal hellfire if they dunnae obey its rules. Canon law, sharia law, halakah law—while ever these systems of law prevail, there'll never be peace on earth. So, am no' gownae miss this opportunity to leak this uranium ledger. Now is our chance—our one and only chance to dismantle this unholy trinity. Our one and only chance to end the Apartheid of Faith. This could be the beginning of the end for the Holy Shepherd."

"Do what you've got to do," said Tristan, looking at his watchTech and wishing the hour was later than it was. "You make the orders around here, Sandhurst, I take 'em."

"Fine," sliding her haunches off the table and dusting her hands as though her work here was done. "Al do it on ma own, shall I? Right, then. But remember, none of the others can ever know. No' Colonel. No' Spider. No' Wacky. They'd never understand."

"I said from the very beginning I'd keep it a secret, didn't I? You know I'm good for that."

"Why dunnae yae stop being such an honourable prick and do it with me?" said Skye, demonstrating her handTech, upon which the uranium ledger was loaded; files she'd retrieved from Babylonian archives and doctored; purchasing files and inventories of uranium—the raw material of nuclear weapons. "Am nervous here," she added. "Ma heart hasn't pounded like this since Duncan Macalister dumped me on Hogmanay by text message."

"Right." Tristan pulled his socks halfway up his shins. It was a habit he'd developed from his school football days when drawing his socks up to his thighs offered him some relief on frosty mornings. Even now he derived a sense of readiness and warmth from pulling them up. "So, all we've got to do to upload this classified document is hit 'Submit', and it'll be leaked for all to see?"

"Aye, it's anonymous, and we won't leave a trace. It's as simple as that."

"Obviously it's simple if you've spent years in the Intelligence Corps."

"So, are yae in?" she said, lightly brushing his elbow with her hand. "C'mon, hun, yae cannae let me do this on ma own. There ain't naw 'i' in 'team'."

"Yeah, but there's a 'u' in 'cunt', Skye Urquhart."

"Very original. So …" she said, clinging to his forearm.

"Do you honestly think it'll work?"

"I think anything can be made believable to folk who disassociate with reason."

"Oh, for fuck's sake, bring it here, you lizard, and let's get it over with before I change my mind."

Tristan held out his hand, and she offered her handTech.

"Right, if yae hold the Tech, al do the dirty work and press it. But a cannae look," she said, pinching her eyes with one hand and holding out her bayonet-finger with the other. "Tell me where to aim, then."

"What is this? Pin the tail on the friggin' donkey? Just bloody press it."

"No' unless yae guide me."

"You're not serious, are you? Oh, for fuck's sake, you are. Listen in, then: up, up, up—down a bit—left now—no, too much, back up a bit—right, down a whisker—now press."

"Is that it?" she said, peeking through the gaps in her fingers. "Are we done?"

"We're done," he said, buffing the crown of his smooth head. At once, his eyes became supercharged with regret, and he glared into the whimsical flicker of candlelight, where his thoughts turned to eternal hellfire and suppositions of it being the most appropriate destination for men of such little conscience.

Skye retracted her hand in the manner of one whose fingers had come into contact with scalding water. As if exhausted from having endured some lengthy loaded march, she backed herself up to the wall, slid down it, and said, "Right, Holy Shepherd, it's yer fockin' move next."

Chapter Twenty-Nine

DON'T BE AFRAID, LITTLE FLEDGLING

It's a strange phenomenon how newfound freedom animates the senses; for when Astrid and Thorsten discovered they'd been pardoned of all criminal charges, things of a typically insipid nature became an ecstasy to relive: water tasted sweeter; the air smelt fresher; fabrics felt softer; colours seemed brighter; and melodies rang clearer.

The midday sun poured out rivers of glittering gold, and the precincts of Athens were mobbed with fans and athletes prior to the closing ceremony of the Olympics. The warm air carried with it the smell of barbecued meat and souvlaki, grilled halloumi and feta, and gyros and olive bread.

Marching at haste down the Athenian avenues, the foragers kept to the shade wherever the shade offered itself, for the heat was stifling, but also because Ulrik's fans were out in throngs, demanding photographs, autographs, hugs, and kisses. Not that Ulrik minded.

"Slow down, you two," said Astrid, fanning her face with a restaurant menu which she'd swiped unremorsefully when passing a table. "I can't keep up."

"But we're late," said Ulrik, who stood now at a crossroads bustling with pedestrians, shading his brow and turning his head this way and that.

"And," interrupted Thor, "we don't want to draw any attention to ourselves."

"It's kind of hard not to draw attention to yourself when you're seven foot tall," said Astrid.

"I hate that," said Thor. "And I hate this prickly heat and these busy streets and all this noise. We need to get out of here."

"Ria told me to meet her here," said Ulrik, diverting the conversation back to his own worries. "And she's not here, is she? What if she's grown tired of waiting? It's your fault for always walking so slow."

"Well," said Astrid, cocking her head as she noticed a slender figure tiptoeing behind Ulrik, "describe to me what she looks like." This newcomer raised a graceful forefinger to her lips, urging Astrid not to alert Ulrik to her presence.

"She's got wavy brown hair," said Ulrik, "brown eyes, and a freckled nose."

On hearing this, Ria slid her sunglasses to the summit of her head, her eyes sparkling with delight.

"Are we looking for someone pretty or … ?" said Thor.

"The prettiest," he said, and Ria flicked her hair over her shoulder upon hearing the compliment. "So don't be embarrassing me in front of her, or I'll probably spend the rest of my life with some woman from Svalbard who stinks of reindeer, like Helga Wolftamer or Frida Hornblower."

At once, Ria girded her arm around Ulrik's waist and nuzzled her nose against his ribs in the manner of an affectionate vixen. A sudden nervousness stole over him, and for a while he stood suspended like a long-standing oak, rigid and rooted to the ground, incapable of thought and speech.

"Hey," said Ria, her face undergoing formidable contortions, "aren't you going to introduce me?"

"Yah, I was about to … Mamma, Pappa, this is my friend Ria."

Ria leant her body away from his as far as was physically possible without toppling over, blinking and pouting all the while with mild disgust. "Ssst, aren't you going to tell them?"

"Tell them?" said Ulrik, tugging his earlobe while looking up into the cloudless ether for answers. "Tell them what?"

"About us. Me and you. Am I just your friend?"

It took him a while, but he finally fathomed out what she was getting at. "Oh, so, I forgot to mention Ria's actually my *girl*friend."

Ria stood erect on her tiptoes, extended her neck, and pouted her lips with pride. Stooping low, Ulrik met her halfway and squashed his lips against hers.

Astrid and Thorsten beamed as all parents do when they witness the transition from fledgling to the fully fledged. Like a butterfly that sheds off its former self and spreads itself anew, Ulrik appeared to undergo a metamorphosis, seeming now so full of symmetry and ready to flutter off on a course of his own choosing.

"Ria Lorenzo Lopez," said Thor, holding his arms wide open to receive her, "it's our pleasure to meet you."

"You must be Thorsten," she said, tilting her head like a puppy in wonder. "It's clear to see who Ulrik inherited his height from."

"Yah, he has my height, but not my strength just yet," he said, trapping Ulrik in an endearing headlock.

"Well, find yourself a good trainer, and we might be cheering for you at the next Olympics. Maybe a giant like you would be suited to the hammer throw or shot put."

The reddening of Thor's cheeks had little to do with his sunburn. He was visibly flattered, and he pressed a palm to his barrel chest and gave a low bow.

"And you must be the wonderful Astrid." Ria leant in and gave her a polite peck on her left cheek—mwah—then on her right—mwah. "Oh, your hair. I love it. Such a beautiful shade of gold. Ugh, I once tried to dye my hair blonde, but it turned out ginger." Turning to Thor and surrendering her hands, "Not that there's anything wrong with being ginger."

"Oh, it's a nightmare to work," said Astrid, deflecting the compliment. "It's taken me hours to plait this morning. Life would be so much simpler if we were boys. They just roll out of bed looking like they do."

"Let's not linger here any longer," said Thor. "There's a mob of teenage girls heading our way."

While Astrid and Ria yakked like long-lost sisters, sharing recommendations of butters, milks, and oils with which to condition one's hair, Ulrik and Thor pressed on down the street. After a prolonged bout of trekking under the scorching sun, they happened upon a quaint cobbled town square surrounded by bustling tavernas and souvenir stores.

"It's much quieter here," said Thor. "Less folk."

It was in the reflection of the nearest shop window that they noticed the brooding figure of a woman—a figure as tall and broad as either Ulrik or Thor—following them and watching them with disturbing blatancy.

"Don't look," said Ria, like the consummate ventriloquist who speaks with minimal effort of the lips. She pushed her sunglasses up the bridge of her nose so the movements of her eyes escaped detection. "That woman there with the red hair and freckles, she's staring at you, Ulrik."

"She's been tracking us for some time," said Astrid, casting a sharp glare to ward off the stalker, who was dressed in slatternly knitwear not too dissimilar to that of the Norwegian style. An uncomfortable choice for such a hot day.

"That's the worst thing about being famous," said Ria, girding Ulrik's arm about her shoulder. "Obsessive fans. Just you wait; you haven't seen nothing yet."

A gleam of self-importance shone in Ulrik's eyes so that they now appeared like two uncut emeralds. Thereafter, a growing commotion ensued in the town square. Several hands belonging to pouting teenagers pointed and waved at Ulrik.

"Well, I don't know about any of you, but I'm getting hungry," said Thor, slapping a tune on his belly and veering towards a pleasant alfresco taverna where an over-familiar waiter intercepted him. "Shall we head in here for cover?"

"My friend," said the waiter, collecting his hands together, "table for how many peoples? Oh, oh, oh! Friends of Ulrik Magnusson, hey? Opa! All of you eat and drink here—for free! Yes, please. Come in."

"Nuh, wait," said Ulrik, who was waving back at his fans as Ria towed him into the seating area.

The lure of a free feast bought everyone's attention; everyone, that is, except Astrid. Glancing back, she noticed that the eyes of the mysterious woman seemed now to be tracking Thor, not Ulrik. But by the time Astrid was escorted to her seat and handed a glass of white wine, the face of this red-haired stalker had disappeared into the swelling crowd surrounding the taverna.

"See, this is my worst nightmare," said Thor, gesturing to the crowd, who were vying for Ulrik's attention. "Trouble is what this is."

"You have to learn to block it out," said Ria, gently tapping Ulrik's cheek to avert his wandering eyes. "Best ignore them, and they'll go away."

But they didn't.

Under the shade of a great parasol the companions dined, and all felt a good deal more bloated for having gorged on too much moussaka and too little salad. There they slumped in their wicker chairs, sipping on sparkling wines and ales and sympathising with each other's tales of trivial offences and revelling in each other's delights as midday meandered into mid-afternoon. Meanwhile, the swelling crowd ballooned to a great size, and from above, the people's heads appeared packed together like dense molecules.

For a while, the foragers got to know Ria, and she got to know them— at least, the outer versions of one another. It's not until folk share some grave experience that the inner soul is laid bare for others to see. Though they didn't have to wait long for such an opportunity, for a growing disturbance some way off interrupted the placid pace of the day.

All bystanders in the vicinity stretched out their necks in unison like a mob of meerkats when, appearing hypnotised, they stand up on their hind legs and look about in coordinated curiosity. Their faces turned from curiosity to concern to horror, though, as chilling screams ricocheted throughout the town square; screams so infrequently heard that when one does hear them, human instinct warns of terrible violence afoot.

A stampede of folk dashed in all directions, tossing their Tech and handbags as though they were burdens no less disposable than common litter.

"Do we get up and run?" said Astrid, as the folk at the surrounding tables scarpered out of the taverna and into the masses.

"Is this not some kind of parade?" said Thor, drawing himself up to his full height and clenching his cubic fists.

Nobody needed to answer him, for a hellish revving of engines was made known to every man, bird, and beast basking in that pedestrian quarter. Four trucks with monstrous tyres came ploughing down the four connecting avenues of the town square, mowing bodies down indiscriminately—fathers, sons, mothers, daughters, babies. Such a hideous pop do skulls make when compressed under forty tonnes, and such a hideous canvas were those lanes of whitewashed buildings, awash now with abstract splashes of vermilion, and bespattered with a slush of bone and brain—a mire of muscle and marrow. Then came an almighty clatter as, one by one, the trucks were overturned by bollards at the edge of the town square; engines groaning like depressed victims, they lay twisted from wall to wall, their oblong bodies penning the survivors in the town square like hapless livestock.

The foragers were sluggish in reacting to these events owing to their heavy consumption of wine, but the surround-sound of screams struck them sober: the guttural gargles of those half-slain; harrowing howls of widows; woeful wails of orphans; the shrill, psychotic chorus of shrieking parents mourning their younglings.

Astrid pressed a hand to her temple to steady her balance, though she felt no touch in her fingertips, and it felt as if it were altogether another hand supporting her head. Numb it was, in a way not too dissimilar to a hand afflicted by frostbite. Feeling faint, she dropped to one knee and waited for the blue haze clouding her vision to subside. In clenching shut her eyes, she sought to escape the metropolitan massacre but saw violent imprints on the back of her eyelids; imprints as vivid as portraits; faces utterly mangled and mauled; bodies squashed paper-flat save for the corrugated tyre treads running hideous patterns across them. No perceptible features remained of these victims, nothing but distorted, abstract blobs of sticky pulp, except for the wigs of hair—all of which were dyed blood-red.

"Saifullah!" screamed Ria, pointing to the assailants who leapt from the overturned trucks and yelled in Arabic while waving crescentic swords. Eight of them, each with a black and white chequered scarf wrapped about their head, came hacking their way through the crowd, lopping off heads with as much ease as bamboo is felled.

"Magnusson," cried one terrorist, whose chin and crooked nose would've intercepted if they were but an inch or two longer.

"Get inside if you want to live," said a bass voice nearby. At first, Astrid supposed it was Thor, but when her senses returned she saw it was the flame-haired stranger from earlier. Up close, this vast woman had a strange familiarity, not because she was known to them, but because she seemed to be of similar stock: northern; grim yet fair; fierce but friendly.

"Let's go!" said Ria, towing Ulrik away by the hand. "We need to get you out of sight."

"Why are they coming after me?"

"Because you're high profile. It's what they do. Kill famous people—to make headlines. Now move. There's no time for questions."

They'd tarried too long, for the doors of the taverna had been barred from the inside, and the steel shutters were being cranked down like a portcullis. The waiters had barricaded themselves in. Who could blame them? For selfishness, not charity, is the ugly agent of life's propagation. The flame-haired woman took offence, and having strode forward, she drove one square shoulder beneath the shutters, stalling them half-way. Then, while she battled against them, Thor and Ulrik sprang into motion and took up a long bench in their arms, carrying it like a battering ram. With it, they charged forward and laid siege to the glass doors of the taverna. On their first strike they rebounded, leaving the window scarred with a mosaic of cracks. On the second strike, the bench burst through and left a jagged star at the centre of the window, wide enough for a person to slip through. There was no time to round off the jagged star, for a scrummage of bodies fought by the entrance to gain admittance.

"You first, Ulrik," said Thor, seizing him by the collar of his tunic. "Astrid, you next," taking her by the hand. "In you go now, Ria," gesturing with a bow. When all three had slipped through the jagged star, Thor took to policing the crowd, fending back men of fighting age and granting priority passage to the women and children. The flame-haired woman, who until now had valiantly stanchioned the shutters and caused them to malfunction, paid no heed to Thor and instead appointed herself a new post: when all others sought asylum, she stood guard, bold of stance and stolid of face.

Watching from the window, Astrid had the aspect of a mannequin—rigid, expressionless, dehumanised—for some way off, a conical mound of bodies was growing: headless bodies, hacked, slashed, latticed, defiled. The clinking and clanking of rattling swords rang like hellish wind chimes while fell voices called out the name "Magnusson".

"Mamma, you're shaking," said Ulrik, who himself was stricken by the worst of tremors. "Come away from the window."

"What about your pappa? He's still out there."

"I'll go."

"No," said Ria, coiling about Ulrik's waist and blocking his path. "It's too dangerous. And that's what Saifullah want. You're Homo Nova. You're too important. And you've only just been discharged from hospital after suffering a stroke. You're in no state to do anything."

At once, a copper head of hair stooped low and entered through the jagged star; but when a hand curled the ginger forelocks about the ears, Astrid's heart shrank and shrivelled upon learning it was the vast woman striding towards them, not Thor.

"Where's my husband?" she said, shaking now as if expecting the worst news.

"Standing guard," the woman said, in a thick Scandinavian accent. Though she didn't stop to discuss the details of his whereabouts. Up close, Astrid saw she had a peculiar condition of the skin which looked not unlike the coarseness of tree bark.

"Hey," said Ria, "you have something stuck in your arm … Is that glass?"

"Who, me?" She lifted her freckled arm and observed the serrated shard protruding from her flesh. Then she plucked it out as though it was no more trouble than a wooden splinter under the skin. Not even as a red ravine spilt forth from the grizzly gash did her face convey any concern. She simply removed her belt, strapped it about her elbow like a tourniquet to stop the bleeding, then made for the exit.

"Wait!" called Ulrik. "Who are you?"

"Embla," she said, unlocking the taverna doors from the inside and bursting through them. "And you are?" But of course she knew who he was.

The scrummage of bodies outside spilt inside, and the taverna quickly became the centre of commotion. Among the inbound faces was a red one, flustered from hard labour, hair bedraggled with sweat and looking like red seaweed: it was Thor, carrying four fledglings—two under each arm—as though they were toys.

"Thorsten!" exclaimed Ria, who was as delighted as anyone to see him.

"Here, Ulrik," said Thor, "take these fledglings to the upper level. Find them a safe space. Keep them occupied."

"Why me? Where are their parents?"

Thor bared his canines, widened his eyes, and shook his head. Bad news.

"Come," said Ulrik, clearing his throat, "come with me, little ones."

But the younglings wouldn't part with Thor, for having told them that he came from the North Pole, he'd won their trust—this giant man with the jolly red cheeks, magnificent beard, big belt, black boots, and the whiff of reindeer about him. It was as if they supposed him to be the heir of Santa Claus himself. Only he did they trust to carry them up the stairs and into an open-plan apartment.

This apartment belonged to the taverna owner, and it could be deduced that he'd invested his entire earnings into his business and spared not a pittance for the upkeep of his home. The surfaces were cold and hard, and so too was the miserable furniture which was buried beneath mountains of laundry, owing perhaps to him being a man who spent so much time hosting guests downstairs that his home upstairs had been deliberately neglected so as to repel them. It was a landscape of cardboard boxes; boxes which seemed not to have been unpacked since his moving in. These were presently being rearranged into seats for the victims and refugees pouring in, and also to cordon off a crèche for the younglings in the corner.

"Mr Claus," said one youngling, tugging at Thor's trouser leg, "my big sister, she's always mean to me, but I will like it if you could please go wake her because I seed her get hurt when she falled asleep in the street."

"Excuse me, Santa-man, please do you know when my daddy is coming to get me? He wears eyeTech and has a moustache, and his favourite thing is to whistle, and m-m-my address is number seven on Station Street—I forgot the rest. But you'll find him out there, sir, I know you will. I won't cry ever again. I'll be a good boy. I promise."

"My Jessie Jackal," said a little girl, producing a sequinned purse which was overflowing with buttons and beads, "I lost my Jessie Jackal. She's got red fur and white socks. I lost her, but if you find her, you can keep my money. I just want my Jessie Jackal back."

"That's okay, little fledglings," said Thor, squatting down to their height and rumpling their hair in turn. "I won't be needing any money. But I need you, all of you, to promise me you'll try your bestest to take care of each other."

"We promise," vowed a chorus of younglings, their tiny honourable hands pressed to their oversized hearts.

But the touching moment was short-lived, for a senior lady raised her voice above all others, causing every object, both animate and inanimate, to flinch and thereafter remain in stationary suspension. "There's a girl," she said, pressing her face to the window and fogging it up with exasperation. "A girl with two Saifullah men—they've taken a young girl hostage! Lord, please, no."

Astrid sped to the window where, looking yonder, plumes of smoke rose in the distance atop a prominent hill—from the Parthenon atop the Acropolis. For millennia it'd stood while empires moved in and out of Athens—the Ottomans, the Byzantines, the Romans—but it was Saifullah of New Babylon who had destroyed it. Down below, there was utter wreckage; life squashed out like insects. And sure enough there was a young girl wearing a black hooded sweater—a most unusual choice of clothing on such a sweltering summer's day. Standing beside her were two Saifullah captors.

"She's so still," said Embla. "In shock, it seems."

"I wish, wish, wish, I had my rifle," said Ria. "I could pick these vermin off so easily from up here."

"Everybody, calm down," said Thor, with the deep rumble of authority. "You're frightening the fledglings. Come now; away from the windows." But even Thor, who'd done so well until now to feign a smile, plugged a fist into the cavern of his mouth, for when he saw the little girl, his jaw dropped, exposing that little stalactite that dangles at the back of the throat of which few folk know either the colloquial or medical name. "That poor girl. I'm going down."

Astrid coiled about his waist and inundated his forearm with kisses while begging him to stay. But he shrugged her off and said that while ever there were little fledglings in danger, he couldn't abandon them. Before he fled downstairs, the taverna owner, who was holding a cardboard box in his arms, intercepted him.

"For your protection, Magnusson, please," said the taverna owner, handing a box of clanking cutlery to him, inside which was a bundle of chef's knives and meat cleavers.

"Exquisite craftsmanship," said Thor, while becoming acquainted with the balance of two long blades.

"Pappa," said Ulrik, "it's too late to be going back out there. They're trying to draw us out. Let us draw the blinds."

"You can't be going out there with those," said Astrid. "What if they have guns?"

"If they had guns, we'd know it," said Ria.

"I'll go with you, Thor," said Embla, who took two blades from the box and, with dextrous hands, juggled them overhead, behind her back, and in front of her, before seizing them during their mad whirring and blurring about the air. Some roguish school was that where she'd been apprenticed; a place where young girls majorette not with batons but with blades.

"Thor, please," said Astrid, hooking her arm through his, and when he shrugged her to one side she collapsed to the floor in a heap about his legs. "You don't know how many of them are still out there. We see only two, but the others could be in hiding—waiting for you."

"Good; I hope to bring them *all* to justice," said Thor, through his gritted square teeth as he scraped the chef's knives together, sending out a sharp ring of steel.

"If you go down there, you'll risk the lives of everybody in here," said a clean-fingered, slender man, obstructing the exit.

Embla, who was closest, towered over this clean-fingered man and sniffed the golden crucifix dangling about his neck. "Smells like a Christian to me. What should we do, godling? Stay here and pray? Look at you," thrusting a cuboid finger through the air. "You, you, you, and you; why are you on your knees praying? Thanking God for sparing you? What about those dead younglings out there? Were they not special enough, huh? Were they not part of God's plan?" The man wearing the crucifix lowered his eyes and stepped aside. A good job too, for had he not, Embla seemed prepared to twist off his head, and perhaps she would've done so with as much ease as an ordinary person unscrews a cap from bottled water. "Well, then, back to your prayers," spitting on the floor. "Hope it makes you feel good about yourselves."

"Don't be afraid. I'll be back soon, little fledgling," said Thor, but instead of addressing a youngling, he rumpled the receding comb-over of the clean-fingered man wearing the crucifix. As he turned out of the door, he called to Astrid and said, "Don't think about following me. You're needed here. For once, listen to me. Don't even …" His words died away as he descended the stairs and headed out with Embla on their heroic errand.

After a few moments, Astrid snuck after them, at all times keeping herself within earshot and always in the shadows.

On the ground floor, Thor stumbled across a cylindrical dustbin and took up its lid as a shield. Embla found another and did likewise. The two of them advanced outside the taverna like Viking raiders with swords and bucklers in hand.

The town square was silent. It was oversubscribed with dead bodies and those who were playing dead.

"Embla, tell me," said Thor, treading with care over the fallen, "where did you learn to wield blades like you do?" She buried her brow down her face as one does when in deep thought or when attempting to stem a flow of tears, but she made no reply. "You're from Norway, aren't you? I know your accent."

"Yah," she said, speaking now in the Norwegian tongue, "I'm from a place on the west coast of Nærøyfjord. You've heard of Gudvangen?"

"You're one of the Gudvangen?" said Thor, speaking now in that near-extinct language. "Yah, I've heard of your people, but I thought you'd disbanded?"

"At one time, our numbers dwindled, but our community has flourished again. People, not just pagans, have sought sanctuary in our village—in our way of life. Free from religious prejudice."

As they headed out further into the violent cemetery, Thor and Embla lunged over bodies—headless, limbless, latticed bodies—keeping their eyes forward as they gained ground on the Saifullah soldiers. Astrid crept along the perimeter of the tavernas, pinching her nose to stop the stench of corpse pulp entering her nostrils.

"They've spotted us," said Thor, clattering his dustbin shield with the chef's knife.

"You take the one on the right," said Embla. "I'll take the left. Spread out and let's draw them away from the little girl."

Astrid flanked the field in the shadows, gaining closer to the little girl.

When Thor and Embla had been spotted, the Saifullah soldiers raised their crescentic swords, shrieking with bloodlust in Arabic. The responses from Thor and Embla were even wilder, for their berserk cries boomed throughout the town square, and their eyes bulged from their kohl-shadowed sockets, and they stuck out their long pointed tongues while clattering their shields. Visibly shaken by the challenge from these red-haired giants, the terrorists conferred among themselves.

"What the ..." muttered Astrid, peeking over a raised flowerbed.

At once, the Saifullah soldiers threw down their swords, removed their black and white chequered scarves, and waved them overhead.

"They're surrendering," said Thor, lowering his knife and shield.

"It's a ruse," said Embla, balancing her blade by the sharp end and eyeing her target. "Don't engage them. Let them advance towards me. I'll draw them off. You get the girl."

The terrorists commenced a horrendous singing, their irksome intonations resembling a droning siren. Sadistic grins spread across their faces as they looked up into the sky, enraptured, it seemed, by the presence of a spirit. And with eyes supercharged with excitement, one gave a subtle nod to the other.

"Allahu akbar—Allahu akbar—Allahu akbar!" they chanted, setting off now at a perilous sprint towards Thor and Embla.

A flash of glinting silver caught the sun; the whirring and blurring of a blade let loose. For almost twenty yards, Embla's dagger kept its flight. Its course never altered, nor did the Saifullah soldier who charged on with extreme love in his eyes and extreme hate in his breast—love for an invisible authority, hate for his fellow human being.

"Get down!" said Embla, diving into a heap of bodies and using her dustbin lid as a shield for cover.

The dagger slotted into the soldier's breast with as much ease as a key slots into its designated lock. A blast threw him and his ally through the air, wreathing them both in flame.

When the shock waves ceased rippling, and when the last rocks fell from the sky, and when the inferno died away, Astrid emerged coughing and saw only a nebula of brown dust and red mist lingering in the air. She called out to Thor and was relieved to hear his voice from behind the curtain of haze.

"Suicide vests," said Embla, choking between her words. "They had suicide vests."

Thor's silhouette emerged holding the hand of the young girl in the black sweater, and with his other hand he groped about the hazy film as one does when making their way through the dark.

"What were you thinking?" said Astrid, storming across the field of corpses and helping Embla to her feet. "That blast could've killed us."

"I thought I told you to stay where it was safe?" said Thor, placing a hand on Astrid's chin and stroking his bulbous thumb over her cheek.

"I told you to do the same thing, but did you listen? Nuh. Do you ever listen? Nuh." She ignored Thor and bent down now to the youngling's height, though the poor creature was paralysed with shock. Perhaps more concerning were the ravines of sweat trickling down her head. "Well, that's a trendy sweater you're wearing. Oh, but it's a little too hot out here for that. Shall we take it off you and get you cooled off somewhere safe?"

Violence had rendered the youngling mute.

"She won't let us take it off," said Thor. "Not me; not anybody. And she won't let me carry her. She'll only go by hand."

"Maybe she's hurt herself," said Astrid, extending her hand. "Oh, you poor creature. Let's get you out of here."

"Don't be afraid, little fledgling. You're safe with us."

The girl slipped her hand in Astrid's, and they walked her back to the taverna, her dainty, innocent sandals squelching the entrails of children underfoot as they went.

When they arrived back in the upper apartment of the taverna, Thor collapsed under the strain of his own weight, and the infants surrounded him, patting his face, pulling his fingers, and tugging his beard—all except the little girl in the black sweater.

"Never think about leaving me again," said Astrid, towering over him. "Stupid, reckless fool."

"Astrid, I want to go home," closing his eyes and drawing in a deep sniff. Then he smiled as though he were daydreaming of Thrudheim and roaring fires and red meat on the bone. "Take me home."

At last, the long-awaited sounds of sirens and the rapid fanning of a quadcopter above signalled the presence of emergency services, at which strangers traded hugs and handshakes. Only one headbutt was exchanged: that between Thor and Embla. But all sense of relief dissipated when they learnt, all of a sudden, that danger of another kind had followed the heroes back to the apartment like a black shadow.

"You're funny," said one youngling to the girl in the black sweater. "Why do you have wires sticking out of you? Are you a robot?"

All voices dropped to an audible murmur; then utter silence prevailed.

"Did you say 'wires'?" asked the clean-fingered man wearing the crucifix. After treading with care to gain a closer look, he threw his spindly arms in the air and fled out of the door yelling, "A bomb! Saifullah have rigged her with explosives!"

Astrid smacked her hands to her mouth and backed away. Sure enough, there were nefarious wires dangling out of the girl's black sweater, and upon closer inspection, she saw, down the baggy opening of the sweater's collar, brown parcels padded about her midriff. Many things happened at once: Thor knelt down and formed a shield around the girl as a stampede rushed forwards and backwards; columns of cardboard boxes toppled over; an old lady fell, or rather was shouldered down the stairs and cracked her head and hip along the way; some people fled through windows and down drainpipes; others found their way up into the attic and onto the rooftops; Ulrik, Embla, and Ria scooped up the younglings, and in making for the exit, they barged over those dithering in their way like skittles.

"Thor, come away from her," said Astrid, reaching out to him from across the cluttered expanse of the room.

"Is everybody out?" he said, drawing circles on the girl's dainty palm as a means of ticklish distraction.

"Everybody except us." She heard Ulrik's heavy footsteps travelling up from the bottom of the stairs, and she told him to clear a path and wait outside because she and Thor were about to head down.

"You go first, Astrid," said Thor. "I don't want to startle the little fledgling."

"Not without you."

"Just go. I'll be right behind you."

"I'm not leaving without you."

"Don't argue. For once, stubborn woman, do as I say."

"Don't leave me, then."

"Okay, I'm getting up. See?" rising with extreme caution, steadying his balance with his arms held out, knees and elbows bent as though he were about to tread across ice.

"I'll wait over by the door," she said, stepping over toppled boxes and drawing herself away from the fatal radius.

"Don't be afraid, little fledgling," said Thor, eyes glistening, lips trembling, nostrils flaring.

The girl, though, who'd stood as rigid and as mute as a waxwork until now, understood only too well that she was being abandoned and hugged Thor's leg for comfort, instigating a faint yet audible click; the click, likely, of some pressure plate activated on the violent vest she was rigged with.

A spectral colour washed over Thor, and he cast Astrid a sharp look. Never had he looked upon her with such emptiness. His eyes widened, yet his pupils shrank to little more than pinpricks; and he seemed not to be staring at her but into the eye sockets of Death. Blinking, throat kinking, not a word escaped his lips.

"Dun be 'fraid, little fledge," said the girl, hugging and patting Thor's vibrating leg to quell his tremor. But like an electrical current, the tremor travelled from one host to another so that the girl's body shook to the same effect, rattling the contraption strapped to her torso.

At once, a mighty blast of flaming wind threw Astrid across the apartment and behind the kitchen counter. Thor and the youngling were swallowed and thereafter spat out as a pink mist. Splinters of tooth, bone, and nail darted like shrapnel in every direction. A hole blew through the roof, and small embers began life like a garden of little red flowers.

Within moments, the blaze spread to all things flammable, so that now the burning, blooming surroundings looked akin to an autumnal forest. Astrid garbled a few words, none of which were intelligible, then pushed herself up. In a state of concussion, she looked around and supposed she'd died and woken up in hell, for the raging inferno consumed the entire floor space, except the quarter which she and Thor occupied (for the blast had flung Thor behind the kitchen counter, too).

"Thor," she said, choking on the smoke as she sidled to her lover's side. His legs were gone, his face had melted, and when she laid a pitying hand on his flesh, his skin pulled away like hot glue. "Oh, your legs. Your poor legs—gone. Oh, your face. Listen to me, stupid. You're too heavy for me to be carrying you. Wake up. We'll find someone who can put you back together. The doctors—they'll be able to fix you. Oh, Thor, I don't care if you don't have legs. Please, just wake up. Say something to me. Anything. It's your Astrid. You're my hero. My Viking. My love. Why won't you wake up?" She pressed her mouth to his charred lips, hoping to break the enchantment of eternal sleep with true love's kiss. "We were supposed to grow old together. Be together forever. Like you said. You promised. You can't break a promise. Why are you being selfish? Oh, you're not selfish. I'm sorry for saying such a thing. I didn't mean it. It's me who's being selfish. I'm just afraid. So, so afraid. I need you. Stay with me. I don't want to live without you. You know I love you, don't you? Please say you do. Or squeeze my hand if you can hear me—or blink your eyes."

She grasped his hand and ran her thumb over his callused cubic knuckles. A faint contraction.

"Oh, Thor, I felt that. Squeeze again if you love me."

A faint contraction ... and then another. But the fingers thereafter stiffened.

Tears escaped her eyes, but they evaporated before they could fall from her chin. The longest lament followed: a severe shrieking that was sure to disfigure her gullet; and the blood vessels of her stinging eyes burst red with dread.

Two giant hands appeared behind the veil of fire—hands that belonged to freckled arms. They seized Astrid by the collar of her tunic and mounted her over a cubic shoulder just as the flames were about to snatch her. "Leave me to die with my husband," said Astrid, wriggling and writhing as the snapping flames commenced their cremation of Thor's remains.

Embla held Astrid firm, and she, as though impervious to fire, never flinched while wading through the field of flame and groping her way through the cloud of soot and smoke, emerging outside with her boots and trousers ablaze; and despite showing signs of grave injury, she never made a single complaint nor any hint of having endured the least bit of torment throughout the rescue.

Chapter Thirty

THE TREATY OF ZION

S cenes of rolling countryside are conducive to mellowing the soul
and unscrambling one's thoughts. Perhaps, though, it isn't growing
greenery and wild scenery which hushes our anxieties but the bliss of
rare solitude and the sheer sparsity of people. For when humankind has
lost its moral way, it does a person good to steer clear of society and be
ignorant of its existence for a while.

Yonder Tristan looked across the rolling shire, shading his eyes from
the westering sun so that his view of nature's rural patchwork stretched
far and wide. Gorse and heather flourished in every dell, dale, glen, and
fen, and their wild molestations were interrupted only by the jigsaw of
dry-stone walling which chopped up plots of moorland in the wonkiest ap-
portioning of property imaginable. A single road, or rather dirt track was
all that connected this solitary house on the hill to the rest of the world.

To look at this sleepy halfway inn, wearing its outer jacket of ironstone
and a neatly thatched cap, it seemed the quintessential countryside
lodging, but ramblers and their spaniels were seldom seen trekking up
in these parts. The Queen Boudicca was a public house in guise only,
the only business conducted here being that of the secret council of
CIGMa in a secret underground war room. It's swinging sign depicted
a red-haired warrioress riding a chariot, her face tattooed in tribal blue;

and before entering, Tristan stopped beneath it (as all the masters did by ritual) and paid his respects to the patron of their guild. Then he scraped the soles of his boots on the doormat and went inside.

Upon entering, he was greeted by one of his comrades, who was presently poring over something at the nearside windowsill. When Duane looked up, his ebony eyes seemed alive with energy, and so, too, did his hair seem alive and as though it might scuttle off his head without warning, for his dyed braids had the semblance of a tropical tarantula's limbs.

"Spider," said Tristan, motioning a nod in his direction, "how goes?"

"Chalky, good to see you. I'll be right with you," said Spider, directing his attention back to his project at the windowsill. As Tristan drew closer, he saw it was a shallow dish of water that Spider hovered over, out of which protruded a sugar cube not unlike a miniature iceberg, beside which was stranded an insect.

"This has to be a world's first: a spider saving a fly."

"It's a honeybee, actually," said Spider, with the sprightly delight of midsummer in his eyes as the bee crawled to the edge of the dish and buzzed off out of the open window.

"Why does it matter? Just fling it outside, and put the damned thing out of its misery."

"Why, when a bit of sugary water is all it needed? Poor blighters get exhausted on summer days like this. If I can save a life, I always choose life."

"Cute."

"Anyway, Chalky," dusting debris off his hands and extending one for the shaking, "how you been keeping?"

"Meh, so-so." Spider's handshake almost tore Tristan's arm from his socket, such was the fuss he made over him.

"Well, come on in, and I'll stick the kettle on. What you having? Cup o' tea? Cup o' coffee? Cold glass o' juice?"

"I'd love a pint o' beer, Spider, but—" The magma chamber of Tristan's stomach rejected the idea. "Phoar, this heartburn. The only thing I can tolerate these days is a pint o' milk."

"Right, let me fetch you a pint o' milk. You head on down. They're all waiting for you."

"Pah! You say 'all' as if we're a troop or a squad. All fucking four of us, you mean? Five, if you count that senile old bastard." Spider cast Tristan a look with one eyebrow astonishingly raised and the other terribly buried, the way he always did whenever profanities were used in his company. "Sorry, Spider. I don't mean to be shitty—oops, I mean I don't mean to be disrespectful. It's just with everything going on, I've not been myself."

"I know, mate, s'all right." When Spider winked, Tristan knew he was forgiven. "We can't change what happened in Athens, but we can choose how we respond to it. Just say 'frog' instead of, you know, the f-word. Say 'for frog's sake' or 'frogging heck'."

"I know you hate swearing, Spider, but I dread to think what gets called out when you and Mrs Webb do it like they do on the Discovery Channel: 'Frog me harder—oh frog, frog, frog!'"

Spider suggested Tristan ask his own mother, if he ever wished to know the truth.

"Oooft," said Tristan, suddenly hunching over the windowsill and clutching at his chest, which Spider mistook for feigned offence in response to his comeback; but it was his heartburn—that internal inferno being stoked in the firepit of his stomach—which incapacitated him.

"You all right, Chalky?"

"Heartburn. Jesus—feels like my stomach's on fire."

"You're too stressed, mate. Here, let me fetch that pint o' milk for you. You head on down."

"Spider—" Tristan thumped his chest as the reflux of acid frothed in his gullet.

"Chalky?"

"Why are you in such a good mood?"

"'Cause it's a good morning …"

"Yeah, but why are you *always* in such a good mood? What's your secret, eh?"

"Well, we're all gonna die one day, and there isn't a sequel. We might as well enjoy it while we're here, mate." Spider went away whistling a whimsical tune and with a song in his breast. He was himself today, as he was yesterday and the day before that. Not that he didn't concern himself with the bubbling trouble of the world (he did), but since joining the military, he'd endeavoured to never willingly allow a bad word, thought, or idea to enter his head.

Tristan made his way down into the dank cellar, where, stacked against the furthest cobbled wall, were half a dozen beer kegs; kegs which seemed ordinary to outward appearances, yet concealed a power source within. When Tristan coupled a bespoke electrical cable to the neck of one particular keg—at the top, where a pipeline ought to be plumbed in—some silent voltage was transferred to it and was thereafter distributed to a network of cable. Hidden pneumatic hinges hissed, causing a slender part of the stone wall to swing open, revealing an annex behind it—the secret chamber, or war room, where members of the presently sat around the grandly carpentered Arthurian round table.

"Tristan, it's no' like yae to be late," said a broad Scottish voice of authority.

"I had …"—thinking of an excuse—"I had things to do, Skye." Tristan's eyes met the floor.

"It's aw right, hun. I know. Come in. Sit yerself doon."

"They got Thorsten. Bastard Saifullah—they got Thorsten. I should've been out there protecting the Magnussons."

Skye shot out of her seat and threw her arms around him. "Yae cannae blame yerself for no' being abroad. Yae were needed here. It's no' yer fault."

"Maybe it *is* our fault, Skye," he said, wriggling his way out of her embrace. "Ulrik might not have made it to the Olympics if we hadn't got involved; if we hadn't bust Ajax Iliadis's legs; if we hadn't bribed those officials."

"Hrumph, what's all this crying about?" said Colonel, stirring from his fireside nap and rolling up to them in his wheelchair. Whenever he spoke, he did so out of the corner of his mouth. "Why's Tristan Nightingfail got a face like smashed-up dog shit? You're in the British Army, lad, not the Salvation Army."

"Colonel," said Tristan, rolling his eyes in good humour, "it's good to see you."

"Flattery won't get you anywhere, Nighting-fail," said Colonel, twiddling his spectacular ivory moustache, which curled about his cheeks like exquisite tusks. "You've had us waiting here like friggin' lizards. I've got no legs, but I can turn up on time. So what's your excuse?"

"I was—erm, I was … polishing my boots. Yeah, polishing my boots, and I lost track of time."

"Polishing your nails, more like."

"Ahem—here we are," interrupted Spider, his long fingers somehow keeping suspended five glasses. "A Brandy Alexander for you, Colonel, and here's your box of snuff; a pint o' milk for you, Chalky; pink gin and tonic for you, Skye; and a lager for you, Waqas."

"Wacky? Sorry, mate," said Tristan, circling the table to intercept his comrade. "Didn't even see you there. How you keeping, you big dosser?"

Waqas stood up, and when making his way around the table he swung his arms in front of him rather than by his side, so broad and bull-necked was he. "Long time no see, Chalky, bro," embracing him. "I'm good. Well … as good as I can be in light of, you know, all this crap going on."

"Here now, what's this shite?" Tristan licked his thumb and lunged for Waqas's goatee with the intention of erasing it. "You've got pen all over your face, Wacky."

"Pen?" Waqas retreated to the corner, where he whipped out his handTech and checked over his features on the screen of his Tech: "Pen? I don't see. Oh, right, my new beard? Funny, aren't you? Well, come at me with that wet thumb again, and, trust me, I'll shove it so far up your arse you'll be able to taste your own crap."

"You know, funnily enough," placing his hands on Waqas's brawny shoulders, "I never trust a person who says 'trust me'. It makes a person sound untrustworthy."

It was a bizarre custom in the forces to insult the person with whom one shares the strongest fellowship; and of all the brethren of CIGMa, Tristan reserved the greatest respect for Wacky, for the biography of

Waqas Akhtar was deserving of a standalone volume. If one is fortunate enough ever to meet an apostate of Islam (one who renounces their faith, an ex-Muslim), then hold this *kuffar* in the highest regard; and if that same *infidel* feels a romantic attraction to those of the same sex, then double your respect, for their sentence of death is twofold under sharia law. Even so, Waqas's parents tried to marry the *haram* (sin) out of him, declaring that once he'd bedded a woman, the evil djinn would be exorcised from his body. But Waqas Akhtar, having no mind for superstition, ran away and underwent a pilgrimage with the British Army instead.

"Sorry to interrupt your scissoring," said Colonel, "but we've important admin to get through. Nighting-fail, thanks for volunteering yourself to fetch me my register. On the double now. By the left, quick, *march*: lef', righ', lef', righ', lef', righ', lef'. The rest of you, form up on parade, you waste of jizz."

When Tristan returned with Colonel's register, they each stood to attention behind their respective seats at the round table, their eyes facing forward, and, with the exception of Tristan, their left breasts decorated with that unifying medal; that gallant token of war with its wine-red ribbon: the Victoria Cross.

"Listen in, then," said Colonel. "Squad!" They struck out their chests. "Squaaaaad, 'shun." All stamped their legs to attention, their boots hitting the ground in tandem. "Squad, stand aaaat ease."

It was a ritual of Colonel's to officiate a headcount with the register. They went along with it, but not because there was any sense in doing so for four troops, but because make-believe kindled in him the nostalgia of better days; days of his youth, when dementia hadn't eroded his intellect and memory.

"Private Appleyard?"

Silence.

"Bombardier Akhtar?"

"Ssssir." Waqas stamped his foot to attention and resumed his relaxed stance.

"Were you born a cocksnogger, Akhtar, or did you study to become one?"

"I was as straight as a ruler before I attested, Sir," said Waqas, s
"If anything, yeah, the Army's to blame for my obsession with s
cocks."

"Nonsense, I'll have none of it. Private Brennan?"

Silence.

"Sergeant Cleghorn?"

Silence.

"Private Foster?"

Silence.

"Sapper Green?"

Silence.

"Green by name, but not by friggin' nature, the jack bastard. Colou
Sergeant Nightingale?"

"Sargh." Tristan stamped his foot to attention and resumed his
relaxed stance.

"Nighting-fail, fall out, and see me after parade. That jacket has more
crinkles in it than my arse crack. Corporal Marshall?"

Silence.

"Gunner Lancaster, or should I say, Sir Nonce-a-lot?"

Silence.

"Private Powell?"

Silence.

"Terrence Powell? Where is that fat battering ram? He's not gone
AWOL again, has he?"

Silence.

"Fusilier Wainwright?"

Silence.

"Captain Urquhart?"

"Saaaaaah." Skye stamped her foot to attention and resumed her
relaxed stance.

"Don't be shy, Urquhart; your mother wasn't. Get that leg up, and
drive your heel into the ground."

"And last but not least, Corporal Webb?"

"Saaaaaur." Spider stamped his foot to attention and resumed his relaxed stance.

"What you grinning at, Webb?"

"No reason, Sir. I'm just happy, Sir. I can't help it, Sir."

"You won't be happy when I take my lawnmower for a spin over those braids, will you, neh?"

Even at his frail age, Colonel brought to them a candle of humour in the depths of their dark despair.

"Well, Skye, I-I-I've … well, I've forgotten what I was going to say," said Colonel, blowing bubbles at his lips. "Oh yes, where's my Hatty? Do you know what time she's coming to get me?"

"Aye, Colonel, she'll be here soon. Why dunnae yae have a wee nap before she comes? Yae need yer beauty sleep."

"A nap. Right. Yes, yes. Will you tell Hatty I've been out fishing with Wilson and Watson? I'll be in bother if she finds out I've been drinking in the NAAFI again."

"Aye, al cover for yae, Sir," she said, wheeling Colonel to his favourite place beside the fire and tucking a tartan blanket over his lap. In the meantime, Spider disappeared to the kitchen and came back with a glass of warm milk in one hand and a pipette in the other. With the pipette, he dispensed a few droplets of medicine into the milk, gave it a good stir, and handed it to Colonel. Shortly after sipping it, almost every loose article not fixed down by nail or screw was vibrating at the mercy of thundering snores. Even the flames of the nearest candles seemed to blow easterly and then westerly with each respective inhalation and exhalation.

"Bless him," said Spider. "He'd be out there fighting Saifullah on the streets if he could."

"I'm telling you, yeah," said Waqas, lighting a cigarette and reclining with his feet upon the table, "there isn't a terrorist alive who'd stand a chance against him in his heyday. He'd talk them to death before a shot was fired."

Tristan and Spider pinched their noses and clenched their mouths to contain their muffled laughter.

"Shh," said Skye, "lower yer volume doon a wee bit."

They were given over to a moment of quietude, their pitying hands clasped to their breasts as they watched their retired commander fall deeper into his slumber. It's a strange paradox how the sufferer of dementia should, in reaching the peak of age and maturity, revert to behaviours of infancy: dependent on others for supervision; dependent on others to get them dressed; dependent on others to clean up their incontinence; dependent on others for their nourishment; dependent on others to lull them to sleep.

"It does him a world of good to get oot into the countryside. Though it breaks ma wee heart every time I have to wheel him back through the doors of that depressing care home."

They took the following silence as an opportunity to wet their necks with their respective drinks. Then came a collective clack as each of their glasses hit the oak table, signalling their emptiness. Spider, being insistent on topping up everyone's drinks, collected their glasses, went away, and returned with a beaming smile, as though the act of fetching his friends a drink was the rarest pleasure to treasure.

"So, Skye," said Tristan, wiping the milk froth from his upper lip, "what's the latest?"

"Right," scraping her chair in closer to the table, "yae'll probably be wondering why av called yaes here at such short notice. Yaes are probably thinking it's to do with the Athens Massacre. But tha's only the half of it. Al come on to that after a wee bit. Before I get to that, I wantae share some *intel* with yaes …"

"Intel?" said Waqas, cocking his head and squinting. The word was usually a precursor to dangerous work.

"Aye: intel. Intel to suggest the Treaty has been broken."

"You mean the Peace Treaty?"

"Aye."

"The Treaty of Zion?"

"Aye, the trilateral agreement between DRUE, Israel, and New Babylon. The one on which the Hoose of Abraham was formed."

"Get fucked," said Waqas cynically, stubbing out his cigarette on the sole of his boot and leaning in to the table.

Spider hummed a tune to cancel out the swearing until he was safe in the knowledge that the foul language had ceased.

"Am no' joking, hun."

"So," said Waqas, taken aback by her seriousness, "you're not pulling our leg, no? The House of Abraham is about to come tumbling down, yeah?"

"Aye; the bedfellows of DRUE have fallen oot … so ma sources tell me."

"Well, cheers to that, guys." Tristan raised his glass but was alone in doing so. "No? What's up with you miserable lot? This is the best news we've had in ages."

"It's no' that simple, Tristan," said Skye. (But of course he knew well the details of what she was about to explain, for he and she were both conspirators in the Treaty's undoing.)

"How so?"

"Am gownae let Wacky explain 'cause I can already see him beavering away at his Tech, and nobody is more clued up on the history of the subject. What yae searching for there, Wacky?"

"This," he said, demonstrating his Tech to the room, upon which was loaded a coffee-coloured document that had an administrative language about it. "We spend so much time talking about the House of Abraham, yeah, but how many of you have actually ever seen the Treaty?"

A graveyard silence filled the war room.

"It was history," continued Waqas, "in the making when Saint-Pierre had this ratified, but trust me, history will remember the day he broke it."

"You might know," continued Waqas, "Saint-Pierre received a Peace Prize for the Treaty, yeah, but do any of you know why?"

"Go on …" said Spider, drumming his fingers impatiently on his kneecaps.

"It's 'cause, yeah, the Treaty ended a 150-year civil war in Israel—or Palestine, whatever you want to call it. I won't lecture you on the history of what's gone on or who I think is right or wrong. All that information is out there for you to make up your own minds. Listen, long story short: Israel (aka Palestine) used to be occupied by mainly two peoples: the

THE

TREATY OF ZION

BETWEEN

THE DEMOCRATIC REPUBLIC OF UNITED EUROPE (DRUE) AND ISRAEL (ZION) AND NEW BABYLON,

The agreement respecting the federation of DRUE,

Israel, and New Babylon,

AS PRONOUNCED

THE HOUSE OF ABRAHAM

SIGNED AT JERUSALEM, APRIL 28TH, 2054

—THE SONS OF ADAM—

DRUE—THE CHRISTIAN REPUBLIC—EMMANUEL SAINT-PIERRE

STATE OF ISRAEL (ZION)—THE JEWISH REPUBLIC—LEVI BEN-DAVID

NEW BABYLON—THE ISLAMIC CALIPHATE—SULTAN BIN IBRAHIM

Jewish population who consider themselves Israelis, and also the Muslim population who considered themselves Palestinians. You following me so far, yeah?"

"So," said Spider, "was there like a clash of beliefs between the Muslims and Jews, or something?"

"Basically, bro, but it's a little more complicated. See, Levi Ben-David, who's the Chief Rabbi and Prime Minister of Israel, had been sponsoring the idea that Israel is the Promised Land and belongs to the Jews—the chosen people."

"What the blinking heck?" said Spider, running a hand through his braids. "Promised Land—promised by who?"

"Promised by God ... in biblical scripture. Hold that thought. Just let me find a Bible quote on my Tech ... Right, got one. Listen, yeah? 'Go in and take possession of the land the Lord swore he would give to your fathers—to Abraham, Isaac, and Jacob—and to their descendants after them' (Deuteronomy 1:8)."

"So," said Tristan, rubbing his neck, "the Chief Rabbi uses Bible quotes as divine justification to do what he wants? Reminds me of another politician."

"Aye, exactly, Tristan," said Skye. "The Holy Shepherd and the Chief Rabbi have a lot in common."

"What happened, then?" said Spider. "Did the Chief Rabbi just force the Palestinians out of the country?"

"Not quite. Along came Emmanuel Saint-Pierre, who at the time was little known to most as DRUE's ambassador to Israel."

"What did he do, Wacky?"

"He gave everybody what they wanted, innit."

"Which was ... ?"

"What he did, yeah, was broker a severance package between the Israelis and Palestinians. Instead of kicking out the Palestinian Muslims, he offered to build them a wealthy new home—New Babylon, the capital of a new caliphate. When Sultan Ibrahim (who is now the Caliph) accepted the deal, it meant Israel remained under the sole occupation of the Jews. Does that make sense, bro?"

"It does; but," said Spider, tapping his lower lip, "what does Saint-Pierre have to gain at this point?"

"A promotion," interjected Skye. "At the time, Saint-Pierre was just an ambassador, but he had his eyes on becoming the Chancellor of DRUE. Ratifying the Treaty was how he won the favour of his peers."

"Not only that, yeah," added Waqas, "but under the terms of the Treaty, New Babylon and Israel would pay a hefty price for membership to DRUE. Don't forget DRUE law supersedes Israeli and Babylonian sovereign law. As the Chancellor, Saint-Pierre has central power over all DRUE's member states."

"Well, if it ended the bloodshed," said Spider, "it was probably for the best."

"Yeah," said Waqas, rolling his eyes, "for the best if you're Jewish. Though I doubt the Palestinian Muslims agree with you. Listen, how would you like it, yeah, if you were told you were no longer welcome in the country you were born in? Told to give back your home and land to the state or face imprisonment? You'd be fucked off, bro. I'm telling you straight."

"Mind your language, Wacky," said Spider, stroking outwardly with his arm like some great oar repelling incoming waves of negativity.

"Soz, Spider. Just winds me up, that's all."

"S'all right, mate." Spider tolerated the profanity since it intrigued him to hear what Waqas had to say. "I know what you're saying, but the Treaty brought peace to the region, didn't it? That's the main thing."

"It *did*," said Waqas. "But as Skye said, yeah, it sounds as though the Treaty is in tatters. It's a dangerous divorce."

"But," said Tristan, "why is that tosser Saint-Pierre pulling out of the Treaty now? Is it not because of the Athens Massacre? Is he not declaring a war on terror? Moving into Saifullah strongholds in Babylon?"

"It's no' the Saifullah attacks which has Saint-Pierre's arsehole twitching," said Skye. "There's something else threatening his regime; some classified papers have been leaked; a dossier which suggests that Babylon has weapons of mass destruction."

"No frogging way. Nuclear weapons, Skye?"

"Aye, tha's what the dossier says, Spider."

"I'll tell you straight, yeah, that's bullshit."

"Why not just say 'hogwash' instead, Wacky?" said Spider, grinding his teeth. "Don't make me come around there and rinse your mouth out with soap and water."

"Listen, bro, don't get mad at me for swearing, yeah? If you're gonna get offended at anything, it should be the dossier. It's a work of fiction, innit."

"Yae dunnae think Babylon has nuclear weapons, Wacky?"

"To be honest with you, Skye, I think you guys need to get your head out of the sand. I'm telling you, someone is out to make a scapegoat of Babylon."

"Honestly, yae talk pure shite sometimes, Wacky. Yae watch too many conspiracy theories."

"Nah, boss, the only conspiracy here is that Babylon has nuclear weapons. C'mon, we've all seen it before."

"Seen what before?" said Skye. "Elaborate."

"All this, yeah? Step one: Western governments claim Middle Eastern country has weapons of mass destruction. Step two: Western governments invade Middle Eastern country. Step three: Western governments plunder natural resource—mainly oil. Step four: locals retaliate and are labelled terrorists for defending their homes. Step five: Western governments drop a weapon of mass destruction on alleged terrorists. Step six: Western governments call off the search for weapons of mass destruction but return as heroes. Nah, stinks of corruption if you ask me."

The aqueous light of Skye's eyes shone with unwavering surety, and for several moments she appeared not to blink or breathe. She simply sat with her hands collected in her lap, spine erect, and pouting her peony-pink lips like a model posing for a portrait.

"Still, I don't get what the big deal is," said Spider. "Most countries have nuclear weapons, don't they? Doesn't mean they'll use 'em."

"Aye, but written into the Peace Treaty is a clause that specifies Babylon canny have or manufacture nuclear weapons. Acquiring nuclear weapons is an act of war, Spider."

"Oh right, but why the frog was that written as a clause to begin with?"

"What it is, yeah," said Waqas, resting his hands beneath his armpits, "it's 'cause of fears the Caliph might seek to reclaim Palestine."

"Skye?" asked Spider, raising his hand and waiting for permission to speak. How timid he was in all but two spheres of life; one: when there were lives in need of saving on the battlefield; and two: when folk were foolish enough to swear in his company. "Skye, can I just ask, do we even know for certain if Babylon does have nuclear weapons?"

"We cannae be certain," said Skye, shaking her head; her long raven ponytail swished this way and that and took a few pendulous swings to settle. "The only way for Saint-Pierre to be certain is for him to invade Babylon. I fully expect, based on ma sources, Saint-Pierre'll deploy forces in Babylon. No' only that, but he'll levy trade sanctions so the Caliph cannae trade or do business with any cunt in the world."

"Saint-Pierre has his hands tied," said Tristan. "If he doesn't confront Babylon, his Christian followers will call him weak. But if he attacks Babylon, he'll lose the support of the Muslim population in DRUE. There could be a revolt."

"Aye, he cannae win either way. The Hoose of Abraham is finally crumbling doon. For as long as I can remember, it's been our mission to separate the State and Church; to weaken the influence of Saint-Pierre; to end the Apartheid of Faith."

"Yeah, no, I get that, Skye." Tristan leant across the table. "But what we gonna do to capitalise on it? We can't just sit idle scratching our scrotums."

Her eyes surveyed the room. "We keep Ulrik Magnusson alive."

"Skye, listen," said Waqas, "I'm sorry, yeah, but I'm not seeing the connection between Ulrik Magnusson and a continental fucking war. How the fuck will keeping Ulrik alive bring down the Holy Shepherd's regime?"

Spider winced at the foul language, as one might when hearing a fork scratch a plate, or the dragging of fingernails on a chalkboard.

"Don't you see, you big dosser?" said Tristan. "Saint-Pierre will have his eyes on Babylon. Ulrik won't be a priority for him right now."

"Tha's exactly ma point. Now do yae see, Wacky, yae carnaptious shitehawk? This is a welcome diversion, and we *do* need to capitalise on it. We need to slip in and get Ulrik oot of danger while we still can. We need him under our close protection."

"To be honest with you, yeah," said Waqas, folding his arms, "I'm not seeing the significance of Ulrik. He's just one person, innit."

"Then yae must be walking roond with yer cunting eyes shut, Wacky." Skye slapped her hand on the table, leaving no drink undisturbed. There are various intimidating looks in the arsenal of leaders which can be deployed to frosty affect, but Skye's expressionless visage was the most disturbing. "Honestly, yae cannae see? It's no' just aboot Ulrik; it's aboot what he represents. It's no' just aboot scientific progress; it's aboot social progression. People'll speak oot again. People are already speaking oot again. They're waking up. Finding their voices. Did yae hear the crowd roar in the aquadrome? Did yae feel their power? There's a silent movement, and many believe Homo Nova is the future of mankind—what with this kaleidoscopic genome and his ability to switch on ancestral genes. If we keep him alive, the spirit of Homo Nova is gownae keep building momentum. Enough, maybe, to spark a revolution. Whether he likes it or no', he's become the figurehead of the faithless, and that makes him very, very important."

Waqas rolled a cigarette and declined to comment.

"Right, what's our first port of call, Skye?" said Spider, who was sitting presently on his hands to prevent himself fidgeting.

"It's funny yae should say 'port', Spider, 'cause Ulrik is holding a public funeral for his dad at the Port of Piraeus."

"A public funeral?"

"See, now," said Tristan, wagging his finger, "that's a disaster waiting to happen. It'll be open season for another Saifullah strike."

"Innit. They'll be sitting ducks."

"Aye, a public funeral is dangerous, but it may be a wee opportunity. I expect the faithless to show their public support in great, great numbers, and I expect there'll be hundreds of drones televising it. The whole world is gownae be watching."

"What are you suggesting, Skye?" said Tristan, reclining on the hind legs of his chair.

"Am sending all three of yaes away to bring him back here." Her searching eyes seemed to interrogate each of them as she glanced at them, one by one. "*But*, we cannae act too hastily. We need to let the vigil play oot before retrieving Ulrik. Obviously, tha's no' gownae be a straightforward task to carry oot."

"He may not come willingly."

"Tha's where yae'll be vital, Tristan, since yae've met him before."

"Just playing Devil's advocate," said Spider, surrendering with apologetic hands, "but he's not going to be keen on leaving his widowed mum behind ..."

"Then bring her, too. I dunnae care if yae have to bring back Ria Lorenzo Lopez and that giant lassie with the red hair. Just make sure yae bring me Ulrik."

"Do we even know who she is yet? The lass with the red hair?"

"No' yet. Am struggling to find any proper trace of her. I'll tell yae more when I know more."

"Right, then," said Tristan, blowing into his palms as though to warm them up for the conflict ahead, "here we go again."

"This is it, lads," said Skye. "I firmly believe keeping Ulrik alive is gownae send progressive ripples across the Continent. If the faithless find the courage to stand up for what they believe in, these ripples are gownae form waves, and before yae know it, a tide; a tide strong enough to wash the Holy Shepherd oot of office. But if Ulrik dies, so does the resistance of the faithless. So, lads, put yer hands doon yer troosers, and let me know if yer bollocks are still there, 'cause am gownae need everybody's best efforts. If yae find a pair of pishflaps doon there, tell me now, and yae can walk away. Anyone wantae leave?"

Silence, save for the thunder of Colonel's snoring.

"Happy with that? Good. Now, all of yaes, take a quick stroll outside, and get yerself some fresh air. When yaes get back, al brief yaes on exactly what we're gownae do."

CHAPTER THIRTY-ONE

DOUBTING THOMAS

The night sky glimmered with sequins of stars.

Not too far away from the Port of Piraeus was a little-known avenue; and in that little-known avenue was a cordoned-off pentagon; and in that cordoned-off pentagon was a marquee; and inside that marquee lay Thorsten's casket. Ulrik couldn't bring himself to confront it, not until the hour of his needing to. Instead, he sat outside on the asphalt, hugging his knees, contemplating death, indulging in thoughts of suicide, toying with the idea that it would be a most agreeable opportunity to catch up on sleep.

The streetlamps out here were bright. Too bright. A strain on his sore, raw eyes. In holding the gaze of one for too long, some ticklish murmur spread throughout his nose like the fizz of carbonated drinks and induced in him a terrible fit of sneezing.

"Tchoo—tchow—tchee—tchar—tchah."

"You know," said Chenglei, emerging from the marquee, "that sneeze ..."

"Yah, I know: it's just like my pappa's. I used to hate it when people said I was like him, so I always tried harder to be less like him. Now I wish,"—pinching his tear ducts—"I wish I was more like him."

"Oh, there's a lot more of him in you than you realise." Cheng lowered himself onto the asphalt, not at all concerned about dirtying his suit. He

420

was wearing his cosmic tie for the occasion—the one depicting galactic matter and nebulae—and he wore, too, his Saturn belt.

For a time, they sat in a subdued stupor, sighing often and saying little. Reminiscing over simpler times.

A short while later, Ulrik dabbed away the blur of tears and noticed Cheng's arm pointing above the urban skyline to a fixed spot in the sky. As Cheng beheld the jewelled realms of the ether, the furrowed lines of grief departed his face, and his cheeks swelled with profound peace.

"Ulrik," eyes dazzling with magic, "that light there—the really, really bright one. Do you see it?"

"Yah, that star you mean?"

"Well, it *was* a star once, yes, but no longer. You see, astronomers suppose it to have passed out of existence over a thousand years ago."

"Huh," said Ulrik, combing the knots out of his beard with his fingers, "if it died over a thousand years ago, why can we still see it?"

"Ah, well, we still see the light of the perished star because it's so far away—thousands of light years away. Which means you're looking at the star as it was thousands of years ago. So my point, you see—" his voice trembled, and he wiggled his Adam's apple as though it was a tie knot in need of adjustment, "—is that even when a star perishes, its light still shines upon us long after it departs the cosmos. Like that star, your pappa will continue to brighten our world in a way which seems as though he's never left our side."

Their solemn heads fell together, and there they huddled, letting rain a deluge of the heaviest tears.

"I've seen too much of death," said Ulrik, wiping the runny mucus from his nostrils with his tunic's sleeve before gathering himself to his feet. "Ivar—dead; Onyx—dead; Pappa—dead. If I were you, Cheng, I'd be staying clear of me." Then he parted the opening flap of the marquee and disappeared inside.

Embla intercepted him on his entry and announced that it was almost time; time to do the unthinkable: time to send Pappa to Valhalla, as had always been his request.

"Are you ready, Ulrik?" said Ria, taking his hands in hers like a bride does the groom's when standing before the altar, looking up at him with everlasting affection in her eyes.

"Nuh," huffing out a regretful sigh, "I'll never be ready." He turned then to the wretched figure in the corner hugging the closed casket: she whose nails were bitten and broken; she whose blonde fronds were brittle and frayed; she whose eyes were bloodshot and black with hate. "Mamma, are you ready? We can't be staying here forever."

She must've tightened her embrace of the casket, for the wood creaked and her hands turned white.

"Ulrik, Astrid," said Cheng, entering the marquee with his solemn head bowed, "before we head out, I've something quite important to say, if I may?"

When neither son nor mother gave him the courtesy of an answer, Ria intervened on their behalf: "Say it, Cheng."

"It might seem a little off topic," stroking his elbow as one does when suffering extreme self-doubt, "and this may not make sense to begin with, but there's an important insight in what I'm about to tell you. So stick with me, okay? You'll think I'm crazy."

Ulrik, Ria, and Embla stood about him with their arms folded and their eyebrows buried halfway down their faces. Astrid kept her cheek pressed to the casket, at all times nuzzling it with her nose.

"Proceed," said Ulrik, gesturing with his hand in the manner of one granting passage. "You have our ears."

"Yes. Right. Good. All right. Shall I begin? Okay. Well, you see, in quantum mechanics there's a particular thought experiment which I've always had a certain fascination with: Schrödinger's cat."

"Cheng, now isn't the time for riddles. My head is weary. Our hearts are heavy."

"No, no, no, please, hear me out. It'll help if I use a prop to demonstrate. Oh, where did I put the damned thing? Where, where, where? Where did I put it?" Cheng rapped his skull with his knuckles and continued to do so until he remembered the whereabouts of this mystery item. After slowing to a halt this self-deprecating rapping of knuckles, he suspended all movement momentarily. Then he thrashed free from the restraints of the rucksack on his back as though it were on fire and unzipped it with ferocious impatience. There it was. The prop he produced from the rucksack looked like a black shoebox of sorts, yet it had a metallic, heavy-duty aspect and seemed more appropriate for the haulage of priceless possessions than any footwear.

"I've seen those vault-boxes before," said Ria, raising a single eyebrow. "Not up close, but on television. Banks use them for depositing, don't they?"

"Banks, jewellers, police departments, antique dealers, drug dealers; they have these vault-boxes for the stowing away of priceless artefacts. Why? Because they're fireproof, waterproof, chemicalproof, bulletproof, and even bombproof. They're said to be the closest thing in the world to being indestructible. As safe as a safe can be."

"Made of a superalloy, I think?" said Ria, her solar eyes accentuated by the flickering of candlelight.

"Indeed it is made of a superalloy," cradling it in his arms as though it were a child of his.

"I'm more interested to know what's inside," said Embla, unfolding her arms and drawing herself up to her full height.

"Well, going back to the thought experiment (Schrödinger's cat), let me describe the contents. I want you to pretend there's a cat inside this very vault-box."

Before she permitted him to continue with his line of reasoning, Ria had Cheng clarify seven times that there was no such cat in the box.

"As I was saying," said Cheng, his face gilded like a pirate who pores over his loot; "imagine in this vault-box there is a cat, and imagine also there is a flask of sulphuric acid. Cruel, I know. But again, I speak metaphorically. Now, as well as a cat and a flask of sulphuric acid, imagine there's a mechanism in there, too."

"Go on ..."

"What if I told you there's exactly a 50 per cent chance the mechanism will be triggered, thereby causing the sulphuric acid to spill?"

"Ssst," said Ria, "the acid will burn the poor cat alive. Don't you think that's insensitive after all that's happened?"

"Sorry, sorry," scratching his badger-hair at the roots, "I know it sounds insensitive to say such things, but it's important."

"Go on, Cheng," said Ulrik. "Tell me, is Ria correct? Will the cat be burned by the acid?"

"Not necessarily. Remember: there's a 50 per cent chance the flask will spill."

"So," said Embla, "how are we to know if the flask of acid has been spilt? The vault-box, you say, is chemicalproof. We can't know by looking at it from the outside."

"Yes, yes, good observations," said Cheng. "Well, you can't know—not until you open the box. And this is the crux of Schrödinger's paradox: you see, there are two possibilities of equal probability: either the acid spills and kills the cat, or it doesn't."

"It's quite simple," said Ulrik. "The cat is either dead or alive."

"Not quite." Cheng shook his giddy head. "Quantum science teaches us that until we open the vault-box, the cat exists in multiple states at once: it's both dead and alive at the same time."

"How can it be both at the same time?"

"Because it's only when we observe the result that we can establish the outcome."

"Okay, Cheng, I believe that makes sense to a mad scientist like you, but I still don't know why you're telling me this."

"What if I were to tell you that inside my vault-box isn't a cat but a book?"

"Then the results of your crazy experiment would be the same. Until we opened the vault-box to see if the acid had spilt, the book would be both burned and not burned—according to your reasoning."

"You're a quick learner, Ulrik," said Cheng, reaching up and rapping his knuckles on his hollow-sounding head.

"So, what book have you got in there?" said Embla, whose complexion seemed, under a certain light, as rough as tree bark.

"You'll see soon enough." Chenglei stowed away the metallic parcel in his rucksack again and withdrew himself to the furthest corner of the marquee, where he checked over its contents one last time. He was so absorbed in his scheme that he hadn't detected Ria creeping up behind him, and she watched him as he rifled through the contents of his rucksack.

"Those vault-boxes aren't cheap toys," said Ria.

"Cheap?" shutting the flap of his rucksack and hugging the bulk of his bag. "Oh no, no, no, certainly not cheap."

"What else has he got in there?" said Embla, her suspicious, corrugated frown intensifying.

"A drone," said Ria, planting her hands on her hips.

"A satellite drone, actually," corrected Cheng.

"Satellite drones cost thousands. Tens of thousands."

"*Hundreds* of thousands. They're the fastest thing money can buy. A satellite drone is the only drone I trust to transport my consignment to outer space."

"Consignment? Outer space?" said Ulrik, sharpening his stare. "What's this about, Cheng?"

Had they not been interrupted, Cheng would've perhaps revealed his scheme, but a growing trampling of boots forewarned them of unexpected visitors. A trio of black shapes handling riot shields and batons burst into the marquee, and the mourners flew back, seeking shields and batons of their own—except Astrid, who kept her cheek pressed to the casket and looked upon the intruders with indifference.

"Halt!" said the lead officer, laying down his riot shield and surrendering his hands. "See? We're friends."

"Ssst, friends, you say?" said Ria. "Friends don't gate-crash funerals. Friends don't cover their faces in the company of friends. Take off your helmets and show yourselves."

So heavily armoured were the trio of trespassers that they looked like contemporary knights in their synthetic breastplates, greaves, pauldrons, and helms.

"Thor is sleeping, Ulrik," whispered Mamma, stirring from her deranged stupor. "Ask your friends to be quiet, or go play outside."

"It's all right, Mamma," he said, placing a hand on her shoulder and giving it a gentle squeeze. Then, through his gritted square teeth: "Our guests, whoever they are, are about to be leaving."

"We're DRUE police, yeah?" said the broadest of the trespassing trio. "We're here for your close protection—to escort you down to the port, innit, Chalky?"

"DRUE police?" said Ria, her face donning a hideous scowl. "What department, huh?"

"We're from," said the lead officer (known to his companions as Chalky), clearing his throat and stepping forward, "we're from a secret service and have come undercover to protect our identity."

"Don't trust them," said Cheng; and like the squirrel who secretes an acorn in some discreet nest, he stowed his rucksack away in a chest and stood guard over it.

"Look, I know this is bad timing," said Chalky, surrendering his palms, "but we've got intel to suggest this marquee is being watched by a clan of Whitehoods. If we don't get a move on sharpish, we could find ourselves in the middle of a raid. Let me be clear: we do not want a Whitehood raid on our hands."

"You rush in here wearing masks," said Embla, holding a plank of wood like a quarterstaff, "and you mean to convince us you're not the raiders? If you are friends, it'd be better to show yourself and be quick about it."

"When it's safe to do so, gladly," said Chalky, treading forward as one might on thin ice.

There was a familiar elocution in this Chalky's voice; a certain intonation; a dull inflexion. Ulrik took a pace closer and said, "Whitehoods, you say? Are you expecting trouble?"

"We're always expecting trouble," said Chalky, exposing a selection of light weaponry concealed about his body.

The tallest of the trio, Spider, or so he was nicknamed, poked his head

426

out of the opening flap of the marquee and turned his frantic head left and right with such animation that the braids of black twine dangling out of his helm whipped and lashed the air. "Chalky," said Spider, with concern in his amiable voice, "we should think about getting a move on, mate."

"If you want to lay your dad to rest," said Chalky, "we ought to go now, like, pronto, like, at the speed of a thousand gazelles."

"Say that again," said Mamma, arousing from her grieving state at once; and with her neck outstretched, she seemed to scrutinise every dimension of Chalky.

Chalky stiffened.

"Listen, yeah?" said the broadest of the trio. "It's a figure of speech, innit."

"Wacky ..." said Chalky warningly, raising his clenched palm. (A hand signal interpreted to mean 'be quiet'.)

"Speed of a thousand gazelles," said Ulrik, taking another step closer to Chalky. "I've heard that, too. Though I've only ever heard it said once before. Said only by a man I met some years ago ..."

The silence of the officers was their greatest concession.

"They're not DRUE police or from any secret service," said Embla, lowering her plank of wood and standing at ease.

"Agreed," said Chenglei. "DRUE police don't have English accents."

Raised whispers broke out among the trio of trespassers. Being wholly convinced now that this Chalky was Tristan, Ulrik reached for the brass tin secreted inside his trouser pocket. Few days had gone by without him laying eyes on the Victoria Cross or reading the poem on that scratchy leaf of paper. When Ulrik shook the brass tin, it gave a muffled rattle.

Chalky ceased all movement and observed a period of silent patriotic staring, as though he'd suddenly heard the faraway peal of a church bell marking the eleventh hour.

"An emblem of gallantry long after bones fade ..." said Ulrik.

"For valour," said Chalky. "May it inspire man in his righteous crusade."

All held their breath.

"Then it is you." A stinging sensation overwhelmed Ulrik's eyes, and his vision became glassy and blurred. Their right hands clasped in an iron grip, and Ulrik's forehead clashed with the officer's helmet in the forager custom. Turning to his family, he said, "These are no strangers, though they wear strange costumes. If you trust me, then trust them. Trust them with your lives."

Embla bowed her head; Ria's ugly scorn faded away; and Cheng retrieved his rucksack from the chest and strapped it to his body, checking the fastenings repeatedly as one might when donning a parachute—such was the life-and-death nature of its contents.

Chalky took up his riot shield, gave it a double smack, rolled his shoulders, creaked his neck, and said, "Spider, Wacky, prepare to move out. We'll go to the port by the safest roads; those being well lit; those being the busiest." Turning to Ulrik: "Who'll be the pallbearers?"

"Me, Ria, Embla, and Mamma ... if you're still up to it?"

"I am," she said, rising to her feet like a gaunt woman twice her age.

"Right, Wacky, you guard the front; Spider, you and I will take care of the rear."

"Cheng," said Ulrik, "I hope you don't mind. With you reading the eulogy, I didn't want to burden you with carrying the casket."

"Don't worry about me," said Cheng, smiling, the paper-fan wrinkles at the corner of his eyes deepening. But everything about his manner today did worry Ulrik.

The pallbearers gathered their respective corners of the casket, and after a bout of deliberate huffing and puffing, they roused their spirits and hoisted it over their shoulders. At once, Ulrik felt a phantom sensation, for he'd expected that, Pappa being the half-giant he was, some great strength would need to be summoned to bear his weight; yet the casket seemed hollow, as if inside were a heap of ash in lieu of a body. Insidious thoughts ran amok in his mind: what remained of Pappa, if anything? Only Mamma knew. She'd looked inside to bid Pappa farewell, but ever since had complained of not being able to recollect his face, perhaps because, having looked upon the horrors of his flame-torn visage, the image had warped her every loving memory of him.

The officers chaperoned the pallbearers into the streets of Athens and into the clamour of the gathering crowd.

"Where the frog did all these people come from?" said Spider.

Drum, drum, "Huh!" went hundreds of voices in unison, and fell silent thereafter.

"Eh, these aren't Whitehoods;" said Chalky, "these are the faithless."

"Not a protest but a vigil. Not protestors but supporters."

When looking into the crowd, Ulrik saw grief wrought into their solemn, sympathetic faces, their expressions not unlike melting plastic. About their necks many wore Mjolnir pendants; around their eyes were black circles of kohl. Grim faces of northern men and women, rendered hard by the weather and harder still by the hardest times. "Don't cry for me or my pappa;" called Ulrik, "cry for your fledglings who inherit this world."

Drum, drum, "Huh!"

The pallbearers shuffled along the causeway, their spines bending as though they were carrying palletised concrete, not because of the weight of the casket but because of the sheer burden of emotional loss.

Drum, drum, "Huh!"

Looking out over the procession of heathenish candlelight, Ulrik saw, rising into view with each step, an entire tongue of land sticking out from the port into the sea. Almost there.

Drum, drum, "Huh!"

On the pallbearers strode, making for the seafront where a Viking longboat bobbed peacefully at the end of a jetty. The dragon-head at the prow had been exquisitely carved and the red raven sails beautifully embroidered.

Much of this had been arranged by Cheng. The funds to carry out the service, however, had been donated by anonymous benefactors who, owing nothing to Ulrik but their deepest sympathies, had delved deep into their pockets to contribute the tithe for liberty.

Drum, drum, "Huh!" Drum, drum, "Huh!" Drum, drum, "Huh!" Reaching a crescendo, the faithless chanted in a frenzy and clashed their wooden sticks against their painted shields as the pallbearers came to a halt at the harbour.

When the companions reached the longboat tethered at the end of the jetty, they passed Thorsten's casket over and mounted it atop a sturdy pyre at the centre of the deck. For a while, they stood about in a tragic trance while saying their last goodbyes. Cheng was first to depart the longboat, then Ria, then Ulrik and Astrid simultaneously, but it was Embla who remained behind when all others had left. From land, they watched her attempt to communicate with the casket her regret about all this; that this road, this rueful road, should come to a dead end when she was ready for a new beginning.

"A dragon without its wings is but a worm," called Ulrik, interrupting Embla's soliloquy. By that, he meant it was time to let down the sails of the longboat.

She turned her left ear to the sound of his call, all the while keeping her eyes facing out to sea to salvage the dignity that might be lost in revealing her crimson face and glistening eyes.

"What gives her the right to stand there?" said Mamma, face stricken with haggardly grief. "What gives her the right to stand there and keep us—Thor's family—waiting here?"

"Let down the wings of the longboat!" boomed Ulrik, letting his wrath be known. Mamma was right. This was his family's time to grieve, not Embla's.

Taking heed, Embla unfurled the red raven sails and leapt back onto land. There, she untethered the ropes, and the midnight breeze escorted Thorsten's casket out into broader waters.

Standing at the edge of the jetty, Ulrik took up his bow and nocked an arrow. Then he passed the bundle of flax wrapped about the neck of the arrow over a torch, and a ginger flame ignited the arrow. Drawing back, he aimed above the horizon, arcing his trajectory. He closed his eyes, and his fingers did what his heart could never do: let go. By the clean twang of the bow, he sensed that the flight path of the arrow was smooth and that his shot had found its mark.

When he opened his eyes, an autumnal blaze was tearing through the sails, and golden flecks of burning ash were floating skyward. Having no wish to watch Pappa's cremation, he turned to face the city while orange and black shadows danced on the solemn faces of those looking out to sea. A short while later, the mast must've crashed down through the bulwarks and splintered the vessel, for there was a penultimate cracking and creaking before a colossal splash.

"Ulrik," said Cheng, holding a deck of cue cards in his sweaty hands, "as promised, I should like to say a few words now, with your permission."

"I don't recommend it," interrupted Chalky, taking him by the elbow and leaning in. "We've outstayed our welcome. Time to go, buddy."

"What is it you're so desperate to say, Cheng?" shaking off Chalky's grip.

"The forbidden truth, Ulrik."

With the approval of the Municipality of Athens, Cheng had gone to extreme lengths to arrange this elevated podium as well as having speakers positioned around the harbour to enable the projection of his voice; without him, the boat pyre and this funeral would never have happened. The least they could do was to let him say a few words. "Say what you need to, Cheng, but, in my pappa's name, make it count."

Cheng took an almighty gulp, swallowing the kink out of his windpipe. In the next moment, he scurried up the scaffold, moving like a beetle with his bulky backpack. When he arrived at the top, he emptied his rucksack of its contents: the vault-box and the satellite drone. Then he stood behind a lectern of sorts, adjusting the microphone and tapping it thrice with a reedy finger. Sensing drama, a flock of drones orbited the scaffold, streaming, broadcasting, televising footage to the Continent and beyond.

"Hi," said Cheng, consulting his cue cards, "my name's Chenglei. I'm a close friend—I mean, I *was* a close friend of Thorsten Magnusson." His Adam's apple seemed to swell in his neck as he choked on his words.

"Sorry, this isn't something I do too often—public speaking. It frightens me. But you see, for the first time in my life, I fear more the consequences of my not speaking out."

Consulting his second cue card: "I've lived a long life, but I've not been so lucky in tallying up friends as I have in tallying up birthdays. You see, Thorsten Magnusson was one of only a few people I've ever been fortunate enough to call a friend. His family became my family. But now he's been taken from me—taken away by the hand of extremist religion." He paused, swallowed, then continued. "Let me ask you this: why send thoughts and prayers after a tragedy to a god who did nothing to prevent its happening? Isn't it time we took responsibility ourselves for all these goings-on?"

People were leaving, and Cheng was visibly hurt by his apparent irrelevance. But Ria was quick to steal his attention: in joining her thumbs and forefingers together, she made the shape of an encouraging heart and mouthed, "Speak from the heart." Cheng nodded. After slipping his cue cards in the back pocket of his trousers, he tilted his chin to the stars.

"The Apartheid of Faith!" he snapped. Many of those leaving turned around to see the source of this new drama. "That's why everybody is here, isn't it? To show solidarity. Well, give me your attention for a few moments longer, and in return I'll give you something worthy of gossip."

Such a suspenseful promise salvaged him some audience. A flock of drones wheeled overhead like vultures around their prey.

"Doubting Thomas," said Cheng, thrusting his arms into the air like the consummate preacher. "For those of you who don't know, Doubting Thomas was one of the Twelve Disciples of Jesus Christ. But Doubting Thomas was different to the other disciples. You see, the story,"—emphasising the word 'story'—"the story goes that after Jesus died on the cross, Doubting Thomas wouldn't believe the rumours that Jesus had risen from the dead. He'd only believe in Jesus' resurrection if he saw him in the flesh. When the other disciples believed the rumours without proof, Jesus said, 'Blessed are those who have not seen me yet believe anyway.' But you see, Doubting Thomas was the scientist of his day. His standard of proof was greater than that of his friends. Yet for this, Thomas is used as an example by the Church of weakness and failure. As though to doubt, to ask questions, is a betrayal of the Lord."

Cheng was taking a gulp of sparkling water when Ulrik looked around to see legions of the crowd clapping with intent. Their number was multiplying.

"Think differently of Thomas," continued Cheng, the profile of his face sharpening to coincide with his wit. "Not Doubting Thomas, then, but Rational Thomas. Analytical Thomas. Intellectual Thomas."

A severe bout of nodding was under way, and the crowd listened with outstretched necks.

"And as in the case of Thomas, we have taught our next generations that to question is a sin. Let us not teach them *what* to think but *how* to think. Right now, DRUE is run by fundamentalists whose orthodoxy goes unquestioned. Unchallenged. We have become a continent of zealots wedded to extremist ideology; and it's made ours a very dangerous continent indeed. But nothing will change unless the Doubting Thomases among you find the courage to ask critical questions."

There were pockets of growing resistance in the crowd. A mob of godlings were making the sign of the cross, and others were holding their rosary beads and other ineffectual charms and talismans, serious in their attempts to pray away the Devil incarnate and ward off his blasphemies.

"Ask questions of your government—of the Holy Shepherd and his House of Abraham. Demand an end to blasphemy laws; demand an end to the halting of scientific progress; demand an end to the censorship of secular philosophy. Don't fight with them in the streets but in the courts; don't engage them with hate and violence but with education and science. Against the House of Abraham, let there be an alliance of science!"

A volley of projectiles peppered him. Coins. Bottled water. Shoes. Rocks.

"Heretic."

"Dissenter."

"Infidel."

"It's okay to talk about evolution," continued Cheng, dodging a grotty sandal. "It's okay to talk about Ulrik Magnusson. It's okay to talk about Homo Nova. We're seeing the advent of a genetic revolution that will benefit the whole of mankind!"

Mouths were whipping up foam from the overuse of profanities.

"Criticism of religion isn't hate speech. If you want examples of hate speech, look no further than the Quran, the Bible, and the Torah. There you'll find pages upon pages of hate, intolerance, bigotry, extremism, and violence. Don't take my word for it. See for yourself what the media refuses to tell you is written within. If you read them, study them, question them, you'll be outraged by them."

"He's gone all-out rogue," said Wacky. "I think I like him."

"This way, now," said Spider, clearing a path through the bodies of the crowd.

"We can't leave without Cheng," said Ulrik, his eyes searching for support from Mamma, but there was little care in her for anything anymore.

"He's beyond recovery," said Chalky, towing Ulrik away by the arm. "And we're now in danger."

At that moment, Cheng held aloft the vault-box and said, "I promised you that if you gave me your attention, I'd give you something worthy of gossip."

The crowd fell into audible murmurs when they saw him power up the satellite drone. Clutched in its talons now was this vault-box—Pandora's contemporary box which, if ever opened, promised to unleash great turbulence and, at the same time, hope.

Ulrik defied Chalky and rooted his feet to the ground.

"Who here has heard of Schrödinger's cat?" announced Cheng. He seemed to grow in stature in accordance with the growth in his confidence. He proceeded to lecture his audience on the rudiments of quantum mechanics and Schrödinger's cat as he had done earlier with the companions in the marquee, telling them the cat in the vault-box existed in two states: being both dead and alive.

"What's he doing?" said Embla.

"He's fucking with them," said Ria, running an exasperated hand through the caramel waves of her hair. "Trolling them."

"Why?"

"Because he's got the biggest balls in DRUE, that's why."

"Listen, yeah?" said Wacky. "We need to move before we get caught up in the middle of a riot. Trust me, things are about to get ugly."

"Move—move—move," said Chalky, jabbing Ulrik in the back with his baton.

Chalky was right. Pockets of the congregation had turned hostile. What was Cheng thinking? To rouse a crowd? To rile a crowd? Time to move.

Wacky and Spider burst through the nucleus of the crowd, and the rest of them followed. So dense was the congregation that it took a great amount of shouldering with those riot shields before they emerged from the outer membrane of bodies. But when they were clear, Chalky turned back momentarily, for following them was a band of strangers.

Chalky reached into the inner pouch of his jacket and drew out a handful of what looked like seeds or pellets. Like the avid gardener, he scattered a row of these seeds on the asphalt, and a haze of tear gas swiftly rose like the morning dew beneath a golden sunrise. Thereafter the companions fled into the inner sanctum of Athens, leaving the strangers groping about in temporary blindness, spluttering like fountain pens at the nib, and coughing up their burning innards.

The companions took refuge in the shadows of a dilapidated alleyway. As far as alleyways go, this was among the foulest, not owing to the hot stink of dog filth but the graffiti which uglified the walls. It wasn't the kind of meaningful graffiti intended to bring colour to a blank canvas, nor was it the kind to provoke political thought or social sentiment. There was nothing abstract about these ghastly squiggles. No redeeming qualities. Nothing. Just clusters of sordid, vulgar vocabulary scribed in monstrous fonts—three-dimensional calligraphy, bubble writing, and illegible zigzagging—in which the rebellious vandal had become fixated upon an arbitrary switching between the upper and lower case from one letter to the next and had made an erroneous habit out of omitting s's from words and appointing z's in their stead.

Spider surveyed the profane literature from top to bottom and shook his head in silence.

"Take a knee, and listen in," whispered Chalky. "Keep your voices down—and your heads while you're at it. Quick count of heads: Ulrik, Astrid, Embla, Ria. Perfect. Now, our quadcopter is parked not so far away from here, but I'm gonna have a look around first. Spider, Wacky, you two wait here while I do a recce. Make sure everybody stays put until I return. Happy with that? Good."

While Chalky scouted ahead, the companions huddled around Ria's watchTech and, having searched for live events streaming in Athens, the search results returned many channels at the top of her news feed. She tuned into one of these broadcasts, and they watched the live event unfold on a screen the size of a postage stamp.

Cheng still stood at the height of the scaffold and at the height of his vigour, the crowd beneath him expanding and contracting like a beating organ. "In this vault-box, however," said Cheng, elaborating on his lecture of Schrödinger's paradox, "there is no cat, but there is a copy of the Holy Quran."

"The Holy Quran?" said Ulrik. "That's the book he was talking about?"

"Shit, shit, shit," said Ria, clasping her hands over her nose. "Burning a Quran—he'll be extradited to Babylon for blasphemy."

"And he could face the death penalty," said Embla.

"Death penalty?" said Ulrik, pinching the broad bridge of his nose.

"My drone will carry the vault-box with the Quran into space," said Cheng. "And upon reaching the thermosphere, there's exactly a 50 per cent chance that the mechanism will trigger and spill the sulphuric acid, subsequently burning the Quran."

"Look, there," said Ria, prodding the sky. The blinking emerald lights of the satellite drone were little more than a pinprick in the sky before vanishing into the abyss against the Milky Way.

"So," said Cheng, "how many of you would protest if this Quran, upon entering space, were to burn? Many more, I expect, than those who protested against the Saifullah attack on these streets three weeks ago. Well, if burning a book offends you more than Saifullah attacks, then you—have—been—radicalised."

So sounded the provocative chants that were so often now the prequel to terror: "Allahu akbar—Allahu akbar—Allahu akbar!"

"Now, I repeat," said Cheng, looking somewhat radicalised himself, "there is a mechanism in this vault-box which means there's exactly a 50 per cent chance that the Quran will burn on entering the thermosphere. I refer you again to Schrödinger's paradox: the Quran now exists in two states: both burned and not burned. Therefore, you are to consider me both *guilty* and *not guilty* of burning the Quran."

There was a collective knitting of eyebrows among the bystanders and a silence in which one would've been privy to the clack of two needles.

"Tell me," said Cheng, leaning back in self-admiration, "tell me how the law deals with someone who's both guilty and not guilty of the same charge? Well, only by observing what's inside the vault-box can you erase the quantum superposition and determine whether I'm truly guilty or not guilty. Good luck ever retrieving it."

"Shut him down—lock him up—shut him down—lock him up!" The protestors shook the scaffold, but for every one of those doing the shaking, there were ten others counterbalancing it.

"I burned a Quran," said Cheng. "Oh no, I didn't. Oh yes, I did. How do you plead, Chenglei? Both guilty and not guilty."

Cheng's sermon was met with another pious protest: peals of church bells sounded throughout Athens; and from the seafront where the mosque was stationed came the wailing of the adhan, the Islamic call to prayer; and from the synagogue came the bleating of the shofar (the ram's-horn trumpet) from its speakers. Louder the Abrahamic factions thundered, vying for spiritual supremacy. Yet the melding of these pious liturgies never amounted to anything more than a terrier's yap when compared to the deep howling of the faithless.

At once, the screen of Ria's watchTech blacked out. Battery dead.

"Schrödinger's Quran;" said Wacky, "that's some serious mind-fuckery, innit."

"Stop swearing, Wacky," said Spider, humming now to cancel out his comrade's foul vocabulary.

"The idiot is going to get himself killed," said Ulrik, tugging at Ria's wrist, urging her to follow. "Come; we have to get him out of there."

A sudden screech pierced the ears of all those in the vicinity, its echo ricocheting throughout the alleyway. Spider and Wacky fell into the prone position and drew out their pistols. But it was a sneeze that had been triggered, not any offensive weapon. It was the distinctive Magnusson way in which their noses rid themselves of pollen and other foreign particles.

"Tchoo—tchow—tchee—tchar—tchah."

"Ulrik," said Mamma, "I wish you'd cover your nose when sneezing."

"It's not me sneezing, Mamma."

They rotated their necks and eyed the culprit: Embla rubbed her nose with the back of her hand. And there passed a wild thought into Ulrik's mind and surely into Mamma's, too, for she broke out of her demented delirium and seized Embla by the throat.

"Who are you?" said Mamma, tightening her chokehold. Though it was as much use as throttling a tree, for Embla's neck (and face, arms, hands, and indeed almost every patch of visible skin) seemed as coarse as that of tree bark.

Like a maiden horse, powerful yet amiable, Embla hung her copper mane over her grass-green eyes. Everything about her anatomy—her square shoulders, her cubic fists, her stooping posture, her brooding brow—and everything about her mannerisms—her inability to hold a gaze under accusation, her tightening of the lips when distressed, her rubbing of her hands as though she were toasting them by the fire, her awful sneeze—all of this implied, when seen at once, that she was a most convincing daughter of Thorsten Magnusson.

CHAPTER THIRTY-TWO

BARKSKIN

Above the alleyway, patrolling cats leapt from one wonky balcony to the next, their curious tails rising like black furls of smoke as they spied on their rowdy subjects below.

"Answer me, stalker," said Astrid, baring her teeth while pinning Embla to the graffitied wall by her throat. "Who are you, bastard girl? Are you a daughter of my husband?"

"My name," said Embla, her face retreating behind her ginger forelocks, "is Embla Magnusson, and I believe Thorsten to have been my pappa."

The news, rather than embolden Astrid's assault, shattered it. Her crumpled, craterous chin appeared like the surface of the moon as her eyes filled and overspilled with tears. She released her grip and sank to a heap on the ground.

"Chalky," said Wacky, communicating through some Tech in his helmet, "better get back here quick, yeah? Shit's about to go down, bro." Supreme was this soldier's handling of operational conflict but diabolical in the arena of the domestic quarrel.

Ulrik rocked back and forth on his heels, gazing absently at Embla, his hot pulse snaking about his temples. Ria appeared in his periphery and took his hand in her gentle fingers. She spoke, perhaps to offer him some words of comfort, but the air between them seemed a vacuum, and her sweet sentiments were lost in the void.

"Who is the mother?" said Mamma, her pallid face glowing in the dark with white-hot fury.

"I never knew my mother," said Embla, who seemed now to have no neck, for she'd buried her chin in her collarbone and raised her shoulders to the altitude of her ears. Her cubic hands retreated into the sanctuaries of her sleeves so that only her fingertips were visible. "My mother never cared to know me."

"Stupid girl." Mamma spat at her feet. "You must know."

"I wish I knew, but only my pappa's name was registered on the birth certificate. I'd hoped that by discovering him I'd find out who she was. And when I first saw you, I supposed you to be her. But I see I was wrong to assume."

"Bah! You thought I could give birth to a monster like you?" said Mamma, snarling in revulsion.

Embla shrugged.

"So tell us," said Ulrik, trying to catch her eyes from beneath her mane of red hair, "what happened to you?"

"Well," dabbing her eyes with a knuckle, "when I was born—so I was told by my carers—my pappa couldn't look at me. I was born early at seven months, and he was convinced I had something wrong with me, convinced I had birth defects. All because I looked a certain way. So he gave me up. Abandoned me at some orphanage when I was only a few days old."

"It's a pity you weren't aborted," said Mamma, who was on all fours and heaving in vast volumes of air.

"That's awful," said Ria, nostrils flaring with wild offence.

"Awful, yes, but I've wished it myself many times," said Embla, nodding, her bottom lip quivering.

Spider and Wacky maintained a strict lookout at opposite ends of the alleyway. Both were embroiled in their Tech and bandying clever jargon about: something to do with rerouting drones through cyber-blockers, gridhawk, and skytrack. Whatever they were doing, it was taxing on their concentration, and they had little attention to spare on domestic diplomacy.

"Tell me, how old are you?" said Mamma, her chest rising and falling at thrice the normal rate.

"Twenty-four."

Mamma paused, and her eyes rolled about her skull as she hearkened back through the chronology of the years: "Twenty-four years ago I *was* with Thor—and we were already married. That would mean you were born just before we moved to Svalbard ... Maybe that's why he was so desperate to escape after all ... Nuh, Thor wouldn't have gone with another woman. He wouldn't have betrayed me. He wouldn't ... But he must have, because you're here. That hair; those eyes; your size. Looking at you now, I see more of him in you than is even in Ulrik." She pressed her forehead to the asphalt and clawed at the ground with her fingernails.

"Mamma," said Ulrik, taking a knee beside her and rubbing her back, "Pappa wouldn't have done that to you. We mustn't be taking the word of a stranger over his."

"You think," said Embla, "I'd come all the way to Greece in search of you if I was lying?"

"Perhaps you have another reason to be intruding." Ulrik drew himself up to his full height. "Why come now? How could it be that for twenty-four years nobody knew of your existence?"

Embla shrugged: "Ever since I turned sixteen I've been searching for Pappa, and until now I hadn't found a single trace of his existence. I found the addresses and knocked on the doors of many other Thorsten Magnussons, but never my pappa's. It was only when I heard, through a chance source, that the father of the Olympian Ulrik Magnusson was called Thorsten, that I tracked you down. I took the next flight to Athens, hoping to find you. And when I saw you together on the day of the Saifullah attack, I knew it was him. Not just another Thorsten Magnusson; it was my pappa."

"Is that the real reason for your coming?" said Ulrik, tilting his chin and surveying closely her lamellated skin. Her curious complexion was not unlike that of tree bark. At first, he and Ria had supposed it to be eczema, but now his suspicions ran deeper.

"Reason? I'm not sure what you mean? Is that not reason enough?"

Ulrik's vine-green eyes contracted, as did his mouth. "Is it because maybe you're like me and have a kaleidoscopic genome? Are you *Homo nova*, too?"

A silence ensued.

"I don't know," she said, shading her face with a hand as one does when exposed to the glare of bright lights.

"You must have an idea. Think. Are you special in any way? Tell me. Tell me anything. Say what you're thinking. Whatever it is, say it."

"I don't know who or what I am—except that I'm your sister."

"*Half*-sister," he corrected. "And who else knows this?" Lowering his voice and checking over his shoulder: "Who else knows you're my half-sister?"

"Nobody knows; I swear on everything dear to me."

"You swear?" said Mamma, crawling closer to Embla like some starving animal. "Bastard girl, if you're anything like your pappa, your word means nothing."

At once, Mamma sprang to her feet, and a murderous shadow passed over her face so that her pupils underwent the darkest dilation. With fingers outspread like terrible talons, she leapt for Embla's throat. But Ulrik foresaw the assault, and just as Mamma was about to seize hold, he charged forward with his shoulder, knocking her to the ground with a seismic clatter.

On scraping the ground, Mamma's cheek was stripped of its skin, leaving behind a burning graze—a moist patch of red that was silvery under a certain light and in which was embedded the tiniest debris. Her cherry lips swelled, and the top lip in particular developed a pitiable protrusion like a duck's bill.

"Mamma, I'm so sorry," masking his shame with both hands. "I didn't mean to."

"Ugh, my mouf," she said, probing her bloody gums with a finger while speaking. "I fink I'm miffing a—I'm miffing a toof. Oh no, no, no, no. My toof. Nobogy move until I fin' my toof." She scoured the cracks of the pavement like a vagrant in search of coins.

"You've lost a tooth?" said Ulrik, stooping down. "Here, let me help you."

"Nuh! Stay back, traitor," she said, hissing like a cornered cat. "You would take her side over mine. Back; I said stay back, traitor." Ulrik cupped his hands over his ears, barring the onslaught of hurtful words. "Just like your pappa, there's a traitor in you. Stay back."

"She doesn't mean that, Ulrik," said Embla, never fully looking up, as though Astrid were a gorgon whose heinous eyes would turn her to stone.

"Don't you speak on my behalf, bastard thing—thing of nightmares."

Four storeys above, a hairy-breasted man swung open his shutters and leant out of his window, brandishing his handTech: "Away! I'm recording you, and my wife is calling the police."

Spider took out a laser pointer and beamed a red dot between the hairy-breasted man's nipples, at which he suspected himself a target of some concentrated gunfire and scrambled back inside for cover. Folk make the worst assumptions when such a harmless little light makes a target of them.

"Don't worry," said Spider, "he isn't recording frog all now."

"I'm dropping this to be sure," said Wacky, pulling a pin from a canister with his teeth and hurling the smoke grenade to one side. "Everybody, gather on me."

A dense cloud of white smoke burst throughout the alleyway, and the companions huddled together. All except Mamma.

"Hey, Astrid," called Spider, beaming his red laser through the smoke to signal his whereabouts, "we're over here by the wall of graffiti."

"Shh, be quiet," she whispered. The rhythm of her footsteps was erratic: she seemed to be altering her course back and forth as though in great indecision. "I need to be somewhere quiet. Away from all this. Away from all of you. So I can forget that any of this ever happened."

"Be gone, then!" boomed Ulrik, still frothing with rage at her calling him a traitor.

A muffled sobbing echoed throughout the alleyway. Faint footsteps commenced again, though this time at a much swifter pace, before ceasing altogether as she fled into the night.

"Oi, Astrid?" called Wacky. "You still there, love?"

No reply.

"Shall I go after her?" said Spider.

"It's too late. Listen, bro …"

They heard it before they could see it, and they felt it before they'd even heard it—the acoustic vibration of their eardrums and the wuthering wind upon their faces. So sudden was the arrival of the quadcopter that its rapid turbines swept away the lingering smokescreen. A whole neighbourhood of hounds went mad at its presence: the mastiffs howled, the spaniels barked, and the terriers yapped as the aircraft descended into the adjacent street.

"Everybody in," shouted Chalky from the cockpit.

"Where the bloody hell have you been?" said Wacky, ushering Embla in first, her inelegant stomp causing the aircraft to dip on one side.

"Cutting about at the fucking seaside. Where the fuck d'ya think I've been, Wack-job?"

"Never mind that. We've got a slight problem, bro."

"What now?"

"Astrid's gone AWOL. An argument broke out, and now she's legged it."

Ulrik interrupted: "After what she said, I don't wish to be seeing her ever again. Leave her. I refuse to go anywhere with her," knotting his arms and tilting his proud chin to the stars.

"You heard the lad," said Chalky, shrugging. "His orders are our orders. Now, in you get. All of you."

Ria was next, then Ulrik, then Wacky, and finally Spider, who slammed the hatch behind him. When seated and strapped in, the quadcopter shot up into the sky and into the black of night. To where, Ulrik knew not. To where, he didn't care.

As the others spoke, he sat with his monstrous brow buried halfway down his face while staring out of the window. Except he wasn't staring out of the window. It was Embla's reflection that he watched with the keenest obsession, hardly blinking as he looked for clues; certain physical clues that might confirm his deep suspicions of her being like him; of her being *Homo nova*; of her being the first.

Chapter Thirty-Three

COLONEL'S PROPHECY

The consummate crow would've been much aggrieved to have taken such a flight as that which the companions took in their quadcopter. After setting out from Athens, some convoluted circumnavigation saw them fly south across violet Saharan skies and avoiding DRUE airspace at all costs. Having then flown west, and after stopping off at Gibraltar for fuel, they altered their course latitudinally and passed over the Celtic sea, somewhere north of which was a rugged coastline—a broken piece of a once grand jigsaw. Even when our ancient earth comprised only one supercontinent (Pangea) did Great Britain sit rudely among her neighbours, her back turned while the rest snuggled in landlocked harmony.

Suddenly, when navigating through a thick margin of grey cloud, the quadcopter shuddered, and the turbulence caused such a riot as to wake Ulrik from his dream, or rather his lucid nightmare. Panting, he clutched at his sweaty neck as though the air were in danger of running out.

"Sorry, my bad," said Spider, who was co-piloting their way through the elements with Tristan.

"I didn't know you were afraid of flying," said Ria, stroking his wrist. "It's okay," nose crinkling. "It's pretty cute."

"Yah, flying ..." said Ulrik, drawing the net of hair out of his face and sweeping it back into a ponytail. "Anyway, how much longer?"

"Almost there, bro," said Waqas, pressing his nose to the window.

As the aircraft descended, the red dawn blundered into view, illuminating the land—a green and growing land—and it seemed to Ulrik a vast emerald ocean, its prairies rolling like surf across the landscape, its moorland ripping like tremendous tides.

"Trust me, you won't be needing sun lotion here," added Waqas.

"Sun lotion?" said Ulrik, cocking his head.

But Waqas wasn't talking to him. Ulrik extended his neck and saw Embla pasting thick dollops of what looked like Icelandic skyr or Greek yoghurt over her arms, legs, face, neck, and shoulders.

"It's moisturiser," she said, lacquering the affected areas for a second time.

"That's a lot of moisturiser," said Ria, rubbing her furrowed forehead as though attempting to erase the deep lines of concern.

"I know, but my skin condition—it feels tight. It's like I'm wearing clothes that are many sizes too small. Don't worry; it doesn't hurt. Although it might hurt my feelings if you were to keep staring ..."

When Embla thought nobody was watching, she tore away strips of dead skin from her elbows and did so with as much ease as one does when peeling the rind of an orange. In his periphery, Ulrik looked on in silent horror, eyeing the excess of Embla's moult collected in her hand. He was deep in the conviction that this was some symptom of hypermethylation; some symptom of a kaleidoscopic genome.

All at once the passengers jerked forward, having been caught unawares of their abrupt landing. Despite their surprise, the foundations of the earth beneath them were a welcome sensation, and so, too, was the pneumatic hiss of the passenger hatch as it flew open. Spider was first out of the quadcopter, and in the manner of a chauffeur, he sped from the cockpit and made his way to the passenger hatch, where he extended his telescopic arm to assist the companions in alighting from the aircraft. Ulrik clasped Spider's hand and climbed out first, and for a moment he stood stretching away his lethargy.

English soil was soft underfoot; softer than the Svalbardian tundra; softer still than the thirsty Grecian earth that he'd come to know of late. There was nothing about for miles, save the solitary cottage with the golden thatched roof to which they'd come. The only other dwellings within a visible radius were the heaths of heather, habitat to elusive grouse and other moorland critters scurrying within.

It was the first time Ulrik had seen the troops' faces in daylight, and Tristan came bounding up to him with arms out wide. Four years, yet not a speck of his Saxon aspect had changed: his bald head was still a great reflector of sunlight; his face was still clean-shaven; and his cold, menacing eyes still flitted about in a state of hyper-vigilance as though he were at all times conducting risk assessments: noting the wind speed and direction, mapping out the contours of the terrain, counting hazards, and conceiving ways of neutralising threats.

"I kept her safe," said Ulrik, embracing him. "Vicky. I kept her safe." When reaching inside his trouser pocket, his hand met with the brass tin, inside which resided that gallant gift he'd been loaned long ago in the Svalbard infirmary. He handed the Victoria Cross back to Tristan, who looked upon his old war medal and was glad to see it untarnished.

"For valour," said Tristan, grasping him on the shoulder and imparting a cold, patriotic stare.

"For valour," returned Ulrik, nodding.

Their reacquaintance was brief, for there came a severe rattling of rickety metal accompanied by a sort of snarling. Turning, Ulrik saw a stranger approaching at speed in a wheelchair, and had he not stepped out of the way at the last second, his knees would've been bashed and his toes would've been crushed on collision. When looking up, the elderly gentleman in the wheelchair drew in a great sniff and examined Ulrik much like a jeweller might when troubled by a counterfeit gemstone. The mottled, sickly hue of his skin was like that of a decaying leaf which in its final stages of disintegration surrenders behind a translucent network of veins and brittle tissue.

"Nightingale," said the gentleman, holding out a polished wooden stick and prodding Ulrik in the chest with the brass end, "what's this piece of turd at the end of my drill stick, neh?"

"Colonel," said Tristan, "this is Ulrik Magnusson. You know … Homo Nova? The lad we were rooting for at the Olympics, remember? Ulrik, this is Colonel Sir John William Ormondroyd. He's like the grandfather of the Guild."

As they exchanged handshakes, Ulrik's grip fell limp while trying to handle his skeletal paw.

"He's got a soggy handshake," said Colonel, speaking out of the corner of his mouth. "I don't trust him."

With the old dog being in the December of mortality, Ulrik thought better of retaliating and kept his mouth clenched. But Colonel continued to berate him.

"Strange-looking fucker, aren't you, Magnusson? Somebody bring me my clippers. I'll not have no shaggy Afghan hound skulking about on my parade."

Colonel was clearly a troubled soul. A compliment might appeal to his better nature. Thus: "I like your hat, Colonel. Where did you buy such a thing?"

"Hrumph, *hat*, he says. You mean my beret, you lanky tosser? My *maroon* beret? Tut-tut-tut. I was in the Paras, boy. Ex-prisoner of war is what I am. And after that I was a Beefeater—a Yeoman Warden of His Majesty's Royal Palace and Fortress. Show some damn respect."

"I wondered how long it'd be before he crowbarred that in," said Waqas, kissing his teeth and rolling his eyes.

"Pipe down, Akhtar. I've more courage in my arse crack than you have in your entire body."

"Come on, Colonel," said Spider, taking the handles of the wheelchair. "Let's get you some breakfast. What do you reckon to some crumpets with jam? Or marmalade? Take your pick."

"Raspberry jam, then," he said, as he was wheeled away across a gravelly path and back into the thatched cottage. "But I don't want none of that seeded crap. I ain't a friggin' bird, you know."

"Don't mind him," said Tristan, patting Ulrik on the back. "It's the brandy talking,"—whispering now behind his hand—"and the dementia."

Ulrik harboured no hate in his breast towards Colonel for this mild humiliation. Besides, his attention was interrupted now by a slender woman in motorcycle leathers. Black was the jacket that was zipped tight across her midriff; black were the knee-high boots she strutted in; and black, too, were her long tresses of hair; though a shock of the severest white affected her face. Such anaemia can wear unhealthily on a person, but on her it was like an angelic stamp of purity which she wore like a fair creature of winter.

"Here she is," said Tristan.

"Morning, Skye," said Waqas. "How you keeping?"

"Aye, am brand new, Wacky," she said, in an arcane accent that sounded like one belonging to secret folk of myth and legend. "Right, ave been watching yaes all for some time, so it's good to finally meet yaes. Am Captain Skye Urquhart, the leader of CIGMa, which, for those of yae that dunnae know yet, stands for Celtic Iceni Guild Masters."

For a moment, Ulrik's eyes met Skye's, but not for too long, in case he drowned in those ice-blue wells.

"And yae must be Ulrik ..." She came close to him. Almost too close. "Yaes even bigger in real life, hun." As she brushed his elbow with her fingertips, an intimate tingle ran throughout his arm.

At once, Ria flicked and fixed her hair with exaggerated movements, tying it up and letting it down again, swishing it forwards and backwards, and running her hands through her caramel waves. Skye did the same, and a contest of hair-flicking ensued which all the men were oblivious to.

"Aye, Homo Nova," continued Skye, combing a lock of hair out of her face and over her ear. "The standard-bearer of a great, great revolution. A living legend. The future of mankind, so they say."

"So, where exactly are we, then?" said Ria, turning up her nose and tightening her pout.

"This," said Tristan, leading them towards the thatched cottage, "this is the home of our guild: the Queen Boudicca Inn." The swinging sign above the doorway depicted a flame-haired woman with stout shoulders

and a square jawline—a woman whom they all agreed was a coinciden-
tal doppelganger of Embla Magnusson. Though not one for frolicsome
social intercourse, Embla retracted her hands into her knitted sleeves
and kept quiet.

"Right," said Waqas, "let's get inside and do proper introductions in
there, shall we? Trust me, it's about to piss it down."

Just as Waqas finished speaking, a pregnant cloud burst, giving birth
to torrents of heavy rain, and the surrounding countryside seemed to
spring to life under the thirst-quenching deluge. Such was how the
wild allotments of Britain were kept great and green—by the perpetual
margin of grey sprinkling from above, the greenest districts being those
which suffer the greyest skies.

With haste, they fled inside, and the companions hurried down into
a cramped cellar and thence into a sort of underground bunker, or war
room as Spider referred to it, or dungeon as Tristan referred to it. Colonel
was carried down the crooked stairs in his wheelchair by Waqas and
Spider as though he were of royal lineage. Never in the fuss of transit
did Colonel's eyes stray from Ulrik, and, twiddling his moustache, he
seemed, given the disturbed expression wrought into the lineaments of
his face, to be working out some dark conundrum.

"Who pays for all these facilities?" said Embla, squinting as she took
stock of the apparatus in the war room. "Weapons. Tech. A war room.
A quadcopter."

"We serve," said Skye, speaking slowly and choosing her words with
extreme caution, "a *royal* benefactor … someone who is very, very
wealthy and very, very motivated to restore our nation's sovereign power
back to its former glory. Understand: CIGMa is all that remains of the
British Army."

"A royal benefactor? You mean like the Royal Family?"

No answer.

"Skye?"

"In yae come now, all of yaes," said Skye, dismissing the question.
"There's lots to discuss."

When Ulrik stood behind a seat at the grandly carpentered round table, Colonel wheeled himself so that he was now seated at his twelve o'clock, never pausing in his unrelenting stare.

When all were in, the cellar wall was sealed behind them; and the candles threw wolfish shadows on the wall where hung woven tapestries bearing coats of arms. Spider came around with a huge teapot, pouring out mugs of tea for everyone and distributing toasted yellow sponges they called crumpets. All were seated and sipping away at their tea, save Ulrik, who stood leaning over the round table, resting on his knuckles with his head lowered like a bull premeditating its charge, for Colonel and he were in a contest of stares.

"Take a seat, hun," said Skye, her pallid face glowing in the dark like a silver moon against the onset of midnight.

Ria took him by the wrist and brought him down into the seat beside her. Even when he sat, he could hardly do so without fidgeting and jerking his leg incessantly, until, that is, Ria gripped his thigh under the table and stroked his kneecap with a delicate thumb. Such was her calming influence.

For the benefit of their guests, the masters gave a history of the Guild and told many stories of how they'd earned their Victoria Crosses and the legacies, too, of those late comrades from bygone generations who'd sat around that very table holding councils of war and peace. But noon was fast approaching, and right now, the only account Ulrik cared to hear was the one concerning the whereabouts and welfare of Chenglei.

"Please, my head is weary," said Ulrik, his feet running away from himself under the table with impatience. "I want to know about Cheng."

"Ulrik," said Tristan, with a grievous sigh, "we don't know where he is, mate. But let me reassure you—"

Ulrik drew his hand high into the air and, with the severity of an axe upon a log, brought it down upon the table, almost cleaving it asunder and shocking the room into silence. He sat in livid speechlessness with his breath held and his eyes stricken wide. Not since he was in the aquadrome had he held his breath for so long.

Ria intervened: "You tell us your history, of your allegiance to the Crown, bore us with politics, but keep from us those details which we are most concerned to hear. Now isn't the time for tea parties or crumpets or complaining about the weather. It's a time for action."

Hesitation pervaded the war room.

"Have you taken a vow of silence?" added Ria, singling out Skye with a striking glare. "We need answers."

"Chenglei Song has been arrested," said Skye, regaining her authority. "That much we do know. Chenglei, or Doubting Thomas as he's known in the headlines, caused quite a scene at yer father's funeral, Ulrik. Brave as he was, what he did was very, very serious. If he's found guilty of burning a Quran, well …"

"What?" said Ulrik, resuming his normal cycle of breathing.

"Well, they're gownae extradite him to Babylon 'cause tha's where the sharia courts are which deal with blasphemy against Islam. It's been that way ever since the Hoose of Abraham was formed."

"Meaning what?"

"Am no' gownae lie to yae, hun; he'll be lucky if he gets away with a public lashing. But it's more likely they'll execute him. Sometimes it's both."

Ulrik yanked at clumps of his hair and seemed in danger of lifting his head off his shoulders. "Babylon," he said, in a voice that seemed faraway even to his own ears. "A death sentence … for burning a book? Madness. They can't do that to Cheng. Surely they can't?"

"Hrumph," said Colonel, nudging Waqas, "what's the matter with that lanky tosser, neh? Is it 'cause he's lost someone dear to him? Aww, diddums."

"Colonel …" said Skye, elevating her eyebrows as a fair warning.

"You're wasting your time with him, Captain Urquhart. He's only bothered for hisself. Thinks he's the only fucker to lose someone now that he's had a slice of real life. What's he want us to do, neh? Get the bugle out and play 'The Last Post' for him?"

Ria's hand throttled the veins and arteries in his shaking leg. "Ulrik, don't."

"Oh, hit a nerve, have I?" said Colonel, shaking his bony fist.

Ulrik stood up with such fervour that he tipped his chair backwards. Unable to make a clear path around the table, he leapt up onto it. The table groaned under his weight, though its legs rallied. All the companions stood up and stood back as he trampled across, clattering fine bone china teacups and saucers with his boots. At all times, Skye stood poised with a hand concealed in her jacket, no doubt pointing at him from within some instrument of violence. As he passed Colonel, the old cripple shrank into his wheelchair and shook like a beaten-up hound.

"All of you, stay away from me," said Ulrik, stepping off the end of the table and glancing about with malice. "I need some time alone. I can't be responsible for my anger if anybody should follow me."

After heaving open the cellar wall, he slipped through the opening and lunged up the stairs, where, at the top, he looked back to see if anyone had followed. Nobody had; though he could still hear their voices. Curious as to what they might say in his absence, he turned his ear in their direction and closed his eyes, which for some reason enhanced his hearing.

"Well, I think Ulrik is a brave young chap," said Spider. "He's been through a lot more than most his age."

"Brave, my eye," said Colonel. "I might be losing my marbles, but you gets to my age and you've seen into enough pairs of eyes to know whose are true and whose are false; shaken enough hands to know who is fierce and who is feeble." He then went on to say a thing which almost every senior citizen has claimed in every single tongue since such claims were made claimable by the evolution of our ancestors' vocal cords: "Back in my day, people had more respect."

"Oh, give it a rest, Colonel," said Tristan. "You only met the kid a few hours ago."

"I only needs me thirty seconds before I knows a man inside out. Sorry, m'dear, but there ain't enough love left in him for you." Ulrik supposed Colonel to be addressing Ria. "He's only enough love for hisself. I only says what you're thinking. I seen what happened in Athens. Coward is what he is. Hiding while Thorsten and our very own Queen Boudicca over here took on Saifullah and rescued all them little nippers. He's wanting everybody to think he's some kind of hero, but he ain't willing to make sacrifices. About anything in life, if I'm uncertain, I says 'I think'; and if I'm certain about anything, I says 'I knows'; and about this Ulrik Magnusson I says I *knows* he's a disease rotting his heart."

Ulrik's clenched fists were bulging with blood. He wanted to scream, but the words died away in his breast.

"Right, Colonel, I think it's time for a wee nap," said Skye.

"Let me finish my piece, Skye Urquhart. I'd sooner bloody well keel over before being silenced. So, as I was saying, yes, I seen that same hunger in Ulrik that I also seen in the worst of men. Success came to him at too young an age; the brat's appetite has been spoilt. You ever brushed your tussepegs with minty toothpaste only to take a sip of orange juice after? Tastes fucking bitter, don't it? That'll be him from now; his whole life'll be a bitter comparison. Unpalatable, I says. His taste for life has been spoilt. Mark my words: his desire to be special will be the ruin of hisself, and not just hisself but the ruin of us all."

Ulrik couldn't listen any longer. He barged out of the back door of the inn and into the wild.

Repetitions of rain unleashed; the smell of the sodden soil was earthy. As he ran full pelt in no particular direction, he came across a heath of heather where, suddenly, he tripped over a hidden rock. A startled coo and a flurry of wings—a covey of grouse scarpered away in search of safer refuge in those idle valleys.

He hardly cared to see if he'd been harmed in the fall, and he lay there with no motive to get up while the rain pattered down on his unflinching face. His eyes rolled back—just for a moment. He battled his eyelids against his exhaustion and tried to open them again, but some physiological reaction held them fast. Limbs sprawled, he succumbed to the wearies of a broken heart and slept in the heath of heather.

CHAPTER THIRTY-FOUR

YOURS UNFAITHFULLY

"Well, Satan, you have been busy in your recruitment," said the Holy Shepherd, scowling down from the abbey window at the armada of trawlers surrounding Mont-Saint-Michel. As below, so above: the Holy Shepherd was surrounded by black clouds sailing across the evening sky in the aspect of corsair ships.

Earlier that day, a tide of protestors garbed in yellow high-visibility vests had descended on the islet to express their rage. Since their arrival, their fell voices had yet to slow in their ceaseless thundering of "Free, free, free Chenglei", and there had as yet been no lapse in their crazed thrusting of their placards which read "I am Doubting Thomas".

"Father, forgive them," tilting his head towards the firmament, the sea breeze rippling his heaven-white hair, "for they know not what they do."

For some time, the Holy Shepherd contemplated a naval response to disperse the nuisance fleet of trawlers, but he postponed that thought for now. Any such controversy would stoke the protestors' rage, and it was perhaps wisest to let their passions shrink to the merest embers rather than to stomp them out. Besides, not only was there domestic trouble here, but there was a growing trouble abroad on his mind, too: that concerning the treachery of Babylon and its alleged arsenal of nuclear weapons. He'd yet to find the solitude to scribe his official sermon to the

Continent in which he'd settle the rumours and quell the unrest. But to apply himself to any cognitive endeavour during the siege of Mont-Saint-Michel was futile, so he stowed his handTech away in his cloak, struck his crook on the stone floor, and moved off from his perch.

He sauntered down into the cloister garden, where all that was green was silvered by moonlight; and as the clouds parted, it was as though a dairy pail were being spilt into the world from the heavens, for a water-fall of milky light poured forth. For a while, he stood under the arches of a pruned enclosure, admiring the exquisite topiary, admiring in par-ticular the shrubbery pruned into the semblance of a dove carrying an olive branch in its beak—a symbol of peace. Yet there was no peace to be found this evening, for his meditations were interrupted by a servant who, after clearing his throat to announce his presence, genuflected and said, "Sorry to disturb you, Holy Shepherd."

"It's quite an ungodly hour, Gabriel," said the Holy Shepherd, leaning on his warped white crook. "You must have something pressing to share …"

"I—" panting profusely, "I came—I came as quickly as I could."

"Catch your breath, will you; a man of my age is loath to waste what precious life he has remaining kept in suspense."

"So sorry, Holy Shepherd," trying to regulate his breathing by gulping down vast helpings of oxygen. "There's someone here. A woman. Claims to be a weather forecaster. Claims to have an important package. A vault-box."

"A vault-box, you say?" said the Holy Shepherd, extending his spine. "Where is this woman?"

"The Archangels are searching her as we speak. But she insists the contents of the vault-box are for your eyes only. She's got us nervous, Holy Shepherd. Says you'd be furious with us if we were to open the box without your approval."

"Do as she says, and bring her up here. Bring her alone."

"But, Holy Shepherd, there could be anything in that vault-box. A bomb. A virus. A poison. Anything."

"Bring—her—up," said the Holy Shepherd, through gritted canines.

"Holy Shepherd, I-I-I'm not sure if that's—"

The Holy Shepherd raised his crook and hooked Gabriel about his neck. As he drew him close, the Holy Shepherd's hot moist breath furled and whirled about Gabriel's face as he whispered, "I am the Shepherd, and you are my lamb. Do as I say."

Gabriel nodded, and at the unhooking of his neck he fled the garden like a nocturnal critter, rustling in and out of bushes and hurdling and hopping hedges as he went. A short while later, he returned with the woman in question, panting even more profusely than when he'd first arrived. She was a bespectacled lady, terribly acned, and advanced with an ungainly gait, as though walking upright was something she'd learnt only recently how to do; her feet slapped the ground like flippers, feet which seemed in danger of walking off in opposite directions. There was nothing hedonistic about her appearance: no highlights in her hair; no augmentations of the face; no make-up; no veneered teeth; no tattoos; no expensive attire, accessories, or accoutrements; not a single trace of narcissism. Just a woman content in the skin God had blessed her with. A woman of faith, likely.

"Holy Shepherd," said Gabriel, "this is Lydia."

"Gabriel, leave us," said the Holy Shepherd, pointing his crook at the garden's exit.

Gabriel bowed low, hiding the concern wrought upon his forehead, and retreated inside the abbey.

"Come closer, Lydia, my lamb," said the Holy Shepherd, eyeing the vault-box in her arms. It was a solid black block with no visible seams. "Step into the light where I can see you."

"Holy Shepherd," said Lydia, edging closer, trembling, "I have a package for you."

"I know you do. Are you a courier of sorts?"

"No, Holy Shepherd. I work in meteorology—weather forecasting. I coordinate a fleet of satellite drones—"

"Lydia, my lamb, before you begin," taking her chin in his hand, "let me tell you that in Proverbs there is a passage: 'Lying lips are an abomination to the Lord—'"

"'But those who act faithfully are His delight,'" she interrupted, with flaming conviction in her eyes. "Yes, Proverbs 12:22, if I remember rightly?"

"Indeed." The Holy Shepherd reclined his head and smiled down his nose at her, feeling safe in the knowledge she was kindred of faith. He motioned his hand over her in the sign of the cross and blessed her for her piety.

"Thank you, Holy Shepherd. I'm here to serve our Father in heaven. And in best serving Him in heaven, I serve the Holy Shepherd here on earth."

"And I'm grateful for your service. Come now; show me the vault-box you've discovered."

"Of course." Lydia knelt on the lawn and laid out the black block on the grass between them. "This is Chenglei Song's vault-box, Holy Shepherd. I watched the footage of the live broadcast in Athens, and when I saw him launching his satellite drone, I just knew he was plotting something heathenish. So I mobilised one of my satellite drones at the same time."

"And your drone intercepted his, I take it?" said the Holy Shepherd, hoping to rush to the story's end. Were Lydia's account a book, he'd have flicked to the last page to discover the conclusion.

"My drone intercepted his, though not in space. It was all an act—the drone going into space. It altered its course. Then it slowed, almost as if it'd been programmed to do so; almost as if it wanted to be followed. So I did: I followed it halfway across the world. It flew across the Atlantic, over the Caribbean, and into the Pacific, where it eventually landed on a remote island, where the box opened of its own accord."

"An island, you say? So a random destination, then? No doubt wasting our time to make fools out of us. A wild goose chase."

"Not random, Holy Shepherd. The drone landed on the Galapagos Islands."

"The Galapagos Islands?"

"Yes, Darwin Island to be exact ..."

"Darwin Island?" Froth gathered on the Holy Shepherd's bottom lip. "And the Quran inside, was it burned? Show it to me. Open the vault-box. Open it now."

With some effort, Lydia prised open the galvanised lid and exposed its contents: "Holy Shepherd, there wasn't a Quran inside, nor was there any sulphuric acid or a mechanism which might trigger a chemical reaction. There was nothing inside which Chenglei Song described."

"What, then? Is that a book I can see? Bring it closer. I'm not wearing my eyeTech."

"Yes, a book," gathering herself to her feet and brushing dirt off her knees. "It came accompanied with this note."

"Pass it to me—the note. Quickly, I say." Not content with waiting, the Holy Shepherd snatched it from her with the urgency of a starving hand when offered bread. He brought the page within an inch of his nose and squinted as he read:

> *Whoever is led to believe that species are mutable, will do good service by conscientiously expressing his conviction, for only thus can the load of prejudice by which this subject is overwhelmed, be removed.*
> — Charles Darwin —

Yours unfaithfully,
Doubting Thomas.

The Holy Shepherd crumpled the note in his venous fist, and his entire skeleton rattled as one might when suffering a surge of some violent voltage.

"The book that came with it, Holy Shepherd, was this," handing him a green leather-bound volume that had pages gilded with gold, and the lettering on the cover was printed in elegant calligraphy: *On the Origin of Species* by Charles Darwin.

"Tell me now, who else has seen this? I need to know." He hooked his crook about her neck and drew her towards him. "It'd be an embarrassment if this were to surface in the news. Who else knows about this, my lamb? Who?"

"Only our Father in heaven, Holy Shepherd. Not even my husband knows. I knew the damage this would do to your reputation if this blasphemy were to get out."

"I believe you, dear child of God," releasing her from the claw of his crook. He turned away and groomed the bristles of his silver beard meditatively: "Now, I have one more favour to ask of you, if you'd be so charitable as to consider it?"

"Anything, Holy Shep—"

"You are to burn a copy of the Quran with sulphuric acid. After which you are to falsify the discovery of the vault-box. You will tell the media Chenglei Song's satellite drone malfunctioned and your drone intercepted it in space. Understand?"

"Holy Shepherd, to lie?" clasping a hand over her face and recoiling as one might in the company of someone carrying a virus.

"If ever there was a righteous lie, it would be this, Lydia. This uprising, all of this, is because of the Continent's lust for its newest idol, Homo Nova. And the heretics rally behind his disciple Chenglei Song, a man who'd see blasphemy normalised—fashionable, even. Imagine what would happen to the Republic if we allowed such a movement to rise. These evolutionists demand that we brainwash our children into believing we're related to bananas and bacteria."

"They remind me of a passage in Romans: 'Claiming to be wise, they became utter fools.'"

"Indeed. Utter, utter fools. So, will you help me quench their fires, Lydia?"

"I don't know, Holy Shepherd. I want to say yes, but I'd be framing an innocent man. Condemning him to death in Babylon."

"Innocent? It's no less than he deserves for inspiring a revolt. Chenglei Song should be whipped, stripped, and nailed high; made to endure the same torment as our saviour Jesus Christ who sacrificed his life for sinners like him."

"Holy Shepherd, to knowingly sin—I couldn't. I shouldn't."

The Holy Shepherd took her by the wrists: "But of course you can, Lydia, my lamb. Pay heed to 1 John 1:9 in which it says if we confess our sins, the Lord is faithful and just and will forgive us our trespasses. I can trust you to make this small sacrifice for the Republic, can't I, my lamb? Just this once? For the good of the Republic?"

"I'll try, Holy Shepherd."

"Excellent," letting go of her wrists so that the supply of blood returned to her extremities. "Now, is there anything else you would ask of me?"

"Not that I can think of, Holy Shepherd."

"There must be something. You can ask of me anything. Go ahead. I see you're thinking of something right now. Something in particular. A light passed over your eyes just then. Go on; seek, and you will find."

"Well, there is one thing."

"Ask, and it will be given to you."

"It's about Ulrik Magnusson. It's something I'm curious to know."

"What of him?"

"Well, he's been missing since the funeral in Athens ..."

"Hmm," said the Holy Shepherd, with a reproachful frown.

"Sorry, I meant no offence, Holy Shepherd. It's just that you were right earlier when you said he's become the Continent's idol. Even my husband has developed an interest in him. He's started to doubt: doubt our origins; doubt our ancestry of Adam and Eve. And it's all because of this talk of Ulrik Magnusson switching on ancestral genes and his kaleidoscopic genome."

"What is it you're asking me, Lydia?"

"Has he disappeared *forever*, if you know what I mean?"

"I think, unless I'm mistaken, you're implying I know something of his whereabouts. Would that it were true, Lydia, but unfortunately, I know nothing. It's my belief that someone somewhere is hiding and protecting him. Our secret services will soon track them down, and when they do, they'll …"

"They'll what?"

"Lydia, my lamb, in times of peril, we must *always* let the scripture guide our hearts; and in this case, I ask you to recall Hebrews 9:22: 'Almost all things are by the law purged with blood, and without the shedding of blood there is no forgiveness.'" The Holy Shepherd gestured with his crook like a conductor when reaching a crescendo, and with a final stroke he waved her be silent.

Lydia paid obeisance to him and sped away with the vault-box in her arms, duty-bound to fulfil her wicked errand.

Chapter Thirty-Five

OPERATION SANDSTORM

There exist few sensations which mellow the anxieties like the tinkling of heavy rain on the windowpane. To be sheltered by impenetrable walls, when all about is external havoc, grants one a fleeting feeling of security. And as Ulrik awoke from the hysteria of his recurring nightmare, he clutched at his sternum, and its diabolical rhythm was swiftly calmed by virtue of that rainy sensation.

With renewed vigour, he sat himself upright, his grass-green eyes roving about here and there; and he deduced, by the rustic design of the room, that he'd been brought back to that lonely inn on the hill, in which the timber beams jutted out from the plaster of the ceiling, brickwork protruded from the chimney breast, and not a patch of floorboard was smothered by carpet or rug. It could be said the anatomy of the room was exposed and in a state of nakedness; and lying in bed next to him was a girl in the self-same state—nude, save for the two scanty bands of underwear veiling her upper and lower half.

When Ria curled up to him and wound her legs about his, he sat as stiff as a corpse. Even when her hot breath tickled his body, and even when she impressed her icy toes on his legs, he somehow suppressed the shudders coursing throughout his frame, such was his determination not to wake her. A few moments later, he took pity on her, for her arm came out in a rash of raised goosebumps, so he sacrificed the greater share of the duvet to cocoon her against the morning chill.

"Um, you're so cuddly, Ulrik," whispered Ria, her nose crinkling at the bridge as she nuzzled her face into his ribs.

"Ah, sorry, I didn't mean to wake you."

"Well, since you have, make it up to me, and play with my hair." She took his hand without consent and ran it through the ends of her caramel tresses. "Did you have any dreams, Ulrik?"

"Nuh," he said, lips tightening. "At least, not that I recall."

"You slept for almost eighteen hours, so you must've dreamt about something."

"I slept for eighteen hours?"

"Uh-hum. Anyway, I know you were dreaming because I heard you talking in your sleep."

"I might've had nightmares, but I prefer not to recall them. Why don't you tell me about your dreams?"

At once, Ria broke free from his embrace and out of the duvet. She seized her hairbrush from the bedside table and held it within a breath's distance of his nose, all the while her nostrils undergoing a tempestuous flaring. "You said her name in your sleep."

"Name? Whose name did I say?" trying to avert his eyes from her bare bronze skin—trying, but failing. How toned she was for one so slender; her concave tummy had deep athletic lines, out of which were sculpted six symmetrical compartments.

"You were saying Skye's name," glaring at him through the contracted slits between her eyelids.

"Oh, you mean her with the black hair? Ria, I don't see why—uh, why are you looking at me like that? What's wrong with you?"

"Nothing is wrong with *me*. It's what's wrong with *you* that should concern you."

"Shh, let's not be arguing. Someone might hear us." He reached out for a hug, but she recoiled.

"I just didn't like the way she looked at you. She better not fucking touch you again. Who does she think she is? Flirting with you right in front of me."

"Flirting? Ria, I don't think she was."

"No, you wouldn't, would you, stupid forager." Ria wound her hairbrush into his beard and tugged at his face to draw him closer: "Promise me you won't entertain her giving you attention. Promise me you only have eyes for me."

"You already know this. Why are you even asking me such a thing?"

"Say it," tilting her head like a puppy. "Say you promise."

"Okay, I promise." She released his beard from the tangles of her hairbrush. "I've given you no reason to distrust me, have I?"

"But she's really pretty, Ulrik," falling into his lap and looking up at him while upside down. "I know I'm being silly, but I don't want to lose you—ever. You're all I've got, and … I like you. A lot. I really, really like you."

"I like you, too, Ria. I'm always telling you this," taking her jaw in both hands and kissing her while upside down. "You're the only one who understands me."

"I know, but I think I like you more than you like me …"

"That's not true. You can't know such a thing."

"But I hate being apart from you, Ulrik. I don't want to go anywhere without you. I *love* being with you."

"From here on in," closing his hand about hers, "it's me and you. Always."

"Good," she said, sticking out her bottom lip in a feigned sulk. "You better mean that."

At her happiest she was a flower of sorts, to which Ulrik was her sunlight, for when he beamed down upon her with the fondest affection, he caused her to open up to him; conversely, in his absence, she shrank away in darkness.

There elapsed a prolonged period which they spent tangled in one another's limbs, rolling about with their lips glued fast. After much frolicking, they lay supine together, staring at the ceiling, catching their breath as though they'd battled through some intense aerobics. For a moment, they almost dozed off again, until deep vocal vibrations travelled up throughout the structural beams of the house. They were coming from downstairs, these low rumblings. It was a voice not dissimilar to Pappa's.

"Embla," he scowled. He kicked off the duvet and strode over to the window, where he threw open the tartan curtains and looked out across the moorland. The last of the owls were returning from their night patrols, and the earliest of the kestrels were departing. "Why is she still here?"

"Ulrik, I know it's hard for you to accept that your pappa—I mean, I know it's hard to come to terms with this, but Embla is your sister, and you're her brother. Don't be calling her your half-sister. Will you at least try being nice? If not for her, then for me? I've become friends with her over the last few weeks. She's like you in so many, many ways."

"How so?"

"Oh, it would be quicker for me to list her differences."

After much squinting and grumbling, Ulrik conceded that he'd put up with Embla's company for now but was opposed to making promises he couldn't keep.

There was a growing commotion downstairs: raised voices, cutlery clanking, and warbled whistles—those, no doubt, of Spider.

"Sounds like they're having breakfast," said Ulrik.

Colonel's croaky, cantankerous voice transmitted better than anyone's throughout the framework of the house: "Why would I use an electric wheelchair when I've still got my friggin' arms, neh?"

"Should we get dressed and go down?" said Ria, the slanting rays of the rising sun catching the amber hue of her eyes.

"Do we have to?" he said, gently stroking her bare bronze shoulder, hoping she'd share his desire to dive back under the duvet and there stay interlocked in one another's embrace for a little while longer.

"Come on, Ulrik; we can't stay in here forever. It'll be fine."

After a series of futile attempts to convince her otherwise, Ulrik abandoned the idea and got dressed in his trousers and tunic, and when they were both ready, Ria led him by the hand downstairs and into the punters' lounge.

The companions were huddled by the fireside, and when they heard Ulrik's cumbersome footsteps approaching, a library silence befell them. His eyes were drawn at once to Embla, who, aware now of his presence, blinked with rapid effect, and she wrung her hands as though she were warming them over a fire—just like Pappa did when he was nervous. Her complexion today was even more cracked than he remembered, and she looked as though she were moulded out of clay that had undergone a period of excessive firing in a kiln.

"Good morning," said the companions, with a simultaneous awkwardness that sounded rehearsed.

Ulrik dispensed a single nod in their direction.

"Well," said Colonel, slapping his knee-stubs, "well, I never. Aha! It's Ulrik Magnusson. What's he doing in the Queen Boudicca?" Colonel introduced himself as if they'd not already been through the uncomfortable rigmarole. The lunatic had forgotten his outburst. Ulrik hadn't. Yet, when looking up at Spider and seeing his benevolent smile, all Ulrik's anger departed his breast and a smile arose on his cheeks, and there was collective relief when Ulrik bent down to Colonel's height and greeted him merrily.

"Good grief," added Colonel, shaking his hand, "he's got the strongest hand I've ever shaken. A fierce hand. A powerful hand. A leader of men, says I. Someone fetch the lad a drink, will yer? Nighting-fail,"—Colonel flung a beer mat with the precision of a shuriken, and it struck Tristan on the shiniest part of his head—"on the double now. At ease, Ulrik, there ain't no top brass here in our NAAFI. Bloody shuffle up, will yer, Wacky? Let the lad sit."

Skye had already created a vacant space, and she stroked the long saddle, beckoning him to join her, to which he obliged. Ria remained standing with her hands planted on her hips and her chest puffed out, pretending to admire the wall art depicting hairy highland cattle.

"How're yae feeling, hun?" said Skye, speaking in a low, prickling whisper so faint it forced Ulrik to lean closer. "Yae've slept a wee bit longer than I expected."

"I feel better for having slept. Though, waking up and remembering everything again—I'm reminded of that evil day in Athens. So I'd prefer not to be talking about myself. Help me forget by talking about something or someone else. How are you?"

"Aye, am brand new, hun," flicking her raven hair behind her shoulder. "Thanks for asking."

He couldn't establish a single word she said but donned a smile anyway. Ria adjusted the aperture of her eyes as one does when staring directly at the sun.

"Take it you'll be wanting some breakfast, bro?" said Waqas, pouring himself a mug of tea from a teapot shaped like a military boot.

"Thanks, but no breakfast for me just yet. There are matters we need to be discussing first. I need to know about Cheng."

"How aboot we talk and eat at the same time?" said Skye, rising from her seat and resting a delicate hand upon his shoulder. "Yer gownae need yer strength, hun."

Skye strode away, driving her heels into the ground, stomping with each step, her jackhammer boots threatening injury to the flagstones beneath. Without another word, the companions followed her down into the cellar and into the war room.

When seated at the round table, Spider served crumpets and scones and toast and blueberry muffins and refused to cease the supply of stodge until Ulrik was beyond bloated.

Tristan propped Colonel up in his chair by the fireside and told him this was his post and that he should be doing them a great service by listening out for enemy movements above their bunker since there was nobody with a more qualified pair of ears for the job. A short while later, though, Colonel's head dropped onto his breast, and a muffled snoring commenced.

For the benefit of Ulrik, Skye inducted him into the politics of the

Treaty of Zion—the history, the names, the places, the agreements, all the conspiring—and revealed that she'd received intelligence to suggest the House of Abraham was at risk of devolution.

"Again, remind me," said Ulrik, "who's this Sultan bin Ibrahim?"

"Sultan bin Ibrahim," said Skye, curling a strand of hair behind her ear, "is the Caliph, and the capital of his caliphate is Babylon."

"And ..." said Ulrik, taking a sharp swallow, "is Sultan bin Ibrahim the leader of—I hate saying their name—Saifullah?"

"Ulrik, hun, when I was serving in the army, ma regiment was the Intelligence Corps, so I have loads and loads of trusted sources when it comes to international affairs. Yet even ma connections cannae say for certain who heads up Saifullah. Some reckon Sultan bin Ibrahim *is* their leader; others say they're funded by Russia; others say it's propaganda."

"But Saifullah are Muslims from Babylon, aren't they? And it was Muslims of Babylon who killed my pappa. Whether or not he leads them, he's a Muslim just like those killers." Ulrik's clenched hands turned red, then white at the knuckles. "So he's responsible for all this."

"I'll answer this one," said Waqas, who had until now been silent on the subject. "Ulrik, a long time ago, I belonged to a Muslim family. I'm not Muslim anymore for my own personal reasons, but I understand what it's like to be called a terrorist—to be guilty by association. What it is, yeah, very few Muslims support Saifullah. Only a small minority, understand. Saifullah are a terrorist group, yeah? They're dogs. Worse, even. Okay, think of it like gardening ..."

"Gardening?"

"Yeah, gardening. Let me explain." Waqas turned to Tristan. "Chalky, do you like gardening?"

"Are you having a laugh? I can't bloody stand it. Worms. Nettles. Itching. Hay fever. Can't think of anything worse. Nope. Not for me. No, thank you."

"And, Spider," said Waqas, "what about you, bro? Are you into gardening?"

"Ahaw, am I. What's not to love about planting new life and seeing it grow and change with the seasons? It's the best way to connect with nature. We rely on flora, and flora relies on us. You know what I mean? What flora breathes in, we breathe out—carbon dioxide; and what flora breathes out, we breathe in—oxygen."

"And, Spider, Chalky, since one of you likes gardening and the other dislikes it, does that mean you disrespect each other?"

Both shook their heads and agreed it was none of their business how they each chose to spend their spare time.

"So," added Waqas, turning to Ulrik, "it's the same with religion, yeah? Religion, like gardening, is just an idea. You get where I'm coming from, bro? It's okay to dislike *gardening*, but that doesn't mean it's okay to hate *gardeners*. And so it's okay to dislike Islam, but it's not okay to hate Muslims."

"Still, Saifullah are Muslim, aren't they?" said Ulrik, not quite understanding Waqas's analogy.

"Ulrik, a few months ago in a quiet village not so far away from here, there was a murder. A lady ran over her husband with a lawnmower, beheaded him with hedge shears, and ground his remains into bonemeal and used him as compost. Since the murderer was a gardener, does that mean we should hold Spider and all other gardeners to account 'cause they share a common interest with this murderer?"

"I suppose not," said Ulrik, leaning back in his chair and scratching the nape of his neck.

"Exactly. People need to understand the difference between a person and their ideas. I've always said no idea should be exempt from criticism. Not gardening, not Islam. I reckon, yeah, that's what your uncle Chenglei was getting at with the whole Schrödinger's Quran thing. A book is a book, innit. A set of ideas. Cheng's attack was an attack on an ideology, not its people."

"I see," said Ulrik, stroking his beard. Upon hearing Chenglei's name, it dawned on him what danger he must be in, so he steered the conversation onto a course of his choosing: "So where exactly is Babylon? That's where Cheng's heading, right? They can't be trialling him, can they? He's both guilty and not guilty at the same time."

"Ulrik, hun," said Skye, pushing herself away from the table and rising to her feet, "they've intercepted Chenglei's drone and vault-box."

"Go on ..."

She came around the table and stopped in her tracks when she was blocked by Ria, so she sidled up to the table's edge beside her and rested her buttocks on it. "There were the remains of a Quran inside the vault-box—badly burnt. It's only a matter of time before they try Chenglei and find him guilty."

Ulrik fell prey to a sudden faintness, but he quickly regained his whereabouts by administering a few exasperated knocks to his temple. "Guilty or not, Cheng's part of my family."

It was the first time Embla had spoken when she leapt in with an utterance so rapid that her words were at first indiscernible: "How-do-we-get-to-Babylon?" After asking her question, she shrank into her chair, lowered her eyes, and withdrew her hands into her sleeves, awaiting an answer, all the while her ginger eyelashes flapping like the wings of an orange butterfly.

All eyes turned to Ulrik.

"Answer her," said Ulrik. "Answer my sister. We can't hide away here while Cheng suffers at the hands of the Caliph. Tell us where Babylon is so we can be on our way."

"I'm telling you it's suicide," said Waqas. "What with everything going on with the Peace Treaty. A war is coming, and there's no way anybody here wants to get caught up in Babylon."

"Ulrik," said Skye, "we thought it'd be better if yae stayed here and helped us track doon yer mamma."

"My mamma is wild at heart and a fair huntress. She's a forager, so for her I'm not worrying. But I do worry for Cheng. I can't deny I'm afraid to go in search of him, but I'm no more afraid of going to Babylon than anywhere else I've freely walked in my life. There's been danger on every road because of who I am. I accept that now. But I won't let that be Cheng's fate. Without him, I'd be a nobody. He's never failed me, so I won't be failing him."

"Ulrik is right," said Tristan, pulling up his socks. "Chenglei saved my bacon when I was stranded in the mountains on Svalbard—on that same night when I saved Ulrik. I owe it to Chenglei to return the favour. I'll go."

"What you gonna do?" said Waqas. "You can't just go barging into Babylon demanding Chenglei's release. Nah, it's fucking reckless, to be honest with you. Especially since the Holy Shepherd is about to declare war. Bloody hell; we'll get ourselves bloody killed in the crossfire."

"Behave swearing, Wacky," said Spider, his ebony eyes bulging from their sockets.

Skye spectated in silence and seemed to be weighing up the terrible odds and the favourable gains of such an operation. While Tristan and Waqas bickered, she strolled to the furthest end of the war room, where upon the wall was mounted a woven map of DRUE and the Middle East. "To answer yae earlier question, Ulrik,"—drumming her flint fingernails at a region inside Iraq—"this is where Babylon is. Yae know how the Vatican is a country inside another, that being Italy? Well, Babylon is an enclave, too, a country inside another, since it exists inside Iraq. Am just thinking aboot how best to enter … aerial or amphibious. The Euphrates River could be an option … hmm."

"Skye, you're not serious, are you?" said Waqas. "This is reckless—fucking reckless."

Until he interrupted, nobody had noticed that Colonel had awoken, and he frightened them with a sound that seemed like a laugh melded with a bark; so aggressive was it that the accumulation of tar on the walls of his lungs sounded as though it'd come unstuck. "Reckless, says Bombardier Akhtar. Reckless, says him, the winner of the Victoria Cross. Shelled and shot at, he was—Bombardier Akhtar. Makes a target of hisself to draw away enemy gunfire from his platoon. There ain't never been a bloke more reckless than that plonker sitting there. Reckless, my eye. Your recklessness has bloody well made a man of you."

"Yeah, and it's made a dead man of many more," said Waqas, gesturing to the tapestries on the wall honouring the fallen.

"I've spent my life," said Ulrik, rising to his feet and leaning on his knuckles on the table, "I've spent my life hiding from the bullies of this world. As a boy, I hid away from Brynolf. In Athens, I ran away scared from the terrorists. Even now, when my friend needs me the most, I'm hiding underground. I don't want to be that person anymore—a coward. Few people remain in this evil world whom I love; Cheng is one, and nothing will stop me from setting out to save him, even if I set out to my own doom—to my own death."

Ria pinched his triceps. "Ssst, don't say that ever again. Don't you dare. Ever."

"Tha's admirable, hun," said Skye, curling a strand of raven hair behind her ear. "Bravery like that is very, very rare, but it won't need to come to that, I can assure yae." She turned to her comrades, "The choice isnae ours whether or no' Ulrik goes to rescue Chenglei. Our choice is simply whether we'll accompany him. Troops, I haven't got any orders to give to yaes today, only choices. Am asking for volunteers to accompany Ulrik to Babylon …"

Embla, wearing an indomitable frown, rapped her knuckles on the table. "I'm in."

Ria drummed her fingernails, making the sound of a swift gallop. "Me too."

There was hesitation from the veterans, and there rose upon Skye's neck a patch of mottled crimson which emboldened her like a badge of fire. Such was her silent wrath that there came a quick succession of responses from the others.

"Goes without saying," said Tristan, with a patriotic stare.

"Count me in," said Spider, blowing into his hands as though they were a conch with which to signal his assent.

"Course I'm going," said Waqas, knotting his arms across his chest. "Someone's gotta keep you pricks alive, haven't they?"

Colonel wheeled over from his post at the fireside and was about to volunteer for the mission until Skye talked him out of it: "We've got some lines of enquiry to pursue as to the whereaboots of Astrid Magnusson, haven't we, Colonel?"

"Oh yes," said Colonel, tapping his nose and winking at her. "We have, haven't we, ma'am?"

"So come on, Sandhurst," said Waqas, "what's the plan?"

"Let me worry aboot the details, hun," said Skye, acknowledging the time on her watchTech. "All of yaes, yae've got a day to prepare yer gear and gather yer full strength. We'll reconvene again tomorrow night at twenty-one hundred hours for a final briefing. The day after tomorrow, yae'll mobilise for Babylon at zero dark thirty on Operation Sandstorm. Happy with that? Good. Now, am no' taking further questions 'cause ave got a shiteload of admin to work through. Fall oot, troops."

CHAPTER THIRTY-SIX

RUSSIAN CONCUSSION

The streetlamps of Athens cast the brightest, whitest rays, but since the laws of physics prohibit the bending of light, the furthest nooks of that secluded alleyway were deprived of any goodly light.

"I need to be sure," whispered Astrid, checking over her shoulder this way and that: "are you saying I only need to drink this tonic, and I'll die peacefully in my sleep?"

"Ezactly, Goldilocks," said the man, tilting his tattered baseball cap lower and retracting his neck until his chin was flush with his collarbone. Better for him to conceal himself, for he was a man offensive to every sense. "No pain will you feel; just tingles, I can assure. It will be over before you can say 'Russian concussion'."

Astrid snatched the colourless phial from his hand and stowed it away in her bra for safekeeping. "Russian concussion ... what drug is this? Some kind of tranquilliser? An opiate? Meth?"

"Yes, drug is very good for making you sleep forever," he said, misunderstanding the question. "You is asking me for Russian concussion, and I has gifting it to you for very special price."

"But why is it called Russian concussion?"

"Ah, me no know why they calling it this. Is just name, I think. Maybe because is dangerous. Peoples will always be blaming Russia for dangerous things. But it isn't come from Russia. Is coming from my home country where I manufacture the best. Why? You no want anymore?"

"Yah, I want it," she said, shrinking into herself. "I was just curious about the name, that's all."

"I has gifting it to you for very special price, unnerstand?" taking one of her blonde plaits in his grimy fingertips and thereafter running it along his upper lip and sniffing it. "We has deal, Goldilocks?"

Astrid clenched her eyes and curled her toes: "Yah, we have a deal."

"Good," licking his teeth and raising his hand above her. Wasting no time, he pressed his palm on the summit of her head and lowered her down inch by inch until she fell to her knees. Then, in carrying out her end of the bargain, she placed a sultry hand under his shirt and held it to his torso, backing him up against the wall where he unbuttoned his tight jeans, bringing them as low as his knees. Her head now hovered within a breath's distance of his gnarled root, and so she stopped herself breathing, for the accumulation of unwashed grunge was a violation of the nostrils not dissimilar to that of festering dairy. Tilting her head upwards, she feigned a look of seduction, eyes half-closed, lips slightly parted. As he seized the back of her neck to draw her closer, she spanked his hands away. Luckily, her feistiness visibly thrilled him, and he submitted to her, mistaking her, it seemed, for a dominatrix. Then she stripped down his jeans, right down to his ankles, and when his legs were suitably tangled, she sprang to her feet at once and knocked him to the ground. In finding herself free, she bolted at full speed and left him scrambling about on his back like a tortoise stranded on its shell, kicking, twisting, turning, flipping, flapping.

Not until Astrid reached her hideout did she allow her fleet feet to slow their pace, and she never chanced a glance back for fear of sacrificing a precious second of her head start. When she reached the fringes of Kesariani Forest, she flew under the canopies of the towering trees; trees which looked like magnificent parasols, some of them open with their great canopies shielding out the sky, and others unopened, tall and thin-looking, like retracted gamps.

Her shelter was situated towards the brow of a green hill, and she followed a marked route of sticks which she'd laid out in the shape of arrows. It was hidden between two slender trees that were chosen for their close proximity. With some lace from a pair of abandoned boots, she'd drawn a sturdy line from one trunk to the other, forming a pitched roof which she'd covered with a thatch of branches and foliage. The height of the roof came no higher than her waist, though she'd hollowed out the earth to give her greater space for manoeuvre, thus keeping the abode discreet and well camouflaged.

She crawled into her leafy lodging and there slumped against a couch of earth. When her eyes adjusted to the dark, she took out the colourless tonic and, turning it over in her fingers, fell into a suicidal fantasy. But then her other hand stole into her jacket pocket of its own volition and took out a white plastic stick of sorts. Each hand was equipped with an artefact—the colourless tonic and the plastic stick—and her eyes passed from one to the other as though she was considering a profound choice: in one hand, a tincture of death; in the other, a promise of life.

For now, she stowed away the phial of Russian concussion and devoted all her attention to this plastic stick—this promise of life. A whiff of urine still emanated from beneath the cap, but instead of recoiling, she drew it closer for inspection. At the stick's centre was a small window in which were visible two bold red stripes: a test result showing positive. She shook the stick, tapped it, whacked it, and cracked it, but those defiant double red stripes endured every assault.

"What should I do?" she said, curling into the foetal position and massaging her womb. "I can't do this alone. Not without your pappa. But we don't have to, do we, bump? There's a way out of this, and neither of us have to be suffering."

She took out the phial of Russian concussion again and bestowed upon it a longing kiss. Then, as she held it against the starlight which came pulsing through a gap in her thatch, it assumed the hue of quicksilver. She was determined to finish the job but deferred its ingestion until she'd carried out one last errand: "We need to write a farewell to your beautiful brother Ulrik before we go."

After sitting upright, she groped about her feet and gained hold of a stash of supplies she'd robbed from a grocery store. In rummaging past several other pregnancy tests—seventeen in total, all of which had tested positive—her hand met a notepad and pencil. With them she scrawled her final words:

Ulrik, my beautiful boy, I miss your face so much. It's about the only thing I can bear to be thinking about.

Her hand faltered, but in squeezing the pencil she summoned the last of her strength to continue writing.

I've spent my time hiding in some woodland. It's on the eastern border of Athens, I think. It's really quiet here besides the occasional hiker. There are barely any drones. You'd love the little shelter I've made, though the bugs ... not so much. I'd forgotten how much I hate creepy things with their extra legs and eyes and wings. They've been feasting on me in my sleep. I'm covered in bumps and bites. It's making me feel lucky to have lived in bug-free Svalbard. I just want us to go back to Thrudheim.

Thinking about Svalbard today got me busy making a spear. My plan was to go hunting tomorrow. I could cure meats and dry fruit under the hot sun. Foraging would make me feel normal again. I suppose I've everything I need to survive here, but I'm sorry, Ulrik, I've nothing here to live for.

You have enough to worry about, and I hate myself for adding to your suffering, but what you are about to read will hurt. I know you'll think of me as selfish, but I hope when your temper cools you'll understand. Maybe you'll even forgive me. I've heard people say no loving parent would ever leave their child behind, but my heart is broken beyond repair. Is it so selfish to end my suffering? You'd help me, I know, but it's not your responsibility to fix me. I want for you the best life. I want you to be happy. It's out of my love that I release you, and I refuse to hold you back from the adventures that await you.

She entered here into details about her being pregnant, but then, not wishing to augment his grief, erased it.

You know, it's a privilege for a person to know they're about to die. Not everybody gets the opportunity to say something for the last time. Here at my end, I'm reminded of your beginning, and I always remember your pappa when he held you on the day you were born. I've never seen his hands shake so much. He was so afraid to move an inch with you. I still remember what he said that evening because it was so unusual to hear him speaking with such emotion: "Ulrik may look different, but I know it's because he's special. Throughout his life, many will love him, but none will ever love him more than I do."

Even though we didn't always say the word "love", I hope you always felt it in your heart. But if you were ever in doubt, my beautiful, beautiful Ulrik, Pappa and I love you so, so much.

Mamma.

Any negative space remaining was littered with x's as though to transfer the last of her love to this crinkled page. Then she tore the sheet from the notepad and, taking out four hair clips, fastened all four corners to the outer thatching of her den.

It was time.

Not wishing to die with bad hair, she tidied her plaits and wore them like thick lengths of twine that ran past her bosoms. Then, just as she was readying herself for her last act, something unwelcome startled the surrounding wildlife. The snapping of twigs, the rustling of leaves, and the sonorous buffeting of wings told of a great exodus of creatures from the forest. Above all else she heard lumbering footsteps: footsteps that were muffled at first, but their thudding grew louder as they drew closer.

When parting the leaves of her thatching, her eyes caught sight of a silhouette of cubic proportions ascending the hillside. She took up her wooden spear. A burning pulse throbbed in her palm. Armed and ready, she crept out of her den and hid behind a tree of colossal girth, watching as the shadow passed in and out of view. Advancing under the starlight, the features of this midnight wanderer were made visible. Tangles of bedraggled red hair fell out from the hood like seaweed, and a forked beard clung to his chin like a flame. When drawing himself to his full height, he appeared to surpass a height of seven foot. Then, when he looked up, an involuntary gasp escaped Astrid's breast and she dropped her spear, for beneath the ridge of his brow was a flash of grass-green like two marbled planets—eyes searching from left to right.

"Thor!" she cried, emerging from behind the tree and bounding down the hill with her arms outstretched. "Thor, I'm here."

A beam of torchlight flashed over her.

"I can't believe you're here, Thor," crashing into him and dispensing a flurry of kisses at his belly. "Tell me it's not a trick."

"Astrid, is that you?" he said, lowering his hood. "I've been looking everywhere for you."

She took a pace back and surveyed the lineaments of his face: "Have you had a haircut, Thor? It looks a little shorter. And why are you dressing in those terrible clothes?"

He heaved in then expelled his breath with a regretful sigh. "Astrid, it's me, Karsten. I didn't mean to get your hopes up."

"Karsten? When and why did you decide to start calling yourself such a name?"

"What? Are you crazy? Astrid, please listen to me," he whispered, shaking her gently by the shoulders. Even when whispering, his foghorn voice boomed across the hillside. "It's me, Karsten—Thor's brother. Remember?"

"Oh, I get it," winking with exaggeration. "You're going by a different name to keep us safe." She draped his hefty arm about her shoulder and huddled into him, but he broke free with an unwelcoming shrug.

Delusion had, with its perverse, flexible logic, rewritten the chronology of her memory; she'd unknowingly invented a future which included Thorsten and had omitted the agony of him ever having fathered a bastard daughter.

"Astrid, you're not yourself," he said, cuffing her wrists with his hands.

"I'm not the one changing my name," she said, breaking free from his vice-like grip. "I'd say it's you who isn't yourself."

He stumbled back a few yards and examined her from boot to brow with the deepest corrugated frown affecting his face.

"Anyway," she added, "now you're here, I won't be needing this …" unfurling her hand and presenting him with the colourless phial. "Russian concussion."

Karsten took it and examined it under the light of his torch. Then he unscrewed the cap and drew in a mighty sniff. "It's still got the security tag attached. Astrid, did you steal this?"

"Nuh—well, I took it from someone, yah. But the rogue deserved it. Wait, what are you doing? Nuh, don't drink it. Stop!" She thumped his chest with minimal effect as he glugged down the deadly tonic. Afterwards, he gave a roar and his eyebrows seemed to stand on end.

"Gah, tastes like liquorice."

"Why did you do that? We need to be getting you to hospital right now before it kills you."

"I think I can handle a little ouzo, Astrid."

"Ouzo? What are you talking about? What is this ouzo?"

"Look," underlining the label with his bulbous knuckle. "Ouzo. It's alcohol. What did you think it was?"

"It's not Russian concussion?" clasping her face in her palms. "But the man said—I thought—I don't understand."

"What don't you understand?"

"He said it would numb the pain. The man said—oh, what does it matter?" She lunged into him and nuzzled into his midriff. "I'm just glad you're here with us."

Great fissures of confusion appeared on his face: "'Us', you say?"

"Yah, us …"

"Who else is here with you?"

She took his palm in her hand and pressed it to her womb, and he recoiled as though he'd been scalded by the touch.

"Astrid, what are you saying? Don't play mind games with me."

She produced the positive pregnancy test, and he raised his hand to conceal the gaping cavern of his mouth. "You're carrying a child?" he mouthed, in a faraway, vacant voice.

"I didn't believe it at first, either," she said, hurrying off into her den and retrieving the stash of pregnancy tests. She emerged again and revealed to him her conclusive proof, seventeen times over. "That's why I did all these. Just to be sure. See?"

Livid veins snaked about his temples, and he turned his back to her and ran his exasperated hands through his hair.

"Aren't you happy?"

"Yah, I am, Astrid. Though, I'm also afraid; afraid of others finding out." Turning on his heel to face her again: "Who else knows?"

"Nobody knows. I'm not so stupid as to be telling anybody. I know it's dangerous."

"More dangerous than you can imagine, Astrid. There's a bounty on our heads—on all genetic links to Homo Nova. The zealots want to eradicate our bloodline. 'A blasphemous bloodline' is what they're saying about us. They've tried to kill me, too. Whitehoods, Astrid; Whitehoods. They're coming for us."

"Oh, is that why you've changed your name and are wearing normal clothes? Maybe I should be changing my name, too. What about Skadi? I've always liked the name Skadi. Do I look like a Skadi? Or maybe some other name?"

"Come on; the forest is no place for a pregnant woman," girding his arm about her and drawing up his hood. "Let's get you out of here."

"Do you think our baby will be like Ulrik? Is that why you're afraid? Because our baby could be born with the same condition?"

"*Our* baby? Hush—hold your tongue until we're somewhere safe. Not another word. Not another breath, if you can help it."

He held her hand and smuggled her throughout the darkness of the forest, and thereafter they rode a sequence of midnight trains and driverless taxis northward bound, heading as far away from Athens as could be achieved in one night.

Even as the wind picked up, her suicide note remained affixed to the herbaceous roof of her shelter by virtue of those trusty hair clips. There it remained until its eventual discovery.

Chapter Thirty-Seven

LETHAL PREPARATIONS

Apprehension pervaded the war room on the eve of their deployment. Supper was had, but in no great portions; words were exchanged, but in no great quantities; though the lavatories, those were used with exceptional frequency.

Having been issued with kit earlier that day, the companions were clad now in their uncreased desert camouflage, listening in as Skye brought her briefing to a close. Then, when all was said that needed to be said, and when all was repeated that needed to be repeated, she bade the companions a good evening and dismissed them.

Ria was first to vacate; she wanted to bathe a little before sleeping since it was uncertain how long it'd be before she could do so again. Embla followed her out, as she'd made a recent habit of doing here, there, and everywhere, though she parted ways with her at the bottom of the staircase and sequestered herself in the punters' lounge, where she was joined by Waqas and Colonel; and together they played dominoes and listened to Colonel's fireside tales for a while. Spider—a man above anxiety—took a stroll outside the inn, whistling and warbling away to a favourite tune of his. Tristan sat on the doorstep, polishing his boots for the seventh time that day, rubbing them with the fervour one might when attempting to summon a genie from a magic lamp. Ulrik and Skye were last to leave,

485

and for a while they remained behind, eyes smouldering under the glow of the expiring candlelight.

They chatted from opposite ends of that grandly carpentered round table about the nature of war, the nature of people, and the nature of nature. Even at this distance, her incredibly long lashes seemed to be fanning him. For some curious reason, they descended into whispers, and she beckoned him to sit next to her. He scraped out a chair from beneath the table and got comfortable beside her. She slackened her leather boots, kicked them aside, and swung her legs over his lap, only asking him afterwards if he minded. He said he didn't.

"I respect yae, Ulrik, for wanting to save yer friend," she said, eddying the wine in her glass. "Yer a great, great guy. I just wish the world had more guys like yae."

"I'm only doing what anybody else would."

"Naw, hun, yer no' like anybody else." Her ice-blue eyes narrowed, kindled with a certain longing. "Yer special."

"As are you, Captain Urquhart. Special, I mean."

"Yae dunnae have to keep calling me Captain Urquhart, Ulrik. I take what I do very, very seriously, but that dusnae mean I take maself seriously. Take away the uniform and am just a normal girl who likes to do normal things—every once in a while ..."

Her eyelashes were fanning him again.

"Anyway, I should probably be getting some rest, Skye. Tomorrow is a big day for me."

"Aye, it's a big day for us all." She brushed his forearm with her hand. A metallic tingle flowed through him like a faint prickle of electricity. "Al find yer maw, Ulrik. I promise."

"You'll find my maw?"

"Agh," rolling her eyes, "where I come from, we say maw instead of mother."

"I see. Well, thank you, Skye. I appreciate all you're doing for me. Tracking down my mamma and helping me rescue Cheng—none of this would be possible without you."

"Well, I appreciate yae, too, Ulrik, hun. But there isnae any need to thank me. Me and yerself—we're friends now, right? And friends look oot for one another." She swung her legs off his lap and stood in front of him—right between his knees. Then she leant over him to part with a hug, and for a long spell they were absorbed in one another's embrace, until Ulrik tapped out. "It's been nice, this," perching her backside up against the table so that it accentuated her curves. "We're gownae have to resume our wee candlelit patter when yae get back. Although, it's probably no' the cleverest idea to tell anybody aboot it—aboot us getting on so well. I wudnae wantae upset anybody."

"Why would it upset anybody?"

"Yer wee lassie Ria dusnae like me, does she, hun? Al bet she thinks there's something between us 'cause we get on so well. I hope her no' liking me dusnae mean us two cannae be friends."

"Well, it's not up to her who I'm friends with. I've had very few friends in my lifetime."

"Right, but yae dunnae have to put up with her being stroppy when yae as famous as yae are. Every lassie in DRUE wants a piece of Homo Nova. So yae might wantae think carefully on which one yae gownae be with ... or two."

"Two?"

Skye shuffled backwards and mounted the table, her legs dangling over the edge, swinging playfully; then her legs lunged forward like pincers, and he found himself suddenly trapped between them. "Hey, one last thing before yae go ..." She pointed to her pouting lips, and her aspect changed from one of dominance to one of innocence.

"Skye, what are you asking of me?"

Her eyelashes doubled their fanning. He knew what it was she was asking.

"Honestly, Ulrik, there isnae any need to look at me like that. It's only a kiss. Yae dunnae need to make such a big deal oot of it. It's no' as if am pestering yae for sex."

It was as though he were stranded at sea, thirsty, when all about was the lure of unpotable seawater, and yet he was desperate to quench his thirst. But to act upon his present desires would be akin to the drinking of that which would lead to his corruption, for once those waters are tasted, a person's thirst becomes unquenchable. Such is the paradox of a kiss: a single sample leaves one thereafter in a state of ravenous longing.

"Skye, I want to, but I can't because—"

"I thought we were friends, Ulrik," she said, with a look of citric offence and tightening her pincer-like legs about his waist.

"We are, but—"

"Am no' gownae beg yae, like. It's just, I thought yae appreciated me and everything am doing for yae."

"I do."

"Just the one kiss, then?" licking the roof of her mouth with her tantalising tongue, which was pierced with a chrome bar. "Am no' gownae tell anyone. And after tomorrow I might no' see yae for a while."

Flutters ran riot in his breast. He checked around to make sure they were still alone before turning his face to hers with his lips pursed. She grasped the back of his neck, preventing his retreat, pressed her peony-pink lips to his, and pressed, too, her pelvis against him. His every tense muscle seemed to melt away into warm wax, except for the thickening throb in his trousers. She must've felt it, for she pushed him away and looked down at his bulge.

"There's me thinking we're just friends, hun."

"Gah, sorry, I didn't mean—" face turning scarlet. "Please don't tell anybody."

A devious smile stretched across her cheeks. Without a further word, she slipped on her boots. Then she got up and spun around on her heel, her tresses of black hair whipping him in the face as she did so. When passing out of the war room, she stomped with her usual gait, proud and assertive as though she were at all times trampling over the graves of Nazis.

There he remained alone, pacing about the war room, rubbing his lips in the hope of erasing any forensic trace of the kiss. He dared not think of

Skye for too long, else his thirst for her might worsen … But how pretty she looked when mounted on the table, subtly reclined, and drawing him in between her legs. He yanked the roots of his hair to expel the treacherous thoughts and did so until his lust subsided. Just friends. That's all. Nothing more … Just friends?

The house grew silent.

He couldn't loiter; that'd be suspicious. He snuffed out the candlelight, snuck out of the war room, and crept up the cellar stairs. After lunging up the next flight of stairs and reaching the landing of the second storey, he noticed a razor of light cutting through at the foot of a door of one particular bedroom—Embla's. She must be awake still.

Ulrik paused for a moment in deep deliberation. His encounter with Skye had burdened him with guilt, so he felt compelled to do something, anything, that might reconcile his conscience. What better than to hurl overboard the emotional ballast which he'd held onto following his acquainting with Embla?

When pressing his ear to the door, he held his breath and listened for signs of life. His impatience got the better of him, and he rapped his knuckles on the door and tried the handle, though it was locked. "Embla," he said, in a hoarse whisper, "it's me, Ulrik. Open up."

Blundering footsteps made gains towards the door from the other side, and when the door flew open, Embla admitted him with the jolliest red cheeks; cheeks not unlike Pappa's.

"Sorry to disturb you," he whispered, clicking the door shut behind him.

"Don't be; I'm glad of the company." Even when she whispered, her bass voice rumbled throughout the walls. "Anyway, I can't sleep in these dwarven beds. Not when my limbs hang out like they do. I think I'd be more comfortable sleeping in a cardboard box."

He shared her misery of sleeplessness in these beds and shared, too, the idea that the people of this world were dwarves, rather than regarding himself as a giant as the tabloids so often did.

"So, what brings you?" she added, wringing her wrists in anxious anticipation. Each blink was executed with a look of forcedness, though he suspected she had little control over these frantic repetitions.

"There's no need to worry, Embla; I'm here to apologise."

"You are?" pressing a palm to her sternum.

"I am."

He apologised for his ill treatment of her since their meeting, though she was adamant there was nothing to forgive. A forager headbutt—that she would accept, if he would but lean in to deal her one. But being at such close range, he was overcome with infatuation of her complexion, and he couldn't help but stare in trance-like wonder: "Your skin—that's no ordinary condition, is it?"

Her head dropped, and her ginger forelocks curtained the greater part of her face.

"Embla, look at me. You're like me, aren't you? You're special. I know you are."

She retreated to the window and there looked upon her own reflection against the onset of darkness: "I'm afraid, Ulrik."

"Of what? Of me?"

"No, no, it's not you I'm afraid of. It's my—" Her cubic face contracted about the centre, and she pinched her tear ducts.

"Your what?"

"Secrets. My, my, my secrets."

"What secrets? Help me understand you, Embla. You know all about me—your brother. Isn't it fair that I should be getting to know my sister?"

She paused for consideration, and after a prolonged silence, roused a spirited "Yes". Then she strode to the centre of the room and looked up at the lightbulb which dangled from the ceiling like a pear at the end of a slender branch. There was no hindrance of a lampshade set about it, and its effulgence was like that of the sun—white-hot and vision-bleaching when staring at it for too long. Then her hand reached up towards it, and without hesitation she unscrewed it from its socket, never once flinching at the heat as she handled it.

Total darkness absorbed the room. The stench of searing flesh filled his nostrils. "You don't feel pain, do you?"

A metallic squeaking was heard above, and when the lightbulb was returned to its socket, light flooded the room again. "I feel emotional pain; the pain of grief," she said, holding up her hand, which was already black and blistering from the burn of the bulb, "but I feel no physical pain."

"Were you born this way, or was this a skill you acquired?"

She veiled her face with a hand and shook her head.

"Nuh? Which one? Please answer me, Embla. Were you born like this, or did something happen to you? Tell me."

"I went through hell."

"How so? What happened? Help me understand."

"It's hard for me to talk about. I've never told anybody before."

"Embla, to feel no pain—that's no shame. Many would kill to have your potential."

"No," she snapped. "Painlessness is no blessing. Try to imagine what it's like for me. When I have a fever, I'm oblivious to it. If you get ill, you'd take medication to make you better, but when I get ill my health deteriorates without me knowing. Not so long ago, my appendix burst, and I almost died. I passed out one day and woke up in hospital. I'm so afraid of something else like that happening. I just want to be normal again."

Grooming his beard: "Normal again, huh? So, you weren't born this way. How, then, did you come by this painlessness?"

"I'm fine now," scratching herself all over as though she'd been brushed by the nettles of anxiety. "I'm fine. But before, I used to do things—things I don't do anymore."

"What things?"

"You can't tell anybody. I hate people knowing about me."

"You'll find no judgement here, Embla," surrendering his palms.

She turned her back to him and rolled up her shirt, exposing her lamellated skin. Disturbing yet beautiful patterns marked her broad

491

back: a network of slender branches like the fronds of a fern or the branches of a tree or the forks of a thunderbolt.

"Are those tattoos?"

"Fractal scars," she said, pulling down her shirt and tucking it in to her trousers again.

"Scars?" Ulrik veiled the horror affecting his face with both hands, and he peered through the gaps between his fingers. "Oh, I'm so sorry. What happened to you?"

"From the beginning, my life has been a grim affair. And many years ago, I looked to extreme ways of coping with my troubles. Whenever I was having a bad time, I'd pinch myself as a distraction. Physical pain helped me forget about everything else. It was my way of escaping the present; my way of ridding myself of the dark thoughts in my mind; my way of taking back control of my feelings. Pain was a distraction. It was gentle to begin with: a pinch here, a scratch there, the occasional bite. But as the circumstances of my life worsened, so did my self-harming. I became addicted—not to pain but addicted to escaping reality. And so I looked for more savage ways to block out my troubles: hitting, cutting, burning myself, throwing myself from heights or in front of moving vehicles ... So, yeah, that's me."

"And your skin ..."

"Over time, my skin hardened in response to the injuries. It's my body's defence—against myself. An overproduction of keratin, so the doctors say."

"Those scars on your back, those are no ordinary scars, are they?"

She shuddered as though she were reliving the trauma: "Electrocution."

"Electro—" He cupped his mouth, intercepting his outburst. "How did you even ... ?"

"I don't want to talk about that."

"That's fine, Embla. Whenever you're ready. You know I'm always here to listen. Some other time, maybe? But only when you're ready."

"I'll say only that it was the most excruciating thing I've ever felt. And it was only after this,"—swallowing with difficulty—"after the electrocution, that I could no longer sense any pain. I don't know why, but after enduring what I did, my body shut down the faculties of pain reception. This painlessness, the doctors tell me, is a condition known as *congenital analgesia*. I don't know much about it, but I've always remembered that it's caused by the rogue expression of one particular gene: *SCN9A*—the gene responsible for transmitting pain signals."

"See, I'm betting you've switched it off ... deactivated it. Then it must be true. You have a kaleidoscopic genome like me."

"I'm not sure about that, but I'd do whatever necessary to reverse this awful affliction."

"You would?"

"I want to feel again, Ulrik. I'm numb to the sensations of life."

"Well, I know that if anybody can help you reverse this, it's Cheng. He's a biologist and knows all about genetics."

"You think Chenglei will help me?"

"He's the most gentle and kind and honourable man. If we can save him from the Caliph, I know he'll do whatever is within his power to help you."

"Then we should get some sleep so that we set out with our full strength tomorrow," gesturing to the time on her watchTech.

"Indeed."

Their heads met for a swift butt, and they bade one another good health. When stopping at the door, he mulled over some words of endearment that came to the forefront of his mind, though he was too shy to face her when articulating his parting words: "Embla, I'll never get over losing Pappa, but finding you has been like finding a part of him. I'm glad you're here with me. We'll face the darkness of this world together."

"We will," she said, in a shaky voice, followed by a light sniffle. "Sleep well, brother."

Out he slipped into the corridor, and there he stood for several moments with his back to the wall, running his hands through his hair in disbelief, his heart drumming out a terrible tempo. Her painlessness—it

493

was a gift! How could she not see? He'd do anything to acquire such a condition. "If only ..."

With haste, he ascended the staircase to the uppermost floor, each stair beneath him groaning in protest under his weight. When reaching the top, he groped about in the darkness for his bedroom door handle and, opening it with extreme caution (to lessen the creak), stole through the gap like a thief in the night.

A muffled snoring came from within the cocoon of duvet where Ria was sprawled in bed, mouth agape, her face caught up in a web of hair. He ought to have clambered in bed there and then, readying himself for tomorrow, but not with all the adrenaline of discovering Embla's secrets could he settle himself for an act so mundane as sleep. So he crept on by and into the bathroom, where he bolted the door behind him.

Within seconds, he'd stripped down and stood in the nude, analysing the inside of his thighs. They were terribly chafed from the days when Coach Lukashenko had him swimming while clothed. He ran his fingertips over the callused regions; a leathery complexion—perhaps it was an overproduction of keratin like Embla's. When looking up at his reflection in the mirror, his pupils dilated as he turned the thought over in his mind: what if I could acquire this painlessness, too?

He triple-checked the lock on the bathroom door before filling the bathtub, the hot tap being the sole lever in employment. Soon after, a turgid cloud of steam lingered in the air, and every mirror, window, chrome feature, and patch of porcelain was wet with condensation, such was the scald of the bathwater.

As he stood over the bathtub, he heaved in and blasted out dragonish rings of vapour from his nostrils. Then he lodged a flannel in his mouth to muffle any cries that might escape in his next act. Suitably psyched, he suspended himself above the scalding water, hands and feet planted on the edges, lowering himself inch by inch before plunging his entire body in.

Within an instant, all save his face turned a deep shade of pink. The stinging agony felt less like a burn and more as though he'd been skinned alive and submerged in saltwater. He twisted and turned—spine terribly contorted, back horribly arched—as he fought against the volcanic scorch of the water; writhing, convulsing, thrashing, splashing, keeping his teeth clenched at all times on the flannel to deny the escape of a single murmur. Feeling his consciousness waning, he scrambled out and rolled about on the floor tiles as though to douse the invisible flames ravaging him.

The ordeal only lasted a matter of seconds, but even that was too long. Yet, after having cooled down, and when his suffering abated, his desire for pain returned. He rose again with obsessive ambition in his eyes, supposing that varying the forms of injury might be a pathway to a faster change in him. Rather than a burn this time, he sought a sharp pain. "Can't stop now," he whispered, tapping his foot on the floor and grooming the end of his beard. "But what next?"

There, upon the windowsill—potted succulents. One in particular: a pint-sized cactus with white needles as thin as whiskers caught his attention. He extended his arm and seized it by the pot. Then, with the manner of one applying a sponge, he scrubbed his midriff with it so that his body afterwards had the aspect of a pincushion.

His cheeks swelled with pride when looking down at his senseless acupuncture, where trickles of blood flowed from every perforation in his flesh. He spent the next twenty minutes plucking out cactus needles and lining them up on the windowsill as though they were a tally of torment endured; each needle representing an incremental gradation—a small step closer to painlessness. When all the needles were unplucked, he flushed away all traces of the ordeal down the toilet and thereafter daubed petroleum jelly over his body to clot the leaking of blood from his veins.

He was so sore and raw that when he got dressed into his nightwear, even the clothes against his back irritated him. But it was a welcome irritation, for he hoped each episode of suffering would bring him closer to painlessness.

He ambled back into the bedroom and shuffled up behind Ria with great care. Her hair smelt of coconut, her skin like lavender. After kissing her on the shoulder, he whispered, "Whatever happens, stay with me."

Half stirring from her slumber, she backed her waist up into him, girded his arm over her, cupped her bosom with his hand, and said, "I'm yours forever."

CHAPTER THIRTY-EIGHT

THE WORD OF THE LORD

The Holy Shepherd knelt in the front pew with his head bowed and his hands interlocked about his rosary beads.

"Father in heaven," he whispered at a decibel almost as inaudible as thought, "you entrusted to me, your vicegerent, the mission of restoring a religious republic. And I know that to enter the gates of heaven, the price of my admission is to fulfil my promise to you: to bring peace and to unite the House of Abraham. But, Lord, unless some divine wisdom wills otherwise, my course is now set to bring the House into ruin; for it's true that New Babylon is in the business of manufacturing nuclear weapons.

"O Divine Master, I've consulted the scripture at length and found your word to be explicit. I understand that the best way to salvage New Babylon is through conquest. But I beseech you, let it be known to me, somehow, if what I'm about to do should condemn me to eternal hell-fire. Give me a sign. Another premonition. Anything. I mean not to tempt you, Lord, but I fear more than anything to wrong you. I fear you with the greatest severity. I fear the torment of the Devil's branding iron. When my mortal time comes to depart this world, I want not to be plunged thereafter into the Devil's molten lake among the blasphemers and buggerers."

His desperate hands turned translucent from clenching them.

"Though perhaps this is a test of my fear? Perhaps this is part of your plan, Lord? I recall in Proverbs 10:27 it says 'Fear of the Lord prolongs life.' Perhaps you ordained that I should continue living at my old age because I *do* fear you and your retribution. That's why in everything I seek instruction from your word—the Holy Bible. 'Your word is a lamp for my feet, a light on my path,' as is written in Psalms; and 'Always, I wait for the Lord, my whole being waits, and in His word, I place all my hope.'"

Silent pause.

"Since I receive no sign, I pray instead, then, for strength and courage. In your word, I place all my hope. Amen."

The Holy Shepherd adjusted the straps of his sandals, drew his robe about his shoulders, and leant on his warped white crook. Then he ascended the stairs before the altar and stood at the pulpit, from which he readied himself to deliver his sermon to a live audience of millions watching on their Tech.

When the cameraman gave a thumbs-up, the Holy Shepherd looked into the camera and read aloud the words rolling on the blue screen. He took up a loaf of bread from the offertory table, tore it into pieces, and said, "Take this, eat this, all of you. This is the body of the Lord, shared out for you." He dipped a piece of bread into his mouth and swallowed before addressing the Continent again in his fragile, wizardly voice:

"Loyal people of the Democratic Republic of United Europe, we live in a period of *great tribulation*," placing vehement emphasis on the latter two words. "The Lord in heaven knows I've strived for everlasting peace on earth; strived to unite the sons of Adam—the descendants of Moses—the heirs of Abraham; but the Almighty Father knows, as is written in Ecclesiastes 3:8, 'There is a time to love, and a time to hate; a time for war, and a time for peace.'

"Let me also remind you of Matthew 24:6–8: 'You shall hear of wars and rumours of wars: see that you be not troubled, for all these things must come to pass, but the end is not yet. For nation shall rise against nation and kingdom against kingdom.'

"My lambs, there is no greater threat to international peace than the proliferation of weapons of mass destruction. It's with regret that I bring you some ill news on that subject: our intelligence services have verified a dossier of evidence exposing the illegal stockpiling of weapons-grade uranium in New Babylon—a raw material used in nuclear weapons. Acquisition of these materials of war is a direct breach of the Treaty of Zion, a pact that I myself arbitrated in the hope of bringing everlasting peace and prosperity to the Middle East.

"The security and safety of the Republic will always be the uppermost priority of government. As the Holy Shepherd of your government, and as a faithful, God-fearing Christian, I cannot allow such a deliberate breach of JOEL—that is, the Journal of European Law—to go unchecked. In times of *great tribulation*, we must always let the scripture guide our conscience, for the word of the Lord is absolute.

"So says the scripture in Jeremiah: 'Sharpen the arrows! Take up the shields! The Lord has aroused the spirit of the kings, because his plan is aimed at Babylon to destroy her, for it is the vengeance of the Lord. Raise a banner against the walls of Babylon; post the guard; station the watchmen; prepare the ambush. Encamp all around her; let no one escape. Repay her according to her deeds; do to her as she has done. For she has defied the Lord, the Holy One of Israel. You who dwell by many waters, rich in treasures, your end has come; the thread of your life is cut.'

"My lambs, I implore you to have faith. Pray, pray, pray, until your knees are sore from kneeling, hearken to the prophecy in Psalm 9:17, and know that 'The wicked shall be burned in hell, as will all the nations that forget God.'

"This IS the word of the Lord. Thanks be to God."

Message: High Importance!

<u>From: the Holy Shepherd</u>

Loyal people of the Democratic Republic of United Europe,

In a matter unrelated to my declaration today, we are in receipt of intelligence concerning the whereabouts and welfare of Olympic swimmer, Ulrik Magnusson. He was last seen attending his father's funeral in Athens at the Port of Piraeus, where he was allegedly abducted by a league of extreme far-right nationalists, known in secret unto themselves as "CIGMa". Anyone who supplies information leading to the arrest and conviction of these dissenters will be rewarded with the most highly favoured blessing of the Holy Shepherd, that being: John 14:14: "If you ask me for anything in my name, I will do it."

May the Lord deliver us from evil,
Amen.